Fatal

I0629278

Blow

Part III of the Fatal Trilogy

Just when you thought the Simmons family survived life's challenges in Part I and II of the Fatal Trilogy, the final installment takes you to the point of no return. A blast from the past turns deadly, sibling rivalry has no limits, murder becomes the norm, and love does not necessarily conquer all. The question of *'who can you trust'* leaves you in suspense until the final chapter.

Library of Congress Control Number (LCCN): 1--769581261

Fiction: Contemporary

ISBN: 978-0-9836488-1-9

Published by:
Dorothy J Morris
www.dorothyjmorris.com

Printed in the USA

First Edition - Paperback and Electronic

Also by Dorothy J Morris:

Fatal Rebounds
Part I of the Fatal Trilogy

Fatal Vengeance
Part II of the Fatal Trilogy

Coming Soon:

"Revolving Doors"

Acknowledgements

I thank God for giving me the desire to write and use my vivid imagination. The positive feedback I received from my first two novels has inspired me to continue my writing journey.

To my dearest friend, Errol Simmons, who graciously volunteered to edit Fatal Blow, the final installment of the Fatal Trilogy. Thank you for your friendship, and for being a wonderful, loving father figure in my life. I love you so much!

I would be remiss if I fail to acknowledge my silent readers: my husband-Andrew Morris, Carolyn Hill, Sandra Fowlks (*Saja Bo Storm, author of the Twisted Trysts series*), Joyce Hillard-Fountain, Marchand McQueen, Keirra Kennedy, Colleen Cates, Marissa Turner, and Donna Giwa-Osagie. Thank you for also being wonderful friends and confidantes. I am so glad you're in my life. Words alone cannot express how much I appreciate you.

Nikkea Smithers, you are an angel in disguise. Thank you for putting me on the right path to publishing the *Fatal Trilogy*. You are an awesome editor, illustrator, consultant, and motivator. I am forever grateful to you.

A special thank you to Michael Reeves and Nicole Clark featured on this book cover; and to the photographer, Juan Stevens, for providing the optics. Your roles were instrumental in bringing two of the main characters (Swag and Carmela) to life.

To all readers, in general, thank you for spreading the word about my novels. I am thankful for your love and support.

Dedicated to the women who helped me raise my daughters: Cassandra Johnson, Emma Simmons, Rosa Mackey, and Gracie Kennedy

Thank you!

Chapter 1
Third Wheel

Thirty-year old Justina Bishop and her husband, Aaron, were living the American dream. They shared a beautiful five-bedroom estate in an upscale community, surrounded by serene lakes and golf courses. Aaron owned and managed several rental properties, and Justina was a legal consultant for a major corporation.

They were in their sun room enjoying each other's company when they heard a knock at the front door.

"Who could that be?" Aaron asked.

Justina shrugged. "I don't know. I'll go find out."

She stood up, walked down the hallway to the front door, and looked through the peep hole. She sighed before she opened the door and came face-to-face with her twenty-year old sister, Carmela Reyes.

Justina and Carmela bore similar features. Both had inherited their mother's full lips and their father's dark black eyes. They were average height, modelesque, had a light complexion, and silky, dark black shoulder-length hair.

"What happened?' Justina asked, as her sister entered her home.

"It's Mom and Dad. They took my car and won't give it back, unless I return to school."

"Well I tend to agree with their decision. I don't know why you decided to drop out of college in your sophomore year."

"*Go figure!*" Carmela said with malice. "It's not like anyone is paying for my education. Unlike you, I had to apply for a student loan."

Justina opened her mouth but held her tongue. She understood her sister's anger. After she graduated from high school, their parents showered her with gifts and money, put her through law school, bought her a condo, and gave her enough money to start her own law firm in Atlanta, Georgia. And when the law firm failed, they put out more money to help her return to Florida.

But things changed with the downward economy. By the time Carmela graduated from high school, their father's construction business folded, and their mother's income as a nurse barely took care of the household bills.

1

"You can stay," Aaron said, after walking up behind his wife and listening to the tail end of their conversation. "Your curfew is midnight."

Carmela rolled her eyes after realizing she had more freedom when she lived at home with her parents.

Two nights later, all *hell broke loose* when she returned home after curfew. In response, Justina asked for the keys to the spare car she had allowed her sister to drive during her stay.

Carmela rebelled by screaming, "I hate you!" Then she grabbed a hand full of Justina's hair with one hand, and socked her in the face with the other.

"Please stop!" Justina cried out, struggling to free her hair from her sister's strong grasp. "You're hurting me," she yelped.

Seconds later, Aaron returned home from work and witnessed Carmela beating the crap out of his wife. When she raised her fist to strike Justina again, he grabbed her hand, and shouted, "Cut it out!"

But Carmela was determined to finish the fight. She yanked her hand away from Aaron and lunged at her sister with all her might. In one swift motion, her brother-in-law grabbed her around the waist and swung her backward. She lost her balance and tumbled to the floor.

Aaron's piercing eyes shifted between the sisters. Then he glanced down at Justina, and asked, "What in the hell is going on?!"

Carmela stood up and folded her arms in a huff. "That *bitch* is not my mother! She can't tell me what to do!"

Justina said between sniffles, "I was…only trying…to help you."

"You need to stay out of my life!"

Fed up with his sister-in-law's rebellious attitude, Aaron turned to her, and barked, "Pack your things and get out of my house!"

Carmela's eyes were filled with rage as she stared at her brother-in-law with contempt. She wanted to kill him.

"Either you leave voluntarily," Aaron stated through gritted teeth, "or I will throw you out, and it won't be pretty."

Taking a deep breath and exhaling, Carmela drew her shoulders back in defeat. She knew she was no match for her brother-in-law. She ran upstairs to pack.

Aaron knelt on the floor beside his wife, and cupped the side of her face. Out of concern, he asked, "Are you all right?"

Looking pitiful, Justina weakly replied, "What's wrong with my sister?"

"I don't know."

Aaron grabbed his wife around the waist to help her stand up.

Huffing and puffing, Carmela flew downstairs with her suitcase. She stopped in her tracks after her brother-in-law blocked her path to the front door.

"What do you want?!" she belted out with gusto.

Aaron said in a firm tone, "I want to inform you that you are no longer welcome in our home. If I catch you anywhere near here, I will file charges and see to it that you go to jail for trespassing."

"*Screw you!*" she spat, before pushing past Aaron and sprinting out the front door in a hurry.

"Good riddance." Aaron swatted at the air and blew out air in frustration. He was happy Carmela was gone but felt sad for his wife.

His heart weakened as tears poured down Justina's face. He wrapped his arms around her and held her close to him. Then he cupped her chin and looked into her eyes. "Honey, I'd understand if you don't feel up to going to the grand opening this evening."

Justina bore a thin smile. "I wouldn't miss it for the world."

She was proud of her childhood friend, who had just opened a new restaurant in Tampa, Florida. She wanted to be there to help celebrate this joyous event.

Aaron asked, "Do you think your friend is going to be happy to see you?"

"I hope so."

"I can't imagine how you might feel. It has been a long time."

"Five years to be exact. I miss her," she thought aloud.

"I'm sure she misses you too."

Aaron kissed her on the forehead and smiled. He frowned after he noticed the small scratch wound above Justina's right eye. He guessed it was the result of the brutal fight with her sister.

"Honey, are you sure you're okay?"

"I'm fine," she weakly replied. "I've been through worse than this."

Several years earlier, Justina was just like her sister, if not worse. She used to be hotheaded, and acted as if the world revolved around her. Among the many consequences of her *ill behavior*, she was physically assaulted and left for dead; held hostage by her business partner; and swindled out of her assets and money by a man she thought she was legally married to - only to discover her marriage was a hoax. To add insult to injury, she contracted an STD from her fake husband.

Justina thought all was lost, until she met and fell *in love* with Aaron. Their union resulted in marital bliss. Her life had changed for the better, and she was able to prosper and regain her self-respect and dignity.

Chapter 2
The Reunion

*T*hirty-year old Regine Simmons was a renowned chef and owner of five restaurants throughout Florida. Her gourmet food was in high demand, and her restaurants received five-star ratings from food critics all over the world.

She had just opened a new restaurant in Tampa, Florida, and invited family, friends, and prominent city officials to the grand opening. The invitation-only event was a formal affair. The men wore tailor-made suits and the women wore glamorous gowns. The turnout was great and everyone was pleased with the array of gourmet food and wine.

Midway through the event, Justina and Aaron arrived at the restaurant in a white limo. They walked through the entrance of the restaurant looking like a handsome couple. Justina wore a royal blue Vera Wang gown, and her husband wore a black suit from Sean Jean's formal men's wear collection. They approached the reception counter with broad smiles.

"Your names?" the hostess asked.

"Mr. and Mrs. Bishop," Justina answered.

"Do you have an invitation?"

Justina said, "No, do *we* need one?"

"Yes you do."

"May I speak with the owner?" Justina quizzed in a soft voice.

For a few seconds, the hostess wavered over her decision. "Wait here. I'll be back."

Standing several feet away was Regine's husband, Guy Simmons. He was the first to notice Justina. "What is she doing here?" he mumbled under his breath.

Regine was enthralled in a humorous conversation with the mayor, before she glanced at her husband and noticed the scowl on his face. Leaning over, she whispered in his ear, "Are you okay?"

Guy did not respond. His eyes were glued on Justina.

Regine's mouth flew open when she turned to see who was dominating her husband's attention. *It was as if hell opened up and out came Lucifer.*

"Justina," she sputtered, while trying with great difficulty to remain calm. "What...is...she...doing here?"

"You didn't invite her?" Guy asked with raised brows.

Regine frowned. "Of course not."

"I'll go take care of it."

Quickly grabbing ahold of her husband's hand, Regine said in a hushed tone, "Please do not cause a scene."

"I won't."

When the hostess spotted Guy in her path, she approached him with a sense of urgency. "Mr. Simmons, we have two uninvited guests."

"I know," Guy curtly replied, as he barged toward the front entrance of the restaurant. He had one thing in mind, and that was to make sure the *party clashers* left the premises, peacefully.

Justina smiled upon seeing her ex-boyfriend. But her smile quickly faded after noting his angry demeanor.

"What are you doing here?!" Guy shouted. Though, he was not loud enough to draw attention.

"I saw the announcement in the newspaper," Justina explained. "We wanted to come and congratulate Regine on her success."

"Regine doesn't want you here. So I suggest you leave."

Frowning, Aaron asked Guy, "Why are you talking to my wife in that manner? She wanted to come and support her friend."

"My wife doesn't need or want your wife's support."

Regine strolled up behind them, and asked Justina in a stern voice, "Why are you here?"

"You wouldn't take my calls."

Regine was stumped for words. For the past two weeks, she had purposely avoided her former friend's phone calls.

"I want to apologize," Justina said, as tears welled up in her eyes. "I was wrong for abusing our friendship. I miss you."

Relaxing her shoulders, Regine's hard stance softened. But Guy was enraged. He stood in front of Justina, and said in a gruff sounding voice, "The best you can do is *go on* with your life, and let us do the same."

Aaron balled up his fists in anger. He was tempted to punch Guy in the face.

Regine sensed things were getting heated. So she turned to Justina, and offered, "Maybe we can meet for lunch. I'll call you tomorrow."

Justina smiled. "I'd appreciate that. We didn't mean to cause a scene. We will leave now."

"That's a good idea," Guy butted in.

Aaron hesitated before he followed Justina out of the restaurant. He did not understand Guy and Regine's outright hatred toward his wife, nor did he understand her desire to reconnect with them.

As soon as they climbed in the limo to return home, Aaron told her, "It is obvious Regine and her husband have some animosity toward you. Why do you want to be friends with them?"

After pondering his question, Justina said, "I admire that you're still in contact with the same friends you grew up with. Regine was my one and only childhood friend."

"What about her husband?" Aaron prodded, after remembering his wife told him Guy had proposed to her several years earlier.

"You have nothing to worry about. Guy is a part of my past. I accepted your hand in marriage, not his."

Aaron smiled but he was worried. Despite his wife's assurances, he did not think it was a good idea for them to reunite.

***

When Regine and Justina met for lunch several days later, both were timid and uncertain of how the meeting was going to end. Justina began the conversation by apologizing to Regine for hurling insults at her throughout her pregnancy; for wreaking havoc on her wedding day; and for trying to seduce her husband. She had long ago accepted that her actions led to the end of their friendship.

Mentally, Regine questioned Justina's earnestness. She wondered if it was another one of her childhood friend's attempts to get close to her husband, *again*. Her concerns were diminished after Justina told her about her past atrocities, including the recent fight with her sister.

"I'm sorry to hear about your troubles," Regine said, after a short pause.

"Please give me a chance to make things right between us," Justina urged. "I'm sorry for everything I did to you in the past."

After taking a deep breath and exhaling, a smile spread across Regine's face. She was ready to start a new chapter in her life.

"I forgive you."

"Thank you," Justina repeated several times, as she jumped out of her chair to embrace Regine. Her gratitude was unmistakable.

But Justina's husband had misgivings. Aaron noticed every time he asked his wife about Guy, she would freak out and become very defensive. He believed she was harboring past feelings for her old flame. Suddenly, he was afraid their happy home could be in jeopardy.

Chapter 3
Love Birds

*T*wenty-six year old Alex Simmons was a successful businessman and co-owner of Trowne Key Estates, a culmination of hotels and resorts around the world. He was thinking about settling down and getting married like his older brother and sister-in-law: *Guy and Regine*.

Alex had always admired their marriage, but he was also aware of the chaos they endured to be a part of each other's lives. Most recently, he was at the grand opening when he witnessed Guy's exchange with Justina Bishop and her husband. It took everything in Alex's power to calm his brother. He had even asked Guy to go on vacation with him, but he declined.

A week later, Alex went on vacation to Daytona Beach, Florida, alone. He was relaxing on the balcony of his beachfront home, when he looked out on the beach and spotted a beautiful young lady sunbathing in a lounge chair. She had on a yellow two-piece bathing suit that matched her butterscotch complexion. A big floppy hat covered her long flowing, curly black hair; and dark sunglasses shielded her hazel brown eyes.

After watching her from afar, Alex went downstairs and strutted on the beach. He approached the young lady with a million dollar smile.

"Hello beautiful."

Twenty-six year old Evian Gant removed her sunglasses and let her eyes drift over Alex's muscular arms and legs. Then her eyes landed on his face. Her mouth gaped open at the sight of his bedroom eyes and deep dimples. "Hello handsome," she cooed, while batting her eyes.

Alex was immediately smitten with Evian. He briefly looked around, before asking, "Are you here alone?"

"Yes, why do you ask?"

"I would like to get to know you better," he slyly remarked.

Evian sat up in the lounge chair and struck a seductive pose. Then she opened her long shapely legs a couple of inches to tease Alex, before asking, "What is your name?"

"Alex Simmons," he replied with an extended hand. "And yours?"

She shook his hand. "I'm Evian Gant. And yes, I would love for you to get to know me better." As if reading his thoughts, she asked, "Would you like to go on a date?"

Alex smiled. "That would be nice."

He was used to women throwing themselves at him, but Evian's forthrightness had turned him on. She was unlike any woman he had ever met. It took him by surprise when he discovered she was a Miss America pageant winner. He also learned Evian was born in the United States, but her parents were West Indians from St. Kitts.

Alex and Evian's one date turned into a romantic three-day rendezvous, followed by a *whirlwind* love affair. Their sexual encounters were filled with lust and desire. They kissed and sexed seemingly day and night.

When they met, Evian had just graduated from medical school, and was about to begin medical residency training. She was studying to become a urological surgeon; a physician who specializes in urinary tracts and the reproductive system of males.

Even though she was career-focused, thoughts of Alex dominated her mind and soul. She found him to be a very charming man. She also found herself falling *head-over-heels in love* with him.

Alex's feelings for Evian were mutual. He was certain he wanted to spend the rest of his life with her, especially after she accepted his proposal to move in with him.

Shortly afterward, Alex invited Guy, Regine, and his stepmother, Jeanine Benedict, to his condo in Tampa, Florida, to meet his new girlfriend. He conversed with his family in the guest room while Evian took on the role of hostess.

For her guests, Evian had purchased the main entrées and a variety of *hors d'oeuvres* from a five-star restaurant. She went into the kitchen to transfer the decadent treats to a silver platter. Then she picked up the tray, put on a happy face, and strolled into the guest room.

She approached Alex's brother first. She thought Guy was handsome like his little brother. They were both tall, and their skin was the shade of cocoa. But Guy was slightly darker and taller.

Evian said to Guy, "Please try one of my appetizers. I made them myself." She lied with ease.

Guy selected a cracker with a sliver of pâte and tasted it. He nodded while devouring the appetizer. "This is good."

Evian smiled. "Thank you."

She breathed a sigh of relief before she approached Alex's sister-in-law with the tray. "Would you like to try one?"

"I would love to." Regine selected a crab tartar and sampled it. "This is delicious. Would you consider sharing your recipe?"

In a temporary trance, Evian found herself gawking at Alex's sister-in-law from head to toe. She noticed Regine's curvaceous figure matched her height; her dark complexion was smooth and ageless; and her big pretty eyes dominated her oval-shaped face.

Alex grew concerned after he caught Evian staring at Regine. He approached her and lightly touched her arm. "Honey, are you okay?"

Evian quickly snapped out of her spell. Then she shoved the tray in front of Alex. "Uh…I'm fine. Try one."

Alex looked at her with genuine concern before he retrieved a tuna tartar from the tray and gobbled it. "Hmmm," he moaned with delight. "Babe, that was good."

Evian smiled. "I'm glad you like it."

Next, she approached Alex's sixty-five year old stepmother, who was tall, slender, and bore a pale complexion. Evian thought Jeanine Benedict was beautiful, and possessed an aura similar to that of *Diahann Carroll*, a professional actress and singer.

Jeanine was sitting on the sofa, when Evian stooped over in her direction with the tray, and asked, "Would you care for an appetizer?"

"No thank you. I'm sure they're fine." Jeanine's tone was cool but polite.

"*O…kay*," Evian uttered under her breath. Slowly, she stood erect and walked toward the kitchen.

After Evian left the guest room, Regine whispered in her husband's ear, "I think she's trying too hard."

Guy nodded. "I agree."

Evian did not know what else to say or do. Being around Alex's family was making her jittery inside. She thought she did everything right to make his family like her. She had even missed a day of medical training to prepare for their visit.

At the last minute, she grabbed the phone in the kitchen to call her best friend, Joyce Jones. Her friend answered her call on the first ring. "I need you to come over right away," she rushed to say. "It's an emergency."

Joyce frowned. "Why? What's going on?"

"I'll explain everything when you get here."

"I'm on my way."

Evian sighed after disconnecting the call. She was happy her friend had honored her request under short notice.

She and Joyce were both in medical residency training at Tampa General Hospital. They met while in medical school. Both had received high marks for their school performance. In addition to being highly intelligent, they were also strikingly beautiful and statuesque.

Polar opposites, Joyce bore a very light pale complexion, light brown hair, and clear blue eyes. She also had a quiet persona. Evian, however, was talkative, and her aggressive personality dominated their friendship.

She was in the kitchen transferring the main entrées from the restaurant containers onto casserole dishes, when she heard a knock at the door. Joyce had finally arrived. She rushed out of the kitchen to greet her friend.

"I'm so happy to see you!" Evian cheered, after she opened the door and hugged her friend.

Joyce stared at her friend in a state of confusion. "We saw each other yesterday. Remember?"

"Of course I do!" Evian continued in a boisterous and animated manner.

After introducing Joyce to Alex's family, Evian grabbed her friend's hand and pulled her into the kitchen.

"What is your problem?" Joyce was annoyed with her friend's frantic behavior.

Evian wrung her hands as she paced the kitchen floor. "I don't know what to do. Alex is amazing, but I don't think his family likes me."

"How do you know?"

"It's the way they've been sizing me up all evening."

"I think you're overreacting."

"What about his stepmother? I believe she hates me."

Joyce snickered. "That's the price you pay for dating the *Baby boy.* Give her time. She'll come around."

Evian sighed. "I hope you're right."

Joyce gently touched her friend's shoulder. "You're a strong woman. Try not to let your insecurities get the best of you. Let's go out there and show them Miss America can compete with the best of them."

Nervously, Evian followed Joyce in the guest room. With her best friend by her side, she came across as confident and self-assured the rest of the evening.

Alex's family eventually warmed up to Evian, but not by much. They had come to terms that Alex was happy, and that was all that mattered to them.

Joyce, on the other hand, believed Alex's family should never let their guard down. She knew her friend was capable of violent acts. In fact, she and Evian shared a dark secret that could have landed them both in jail for the rest of their lives.

***

After dinner, Alex pulled Guy aside to talk in private. "What do you think of Evian?" he asked his brother.

"I think she's nice."

"I'm thinking about asking her to marry me."

Guy frowned. "Are you sure? I mean…I think you need time to get to know her better."

"I feel as though I've known her my entire life."

"Have you met or spoken with her parents?"

"No, not yet. I'm working on it."

"What do you mean?"

"Evian thinks it's too early for me to meet her parents."

"Alex, what you're telling me doesn't make any sense. Are you sure she's not hiding anything?"

"No. Why do you ask?"

"I just think it's strange that you haven't at least spoken with her parents over the phone. You've been dating Evian for several months, and she lives with you."

Alex shrugged. "Evian is in medical training, so I understand. I'll meet her parents soon enough."

Guy bore a thin smile even though he had doubts about Alex's girl-friend. He and Regine guessed Evian lied about cooking the entrees and appetizers she served them. He questioned what other lies she told, or the secrets she harbored.

Chapter 4

The Grass Ain't Greener

*C*armela left her sister's home in a fit of rage, and vowed to never return. But she did not realize how dramatically her life would change, when she called her twenty-five-year old boyfriend, Robert *"Swag"* Collins, to come to her rescue.

The day Swag retrieved Carmela from her sister's home, he sensed something was wrong. He asked, "Are you okay?"

"I have no place to go," she admitted, sounding pathetic.

"Are you still in school?"

Carmela shook her head. "If it's okay with you, I'd rather not talk about it." She was too ashamed to admit she lost interest in school after receiving failing grades in practically all of her classes.

Swag smirked as he thought of ways to use her misfortune to his advantage. He had easily convinced her to stay with him.

Shortly after Carmela moved in with Swag, she lost her virginity and started jumping hoops to please him. She did not realize he was using her, even when he persuaded her to drink alcohol, smoke marijuana, and snort cocaine. Then he introduced Carmela to a life of glamour and glitter, changing her image from *Fuddy Dud* to *Fly Girl*. Lastly, he taught her how to shoot a gun, to protect herself.

Satisfied with her new makeover and vibe, Swag took Carmela to a *five-star* hotel to introduce her to her first john. Though, he had withheld that minor detail, until the time was right.

"Why are you bringing me here?" Carmela asked, as Swag escorted her to a room on the penthouse level.

"I have someone I want you to meet."

Earlier, he had insisted she wear a red skintight mini-dress with matching six-inch pumps.

Carmela thought they were going on a date, especially after Swag dressed in a purple three-piece suit, white dress shirt, and red tie. His gold pinky ring, gold chains, and white Stacy Adams hat and shoes made him look the role of a professional pimp.

When they made it to the hotel room, a tall black, middle-age man in a business suit opened the door and let them inside.

"Hello," the man said, while eyeing Carmela like a piece of meat.

Swag stood back and gloated. "I told you she was *fine*."

The man smiled. "Yes, she is."

Confused, Carmela's eyes shifted back and forth between Swag and the stranger. "What's...going...on?" she asked in a choppy, nervous voice.

"Babe," Swag said, as he cupped the side of her face. "I want you to make this man feel good. He's paying big bucks for you."

"This is crazy!" she shouted in defiance. "I want to go home."

Carmela turned to leave, but Swag grabbed her arm and swung her around. "You're not going anywhere! You owe me!"

Biting her bottom lip, Carmela agreed with Swag's assessment. She thought if it were not for him, she could have ended up on the streets. Not only did Swag provide a place for her to live, but he also exposed her to a life of luxury. She had become accustomed to wearing designer clothes and eating at restaurants that catered to the rich and famous.

The man grew uncomfortable with the scene played out in front of him. "C'mon," he said to Swag, "do you have to be this aggressive?"

"You're paying for a service," Swag replied in a rough tone. "I expect you to get your money's worth."

"I don't want her to do anything against her will."

Carmela squirmed and winced from pain after Swag's grip on her arm tightened. "I'll do it!" she blurted out, after she failed to pull her arm from his grasp.

"You can let her go," the man intervened. "Come back for her in an hour."

After releasing her arm, Swag stepped back and glared at Carmela through slanted eyes. It was his way of hinting she better not screw up his business arrangement. Then he walked out of the hotel room and shut the door behind him.

The man turned to Carmela, and asked, "Would you like something to drink?"

"Yes." Her voice was soft and fragile.

He poured her a glass of pure Vodka and handed it to her.

Carmela drank the clear liquid in one gulp. Within seconds, the liquor had quickly taken over her senses. She felt loose and ready for whatever.

Over the next hour, Carmela experienced the role of a professional Call Girl. She was surprised the man was gentle with her. He did not make her feel like a whore. He wanted to sexually satisfy her. When the deed was over, he left a hefty tip.

After that night, Swag began to open up to Carmela about his *Call Girl* business and escorts. Though, he assured her that she was his number one girl.

Carmela knew she could have easily walked away from Swag, but she allowed pride to get in the way of common sense. Of course, staying with Swag meant she spent most nights in hotel rooms with various johns.

Initially, she thought Swag was the best thing that ever happened to her. She believed they met by chance. But she did not know she was strategically targeted.

Several months earlier, Carmela was sitting on a bench at a bus stop in front of the library. Swag spotted her reading a text book as he drove by in his BMW. He put his gear in reverse and backed up to the bus stop.

He studied Carmela's features and guessed she was in school based on her attire. She had on a white dress shirt, a black skirt, and four-inch heels. Her *makeup-free* face was too conservative for his personal taste, but he figured she was what he had in mind for his line of business.

"You need a ride?" Swag asked, while yelling out the passenger window.

"No," Carmela said in a soft whisper.

"Can I ask you a question?" he persisted.

Reluctantly, she stood up and walked over to the passenger side of his car. "How may I help you?"

"You're a pretty young thing. You know that?"

Carmela blushed.

He asked, "Where are you headed?"

"To my dorm."

"Let me give you a ride."

Not wanting her to reject his request, Swag leaned across the passenger seat and threw the door open.

Carmela hesitated before she climbed in and glimpsed at Swag from the corner of her eyes. She acknowledged no one as good-looking or as smooth talking as Swag had ever approached her. His dark brown eyes were captivating, his low hair cut revealed soft wavy hair, and his chiseled nose and *just right* lips reminded her of LL Cool J, an American rapper. Carmela also thought Swag's nickname personified his muscular build and sexy cool looks.

In retrospect, she did not know what compelled her to get in the car with him that day. She now realized she did not know Swag as well as she thought she did. More importantly, she wished she was aware of his line of work before she decided to move in with him.

Chapter 5
Family Matters

*R*egine Simmons was home preparing dinner for her family when the phone rang. She glanced at the *Caller ID* before wiping her hands on a dish towel, and reaching for the phone on the kitchen wall.

"Hi Justina," she greeted with a warm smile.

"Hello Regine, it's nice to hear your voice."

"Same here. How are you?"

"I'm fine," Justina replied in an almost inaudible tone. But she was not fine, and her sister was the primary cause of her distress.

Regine detected sadness in her friend's voice. She asked out of concern, "Is everything okay?"

"Yes, why do you ask?"

"You sound like you just lost your best friend."

Justina winced after conjuring memories of how she and her childhood friend fell out of friendship years earlier. They were both in a relationship with Guy Simmons but at different times. The love triangle ended when he had asked Regine for her hand in marriage. But it was only after his proposal to Justina failed, miserably.

"Justina, are you still there?" Regine asked, after she was met with silence on the other end of the line.

"Yes, I'm here."

"What's going on?"

"It's Carmela. I'm worried about her."

"I'm sure she's fine. Try not to worry."

"But I keep having visions that she's out there on the streets doing unthinkable things to survive."

"If she is, that's not your fault. Carmela knows right from wrong."

"I suppose you're right."

"Pray about the matter," Regine said in a comforting voice. "Then let go and let God."

Comforted by her friend's words of encouragement, Justina relaxed and managed a thin smile. "What would I do without you?"

"You're going to be okay. God will see you through this."

Justina let out a sigh after disconnecting the call.

When Regine heard the dial tone, she turned around and was startled to see her *not-so-happy* grandmother standing in front of her with her hands on her hips and a scowl on her face.

"Grandma Bessie," Regine said while returning the phone to its cradle, "what are you doing in the kitchen?"

"Why are you talking to Justina after all the nasty things she's done to you and this family?"

"That was a long time ago."

"Humph, I don't trust *that girl* as far as I can throw her."

"Justina is married," Regine emphasized, to lessen her grandmother's worries.

Bessie wielded her index finger in the air, and warned, "Mark my words. That girl ain't nothing but trouble."

"I can assure you that Justina has changed. I feel it in my spirit."

"Not that heifer," Bessie groaned. "I swear she's Satan's daughter." She looked at her granddaughter with grave disappointment before exiting the kitchen.

Regine knew her grandmother was trying to protect her, but thought she was wrong about Justina, *this time*. She reasoned she and her friend had matured, and had learned from their past mistakes.

Shortly after Grandmother Bessie left the kitchen, Guy walked in smiling at the sight of his wife retrieving a perfectly baked pot roast from the oven. Then he spotted the spinach casserole and macaroni and cheese on the stovetop. He commented, "Everything looks good and smells good."

"Thank you." Regine chuckled as she eyed his waistline. "Got beef?"

Guy laughed and patted his slightly bulging belly. "If you keep feeding me like this, I'm going to have to go on a diet."

At six feet, four inches tall and weighing two-hundred twenty pounds of mostly muscle, Guy was considered fit and in shape. He towered over Regine by six inches.

Guy looked at his wife through dreamy eyes. He loved everything about Regine, from her deep chocolate complexion to her sparkling brown eyes. Approaching her from behind, he wrapped his arms around her waist and whispered in her ear, "I love you."

Regine was uneasy with her husband's display of affection. She pulled out of his embrace, then busied herself by cutting the pot roast and placing slices on a large platter.

Guy was puzzled. Lately, his wife seemed turned off every time he tried to cuddle with her. They had not had sex in over a month.

"What is it?" he asked, trying to make sense of her reaction.

"I don't know what you're talking about."

Guy peered at his wife sideways, but Regine purposely kept her back to him. He had a feeling she was hiding something. Changing the subject, he asked, "What was your grandmother complaining about earlier? She walked by me, yelling, *Satan, the devil, is a liar!*"

"She's talking about Justina. Grandma Bessie doesn't like the idea that we're friends again."

Guy understood her grandmother's concerns. After all, Justina had caused his wife a lot of grief in the past.

Regine grabbed the platter of pot roast. Then she beckoned Guy to put on kitchen gloves to transport the white porcelain serving bowls filled with spinach casserole and macaroni and cheese to the dining room.

As soon as Guy placed the food on the table, he curiously asked, "How do you feel about befriending Justina, again?"

"I don't have a problem with it," Regine answered, after she placed the platter of sliced pot roast in the center of the dining table. "Justina's dealing with a lot."

"I know."

Over time, Guy had forgiven Justina at his wife's urging. He had completely let his guard down after learning of her past struggles. In fact, he and Justina became friendly and started engaging in small talk whenever they were in each other's presence.

But Guy's true feelings for Justina were tested when she and her husband, Aaron, came over to their home for cocktails one evening. As soon as Regine excused herself to go into the kitchen to prepare the drinks, Justina asked Guy to show her to the powder room.

Guy hesitated before he guided Justina down the hallway to the guest restroom. He was caught off guard when she stepped in front of him and stared into his eyes.

"What is it?" he asked with a hint of annoyance.

"Do you hate me?"

"What kind of question is that? You almost ruined my life."

"I was young and stupid."

Justina raised her hand and cupped the side of his face. "I'm sorry if I hurt you."

Guy removed her hand but it was before his heart *pitter-pattered* from her hand touch. "I think we both made the right decision."

"I want us to be friends," Justina said, as she extended her hand as a friendly gesture.

He nodded. "That's doable."

After they shook hands, there was a bolt of electricity between them. Neither said a word after realizing they still had feelings for each other.

Guy felt uncomfortable being that close to Justina. He quickly headed back down the hallway to the guest room. When Justina returned from the powder room several minutes later, he purposely kept his eyes focused on Regine the rest of the evening.

After that awkward encounter, Guy made sure he was never left alone with his ex-lover again. He had put all his time and energy into building a stronger bond with his wife. It was his attempt to dispel the notion that he still might be in-love with Justina.

Guy looked on as Regine arranged the food in the center of the dining table. Then she retrieved crystal glassware, cloth napkins, utensils, and gold rim plates from the china cabinet, and placed them on the table.

"I wish Alex could have made it over for dinner," Regine said, as she set the table for five.

"Me too," Guy said with a slight frown. "I think his decision had something to do with his girlfriend. Alex told me he wants to marry her."

Regine stared at her husband in disbelief. "Are you serious?"

"I'm afraid so."

Early on, Guy had a funny feeling about his brother's girlfriend. He tried to convince Alex to hold off on asking Evian to marry him, but his brother was *in love.* From personal experience, Guy knew love made one do crazy things. His brief fling with Justina quickly came to mind.

"Don't worry," Regine encouraged. "Alex's new girlfriend doesn't seem like all the other lunatics he has dealt with in the past."

"I hope you're right," Guy said, after admiring the way Regine set the table. "Do you need me to do anything else?"

"Please tell everyone to meet in the dining room for dinner."

"Sure thing."

***

In the living room, Grandma Bessie Croswell sat on the love seat with her husband, Deacon Alfred Franklin. They were winding down after driving sixteen hours from Virginia to Clearwater, Florida. It was the start of their two-week vacation with her granddaughter, Regine, and her family.

Seventy-four year old Bessie was a dark-skinned robust woman with a good mind and a good heart. She and the deacon married four years ago. Bessie was ten years older than her husband, but she did not look or act it. There was no doubt that she loved the deacon with all her heart.

Deacon Franklin stood six feet and weighed two-hundred pounds. A reformed gangster, he opted to turn his life over to the *Lord* after serving twenty years in prison for murder. Shortly after, he and Bessie started courting and subsequently married.

The deacon loved Bessie as much as she loved him, if not more. He had repeatedly proven he was willing to do anything to make sure he protected his wife and anyone close and dear to her. In fact, he murdered two young men who dated and harmed her granddaughter in the past. So he grew concerned when Bessie told him she was troubled over Justina and Regine's reunion.

"What do you want me to do?" he asked, after rubbing his beard.

"Nothing." Bessie shook her head for added affect. She did not want any more bloodshed on her husband's hands, or guilt on her conscience. She placed her hand on top of his, and spoke in a pleading tone. "Promise you won't do anything crazy."

"I'll do anything to make you happy."

"You don't have to do anything. Regine knows what she's doing."

Though, Bessie thought her granddaughter was making a big mistake by associating with the likes of Justina Bishop.

Undeterred, the deacon was going to make sure nothing ever happened to Regine, even if he had to do things under the radar.

Their conversation came to an end when Guy walked into the living room and told them the food was ready.

"It's about time," Bessie teased, as she stood up with her husband on her heels.

Guy laughed as he went upstairs to fetch his son; four-year old Kevin Charlie, nicknamed KC. He was Guy and Regine's only child, and the spitting image of his maternal grandfather.

When Guy and KC arrived in the dining room, Regine, Grandmother Bessie and Deacon Franklin were seated at the table. KC sat in the seat next to his mother while Guy sat at the head of the table.

Everyone bowed their heads while Guy prayed over the food. He closed the prayer, by saying, "We ask that you continue to watch over our family as we look forward to a brighter future."

"Amen," everyone said in unison.

Bessie's head remained bowed, as she prayed, *"My granddaughter is dealing with her so-called friend again. Please give me the strength to keep from hurting that evil witch."*

Then she hurriedly picked up her fork and dug into her food before anyone noticed her brief moment of fierceness.

Chapter 6
Put a Ring on It

*O*n their six-month anniversary, Alex planned a special evening for his girlfriend. Without her knowledge, he invited their friends and family members to a banquet hall to hear a surprise announcement. He used the phone in his corporate office to finalize last minute details with the owner of Evian's favorite Italian restaurant. Then he called her at home.

"Where are we going?" she asked, after Alex told her he was taking her out to dinner.

"Labella Sintos."

Evian grinned. "Sounds nice. What time are you picking me up?"

"I'll send a limo to pick you up at seven."

"Why aren't you picking me up?"

"I have a business meeting this evening in the same area," Alex fibbed. "So I thought I'd send a limo for you, and meet you at the restaurant."

"Okay."

"One more thing. I left a surprise for you in the closet. I want you to wear it tonight."

Eagerly, Evian threw the phone on its cradle and rushed to her closet. Air was caught in her throat as she eyed the most beautiful gown she had ever seen. It was a red, three-dimensional, strapless A-line gown by Michael Kors.

She hurriedly slipped it on and stood before the mirror. Turning from side-to-side, she admired the way the gown accentuated her slim physique. She retrieved ruby red earrings and a matching necklace from her vanity dresser to complete her attire.

After applying makeup, she grabbed her silver rhinestone clutch and headed out the front door just as the limo arrived. She climbed in the backseat and smiled at the sight of a long stem rose. Then she turned to her right and spotted a bottle of red wine in an ice bucket with a note that read: *You are the love of my life*.

Evian smelled the rose before pouring herself a glass of wine. Smiling from ear-to-ear, she was used to getting flowers and gifts from Alex. But she had a feeling this evening would be different.

When the limo pulled in front of the restaurant, Evian looked around and was disappointed Alex was not present to greet her. She climbed out of the limo, walked inside the restaurant, and approached the reception counter. Again, Alex was nowhere in sight.

"Are you Evian Gant?" the hostess asked her.

"Yes."

"Please follow me."

The hostess guided her to a banquet room in the back of the restaurant. To Evian's delight, the room was decorated with red and white balloons; and red rose bouquets in crystal vases were centered on each table. Her mouth flew open once she spotted her parents, her best friend, Joyce, and several colleagues sitting at tables on one side of the room. Then she scanned the other side of the room and noticed Alex's family and friends.

She remained motionless when a new rhythm and blues singer, Xavier Harris, stood in front of the room, and began singing, "Lately" by Tyrese Gibson.

While Xavier belted out sonatas, Alex walked through a side entrance in a white tuxedo, looking dapper. He approached Evian, then held her hand and kissed her on the cheek. "I'm glad you made it. You look beautiful."

"What's going on?" Her question bordered on hysteria.

"I want you to hear this song. The words exemplify what you mean to me." Both Alex and Evian turned to Xavier, as he sang:

"...I can't imagine life...without you by my side.

This is love babe...that I'm feeling.

And I'm hoping that you're feeling the same way..."

On the last note, Xavier was met with a loud applause and a standing ovation.

Shortly afterward, Alex guided Evian up the aisle in front of the room. He thanked Xavier for singing his song of choice. Then he turned to his guests and spoke over the microphone.

"Ladies and Gentlemen! Can I please have your attention? I have a special announcement. Today is special because I know in my heart that I've found the woman I want to spend the rest of my life with."

He knelt on one knee and retrieved a small box from his coat pocket. While looking into Evian's wide eyes, he revealed a five-carat diamond engagement ring. "Will you marry me?" Alex asked, taking delight in her surprised reaction.

Evian was close to tears. She looked to her mother and father who nodded their approval. Then she turned back to Alex, and said in a shaky voice, "Yes...I will...marry you."

Alex was elated as he stood up and slid the ring on Evian's finger. Then he picked her off the floor and gently swung her from side to side. "You just made me the happiest man in the world!"

Their guests surrounded them and showered them with well wishes. Then everyone ate, drank, and danced to a live band the rest of the evening.

Alex was on *cloud nine*, and assumed his girlfriend felt the same way. The evening had turned out as he had expected. He smiled after his stepmother and siblings embraced his new fiancé.

One of Alex's twin sisters, Dana, waited until everyone dispersed, before muttering in her future sister-in-law's ear, "I'm only tolerating you for my brother's sake. If you hurt him, you will regret it."

After belting out soft but wicked laughter, Evian touched Dana's arm. "Lighten up, *lil sis*. I love your brother to death." On that note, she walked away with a wide grin. She decided she had more pressing issues to deal with than to be worried about Dana's little threat.

But Dana was burning up inside from anger. She and her twin sister, Cassie, became overprotective of their family after experiencing turbulent growing pains, a year earlier.

Dana's first boyfriend had wound up dead, and Cassie was a victim of blackmail after the perpetrator assumed she was gay. Her sexual preference was even a mystery to her family, until she showed up at her high school graduation party with her new boyfriend.

From across the room, Jeanine saw the scowl on her stepdaughter's face. She walked over to her, and asked, "Are you okay?"

With her eyes glued on Evian, Dana mumbled under her breath, "I don't trust her."

Jeanine cupped her stepdaughter's chin with her thumb and forefinger, before speaking in a levelheaded tone, "Your brothers don't need their little sisters watching over them. Besides," she added with a mischievous grin, "that's what I'm here for."

Dana relaxed her shoulders and managed a soft smile. Her stepmother's assurance had eased her worries, but only a little.

Several feet away, Evian put on a plastered smile as she mingled with her guests. She was having a hard time enjoying herself, because a deep-rooted secret haunted her the entire evening.

When her best friend approached her, she asked, "Did you know about the engagement party?"

"No. This was all Alex's doing. I didn't find out until a couple of hours ago. He told me you wanted to meet me here for dinner. I think everyone was just as surprised as you."

Evian froze in place after she spotted her parents walking in her direction.

"My darling, Evian!" Mrs. Gant said with a burst of excitement. "We're so happy for you!" She gave her daughter a warm hug and stood back to get a closer look at Evian's gown. "You look heavenly!"

"I agree," her husband chimed in, after giving Evian a warm hug.

Hastily, Evian pulled away from her father's embrace. Then she turned to Joyce and asked for some time alone with her parents. She waited until her friend was out of ear shot, before she asked her mother and father, "Why didn't you tell me you were coming?"

"And ruin the surprise?" her mother said with a wide smile.

Her father interjected, by saying, "Alex Simmons is a good man. He's unlike the idiots you've dealt with in the past. I think he will do right by you."

"What did you tell him?" Evian asked her father in a hushed voice.

"Nothing," her mother intervened. "We want you to be happy. Your past has nothing to do with your future."

Flinching, her father did not agree. He believed the past had a way of catching up with the future.

"Finally!" Alex cheered, as he approached Evian's parents and gave them a bear hug. "I get a chance to meet my future in-laws."

Evian's father said, "You've found yourself a fine young woman."

Alex smiled. "I'm a very lucky man."

Mrs. Gant asked, "You two are not going to get married any time soon, are you?"

"*Mom!*" Evian scolded. "Alex just proposed to me, so it'll be a while before we're able to set a date."

Alex turned to his fiancé with a knowing gaze. "I was hoping we can marry this fall."

Stammering, Evian said, "Alex, honey…it takes…more than a… couple of months to plan a wedding."

"I've been secretly planning our wedding for months."

"But…how?" she asked with wrinkled brows.

"Do you remember when I asked you about the type of wedding you wanted?" Alex did not wait for her response, before adding, "Let's just say, I took notes."

Evian remembered. At the time, she thought Alex was just hinting he wanted to marry her. Teary-eyed and speechless, she recalled telling him she would love to marry in the fall.

Breaking the silence, Alex said to Evian's parents, "I'm glad you made it here under short notice. Hopefully, you'll be able to make it to our wedding."

Mrs. Gant chuckled. "We wouldn't miss it for the world. I'm glad you invited us to the engagement party." Her husband added, "It was generous of you to send plane tickets, and put us up in a hotel."

"It was my pleasure. Stay as long as you like."

"My parents are leaving tomorrow," Evian stated with certainty.

Alex asked, "Why so soon?"

Evian's parents looked at each other in bewilderment. They wanted to stay longer, but it was obvious their daughter objected to that idea.

"Something came up," Mrs. Gant said to Alex, after glimpsing at her daughter. "We have to leave as soon as possible."

Alex looked at Evian's parents with genuine concern. "I hope everything's okay. Maybe *we* can fly to St. Kitts to spend time with both of you, before the wedding."

"That's not possible!" Evian hurriedly chimed in. "I'm still in medical training, and Alex is busy running his company."

Sensing his fiancé's uneasiness, Alex said, "When the time is right, we'll be able to sit down and chat before the wedding."

"That sounds like a plan." Mr. Gant welcomed the idea, until he detected the scowl on his daughter's face. "We'll be leaving now. Please take care of our daughter."

"She's in good hands."

Mr. and Mrs. Gant bid Evian and Alex farewell with hugs and kisses. Then they walked out of the banquet room with droopy shoulders and sad eyes.

Holding back tears, Mrs. Gant assumed their one and only child was ashamed of them. After all, they were considered common folk living on a fixed income. She and her husband had recently retired from government jobs in the United States before relocating to St. Kitts.

Unlike his wife's point of view, Mr. Gant believed their daughter wanted them to leave because she was trying to keep them from revealing a secret that could possibly alter her future with Alex.

Chapter 7
Shock and Awe

Six months after the big fall out with her sister, Carmela returned to Aaron and Justina's home with her tail between her legs. She was sickened by the thought of asking her sister if she could stay with her *again*. After she rang the doorbell, she leaned on one leg, crossed her arms, and waited to be greeted by the person she despised the most.

Justina was on her way to work when she heard the doorbell chime. She grabbed her car keys and briefcase before she opened the front door and noticed her feisty sister on her doorstep. She gasped after looking at Carmela from head to toe.

Her sister's bold, colorful makeup made her look ten years older. A red halter-top barely covered her small, perky B-cup breasts. Around Carmela's waist, was a black flounce mini-skirt. It was so high up her thighs, a slight breeze could have easily revealed her pink panties. Six-inch platform boots completed her *hooker-like* appearance.

Justina wondered what happened to her one and only sibling, a straight "A" student throughout high school. She stared at her sister, while struggling to say, "What...are...you doing here?"

Carmela dryly admitted, "I have no place to go. Can I stay here with you?"

"Um...sure," Justina stammered. But she was not sure. When her sister showed up at her doorstep six months earlier, they had fought like cats and dogs. She feared a repeat of that infamous day.

Carmela asked with an attitude, "Aren't you going to let me in?"

"Uh...yes."

Justina slowly stepped aside and held the door open.

After grabbing her suitcase, Carmela entered her sister's home, rolling her eyes and dragging her feet. She had the urge to tell her sister how she really felt about her. Instead, she twisted her mouth, before asking in a harsh tone, "Where's my bedroom?"

Justina placed her purse and briefcase on the console in the foyer, after deciding to stay home from work. Then she turned to her sister and responded in a not so enthusiastic manner. "You can go to the guest bedroom upstairs, down the hall from our bedroom."

After strutting toward the staircase, Carmela turned around, and asked, "Where is your husband?"

"He's out of town on business. He should be home this evening."

"I look forward to seeing him again."

In all honesty, Carmela never liked her brother-in-law. She always thought he was pompous and arrogant.

With her nose in the air, she walked upstairs, acting as if she paid the bills and lived there her entire life. She entered the guest bedroom, locked the door behind her, and dived in the queen size bed, fully clothed.

Suddenly, Justina felt uneasy with the idea of her sister and husband under the same roof. She shrugged off her discomfort as she walked in the den to make an important phone call.

"Carmela is here with me," she said, as soon as her mother answered her call.

"Thank God!" her mother cried out with relief. "Please see if you can convince your sister to come home."

"I'll do my best." Justina paused, before asking, "How's Dad?"

A week earlier, her father underwent surgery to have a heart stent implanted after blockage was found during an annual checkup.

"Your dad is recovering well," her mother assured her. "He's going to be happy to hear the news about Carmela."

Justina smiled. "Give him my love."

"Will do."

After disconnecting the call, Justina went upstairs to talk to her sister. She knocked on the guest bedroom door, but there was no answer. Then she turned the doorknob and discovered it was locked.

Justina inched closer to the door, and said in a soft-spoken voice, "Please open the door. I need to talk to you."

Carmela rolled her eyes and sucked her teeth, before muttering, "Justina thinks she's better than me because she's married to a rich man." She shook her head, and said in a low voice, "*If only she knew what I know.*"

Justina banged on the door and raised her voice, "Open the door!"

"I don't feel like talking!" Carmela hollered back.

After taking a deep breath and exhaling, Justina retreated to her bedroom. She wanted to believe her sister had changed since she last saw her. But Carmela's brash disposition proved otherwise.

***

Aaron Bishop had taken a *red-eye* flight home from a business trip. He walked through the front door and put his car keys and briefcase on the console in the foyer. Then he took off his jacket and put it on the coat rack.

As usual, he stopped in front of the full length mirror in the hallway, to flex his arms and push out his chest. He had always taken pride in toning his muscular physique, which complimented his brown complexion and medium build.

He stood five feet' eight inches tall, and weighed one-hundred seventy-five pounds. A dimple in his left cheek accentuated his smile and bright white teeth. Although Aaron appeared wholesome wearing bifocal glasses and business suits, he was far from perfect. He had a weakness: *women, women, women, and more women!*

"Honey, I'm home!" he announced, as soon as he walked in the den, loosening his tie.

Justina did not hear Aaron. She was sitting on the sofa in a daze. She could not understand why her sister refused to talk to her all day. During lunch, she tried to strike up a conversation by asking questions, but Carmela's answers were restricted to a simple *yes* or *no*.

"What's wrong?" Aaron asked, fearing the worst.

Justina remained quiet and in deep thought.

When she did not respond, Aaron sat beside her on the sofa and placed his hand on top of hers. "Honey, talk to me."

Snapping out of her revere, Justina glimpsed at her husband and murmured, "Oh…hi. How was your trip?"

"It was okay. How are you?"

"My sister stopped by."

Aaron paused, before asking, "How is she?"

"She's okay."

"Good. I hope her visit was pleasant for you."

"Oh…um…Carmela is going to stay with us for a little while."

"Over my dead body!"

Aaron's voice was so loud, it reverberated off the walls in the den.

When he told Carmela she was no longer welcome in his and Justina's home several months earlier, he had meant every word. He could not forget how hopeless he felt when he witnessed his sister-in-law brutally beating his wife.

In a pleading tone, Justina said, "Aaron, please let Carmela stay with us. She's my sister."

"I don't care! Carmela's an ungrateful, selfish bitch!"

"Well…well…well," Carmela sang, from the top of the stairs. "Look who finally showed up."

Earlier, she spotted Aaron pulling up in the driveway from the guest bedroom window. She cracked open the bedroom door and overheard her brother-in-law objecting to her stay.

While descending the stairs, she twisted her lips and kept her eyes focused on Aaron until they stood toe to toe. "Now I see how you *really* feel about me," Carmela sassed with folded arms.

"I never made it a secret," Aaron spitefully retorted. "You need to leave now."

"What are you going to do if I don't?" Carmela talked back with a wide grin. "I suggest you chill out, if you know what's good for you."

Aaron experienced a knee-jerk reaction. Sweat began forming on his forehead and his heart was beating at the speed of lightning. He feared his sister-in-law was going to reveal secrets that could possibly destroy his marriage.

Carmela giggled as silence filled the air. She knew she could turn Aaron's world upside down. But doing that, she thought, would expose her own demons. So she pretended to have the upper hand.

"Don't worry," she coyly told her brother-in-law. "I'll be out of your house soon enough."

Aaron turned to Justina, and ordered, "Take care of this." He stared down his sister-in-law before he pounced upstairs to the master bedroom, slamming the door behind him.

The altercation with Carmela reminded him of the time he and his father argued over a serious matter. They had not seen each other since. Just like he walked out of his father's life, Aaron wanted Justina to do the same with her sister. He could not understand why his wife could not see through Carmela's lies and self-serving antics.

After Aaron went upstairs, Justina realized the situation had gone awry. She turned to her sister, and said, "I think it's best if you return home to mom and dads. They're worried sick about you."

"I'll leave," Carmela snarled, "but I'm not going home. *Ever!*" she sharply added, before turning her back to her sister in a huff.

Suddenly, Justina had a change of heart. She wanted to help her sister get off the streets. "Please don't go," she said in desperation. "You can stay."

Carmela turned around and eyed her sister with suspicion. "Why do you want me to stay?"

"I don't want anything to happen to you," Justina sincerely admitted. "I'd feel better if you were here with us."

While mulling over her sister's request, Carmela realized she had no choice. She needed money badly, and her unknowing sister was a part of the equation.

"I'll stay," Carmela said with a hint of defiance.

"Just one thing," Justina said, as an afterthought.

"What is it?"

"Don't get into a fight with Aaron."

"You don't have to worry about me," Carmela griped. "I don't know why you married that *jerk* in the first place."

"Enough!" Justina screamed. "I will not let you stay here and disrespect my husband."

Carmela rolled her eyes skyward, mocking her sister's anger.

"It's been a long day," Justina said in a calm voice. "Go to your room and get some rest before dinner."

"That's a splendid idea!" Carmela replied in a fake, high-pitched voice, before she turned and headed upstairs.

Justina's eyes shifted toward heaven as she prayed the tension in her home would soon subside. Then she marched upstairs to try and convince her husband he had no reason to be concerned about Carmela.

Aaron had taken off his business clothes and changed into his workout gear. He spotted Justina as soon as she strolled into their bedroom. "I hope you came in here to tell me your sister is leaving."

"Honey, let's not get bent out of shape. Carmela will only be here for a little while."

"Oh...no...she's...not!" he shouted, placing emphasis on every word.

"Please...Aaron," Justina cried out, as tears welled in her eyes. "I don't want to lose my sister, again."

"You don't have to worry about that, as long as you and your parents continue to cater to her."

"You...don't...understand," Justina pressed on in a shaky voice. "I have a feeling my sister's been dealing with ruthless people."

"Whose fault is that? No one put a gun to her head and forced her in the streets."

Justina's heart ached in response to her husband's remarks. There was nothing she could do or say to negate the truth.

Aaron hesitated before he walked past Justina, to exit their bedroom. As an afterthought, he turned around, and said, "Your sister can stay. But tell her to stay out of my way."

Justina smiled as a glimmer of hope filled her eyes. "Thank you."

"Don't thank me yet. Your sister has a flair for drama."

Chapter 8
Love is Fragile

On Sunday, Regine woke up early to meet her business partner, Lamar Greene, to discuss the grand opening plans for a new restaurant in Miami, Florida. She had come to rely on him for much needed advice and support. Even though her husband had always supported her endeavors, Regine believed Lamar was her biggest asset.

While rummaging around in the bedroom, Regine made a concerted effort to be as quiet as possible. She did not want to wake her husband. Her efforts failed when Guy's eyes fluttered opened.

He rolled over and peered at the neon-lit clock on the wall. Then he sat up in bed and turned on the lamp on the nightstand. He spotted Regine standing in front of the floor mirror in her black Jones New York pants suit. Then he watched her stroll over to her vanity dresser.

In a groggy voice, he said, "Why are you up so early?"

Regine put on her watch and earrings, as she explained, "I thought I told you I had to meet with Lamar this morning, to discuss our plans for the grand opening in Miami."

Guy could not recall the alleged conversation with his wife. First of all, it was Sunday. Regine never worked on Sunday unless it was urgent. Secondly, Guy was sure she never told him about her meeting with Lamar.

"When is the grand opening?" he probed out of curiosity.

"In two weeks."

Lightly scratching the top of his head, Guy was certain this was his first time hearing about the grand opening. He sat up in bed, and said, 'I'll go with you this morning to meet with Lamar."

Regine waved her hand, rejecting the idea. "That's not necessary."

"I want to come and support you."

"It's not a big deal."

Guy frowned. Regine's nonchalant attitude irked him. He had always supported her. But she made it clear she no longer needed him.

After grabbing her purse, Regine walked over to Guy and brushed her lips across his cheek. "I'll see you later." She ignored his quizzical stare as she strolled out of their bedroom and closed the door behind her.

Guy was unable to return to sleep. He got out of bed and headed for the shower. He made a mental note to stop by his office to review a potential investor's business proposal.

Ever since he became the primary owner and CEO of Calvent Lucent Technology, business had been booming at a steady pace. It had even made the Fortune 500 listing three years in a row. Guy was certain the deal with the new investor would increase the company's revenue.

As soon as he dressed for work, he walked in the kitchen and was surprised to find Regine's grandmother sitting at the table, reading her Bible. "Good morning, Grandma Bessie. What are you doing up so early?"

"Morning, Guy," she said with a warm smile. "I heard you mulling around the house earlier. I thought you left."

"No, that was Regine."

"Where did she go?"

"She had to go to work to meet with Lamar."

Bessie frowned. "This time of morning? And on a Sunday?"

"My thoughts exactly," Guy replied, as he walked over to the kitchen counter to pour himself a cup of coffee. Then he turned to Bessie, and explained in a tone laced with sarcasm, "Regine and Lamar are buddies. She doesn't need me anymore."

Bessie understood why Guy felt uncomfortable with Regine's business partner. Her granddaughter had always spoken positively about Lamar. It was not only the things Regine told her about him, it was the way she said it. Her eyes and gestures spoke volumes. But Bessie refused to believe her granddaughter was having an affair. She figured Guy had his own suspicions.

"Did she tell you why she had to meet with Lamar?" Bessie inquired.

Guy sipped his coffee, before answering, "They're meeting this morning to discuss the grand opening in Miami."

"I don't mean to pry, but what's going on between you two?"

"Why do you ask?"

"Something doesn't seem right."

"Don't worry," Guy tried to assure her. "We're fine."

Even as he said the words, he was not sure. He checked his watch before placing his coffee mug in the sink. "I have to go to work. I'll see you this evening."

"Son, have a nice day and try not to worry."

Guy smiled before he turned to leave. But his heart was aching. More than once, it had crossed his mind that Lamar and Regine could be having an affair. He was overcome with grief.

After Guy left for work, Bessie remained at the kitchen table, thinking about her granddaughter. First, Regine decided to reconnect with Justina Bishop, the same young woman who made her granddaughter's life a living hell. Now her granddaughter might be letting her relationship with Lamar Greene affect her marriage.

Bessie thought, at this rate, Regine and Guy could end up in divorce court. She prayed for God's divine intervention. Then she phoned Regine's father for help.

***

Forty-eight year old Kevin Graham was handsome but rugged. He was dark complected, and had a lightly graying goatee. The same body type as Denzel Washington's, Kevin stood five feet' ten-inches tall and weighed two hundred pounds. Often, he sported black suits, a trench coat, dark shades, and a Godfather hat that made him appear invincible and in control.

A formidable crime lord, Kevin was a no-nonsense man. Whenever he opened his mouth, he did not mince words. He was a man to be feared and with good reason. He murdered everyone that ever crossed him. He was ruthless, unrelenting, and calculating.

He assumed someone had wronged his oldest daughter when he received Bessie's phone call. "What's up?" he answered her call in a gruff manner.

"It's Regine."

"What's going on?"

Bessie explained her issues involving her granddaughter, and answered Kevin's questions regarding Regine and Lamar's business relationship. "Whatever you do," she cautioned, "do not hurt anyone."

"I hear you." Kevin heard her but he was not feeling her.

Bessie continued, "What about Guy? Will you talk to him?"

"As far as I'm concerned, Guy doesn't deserve Regine."

Perplexed, Bessie said, "Kevin, what are you saying?"

"My daughter deserves someone who can protect her."

"Kevin, you can't blame Guy for what happened in the past."

"Yes I can!" he said in anger. "Do you know how I felt when my daughter was kidnapped, and her *stupid ass* husband sat on the side line and watched it happen."

"Kevin, you're wrong for blaming Guy for that. He is a good man. Would you rather Regine be with someone like you?"

Briefly closing his eyes, Bessie's words had hit home. The answer was *no*; he did not want his daughter to be with a hardcore criminal.

"Will you at least talk to Regine?" Bessie urged.

"I can do that."

Bessie smiled. "Now what about her sisters? Don't you think it's time they meet?"

Kevin remained quiet. Several years earlier, he had confided in Bessie about his other children. His daughters all lived on the East Coast. Regine was the oldest.

Unlike his other children, Kevin was estranged from his youngest daughter, who was adopted by her stepfather. Kevin's role in her life was minimal, but he would periodically follow up with her mother to see if she needed anything.

After pondering Bessie's question, Kevin was certain of his stance. With his criminal history, he thought it was too dangerous for them to meet. "It's not a good idea," he finally answered her.

"They have a right to know."

"I'll think about it," Kevin said to appease Bessie. "I gotta go."

"Kevin!" Bessie called out, before disconnecting the call. "You can't go around killing people over your children."

"I'll do whatever it takes."

Kevin abruptly disconnected the call. Then he thought back to the last time one of his daughter's was wronged by her boyfriend. He and his henchmen abducted the young man, and transported him to a vacant lot behind an old manufacturing building.

Kevin stood by while his henchmen poured gasoline over the young man's body.

"Please!" the young man sobbed, while tears flooded his face. "I promise, whatever I did, it won't happen again."

Kevin looked closely at the young man through hardcore eyes. "Let me get this right," he said in a condescending manner. "You fucked with my daughter. Now you're trying to act innocent?"

The young man thought long and hard before the truth hit him in the face. He knew exactly who Kevin was referring to; it was his ex-girlfriend. She looked like her father. Their similarities were unmistakable.

Stuttering, the young man begged for dear life, "I...I...didn't mean to hurt her. It...was...a misunderstanding."

"Shut the hell up!" Kevin exclaimed, before he tightened his right fist and punched the young man in the face, forcing him to fall backward.

Kevin removed a lighter from his coat pocket, fired up the cigar he had been holding in his left hand, and took a long puff. He flicked his lighter once more, threw it on the young man, and shouted, *"Die mutha fucka!"*

The young man screamed and howled before succumbing to the flames. His death was imminent.

Kevin felt satisfied with the execution. He walked away, and left his loyal associates to clean up the mess.

Chapter 9
Sweet and Sour

With the engagement party out of the way, Alex took Evian out to breakfast at a quaint restaurant overlooking the Tampa Bay pier. He thought it would be a great idea to divulge their wedding plans in an intimate setting. Evian, on the other hand, had been trying to avoid the subject of marriage since Alex proposed to her. She was relieved he had remained mum on the subject during their drive to the restaurant.

Unfortunately for Evian, Alex broached the subject after their food orders were delivered to their table. While eating, he explained how he had hired a reputable wedding coordinator to ensure Evian had the fairy tale wedding of her dreams. He also stated he had rented a historic wedding chapel, situated on a small private island along the Gulf Coast.

Evian's mouth flew open in surprise when he told her he had rented a horse and carriage to transport her to the chapel.

"Wow," she whispered in amazement. "I don't know what to say."

Proud of his efforts, Alex continued to boast, "Guy is going to be my best man, and my three closest friends agreed to be the groomsmen. I've already made arrangements to have everyone fitted for their tuxedos. All you have to do is ask your best friend, Joyce, to be your maid of honor, select your bridesmaids, and pick out a wedding dress."

Evian removed her cloth napkin from her lap and placed it on her plate of sparsely eaten food. Suddenly, she lost her appetite. She realized Alex had exerted a lot of energy in making their wedding day special.

"I still don't know about this," she muttered under her breath.

"Know about what?"

Casting her eyes downward, Evian struggled to say, "I think... we're...rushing things."

Alex dropped his fork in his plate and glared at Evian. "What do you want to do?" he asked out of frustration.

Evian lowered her eyes as she spoke in a soft tone. "I want us to wait a little longer before we marry."

"When do you want to marry me?"

"Please don't take this the wrong way. I want to marry you, but not now."

After shaking his head in disbelief, Alex removed his cloth napkin from his lap and placed it on the table. Then he pushed his chair back, stood up, and retrieved his wallet from his pants pocket.

"What's wrong?" Evian asked, astonished by his reaction.

"Let's go home."

He avoided eye-contact as he threw a couple of one-hundred dollar bills on the table, returned his wallet to his pants pocket, and headed toward the exit.

Evian remained seated for a few seconds before she followed Alex out of the restaurant. She noticed he was already behind the steering wheel of his Lamborghini. She was hesitant as she opened the passenger door and climbed in.

Alex waited until his fiancé buckled up, before asking, "How long do I have to wait before you decide to marry me?"

Evian said in a baby-like voice, "I'm not sure."

Sighing, Alex thought the money and time he had put into expediting their wedding plans had been in vain. He backed out of the parking space and headed home.

During the drive, thoughts about their relationship swirled around in his head. He believed if Evian had doubts about him now, there was nothing he could do to change her mind in the future.

Evian was also thinking about their relationship. She did not blame Alex for being upset with her. She wanted to marry him, but first she had to deal with an issue from her past. It was the same issue that saturated her thoughts and made it difficult for her to enjoy her surprise engagement party.

Up to this point, she had tried everything in her power to keep Alex from finding out about her *Little Big Secret*. Resorting to murder had crossed her mind.

Alex was in a somber mood, as he and Evian arrived home in utter silence. He did not look in her direction after he put his gear in park and climbed out of his car. He entered his condo and strolled out on the deck to call his brother.

Guy answered on the first ring. "Hi Alex. What's going on?"

"Evian is having reservations about marrying me this fall."

Gasping in surprise, Guy sat up in the chair in his office, and asked, "What happened?"

"She wants to wait."

"I'm sorry to hear this. But maybe this is a sign that you might be rushing things."

"Yeah, I thought about that. I misunderstood her intentions."

"Don't beat yourself up. You never know, she may change her mind."

"I hope you're right."

"Hang in there, little brother. Things will work out."

"Thanks for listening."

"No problem."

Next, Alex called the wedding coordinator. His directive was short and to the point, as he said, *"Cancel everything. The wedding is off."* He disconnected the call before she had the opportunity to question him about the sudden change in plans.

Alex walked over to the patio bar and poured Vodka in a shot glass. He downed the liquor, and immediately refilled the glass. He was trying to soothe his broken heart.

Prior to asking Evian to marry him, Alex thought long and hard over his decision. This was his second attempt to try and do the right thing.

Rhaunda Coleman was the first woman he had asked to marry. She was a virgin and a *die-hard* Christian. She had forgiven him for being unfaithful throughout their relationship. But she ended up shooting him after she found out about his fling with her best friend, Alecia Kellam.

Shortly after he was released from the hospital, Rhaunda's mother, Elizabeth Coleman, called him. Her voice was filled with anger and resentment. "It's because of you," she shouted with fury, "my daughter is locked up!"

"I'm sorry your daughter is in a mental institution," Alex corrected her, in a calm voice. "Why didn't you tell me about her mental condition?"

"Because it was none of your *damn* business!"

"It *was* my business. Your daughter shot me."

"You pushed her to do it," Elizabeth sobbed. Her voice was caught in her throat and her lips from quivering from rage.

"I'm sorry you feel that way, but you knew your daughter's medical history played a role...."

Elizabeth interrupted Alex, by yelling and crying, "You're going to pay for what you did to my family!"

"I didn't do anything to your family."

"My husband is locked up and he's not eligible for parole for ten years!"

"Again, that is not my fault. Your husband tried to blackmail the doctor that saved my stepmother's life."

"To hell with that!" Elizabeth continued to spew hate. "You and that bitch, Alecia, are going to get yours!" On that note, she slammed the phone on its cradle.

Alex listened to the dial tone before hanging up the phone. He thought about calling the police but concluded Elizabeth would not pose a threat to him or Alecia Kellam. He could not understand why she felt he was responsible for landing her husband in jail.

Before Rhaunda Coleman was identified as the culprit who shot Alex, her friend, Alecia, was put in jail after she was suspected of shooting him. Rhaunda's father, Pastor Coleman, was afraid the police detectives would learn the truth about his daughter's involvement, so he tried to blackmail Alecia's father, Dr. Kellam – *the same doctor who had given a drug for stage IV breast cancer to Alex's stepmother.*

The pastor was aware the cancer drug was not approved by the Food and Drug Administration, and was considered illegal if administered in the United States. He used this tidbit of information to send a letter to Dr. Kellam stating that if his daughter, Alecia, did not confess to shooting Alex, he would report the doctor to the medical board.

Worried that his medical license would be in jeopardy, the letter had sent shock waves throughout the doctor's body. He immediately died of a heart attack. The pastor almost got away with blackmail, but the authorities got ahold of the letter.

The doctor did not live long enough to see that his daughter was acquitted of all charges, and to see that Jeanine Benedict was alive and well because of the cancer drug.

Reflecting on his near-death experience, Alex felt lucky to be alive. Though, he felt bad for Rhaunda and her family. He made a promise to himself and to God, to never hurt another woman. He could not help but wonder if Evian's reluctance to marry him was God's way of punishing him for his past mistakes.

Chapter 10
Crash and Burn

Carmela was still sizzling in anger from her recent confrontation with her brother-in-law. For the past three days, both had been successful at not uttering one word as they crossed paths. But the truce ended when Justina insisted they all dine together. She was hoping her sister and husband could patch up their relationship.

Over brunch, there was awkward silence. But it did not stop Aaron and Carmela from shooting daggers at each other. Justina hopelessly sat on the sidelines witnessing her husband and sister's exchanges.

Aaron grew furious after he caught his sister-in-law rolling her eyes and shaking her head. "What is your problem?!" he shouted at her.

"I know you're not talking to me," Carmela flippantly replied with a head roll.

Justina intervened before things got out of control. She gently touched Aaron's hand. "Honey, please don't start."

He abruptly snatched his hand away from Justina and pushed his chair back. "I don't know how much longer I can deal with this," he said, before he stood up and headed out of the dining room.

"Where are you going?" Justina asked him.

Aaron turned around with a dirty look on his face. "I'm going out. I'll be back later."

He grabbed his car keys off the console in the foyer and darted out the front door. Upon climbing in his car, he retrieved his cell phone from his coat pocket and dialed the phone number he knew by heart.

"Hello," he said, as soon as the owner of the *Call Girl Service* answered his call. "Can you take care of me now?"

"What are you looking for?"

"A threesome," Aaron answered. "A man and a woman."

"Same location, right?"

"Right."

Aaron performed his treacherous deeds at a sleazy hotel on the south side of Tampa. He figured no one would catch him in a place like that.

"I can hook you up," the owner said, after deciding which escort he could pair Aaron with. He figured he would call in a favor from one of his associates to find a male escort for the threesome.

Aaron asked, "How much are you going to charge me?"

"Five thousand."

"I'll be there."

Aaron hung up the phone with a look of satisfaction. Having sex with multiple women at the same time was the norm for him. Sex with a man, he thought to himself, would be an experience of a lifetime.

Sitting quietly at the dining room table, Justina was saddened by her husband's departure. She became furious after noting the smug grin on her sister's face.

"Carmela, what happened to our agreement? You promised not to get in Aaron's way."

"I didn't start it!"

Incensed, Carmela stood up and ran upstairs to the guest bedroom. At this rate, she knew the objective for visiting her sister would be impossible to achieve. She retrieved her cell phone from her purse to call her boyfriend.

"Hi there." She tried to sound upbeat as soon as she heard his voice. But her tone fell flat.

"Did you ask your sister for the money yet?" Swag sounded harsh and impatient.

"Not yet."

"Watcha waiting for?!"

Carmela blew out air in frustration, before explaining, "It's going to take a little longer than I thought."

"Damn!" Swag exclaimed.

"I just need a little more time."

"Make it happen." His directive was laden with disappointment.

"I promise," she said in an almost pleading voice.

"Don't call me back until you got the money."

Swag abruptly disconnected the call. The only thing that kept him from going off on Carmela was his dealings with her brother-in-law. He expected to get paid five thousand dollars for the threesome he had just arranged for Aaron.

Carmela was befuddled after Swag hung up on her. She had second-thoughts about her occupation as an escort for her boyfriend's *Call Girl Service*. But the one thing that remained constant in her life was the love she had for Swag. She worshipped the ground he walked on.

Several days earlier, her love was tested when he asked her to borrow money from her sister. She was willing to do anything to please him, but asking Justina for money was not what she had in mind.

"Are you crazy?!" she told him with a baffled look on her face. "I can't stand my sister."

"Listen babe," Swag cooed in a comforting voice. "I get it. You and your sister got beef with one another. But I need money to pay off a debt. If I don't get the money, they're going to kill me."

"Who's going to kill you?"

"Some people I owe."

"What happened to the money you've been getting from your escort service?"

"It's not enough. I need fifty grand."

"Fifty-thousand?" Carmela's brows shot up in surprise. "My sister is not going to give me that kind of money."

"Can you get half of it?" Swag was willing to compromise.

"I haven't spoken to my sister in months. I'm not sure if she would even open her front door for me."

"Why not?"

"We had a fight, remember?"

"That happened a while ago," Swag reasoned. He cupped her face and kissed her lips. "Don't you love me, babe?"

She cracked a smile.

"Will you do this one favor for me?" he persisted in a whiny voice.

Carmela could not tell Swag *no* even if she wanted to.

Ever since she told him about Justina and her brother-in-law's wealth, Swag had been holding on to that information for a moment like this. He saw dollar signs and wanted a piece of the pie. So he lied to Carmela by telling her he needed money to pay off a debt.

Flashing back to the present, Carmela slouched on the edge of the bed. She was wondering how she was going to get the money from her sister, to give to her boyfriend. Then it suddenly dawned on her that she should try to get the money from her brother-in-law. She reasoned Aaron loved Justina and had a lot to lose.

Her cheeks flushed as she began to put the pieces of her plan together. *Blackmail* was a huge gamble, but she thought it was the best option.

Chapter 11
Basic Instincts

*A*s soon as Regine drove into her designated parking space in front of the restaurant, Lamar pulled up in his car and parked next to her. She was happy to see him, especially since she had been daydreaming about him the entire weekend. She had long ago determined that if she were not married, Lamar would be a potential mate.

Both smiled at each other before grabbing their briefcases and climbing out of their cars.

Lamar beamed, as he sang, "*Good morning, Mrs. Simmons!*"

"Good morning," Regine replied with hearty laughter, while locking the car door with the remote.

Smiling broadly, Lamar ogled her from head to toe. "You look heavenly in your business suit. In fact, you look beautiful in anything you wear."

Regine blushed. "Thank you." She welcomed his kind words, which prompted her to take a closer look at Lamar.

She thought he looked handsome in his two-piece navy blue designer suit with matching Magnanni shoes. She noted his pitch-black hair hinted strands of gray, and his well-groomed haircut made him looked distinguished. She also recognized his tall slim build gave him a sexy swag. And judging by his even skin color, Regine sensed Lamar spent a lot of time in the sun.

When they walked up the path to the front entrance of the restaurant, Lamar unlocked the door and stood back to allow Regine to enter first. He took a whiff of her perfume as she passed by him.

"Hmmm…you smell good," he commented with a sly grin. "Coco Chanel, right?"

Turning around, Regine asked, "How did you know?"

"I make it my business to know vital facts about the woman I admire."

Regine gasped and experienced a *Waiting to Exhale* moment. She was captivated by Lamar's words.

"Mrs. Simmons," he said as he stepped within inches of her face, "you are breathtaking."

Regine broke out in nervous laughter. "Stop playing around, Lamar. We have to open the restaurant in a couple of hours."

"Or, we can let our manager take over," he said with dreamy eyes. "So I can take you to the beach."

For a fleeting moment, Regine considered Lamar's suggestion before assuming he was joking, again. She took a step backward and checked her watch. "Let's meet in my office in thirty minutes, to discuss the grand opening for the new restaurant in Miami." Then she headed to her office.

"I'll do anything for you," Lamar silently thought to himself. He chuckled before heading down the hallway to his office.

Once inside, he rested against the back of the door. His heart was beating fast. He looked down at the noticeable *boner* protruding in the crotch of his pants. Regine had turned him on in the worst way.

At that moment, Lamar felt as though he had just taken a bite out of forbidden fruit. Normally, he drew the line when it came to married women. But ever since their first meeting, he could not get Regine out of his thoughts. With control and willpower, Lamar kept his true feelings to himself. He settled with being her protector and guardian.

A year earlier, Regine was kidnapped and Lamar was instrumental in rescuing her from her captor. He recounted the time he called her husband to explain she might be in trouble with Bryce Jennings, who was Lamar's potential business partner at the time.

Regine was rescued an hour later, thanks primarily to her father, Kevin Graham. Subsequently, Bryce Jennings was put to death at the hands of Kevin's henchmen.

After Lamar called and reported Regine's life was in danger, it had meant a lot to her father. So much so that Kevin paid Lamar a visit at his home several days later.

Lamar opened his front door and his mouth flew open from the sight of Regine's father.

Kevin extended his hand. "I want to thank you for saving my daughter's life."

"But I didn't do anything," Lamar stated, as he shook Kevin's hand.

"Yes you did. You cared enough about my daughter to realize something was wrong."

Lamar nodded in understanding.

"I need a huge favor," Kevin said.

"Anything."

Kevin handed Lamar a business card with his cell number. "From now on, call me if my daughter is in trouble."

Reluctantly, Lamar retrieved the card from Kevin's hand. He did not know what to make of his new acquaintance.

Then Kevin retrieved a wad of cash from his wallet and extended it to Lamar. "This is for your troubles."

"I can't take your money," Lamar explained.

Frowning, Kevin tilted his head to one side, and asked, "Why not?"

"Because I *love* taking care of Regine." Lamar's tone was boastful and filled with desire.

Kevin raised a brow. He mentally questioned the meaning behind Lamar's statement.

"I mean. I would do anything to protect her," Lamar clarified, hoping his comments were not taken out of context.

"Cool. But don't get it twisted. If you hurt my baby, I will *fuck* you up."

Kevin stared at Lamar before he returned the cash to his wallet. He gave his henchman a head-jerk, signaling it was time to leave. Then he turned to Lamar, and said, "I'll be in touch. Don't let me down."

"I won't, sir. You have my word."

Swallowing hard and out of fear, Lamar believed Kevin was a man of his word. He knew he had two options when it came to Regine. He could honor her father's request to protect her; or he could pursue her and put himself at risk, at the hands of her father.

Ever since that one encounter, Kevin and Lamar stayed in contact by phone. Regine never suspected anything, and her father wanted to keep it that way. As far as Lamar was concerned, he and Kevin had established a good rapport. So he was surprised when Regine's father walked in the restaurant, looking unpleased to see him.

"Hi," Lamar greeted Kevin with a nervous smile.

"Where's my daughter?" Kevin asked, after browsing the restaurant for Regine.

"She's in her office. Do you want me to go get her?"

"No, it's okay."

Kevin thought about confronting Lamar but changed his mind. As per Bessie's request, his objective was to clear up some things with his daughter. He headed toward the back of the restaurant and entered her office with a broad smile.

"Hi *Babygirl*."

Regine's eyes lit up upon seeing her father. "Hi Daddy!" She jumped out of her chair and ran into his open arms.

Kevin smiled and embraced her. "How are you doing?"

"I'm fine. It's good to see you."

"Have a seat *Babygirl*. We need to talk."

"What's wrong?"

"Your grandmother asked me to talk to you."

"Oh brother," Regine moaned, as she walked around her desk and sat in her chair.

Kevin took a seat on the opposite side of her desk, before asking, "What's this I hear about you and Justina being friends again?"

Regine sighed before she leaned toward her father. "Dad, I appreciate your concern, but I do believe in redemption. Or, are you forgetting I forgave you, for letting me believe you were dead the first twenty years of my life?"

His daughter's words stung, but Kevin was steadfast on remaining focused. He had already decided to silence Justina for good, if she ever became a problem for his daughter. So he changed the subject, by asking, "Is there something going on between you and Lamar?"

Stunned by the question, it took a couple of seconds before Regine collected her thoughts. "No," she finally answered. "We're just business partners. Why do you ask?"

"How well do you know him?"

"Well enough. He really is a sweet guy."

"I just want you to be careful around him."

Regine frowned. "Is there something I should know about my business partner?"

Kevin liked Lamar but believed he was no different from Guy; both men were considered weak in his eyes. He bore a wide grin, before admitting, "I'm not in a position to give you relationship advice. You deserve to be happy."

Regine smiled. "Thank you, Daddy. I'm glad you feel that way."

Kevin stood up, walked around her desk, and gave her a kiss on the forehead. "You take care of yourself."

"You too."

Like a thief in the night, he left through the back entrance of the restaurant.

Regine remained in her office long after Kevin left. She mulled over their conversation and her father's warning about her business partner. After all, she met Lamar under unusual circumstances.

Three years earlier, she had opened her first restaurant in St. Petersburg, Florida. That was around the same time Lamar walked through the entrance, suited-up and looking spiffy.

"Can I speak with the owner?" he asked Regine.

"Who are you?"

"Lamar Greene."

"Lamar?" she asked with raised brows. She acknowledged he was the first white man she had ever met with that name.

"My mother lived in Lamar, Colorado in her youth. Let's just say the name stuck with her and here I am."

"That's an amazing revelation. My name is Regine Simmons, the owner of this establishment. How may I help you?"

"You're the owner?" he asked in amazement.

Regine smirked. "What surprises you most?" she asked in a playful manner. "Is it because I'm a woman, black, or both?"

"I didn't mean anything by…."

Chuckling, she stood back and watched Lamar try to squirm out of her line of questioning. "I'm just kidding. How may I help you?"

"I'm interested in your restaurant."

"My restaurant is not for sale."

"I don't want to buy it. I would like to invest in your restaurant business, and possibly help you expand."

"Do you have restaurant experience?"

"I've managed several businesses. I think I can be a valuable asset to you." Lamar failed to mention he never worked in the restaurant industry.

Regine invited him to her office to discuss his proposition. It took them a while before they agreed to the terms of their new business relationship. She was satisfied with her decision.

Unbeknown to Regine, her father had commissioned one of his associate's to conduct some research on Lamar, but was not able to find any background information. Kevin did not worry too much about it, until recently.

After leaving the restaurant, he thought about taking Lamar completely out of the picture. He was concerned his daughter might have stronger feelings for Lamar than she let on. It did not help that he discovered some shocking revelations about Lamar's live-in girlfriend. Kevin had a feeling he would be crossing paths with her in the very near future. He ordered one of his men to follow her, while he dealt with Lamar.

Chapter 12
The Little Big Secret

*A*fter becoming Miss America, Evian was immediately thrown into the spotlight. She had honored numerous requests for speaking engagements and fundraising events. Over a year's time, she travelled around the country with her rhinestone tiara, orating *safe-sex* lectures.

When her duties as Miss America came to an end, Evian went to St. Kitts to visit her parents. They lived in a hillside villa, which was in view of the Atlantic Ocean and the Caribbean Sea. Evian believed a vacation on the island would be a nice transition to civilian life.

One day, she and her parents went to the Marina in Basseterreon to dine at a well-known seafood restaurant. They were outside on the patio enjoying the ocean view, when Evian scanned the port and spotted a dark, handsome West Indian docking a brand new state-of-the-art fishing boat.

As the young man climbed out of the boat, he caught Evian staring at him. He smiled and tilted his hat as a friendly gesture.

Evian chuckled and turned away from him.

Several minutes later, the stranger entered the patio area of the restaurant and approached their table. He said in a chipper voice, "Greetings. My name is Pierre Michel. How do you do?"

Evian and her mother smiled. But her father spoke up after taking note of the young man's fishing gear. "Hello, young lad. Did you catch any fish today?"

"Today was not good, but I'll be back tomorrow," Pierre replied, before turning to Evian. "Would you like to come with me?"

"That's a great idea," her father interjected. He knew his daughter was mentally drained from her duties as Miss America, and thought a date with Pierre would boost her spirits.

"Well?" Pierre asked, waiting for Evian's answer.

"Sure."

After formal introductions, Evian wrote her name, address, and phone number on a napkin and handed it to Pierre.

The next day, they went on a fishing expedition and discovered they enjoyed each other's company. But Pierre failed to tell Evian that expenses accrued from their excursion was courtesy of his employer, including use of the fishing boat.

He used his charm and attentiveness to *woo* Evian. Though, he was not aware he was in the company of a public figure from America, and Evian wanted to keep it that way. She had even told her parents not to reveal her status.

Two weeks later, Pierre proposed to her at a local restaurant. Evian's mouth flew open from shock. Then a smile spread across her face. Pierre's genuine warmth and attentiveness made it easy for her to marry him on a whim. Her parents told her it was a mistake to marry so soon, but Evian was certain Pierre was the man of her dreams.

As soon as she said "I do," she knew she had made a mistake. In fact, she had made a lot of assumptions about Pierre, and was proven wrong on all accounts.

Firstly, Evian never thought to ask Pierre about his profession or his background. She had assumed he was wealthy, and living off investments. She later discovered he received most of his income from fishing. Pierre earned ten pounds a day, or fifteen dollars if converted to American dollars.

Secondly, Evian assumed Pierre owned and lived in the palace they frequented during their courtship. She was dismayed to learn Pierre housesat for the owner during the summer months.

The night they married, Pierre insisted Evian pack up her things at her parents' cottage and move into his home. Actually, he lived in a *jacal* or hut made of scrap boards and bricks covered in plaster; the roof was made of linoleum tiles; and pieces of cloth and plastic covered large holes that used to be windows.

The condition of Pierre's makeshift home was the result of Hurricane George in 1988. It was one of the biggest storms to ever hit the Caribbean islands. Pierre purchased the property as a fixer-upper, two years ago.

"I did all the repairs myself," he bragged, feeling good about his accomplishments.

"Uh...wow," Evian uttered. Shocked by the condition of Pierre's home, she was unable to form a full sentence.

Pierre continued to blow his own horn. "When I make more money, this is going to be our own palace."

Evian wanted to cry. She believed Pierre misled her about his financial situation. Though, she loved him and was willing to make their marriage work.

After living in his hut for one week, Evian came to admire the authenticity of sub-standard living. But she could not deny she was a spoiled American. She desired creature comforts, including air conditioning and running water.

One day, after Pierre went to work, Evian executed plans to try to make the best of a bad situation. She decided to spend some of the money she won from the Miss America pageant on making the hut sturdy and comfortable. She hired a construction contractor to install windows, tile floors, and plumbing for running water. Then she went furniture shopping to spruce up the interior of the hut.

Pierre returned home that evening and spotted construction workers in front of his hut. Then he noticed the ladders, tons of plywood, and glass windows stacked against the side of his home.

"What's going on?" he asked one of the workers.

"We were hired by the Missus."

Pierre barged inside his home to confront Evian. But she was nowhere in sight. He looked around and noted his used furniture had been replaced with expensive imported pieces.

Right away, he rushed outside and told the workers to leave his property. Then he started removing the new furniture out of his hut. He was in the process of removing newly framed pictures from the wall when Evian walked inside their hut with a bag of groceries.

"Pierre, what are you doing?!" she asked in panic.

"You tell me!" he screamed to the top of his lungs. "I invited you to my home, and you are not satisfied."

"You don't understand...."

"No, you don't understand!" he cut her off in mid-sentence. "I am the head of this household! As my wife, you are to do what I tell you!"

"I am not your slave!" Evian cried out, as she slammed the bag of groceries on the kitchen table.

Pierre began breathing hard and panting from anger. "I don't know how things are done in the United States, but here in St. Kitts, you must respect your husband!"

"I'm not going to stand here and tolerate...."

Pierre flew across the room and slapped Evian across the face in mid-sentence. She tumbled to the floor. Hunkering over, she feared he was going to strike her again.

Instantly, Pierre was remorseful. He dropped to the floor and scooped Evian in his arms. "I'm sorry. You made me do this to you."

Evian looked at her husband like he was crazy.

"Forgive me," he pleaded. "I promise I will never hurt you again." Then he cupped her face and removed strands of hair from her eyes. "Just so you know," he warned, "I will never consent to a divorce. You and I are made for each other. I love you with all my heart."

Later on, Evian set out to give her husband some of his own medicine. She cooked dinner and doused his food with rat poison.

Pierre became nauseous an hour later. He ran outside and threw up on the side of his hut. He did not see Evian when she snuck up behind him and whacked him on the back of his head with a large iron skillet.

"So you're a woman beater!" Evian hollered, not caring if neighbors could hear her. "You messed with the wrong woman *this time*!"

Before Pierre could stand up to defend himself, Evian whacked him again. She repeatedly beat him with the skillet until he fell to the ground. She left him there moaning and groaning from pain.

Quickly, she ran back inside the hut, packed her bags, and caught a cab to get as far away from Pierre as possible. Tears pouring down her face, she made a promise to herself that the next man that came into her life was going to be financially secure and successful.

When the cab arrived in front of her parents' home, Evian jumped out of the car with her bags and ran up the front steps. She banged on the front door nonstop until the door flew open.

"What happened?!" her mother hysterically screamed. She broke out in tears after spotting a large mound on the side of her daughter's face.

Tears gushing down her face, Evian pushed past her mother and rushed toward her father.

"I'm going to kill that bastard!" her father shrieked, when Evian went into his arms, weeping.

"Please Dad," Evian said between tearful sobs, "leave well enough alone. I'm going back to the United States. I think it's for the best."

"Are you sure?" her mother asked.

Evian nodded. "Yes."

She was relieved Pierre never discovered she was crowned Miss America. Otherwise, Evian assumed it would have been easy for him to find her.

***

Upon arriving in Florida, Evian went out of her way to keep a low profile. She had even decided not to date anyone. But she changed her mind the day Alex approached her on the beach. She could not resist his gorgeous face and buff body. She was thrilled after learning he was not only handsome but rich. More importantly, he treated her like a queen. She thought meeting a man like Alex only happened once in a lifetime.

Four months into their relationship, Alex started hinting he wanted to marry her. Evian wanted to marry him too, but knew she had to take actions to dissolve her marriage to Pierre. She called an acquaintance, Shebby Winfield, for assistance. She knew Shebby practiced law and provided free legal advice from time to time.

"Hello Shebby. This is Evian Gant. We met a couple of years ago at the NAACP convention."

"I remember you," Shebby said with a smile in her voice.

To cut through the niceties, Evian said, "I'm calling because I'm married and I want a divorce. I need to know if you can help me."

"Where did you marry?"

"St. Kitts." Evian paused, before adding, "I want to get remarried right away. Is that going to be a problem?"

"The divorce laws are different in that region of the world. I believe the court system requires mutual consent from both parties in order to quickly terminate the marriage."

Exasperated, Evian asked, "Are you serious?"

"I'm afraid so. But if your husband doesn't agree to the divorce, I can help you with the necessary paperwork."

Evian thanked Shebby before disconnecting the call. Then she nervously dialed her husband's number. "Hello Pierre."

"I want you to come home." His tone was demanding.

"Pierre, I don't want to be with you. I want a divorce."

"I love you, Evian."

"But I don't love you."

Pierre did not respond right away. He did not want to believe Evian did not love him. "I want to see you," he insisted.

"Why? So you can hit me again?" In that instant, Evian wished she had killed him when she had the opportunity.

"It was an accident," Pierre explained. "I never meant to hurt you."

"But you did hurt me, and it wasn't an accident."

"I'm sorry. Please give me a chance to make it up to you."

"It's too late," Evian said in a firm tone.

Pierre shook his head as if shaking away his wife's last remark. "Let's get together to talk about this in person."

"There's nothing to talk about." Evian abruptly hung up the phone.

Even though Pierre had made it clear he would not consent to a divorce, she hoped he would change his mind once he received a formal dissolution of marriage notice through the court system. She met with Shebby to file the necessary paperwork the next day. And from that day forward, she checked her P O Box like clockwork, looking for a divorce decree.

Chapter 13
Plan B

Early Monday morning, Carmela cracked open the guest bedroom door, to listen for signs of when her brother-in-law would be leaving for work. She heard Aaron exit his bedroom and walk downstairs. Then he strolled out the front door a few minutes later.

As if on cue, Carmela bolted downstairs and burst through the front door. She caught up with her brother-in-law just as he climbed behind the wheel of his Mercedes Benz. "Hey Aaron!" she called out, while running to the driver's side of his car.

Aaron closed his car door and buckled his seatbelt, then turned to Carmela with a frown on his face. He hesitated before pressing the button to roll down his window. "What do you want?!" he growled, making it clear her presence was annoying him.

"I need a favor."

"Save it!" he sharply countered. "Whatever you're scheming, save it for someone who believes your lies."

Arms crossed and pouting, Carmela asked, "What's up with the animosity? I've never done anything to you."

"Because I'm smart enough to see right through you. I know *your kind.*"

Fed up with Aaron's better-than-you attitude, Carmela uncrossed her arms, put her hands on her hips, and gazed at him with slanted eyes. "You should know my kind," she sassed. "As it seems you're with *my kind* when it's convenient for you."

Aaron bit his bottom lip. Carmela's comments had gotten his attention. "What do you want?"

"Twenty-five thousand dollars."

His brows shot up in amazement. "Are you crazy?! You're not getting a single dime from me."

"That's not a problem. I'm sure my sister would love to know where you hang out on the weekends."

Aaron grimaced. "I don't have that kind of money lying around."

"Of course not, silly," she said in a whimsical voice. "That's what banks are for."

Groaning aloud, Aaron realized he needed to get rid of her. "If I give you the money," he reasoned, "will you leave my home?"

"That depends."

"On what?"

"Whether my sister insists that I stay."

"Make sure you convince her that it's for the best."

Aaron checked his watch to gauge whether he could make it to the bank before his ten o'clock meeting. Shaking his head, he knew it would be impossible. He glanced at Carmela, and said, "Meet me downtown, at the Bank of Bradenton, around noon."

"Sure honey!" Carmela sang in a high-pitched voice, followed by a big fake smile.

Carmela's cynicism was getting on Aaron's last nerves. He stared straight ahead, as he said, "Make sure you show up at the bank with your suitcase. I do not want to see you when I return home this evening."

"Anything for you," Carmela mocked, taking pleasure in taunting him.

With the quickness, Aaron put on his shades, turned the ignition, and backed out of the driveway. He had a feeling *twenty-five thousand dollars* would not be enough to keep Carmela quiet about his double life. For a split second, he wished he had the willpower to make her disappear, forever.

Carmela stood in the driveway gloating. She was excited her blackmail scheme was going as planned. Feeling rejuvenated, she walked back inside the house and found Justina preparing to leave for work.

"Hi Big Sis!" she happily called out.

Justina frowned. She had blamed her sister after her husband stayed out most of the night. "Hi Carmela," she dryly stated. "Did you sleep well last night?"

"Yes, I did!" Carmela stressed, her voice filled with enthusiasm. "The plush blanket and feathery light pillows suited me just fine," she playfully added.

Justina raised a brow. She wondered what contributed to her sister's cheerful mood. "I'm leaving for work. Maybe we can go out to dinner to talk about what happened yesterday."

"Sounds nice, but I don't want to overstay my welcome." Carmela was attempting to adhere to the deal she made with Aaron.

Justina approached her sister with a warm smile. She was ready to let sleeping dogs lie. "I'm sorry I got angry with you."

"It's okay. It was my fault." Carmela said anything to rush her sister out of the house.

"We can talk about this tonight over dinner, okay?"

"Sure," Carmela said to appease her sister.

Justina smiled. "Everyone wants you to do well." She hugged her sister, while professing, "I love you."

In a haphazard manner, Carmela pulled out of her sister's embrace. She felt obligated to say something nice. So she lied, "I love you too. I won't let you down."

"That would mean the world to me." Justina turned to leave after stopping in the foyer to retrieve her briefcase.

As soon as her sister walked out the front door, Carmela briefly closed her eyes, before running upstairs, screaming, *"Oh hell-to-the-no!* I can't stay here another day! I have to leave this house before Justina get on my last nerves!"

Carmela packed her things, strolled downstairs with her suitcase and placed it near the front door. Then she called a local cab company to pick her up at noon.

To pass time, she walked around the house, snooping in Justina and Aaron's things. She struck gold when she walked into their bedroom and found her sister's jewelry box in the top dresser drawer. She helped herself to a gold watch and a gold bracelet. She figured Justina would not miss the items, as the box was filled with an abundance of priceless jewels.

Chapter 14
Something's Gotta Give

Even though Bessie spoke with Kevin about his daughter's relationship with Lamar and Justina, she still believed Guy and Regine's marriage was unstable. So the next day, she beckoned her granddaughter to follow her into the living room to chat. She sat on the loveseat while Regine sat on the sofa, across from her.

With a worried look on her face, Regine asked, "What's going on, Grandma?"

"You haven't been yourself lately. Is something troubling you?"

"I'm fine."

"How's your business partner?"

Regine smiled. "Lamar is great. If it were not for him, I don't know what I would do." Then she went on to explain how helpful Lamar had been to her and her restaurant business.

Bessie listened while Regine talked about Lamar nonstop. Everything she said about him was positive and glowing. It had been awhile since Bessie heard her granddaughter talk about Guy in the same manner. She asked, "What about your husband?"

When Regine opened her mouth to respond, Guy walked in the living room, and asked, "What about me?"

Swerving her neck around, Regine came face-to-face with her husband. She was getting ready to tell her grandmother the truth; she was no longer *in love* with Guy. She cared about him, but things between them had changed ever since she was kidnapped a year earlier. Unlike when she first met her husband, Regine was stronger, wiser and more self-assured.

"Guy, why don't you have a seat?" Bessie insisted. "I have something to say."

Obediently, he sat next to Regine on the sofa.

"Something is going on between you two," Bessie acknowledged, "and I want y'all to fix it."

"This conversation is for Regine," Guy said while looking at his wife. "She's the one that can't see Lamar has a thing for her." He did not have proof, but he had a hunch.

Lately, Guy noticed the way Lamar had been calling Regine at all times of night. Their conversations were business related, but Guy was displeased with the way Regine responded to Lamar's phone calls. She would end the calls with a smile or a gesture that said they were too close to be just business partners.

Regine turned to Guy with hatred in her eyes. "You've got a lot of nerve. Not so long ago, you left me for my best friend. Remember? You even asked Justina to marry you."

Digesting Regine's remarks, Guy felt like someone took a sledge-hammer and aimed it at his heart. He thought his wife had gotten past his indiscretions, but it was obvious to him that she was holding on to *ill* feelings. "Do you want to have an affair to get back at me?" he asked his wife, after momentary silence.

Regine stared at her husband with a blank face. Truth was, she did not harbor negative feelings toward her husband or Justina. It was her way of trying to distract Guy from making inferences about her rela-tionship with Lamar. She briefly looked at Grandma Bessie, before turning to Guy. "I never cheated on you," she truthfully admitted.

"But it has crossed your mind," Guy countered.

Regine did not know what to say. Her answer was *yes;* having an affair with Lamar had crossed her mind.

"Regine," Bessie cut in, "if what Guy is saying is true, you need to think twice. Life is too short to hold grudges."

"Grandma, it's more complicated than that."

"Explain it to me," Guy said in a calm manner. "I'm willing to do anything and everything to make our marriage work. But I can't do it alone. I love you," he whispered, while cupping the side of her face. "I can't see myself living without you. I'm sorry for ever hurting you."

Suddenly, tears burned the back of Regine's eyes. Spellbound by her husband's heart-felt apology, she felt compelled to say, "I'm will-ing to work on our marriage."

Grandma Bessie clasped her hands in relief. "Well, that settles it. It looks like you two are going to be all right. Now you can head up to bed and take care of business."

Guy burst out in laughter, but Regine's mouth flew open in sur-prise. She stared at her grandmother in disbelief.

"Don't look at me like that," Bessie chided Regine. "I know what goes on in the bedroom. Y'all go 'head on. I'll take care of KC."

Guy and Regine looked at each other and burst out laughing. Then they headed upstairs, hand-in-hand.

Bessie was satisfied with Guy and Regine's attempt at reconcilia-tion. She remained seated with her eyes closed. Then she prayed for

God to watch over them and give them strength to survive whatever obstacles they encountered.

In the bedroom, things did not start out as Guy had anticipated. When he kissed Regine, her lips felt like ice.

"Honey," he softly cooed, "what's wrong?"

"I don't know."

"Please talk to me."

Regine avoided eye contact, as she said, "I'm not sure I want to make love to you. Things have changed between us."

"Can we at least try?" he begged with outstretched hands.

Nodding, Regine reluctantly submitted to Guy's wishes.

In slow motion, Guy ravished her lips even though she showed resistance to his touch. Then he removed her clothes and kissed her breasts. Hoping to arouse her, he slipped his hand in her panties.

Regine closed her eyes and imagined it was Lamar's hands massaging her *vajay-jay*. Then she imagined it was Lamar's mouth sucking her breasts. Her heartbeat sped up with each kiss.

Guy guided her to their bed after removing his clothes. He climbed on top of her and inserted his manhood.

With each thrust, he became aroused and so did Regine. For the first time in a long time, Guy thought there was hope for their marriage. He was excited at the way Regine responded to his sexual prowess.

Closing his eyes, he acknowledged their lovemaking was intense and lengthy. Guy made love to Regine as if it was their very last time. He wanted her to feel the sensation, long after his release.

An hour later, Regine started shivering from satisfaction. She voiced her contentment, by screaming, *"Yes! Yes! Oh Lamar!"* Her face was glowing as she reached the point of ecstasy.

Guy, too, was about to climax. But he froze in place when he heard Lamar's name slip from his wife's mouth.

Regine noticed his reaction and opened her eyes. "What's the matter?"

"You called me Lamar!"

Guy was outraged as he rolled off her and climbed out of bed.

At a loss for words, Regine did not know how to respond. She had allowed her thoughts of Lamar to take over her body and soul. She could not think of a good reason for calling out his name.

Lowering her eyes, she said in a soft voice, "I'm sorry."

"I need to be alone for now." Guy put on his robe and rushed out of their bedroom steaming mad.

Chapter 15
Pursuit of Happiness

Evian was relieved when she received a notice from the court system in St. Kitts. But her hopes were quickly dashed after learning Pierre was contesting their divorce. The notice also stated he was requesting spousal support. She immediately called her parents.

"The nerve of him!" Evian screamed over the phone. "That son of a bitch was happy living in a freakin' hut. Now he wants my money! It's not going to happen."

"Why don't you pay the money to get him out of your life?" Mrs. Gant suggested over the speaker phone. "The sooner you get Pierre out of your life, the sooner you can begin a wonderful life with Alex." She turned to her husband who nodded in agreement.

"Mom, you don't understand," Evian said while sobbing. "If I'm forced to pay alimony, I'll never be able to get him out of my life."

"Did you tell Alex about Pierre yet?" her father inquired. "You must tell him sooner than later."

Evian sighed. "I wish it was that simple. I'm afraid of losing Alex. I'm going to hire an attorney to appeal the court's decision. Hopefully, they'll see things my way."

"I hope you know what you're doing," her father said. "Please keep us informed, and let us know if we can help."

Evian disconnected the call and dwelled on the matter. She was tired of walking around Alex on eggshells. She regretted ever getting involved with Pierre, and was willing to do anything to make him disappear from her life.

Pierre, on the other hand, wanted to fight for his marriage. He was devastated when he learned Evian had returned to the United States. But he went ballistic when he received her request for a divorce. He had contested the divorce and asked for financial support out of spite. He did not want Evian's money, but he needed her to see he was willing to do anything to save their marriage.

Driven and determined, Pierre decided to visit his in-laws after receiving the petition from the court system.

Evian's mother greeted him at the door with a frown on her face. "What do you want?"

"I want you to convince Evian to come back home to me."

Evian's mother frowned before inviting Pierre in her home. Then she excused herself and went to alert her husband of Pierre's visit.

Making himself comfortable, Pierre sat on the sofa and glanced down at the coffee table. He noticed a magazine was open to a page that featured Evian's picture. Blinking, he thought his eyes were playing tricks on him. In the photo, Evian had on a white beaded fairytale gown and donned a tiara. Then Pierre noticed she was wearing a sash with the Miss America title. Instinctively, he flipped the magazine to view the front cover.

"What are you doing here?!" Evian's father blasted, barging out of his bedroom with his robe on. He was only inches from Pierre's face.

Pierre dropped the magazine and drew back. "I want my wife back," he timidly admitted. "She needs to be with me."

"You need to sign the divorce decree, and get on with your life. My daughter does not want you."

Pierre became livid, as he explained, "Evian is my wife."

"What do you want?" Mrs. Gant asked. "We will pay you."

Frowning, Pierre was offended by her offer. "You don't have enough money to buy me out of your daughter's life."

"Evian is never coming back to you," Mr. Gant made clear. "She's going to marry someone that treats her like the queen she is."

"I need to see her face-to-face. I need her to tell me she doesn't want to be with me."

"Hasn't she made herself clear, already?" Mrs. Gant stated. "She left St. Kitts to get away from you."

Pierre huffed and puffed, before shouting, "I'm not going to give up on Evian without a fight!"

Mr. Gant grabbed Pierre by the collar and threw him against the front door. "You are to leave our daughter alone!"

After squirming out of Mr. Gant's stronghold, Pierre yelled, "I will find her, if it's the last thing I do!" Then he sprinted out of their home in a hurry.

Pierre was spitting mad. He tried everything to get his wife back, but was faced with major obstacles. The primary obstacle was *money*. He did not have enough money to fly to the United States, or hire a private detective to find Evian.

Then he remembered the picture of Evian in the magazine. His eyes welled up upon visualizing his wife's picture. He was in awe to have discovered he was married to a beauty queen. He felt hopeful when he went to the library and found a phone number for the magazine company. He eagerly dialed the one-eight hundred number.

"Hello," the operator said. "May I help you?"

"Hi, my name is Pierre Michel. I'm looking for my wife, Evian Gant. Your company wrote a story about her in your magazine. She was crowned Miss America. Can you help me find her?"

"Hold on."

After hearing Pierre's revelation, the operator put him through to the executive staff. His call was subsequently routed to the owner of the magazine company.

"Hello Mr. Michel. My name is Mr. Hodges, the CEO and owner of this company. Is it true you are married to Evian Gant, the Miss America title holder?"

"Yes."

"Who can verify what you're saying?"

"Her parents. They were present when we married."

"Do you have wedding pictures?"

"Yes, her father took pictures of our special day."

"And where are you calling from?" the owner continued to probe.

"St. Kitts."

Figuring an interview with Pierre could be a great cover story, Mr. Hodges asked, "Do you have a passport?"

"No, I do not."

"Don't worry. We'll take care of everything on our end."

Pierre was not sure if Mr. Hodges understood his quest, so he asked, "Can you help me find my wife?"

"Of course. Do you have a number where we can reach you?"

After Pierre provided his phone number, Mr. Hodges told him a travel coordinator would be contacting him, to help him apply for a passport and a temporary visa. He also told Pierre he would be compensated for his cooperation.

Breathing a sigh of relief, Pierre felt as if he was getting closer to finding his wife. In fact, the conversation with Mr. Hodges had caused him to reflect on the day he and Evian married.

Pierre wore a borrowed suit and Evian had on a simple white gown. Her hair was tied back in a French twist. It was a small wedding ceremony attended by Pierre's friends and Evian's parents.

Evian was smiling throughout the wedding ceremony. But her moment of joy turned to sadness after Pierre invited her to his home.

Pierre knew Evian was accustomed to an American lifestyle, but was hoping their love for one another would be enough. Obviously, he was mistaken after she poisoned and beat the crap out of him before walking out of his life. But that did not stop Pierre from looking for his wife with the hope of bringing her home one day.

Chapter 16
The Plot Thickens

Ever since Dan Bellam was released from jail, he found it difficult to find a job. He thought by using his former cellmate's name and identity, his job prospects would have been easier. One day he lucked up when he was hired as a chauffeur for a private company. The company lent him a black SUV to drive while chauffeuring. He also had the benefit of using the vehicle for personal use.

While off duty, he put all his energy into finding his nemesis: *Justina Reyes*. His research revealed she was married to Aaron Bishop. Justina and her husband were highly regarded in their community, so it was easy for Dan to locate their residence in Bradenton, Florida.

Dan used his work vehicle to spy on Justina. For the past three weeks, he carefully scoped out her comings and goings. He was parked across the street from her home when he spotted her walking out the front door and heading to her car. He was going to follow her, but he was curious to learn more about Justina's houseguest, whom he had spotted three days earlier.

He waited several hours for the mystery person to walk out the front door. Dan sat up in his truck after she stood outside near the road with her suitcase. Then he waited a little while before he started the ignition and drove in front of her. He reached across the passenger seat, and yelled out the window, "Hey there! You need a ride?"

Carmela checked her watch and noted her cab was late. Time was of the essence, so she strolled over to the black SUV, and asked, "Where are you headed?"

"Nowhere in particular. I just left a friend's house not far from here." Dan lied with confidence.

Boldly, Carmela opened the rear door and threw her suitcase in the backseat. Then she climbed in the front passenger seat. "Can you drop me off at the bank?"

"Sure, which one?"

"Downtown, to the Bank of Bradenton. I'll figure it out from there."

After Dan drove onto the highway, he glanced at Carmela and noticed she was eerily quiet. "You want to tell me what you're thinking about?"

"Nope," she replied, as she continued to look out the passenger window.

"What is your name?"

She turned to him, and answered, "Carmela. What's yours?"

"Dan," he replied with a creepy grin.

Frowning, Carmela drew closer to the passenger door. "Sorry, *Mister*. I don't do old men."

She told an untruth. Many of the men she slept with were older than Dan. But they were usually rich and much cleaner looking.

"I'm not like that," Dan explained, surprised by her insinuation. He needed to get more information from her, so he asked, "Do you want to stop somewhere to get a bite to eat?"

Before she could answer him, her stomach growled and they cracked up laughing.

They went to Burger King for lunch. Initially, their conversation was light, until Dan started asking Carmela personal questions. "Are you close with your family?" he asked out of curiosity.

"Not really. I hate my sister."

"Your sister?"

"Yeah, I just left her house."

"Why do you feel that way about your sister?"

"It's a long story, but *payback* is a bitch."

"Payback?" he inquired.

She nodded.

Thanks to Carmela, Dan learned a lot about Justina over lunch. She had even told him she was going to the bank to get some money from her brother-in-law. He thought that was vital information.

When he drove into the parking space across the street from the Bank of Bradenton, Carmela grabbed her suitcase from the backseat and asked him to wait for her.

Dan asked, "Why are you taking your suitcase?"

"Collateral," she answered, not caring to elaborate.

"You sure you don't want me to come with you?"

"I'm sure."

Carmela strolled to the bank entrance, then briefly looked back to make sure Dan did not leave. She needed him to transport her out of Bradenton.

As she entered the bank, she spotted Aaron standing near the door entrance. She acknowledged him with a fake smile.

"Who's your friend?" Aaron asked, letting her know he had gotten a glimpse of the driver.

"None of your *damn* business!" Carmela snapped, while cutting her eyes. "You got my money?"

Aaron handed her an envelope full of cash.

Carmela put the suitcase on the floor before she snatched the envelope out of his hand. She opened the envelope and eyed the money.

Aaron said "It's all there."

"It better be," she flippantly replied with an eye roll.

He closed the gap between them and his breath covered her face, as he cautioned, "I never want to see you again. If I do, you're going to wish you were dead."

Carmela laughed. "And what are you going to do to me?"

"Don't play with me!" he bellowed.

Incensed, Carmela stopped cackling and turned serious. "Listen asshole," she said between gnashed teeth. "You're not in a position to threaten me. I'm not the one around here *double-dipping*. Then again, maybe my sister should know about you."

"Keep your damn mouth closed!" Aaron yelled, a little too loud.

Standing several feet away, the security guard shifted his eyes between Aaron and Carmela, before asking, "Is there a problem?"

"No," Carmela answered. "We're just having a family disagreement."

"Take it outside," the security guard ordered.

Without saying another word, Carmela picked up her suitcase and followed Aaron out of the bank.

Near the bank entrance, Aaron looked around to make sure no one was present. Then he turned to her, and said in a low voice, "Please don't tell Justina about me. I gave you what you wanted."

"I appreciate it," Carmela said, as she held up the manila envelope. "And you don't have to worry about me telling my sister your secret."

Truth was, Swag told Carmela she better not mess up his arrangement with her brother-in-law, especially since Aaron was his best paying customer. She found out he was her boyfriend's customer by accident.

One day, one of Swag's *Call Girls* got sick, so he sent Carmela in her place. Aaron was shocked and speechless when she walked in his hotel room wearing an overcoat over a cat suit.

"Carmela!" Aaron shrieked, as he tried to cover up his naked body with a blanket. "What are you doing here?"

"I would ask you the same thing, but the truth is obvious."

Aaron was caught like a deer with headlights. He quickly put on his slacks. "This...was...a mistake," he stuttered. "I don't normally do this."

With a smirk on her face, Carmela took joy in watching Aaron try to explain away his indiscretion.

"You got to believe me," he implored, putting on his dress shirt.

"Yeah right." Rolling her eyes, Carmela was not buying Aaron's lie.

Hurriedly, he put on his shoes and grabbed his car keys. "Can you keep…this between us?" he asked in a shaky voice.

Carmela simply said, "Sure, whatever."

Aaron went in his wallet, retrieved a one-hundred dollar bill and extended it to her. "This should be enough for your troubles."

"What about the thousand dollars you owe me for tonight?"

Exasperated, Aaron said, "We didn't do anything."

"Whose fault is that?"

"Can't we pretend like tonight never happened?'

Carmela went inside her purse and pulled out a gun. With her finger on the trigger, she aimed the gun at his forehead. "Pay now or pay now," she threatened. "It's your choice." Her stance was bold and fearless.

Swag had trained her for this type of situation. He told her the only things *johns* understand was the power of a gun.

Aaron's hands were shaking as he retrieved an envelope filled with money from his shirt pocket and handed it to her. He did not wait around and watch her count the money. Instead, he fled the scene like a bat out of hell.

That incident happened three months ago, and Aaron still had not learned his lesson. He was still entertaining *Call Girls* every weekend.

Leaving her brother-in-law standing in front of the bank, Carmela grabbed her suitcase and rushed to the SUV. "Thanks for waiting for me," she said to Dan, after climbing in the passenger seat.

His eyes shifted to the envelope. "What are you going to do with all that money?"

"It's for my boyfriend."

Perplexed, he asked, "Come again?"

"My brother-in-law gave me a loan."

"Tell me about the loan," he insisted.

"I don't think so."

"Well, can I get a couple of bills for gas?"

Carmela twisted her mouth as she thought about his request. Then she opened the envelope, retrieved one of the one-hundred dollar bills and handed it to him.

Dan opened his mouth to demand more money, but closed it after realizing he could potentially get more than Carmela was willing to offer. He knew she was lying about the loan Aaron had supposedly given her. If he had to guess, he believed it was *hush money*. Dan had planned on using whatever Carmela had on Aaron' to his advantage.

After assessing the matter, he turned to her, and said, "Maybe you and I can work together, to get more money from your brother-in-law."

She looked at him sideways, before asking, "Are you crazy? Aaron would never go for that."

"What about your sister?"

"Nah…that would never work."

Dan cupped his chin. Then he smiled broadly, as if he had just won the lottery. "What if she thought you were kidnapped?"

Carmela cracked up laughing. "She won't believe it."

"What if I convince her?"

With her forehead scrunched up, Carmela considered what Dan was suggesting. "Do you think it will work?"

"Just leave everything to me."

"Hmmm," Carmela moaned, signaling his plan seemed plausible. "Before we do anything, I need to discuss this with my boyfriend."

"Where is he?"

"In Tampa."

"That's perfect," Dan said, as he pulled onto the highway and headed northbound. "Call your boyfriend, and tell him to meet us at the Cameroon hotel in Tampa."

"Why? What's on your mind?"

"Trust me, you won't have any regrets. My plan is certain to make us a ton of money."

Chapter 17
Shaky Grounds

*D*uring Alex and Evian's engagement party, Jeanine Benedict peered across the table and noticed the tension between her older son and daughter-in-law. She thought Regine seemed detached from Guy; not only physically but emotionally. Then she looked over at Alex, who appeared happy and in-love. But his fiancé seemed distracted.

When Alex told Jeanine he was going to ask Evian to marry him, she was not sure if he was making the right decision. So she contacted her private detective, Tim Carter, to find out if Alex's fiancé had any baggage she should be aware of. Within twenty-four hours, Tim gave Jeanine a *"thumbs up"* after he conducted extensive background research on Evian Gant throughout the United States.

Jeanine was satisfied with the investigative report, but she was still unsure about her future daughter-in-law. It did not help that her stepdaughter, Dana, had expressed misgivings about Evian.

Raymond Brown, Jeanine's beau, was sitting next to her at the engagement party. He became concerned after he noted worry lines etched across her forehead. He touched her hand, and asked, "Are you okay?"

She bore a faint smile. "Yes, I'm fine."

Raymond wondered what caused Jeanine's blissful smile to turn upside down. He had a feeling her somber outlook had something to do with her children. He cared deeply for her, and was willing to do anything to lessen her worries.

They met during a chance encounter, four months earlier. Jeanine was leaving her doctor's office when she bumped into Raymond by accident. "Excuse me," she yelped, startled by his presence.

Raymond was awestruck by her beauty. He undressed her with his eyes, before remarking, "You can bump into me any day."

Jeanine blushed in response. Then she took a closer look at Raymond and noted his distinct features. He stood five feet' ten inches tall, had a golden-brown complexion, and a receding hairline. She was attracted to Raymond, because he reminded her of her deceased father.

"Can I help you to your car?" he asked, holding the door for her.

"No, that won't be necessary. My driver is waiting for me." She smiled as she walked past him en route to her waiting car.

Raymond galloped in two long strides to catch up with her. "Uh… excuse me. I'm sorry I didn't get your name."

Jeanine turned around, and asked, "Why do you want my name?"

"I was wondering if you'd be interested in having dinner with me."

"I'm sorry, but I don't know you."

"I think I know your doctor."

"And how do you know my doctor?"

"He's my childhood friend," Raymond explained. "And if you don't believe me, you can ask him yourself."

At that very moment, Jeanine's doctor walked out of his office and approached Raymond. "Hey Buddy!" he said, as he gave his friend a manly hug. "I was wondering what happened to you."

Smirking, Raymond gave Jeanine a knowing look.

She asked her doctor, "Can you vouch for this man?"

"Not only can I vouch for him," the doctor told her, "I can tell you Raymond is a good man. If you wish, I can tell you his childhood secrets."

"C'mon man," Raymond cut in with a light chuckle. "Don't go too far." He turned to Jeanine, and asked, "Can I take you out on a date?"

Jeanine retrieved her business card from her purse and handed it to him. "Call me on my cell phone," she instructed. She smiled as she strolled to her waiting car.

Since their chance encounter, Jeanine and Raymond grew closer. She became the *yin* to his *yang*, and vice versa.

The night before the engagement party, Jeanine told Raymond the story about her late husband, Charlie Simmons, and his mistress, Dottie Smith.

Jeanine was calm, as she explained, "Charlie was seeing Dottie for over a decade before I found out about them. They had given birth to two sons, Guy and Alex, who were eleven and eight at the time. Eventually, I forgave Charlie and asked him to stop seeing Dottie. It wasn't long before I discovered he started seeing her again. That's when I learned Dottie had given birth to twin girls."

"So he left you for her?" Raymond asked.

"It wasn't that simple. I believe his mistress experienced a nervous breakdown. She was behind the steering wheel when she drove off a cliff, taking Charlie with her. The car went up in flames as soon as it rolled to the bottom of the mountain."

Raymond exhaled after listening to Jeanine rehash her painful past. He held her hand, and sincerely said, "I'm sorry for your loss."

"I'm not sorry. If it were not for Charlie and Dottie, I wouldn't have the most beautiful children in the world."

Jeanine had stepped up to the plate as an unofficial guardian of her stepchildren after Charlie and Dottie were pronounced dead. She loved the children as if they were her own. Throughout their lives, she used her resources to help them escape near-death situations.

Raymond cupped her face and looked into her eyes. "I'm not your husband. I'll never betray you."

Jeanine bore a faint smile. She wanted to believe him.

"Give me a chance to make you happy. You won't regret it." Before Jeanine could respond, he reached over and stroked the side of her face. Then he gave her a long passionate kiss.

Her body went limp. She had not felt that way in years, and did not want the moment to end.

Raymond removed her blouse and tried to remove her bra, but Jeanine held up her hands to stop him. He was persistent, as he pleaded, "Let me make love to you."

"There's something you should know about me."

"Whatever it is, I don't care. Can't you see I'm crazy about you? I love you. I love everything about you."

Sensing her hesitancy, Raymond kissed her on the lips. "Please give me the opportunity to show you how much you mean to me."

Jeanine was unsure of whether she should tell Raymond she had undergone a double mastectomy a year earlier. Scars from breast reconstruction were faint but visible. She looked into his sincere eyes and slowly uncrossed her arms. She had given in to Raymond's pleas.

Raymond relished the moment, planting kisses on every inch of her body. Then he made love to her as if it was no tomorrow.

Toward the end of their intense lovemaking, Jeanine knew Raymond loved her. She recognized he treated her as if she was priceless. Her doubts about him had gradually dissipated.

Raymond wrapped his arms around her and fell asleep. However, Jeanine's eyes remained open. She had a strange feeling her stepsons' lives were getting ready to spiral out of control. Before that happened, she was prepared to use her power and resources to protect them at any cost.

Chapter 18
As the World Turns

*A*lex woke up early to go to work. He glanced over at his fiancé who was sound asleep. Although he was not sure about his future with Evian, he could not deny he loved her, deeply. He kissed her on the cheek before climbing out of bed. As soon as he put on his dress clothes and shoes, his cell phone rang. He glanced at the caller ID and noted it was his secretary. He answered her call on the second ring.

"Mr. Simmons," the secretary said in a hushed whisper, "a woman is here to see you."

"Who is she?"

"She refused to give me her name."

"Did she say what she wanted?"

"No," the secretary replied, while keeping her eyes on Alex's visitor. "But she said it was a matter of life and death."

His brows shot up in response. "It sounds serious."

"I think it is."

"Give me an hour. I'll be there as soon as I can."

Evian rolled over in bed after Alex disconnected the call. She had overheard his responses to his secretary. "What's going on?"

"Nothing serious, I hope. I'll see you later," he said, after he kissed her on the cheek and walked out of their bedroom.

"Okay, be safe."

Evian assumed Alex was still disappointed in her for not agreeing to marry him this fall. So she wanted to do something nice to take his mind off their minor setback. A smile spread across her face as she thought of a plan to seduce him with food and passion.

***

Alecia Kellam had just arrived in Tampa, Florida, after taking the first flight out of Baltimore, Maryland. She had booked a return flight later on that evening. She had instructed the cab driver to take her directly to Trowne Key's corporate office.

When she took the elevator to the Executive floor, she approached the secretary with a nervous smile. She became anxious after discovering Alex was not in his office. So she begged the secretary to call him at home. She did not provide her name for fear Alex would not show up.

An hour later, Alex walked in his office and was surprised to find his ex-lover in his office. She was slumped over in the reception chair with her face buried in her hands. "Alecia," he said as he approached her, "what are you doing here?"

"I'm so happy you came!" she said, as she jumped out of her chair. Her eyes were red and swollen from crying.

Alex was confused by her presence and distraught behavior. He turned to his secretary for answers. But his secretary was teary-eyed and moved by Alecia's emotional state. She grabbed the tissue box from her desk and pointed it in Alecia's direction. "Miss, please take one."

"Thank you." Alecia grabbed a tissue and wiped her eyes.

Alex turned to his secretary. "Clear my calendar and hold all calls." Then he said to Alecia, "Please follow me to my office."

She strolled in his office and sat in the chair across from his desk. She said with a choppy voice, "I know...you're surprised...to see me."

Nodding, Alex said, "Yes, it is a surprise. Why didn't you call and tell me you were coming?"

She was choked up, and found it difficult to speak.

"What's going on?" he probed, attempting to seek an explanation for her emotional state.

Between sobs, she said, "I...have...a baby."

"I'm happy for you, but I don't understand why you want to see me." "My...baby," she continued to weep. "He's...dying."

"I'm sorry to hear this. What's wrong with him?"

"His bone marrow is not producing enough white blood cells. The doctor told me he needs a bone marrow transplant to save his life. I'm not a match," she added with sorrow in her voice.

"Have you asked your baby's father?"

"My baby has a rare blood type," Alecia stated, purposely ignoring Alex's question.

"I'm B negative," Alex thought aloud.

Alecia sighed in relief. Her son was also B negative. "I would like for you to go to Johns Hopkins hospital in Baltimore, Maryland. The doctor will perform a series of tests, to see if you're a good match for the bone marrow transplant."

Alex frowned. "I'm confused. Why are you asking me?"

Without answering his question, Alecia said, "My baby's name is Alexander Simmons. He's three months old."

Crooking his head to one-side, Alex acknowledged the baby's name was similar to his. He mentally calculated the baby's age and the last and only time he and Alecia had sex, which was a year ago. He guessed she was hinting he was her child's father.

Alecia nodded before confirming, "Alexander Simmons is your son."

Eyes bulging, Alex stared at Alecia in disbelief. Her confession was hard for him to digest. It seemed everything around him stopped while his thoughts spiraled out of control.

"Why didn't you tell me about the baby?" he asked, after getting ahold of his bearings.

"I felt bad for what I did to you."

As if it were yesterday, Alecia remembered when she took advantage of Alex. She had slipped a *date rape drug* in his drink and waited until the drug took over his senses. Then she undressed him and climbed on top of his erect penis. That was the same night her baby was conceived, and the only time they had sex.

"Both of us had issues," Alex replied, accepting some of the blame.

He was referring to the ultimatum Alecia had given him a year ago. He had agreed to marry her in exchange for making sure his stepmother received the cure for stage IV breast cancer.

Alex asked Alecia, "How do you know your son is my baby?"

"He looks just like you." She retrieved a photo from her purse and slid it across the desk. "You can keep the picture."

Slowly, Alex picked up the picture and analyzed the baby's features. "Wow," he said, after he noticed striking similarities.

"You can take a DNA test if you'd like," she offered. "Can you make it to the hospital tomorrow?"

Alex was not convinced Alecia's son was his baby. But he needed to go to the hospital to make sure. "I'll be there in the morning," he finally said.

"Thank you."

Alex remained seated long after Alecia walked out of his office. He told his secretary to cancel his appointments the rest of the day. Then he browsed the internet sites to read information about the bone marrow transplant procedure.

***

On the drive home, Alex thought about the day's events. He came to grips that Evian wanted to delay marrying him. Then Alecia dropped by his office and told him he was her son's father.

He entered his condo as jazz music blared from the BOSE stereo system. Quietly, Alex crept down the hall toward a candle-lit room. He found Evian in the den, looking scrumptious in black lingerie. She was drinking a glass of wine.

"Hello sexy," she purred like a cat.

Alex smiled, taking in the mood. "What's the occasion?"

"You," she answered with a devilish grin.

"Me? What did I do to deserve this?"

Evian approached Alex with hunger in her eyes. Then she wrapped her arms around his waist, pulling him close to her. "I realize I was being selfish, especially after all you went through to plan our wedding."

"Did you change your mind about marrying me this fall?" His heart was filled with hope as he waited for her answer.

"I think we should table this topic until I feed you," Evian said, as she summoned Alex to the dining room.

After noting the tossed salad, steak, potatoes, and red wine, he turned to her with a surprised look on his face. "Wow. You did all this for me?"

She smiled. "Of course."

After Alex cleaned his plate, Evian sat in his lap and ravished his lips. Then she dropped to her knees, unzipped his pants, and pulled out seven inches of heaven. His knees buckled during the blowjob.

Before climaxing, he removed her lingerie, turned her around, and bent her over on the dining table. Eagerly, he inserted his manhood inside of her. With each thrust, Evian trembled from pure satisfaction. Both had an orgasm at the same time.

Looking forward to round two, Alex led Evian to their bedroom. He removed her robe and kissed her naked body like an animal relishing his last meal. Then he repeatedly plunged inside her.

Evian moaned and screamed with delight.

Their lovemaking was intense and exciting. After climaxing at the same time, they cuddled next to each other.

Alex's mind was in a different place, but not for long. His stomach was twisted in knots. He rolled over on his back and stared at the ceiling. He was thinking about Alecia and the baby.

"What is it honey?" Evian asked, after realizing Alex did not seem like his usual self.

"I think I have a baby."

Her brows shot up, as she asked, "What are you talking about?"

"I met with Alecia Kellam this morning," he stoically replied. "She told me I'm her baby's father."

Evian sat up in bed. She felt uneasy about this new revelation. "Is she the same girl you told me about earlier?"

"Yes."

"What are you going to do?"

"If I am the father, I'm going to step up to the plate."

"What about me?" she whined, feeling insecure.

Alex cupped the side of her face. "You are the love of my life. I don't want to lose you."

Evian briefly closed her eyes and wondered how the baby might impact her future with Alex. One thing she knew for sure: *She did not want to deal with any baby-mama drama.*

"Is Alecia married?" Evian asked, hoping he would say *yes.*

"I don't know. Right now my focus is on the baby. He's in the hospital."

"What's wrong with the baby?"

"Alecia told me he needs a bone marrow transplant. His blood type is B negative, and so is mine."

"It's a boy?"

"Yes," Alex acknowledged with an inward grin.

"How old is he?"

"Three months." Alex paused, before volunteering, "I have to go to Baltimore in the morning to help save his life."

"I see," Evian said with a jittery undertone.

Alex and Evian remained quiet as they cuddled next to each other. Their minds were clouded with thoughts of Alecia and the baby.

Chapter 19
Whistle Blower

Swag was sitting in the parking lot of the Cameroon hotel in Tampa, waiting for Carmela. He was excited when she told him about her new acquaintance's plans to make them a lot of money. He was also blown away when Carmela told him she blackmailed Aaron into giving her twenty-five thousand dollars.

He climbed out of his car when Carmela and Dan arrived at the hotel. Playing it cool, Swag leaned on the driver's door with his arms crossed. He let his guard down after Carmela jumped out of the SUV and ran toward him.

"Hey Baby!" she squealed with excitement.

Swag felt her energy. He was not a *touchy-feely* person but made an exception for Carmela. He opened his arms and embraced her. "Watcha got for me?" he asked, while resting his arms around her waist.

Carmela handed him the envelope. "It's all there. Twenty-five *Gs*." Then she held up her wrist to show him the gold watch and bracelet. "I stole these from Justina."

"That's my girl," Swag proudly stated. He opened the envelope and ogled the money with dollar signs in his eyes.

"Oh," Carmela said, as an afterthought. "I gave my new friend a hundred dollars for giving me a ride here."

Swag glanced at Dan, who was climbing out of the SUV. Then he walked over and approached him with his fist extended. "Hey man, what's going on?"

Dan gave Swag a fist bump. "Let's go to my hotel room and talk. I have a plan that will make us a ton of money."

"Cool. Let's do this."

For the next hour or so, Dan explained his plan to get a ransom for Carmela. He even thought of a backup plan in case Justina and Aaron called the police. Dan directed his attention to Carmela, when he asked, "Do you have anything I can show your sister, to convince her that you are being held captive against your will?"

"Babe," Swag interjected, "what about that watch your sister gave you?"

Carmela unfastened the latch and handed the silver Rolex watch to Dan. When Justina gave it to her on her sixteenth birthday, it had meant so much. Now she could care less.

"I promise," Dan said, "you'll get it back."

Carmela shrugged, nonchalantly.

"Oh, one more thing," Dan said. "I need your cell phone."

"Why?" Carmela asked, while handing her phone to him.

Dan removed the battery from her cell phone and put both her cell phone and the battery in his pocket. "Your sister is going to try to reach you. You need to give the appearance that you can't be reached. I'll replace your cell phone tomorrow," he added to appease Carmela.

"How much money are *we* going to ask for?" Swag asked Dan.

Dan's eyes shot skyward for a brief second while mulling over Swag's question. "Based on my research," he finally replied, "Aaron owns several rental properties. We should ask for a half a million."

Carmela's mouth flew open and her eyes grew wide. "That's a lot of money. Aaron doesn't even like me."

"It doesn't matter," Dan replied, while giving Carmela a knowing gaze. "I think he has proven he is willing to do anything to make your sister happy. I believe he will pay the ransom."

Swag rubbed his hands back and forth, feeling an adrenaline rush. In his head, he was thinking of ways to spend the ransom money.

"We should split the ransom fifty/fifty," Dan suggested.

"Fifty/fifty?" Swag questioned. "What about my girl?"

"I thought you would be willing to share your half with her."

"You thought wrong. My girl is taking the biggest risk. So what about breaking her off?"

Blinking, Dan knew he was being swindled. He twisted his mouth, before asking, "How much are we talking about?"

"One-hundred thousand should be enough," Swag answered with a straight face.

"I think that's fair." Dan wanted to object, but thought it was best not to get into a scuffle with Swag. "I'm going to pay Justina a visit first thing in the morning."

Smirking, Swag was satisfied with Dan's plans. He no longer viewed Carmela as his employee. In his eyes, she was a *goldmine*.

The day before, he had arranged a threesome for Aaron and was paid five thousand dollars. And today, Carmela had managed to swindle Aaron out of twenty-five thousand dollars. Now he was expecting a windfall of a half-million dollars from the same man. This was too real to be true, Swag thought to himself.

Justina returned home from work looking forward to going to dinner with her sister. "Carmela!" she called out, as soon as she walked through the front door.

When her sister did not respond, she strutted in the entertainment room expecting to find her there. Instead, Justina found her husband sitting on the couch, nursing a glass of wine.

"Where is she?"

"She's not here." Aaron's tone was neutral. He did not want to let on that he was excited because Carmela left their home.

"What did you say to her?"

"Nothing."

"Don't lie to me!" Justina screamed.

Aaron stood up and approached his wife. Then he looked her dead in the eyes, and said, "I swear. I did not say anything to her."

"Why didn't you call and tell me she wasn't here?"

Aaron shrugged. "I just got here."

"Oh," Justina muttered with sadness in her voice.

"Carmela's fine," he said with confidence. "Why don't you call her?"

Justina rushed to pick up the phone on the tabletop. She was disappointed when her call went straight to Carmela's voicemail.

"I'm sure she'll call you as soon as she gets your message," Aaron said, after Justina returned the phone to its cradle.

"I hope so."

"Do you want to go out tonight? We have a lot to celebrate."

"What's the occasion?"

"We have peace in our home again!" Aaron gushed.

Justina gave him the evil eyes, before hollering, "You are so insensitive! My sister could be out there on the streets doing God knows what, and all you care about is peace!" She turned her back to Aaron and headed upstairs to their bedroom.

"I'm sorry!" Aaron yelled to her back, but figured his apology fell on deaf ears. He sat on the edge of the sofa and buried his head in his hands. He realized he did not handle the situation, tactfully.

Chapter 20
Close Encounters

*G*uy was at work but his heart was not in it. He was still upset with Regine for calling out Lamar's name the last time they made love. He asked her if she ever had sex with her business partner and she said *no*. He believed her, but was still suspicious of their relationship.

Around noon, Guy got off work to pay his wife a surprise visit at her restaurant in Tampa, Florida. He parked on the side of the building, climbed out of his car, and walked up the pathway to the restaurant. Coincidentally, he opened the door and stood face-to-face with Regine's business partner.

Lamar was startled by Guy's presence. "Hi," he greeted in an uneasy manner. "What are you doing here?"

"Since when do I need an appointment to see my wife?"

"Uh…I…I mean…*we* weren't expecting you."

Guy made a mental note to do more drive-bys. He thought Lamar was becoming too comfortable with his nonexistence. He determined now would be a good opportunity to get some things off his chest, so he asked, "Can we talk in private?"

Lamar opened his mouth to respond but closed it after he turned back and spotted Regine approaching them.

"What are you doing here?" Regine asked Guy.

"I was hoping we can go out to lunch."

"I'm sort of busy," Regine explained. "Do you mind if we eat here?"

"I want to take you somewhere else, so we can talk in private."

Feeling like the third wheel, Lamar said to Regine, "I have to go now. I'll call you when I arrive in Miami."

"Why in the *hell* would you do that?!" Guy questioned in anger.

Regine glared at her husband. She could not understand his rude behavior.

Lamar said to Guy, "We thought it was a good idea for me to head to Miami in advance of the grand opening. Regine asked me to call and make sure the plans were on schedule."

"Can't you send her a text message?" Guy countered, not caring how his question was perceived.

Lamar looked at Regine before responding to Guy. "I suppose so."

"Great!" Guy cheered, pretending to smile. "We'll expect your text message soon."

Nervously, Lamar redirected his gaze to Regine. "I'll see you later." He did not look back as he headed to his car and drove away.

"What was that about?" Regine asked Guy.

"You know *damn* well what that was about!"

Folding her arms and leaning on one leg, Regine snapped, "I have no idea what you're talking about. So explain it to me."

"You don't think I see what's going on? Lamar is *in love* with you. Are you too blind to see that?"

"You're insane. That man has given me nothing but respect. There's nothing going on between us."

"Did you tell Lamar?"

"Tell him what?"

"That there's nothing going on between you two."

"I can't do this." She turned her back to Guy and walked away.

"Regine!" he called out. "Come back here! We need to talk about this!"

She heard him but kept walking toward her office.

At his wits end, Guy clasped his hands on top of his head and gazed at the sky. He whispered aloud, *"What if I jumped to the wrong conclusions?"*

Regine was livid as she walked in her office, shutting the door behind her. "How dare he come here and accuse me of the unthinkable!" She flopped in the chair behind her desk, rested her head in her hands, and started weeping.

Twenty minutes later, Lamar opened the door to her office and walked in. "Mrs. Simmons, are you okay?"

She lifted her head and dried her tears with her fingers. "Lamar, what are you doing here?"

Earlier, Lamar had parked down the street from the restaurant, and waited for Guy to leave. Then he made a U-turn and returned to the restaurant.

"I was worried about you," he admitted, clearly moved by Regine's tears. "Are you okay?"

Her voice shook as she nodded, and said, "Yes, I'm fine."

Lamar walked around her desk and knelt down beside her chair. He cupped her face and looked into her eyes. "I can't go to Miami, until I know for sure you're okay."

On impulse, he opened his arms and Regine fell into his embrace. She felt safe and protected.

Lamar hugged her tightly. He did not want to let go. "I care about you. I'll die if something ever happened to you."

"What about Leslie, your girlfriend?" Regine quizzed, as soon as she looked into his eyes.

"It's not serious. I can't see myself spending the rest of my life with her. I love you."

Regine felt the same way but was afraid to admit it.

"Did you hear me?" he asked to be sure.

"I love you too, but I'm married."

"I know. When the time is right, we will be together. Will Guy be coming to Miami with you?"

"I'm not sure. I doubt it."

"Good. We'll have time to talk before the grand opening."

Lamar checked his watch before turning back to Regine. "I have to leave, *my love.* You can reach me on my cell phone if you want to talk." Then he dreamily said, "Good-bye, for now."

Regine blushed after Lamar kissed her on the lips. There was a moment of silence as their eyes connected. Even though her heart fluttered, she felt guilty about his kiss and their confessions of love for one another.

However, Lamar was satisfied he and Regine were on the same page. Smiling broadly, he stood up and walked out of her office. Winning Regine's heart was only part of the equation, he thought to himself. Now he was trying to figure out a way to make her father understand that his feelings for her were genuine. He believed Kevin Graham's blessing would seal the deal for his and Regine's union.

Before heading to the airport, Lamar returned home to pack for the trip to Miami. He also wanted to talk with Leslie Holloway, his live-in girlfriend. He decided to end their relationship after picking up good vibes from Regine. He hoped Leslie would understand his plight.

Lamar unlocked the front door and walked in their condo. He discovered Leslie running on the treadmill in the exercise room. She did not see him, as her back was turned to him and hip-hop music was blaring from the Bose stereo. He smiled after admiring her fit body. Then he headed to the bedroom to pack his suitcase.

While packing, he was thinking of ways to break up with Leslie without causing drama. He grinned after strolling into his home office to search for the deed to the condo. Then he returned to the exercise room and turned off the music.

Alarmed, Leslie stopped running on the treadmill and looked back. "Hey you!" she said with a wide grin. "I didn't hear you come in."

"I came in a little while ago. Can we talk?"

"Sure." She turned off the treadmill, drank a swig of water, and wiped perspiration from her face with a towel. "What's going on?" she asked, breathing hard from the rigorous workout.

"I'm *in love* with Regine," he confessed. "I'm going to move out of the condo after I return from Miami."

Leslie's heart leapt from hearing his confession. "That's it!" she said in anger. "For the past year, I've waited on you, hand and foot, for nothing!"

"It wasn't exactly for nothing," Lamar lamented. "I took very good care of you."

Leslie had prepared herself for this moment, but she still felt betrayed. She had been through this before with an old boyfriend. Their affair fizzled in the wake of tragedy.

"You can continue living here," Lamar said, to minimize the impact of their breakup. Then he held up a document in his hand and extended it to her. "Here's the deed to the condo." When Leslie remained mum, he added, "I want us to remain friends."

Unable to think of anything to say, she continued to stare in space.

"If you need to reach me, I will be staying at the Hilton hotel in downtown Miami."

Lamar walked toward the kitchen and placed the deed to the condo on the kitchen counter. He briefly looked back at her before he grabbed his suitcase and headed out the front door. Upon stepping outside, he took a deep breath and exhaled with relief. Then he climbed in his car and headed to the airport.

***

Leslie remained in one place long after Lamar left for the airport. With nostrils flaring and heavy breathing, she grew angrier by the second. Ultimately, she became a woman scorned. She destroyed every picture she and Lamar had ever taken together. Then she marched upstairs to his walk-in closet, pulled his clothes from the hangers, and threw them on the floor.

Next, she grabbed his clothes, marched downstairs and threw them out the front door. She performed this task repeatedly until everything that belonged to Lamar was outside of their condo. Then she called her *home girls,* Nicky Cannon and Marissa Carey, and told them she was selling all of Lamar's things for a good price.

Her girlfriends arrived at her condo in record time. Before the selling began, Leslie told them Lamar was leaving her for Regine.

"Are you serious?" Marissa was shocked and dismayed. She had always believed Lamar worshipped the ground Leslie walked on.

Nicky said, "I wouldn't let Lamar get away with this."

"What are you talking about?" Marissa asked, while scanning the beautifully decorated condo. "Leslie is set for life. Look at this *bad ass* condo he gave her."

"Nah," Nicky disagreed while bobbing her head, animatedly. "He owes her more than a condo."

Leslie asked Nicky, "What do you have in mind?"

"Do you know where Lamar is staying?"

"At the Hilton, in downtown Miami."

Nicky bore a mischievous grin. "That's good. One of my girl-friends work at the Hilton. I'm sure she can help arrange Lamar's demise."

"Are you crazy?!" Marissa exclaimed. "Don't be a fool, Leslie. Lamar has plenty of money. He gave you this condo, and if you play your cards right, you can have more than this."

"How? He's leaving me for his business partner."

"He's generous," Marissa explained.

Leslie nodded. "I suppose you're right."

"I can't tell you what to do," Nicky said as she turned to Leslie, "but call me if you change your mind about getting even with La-mar."

"Do not listen to Nicky," Marissa butted in. "Once Lamar realizes you're a special woman, he's going to come to his senses."

Leslie had her doubts. She resumed selling his items, and made over five thousand dollars. Though, she considered it chump-change compared to the weekly allowance Lamar had been giving her.

After her friends left, Leslie sat on the sofa and mulled over her situation. Then she reflected on her first encounter with Lamar, which was a year earlier. She was a secretary sitting behind the reception desk at a law firm in Tampa, Florida, when Lamar walked in to con-firm his appointment. Both had greeted each other with warm smiles followed by flirty gestures. It was obvious that they were attracted to each other.

Leslie had readily accepted Lamar's offer to go out on a date. They did not have anything in common but enjoyed each other's company. In fact, she did not ask Lamar if she could move in with him. One day, she quit her job and showed up at his condo with two suitcases. They had been living together ever since.

Throughout Leslie's entire adult life, she had always depended on men for financial support. She realized she was getting older, and her pretty face and firm body was aging. She was afraid the gravy train was coming to a complete stop. Lamar was her last *white hope*.

"He won't get away with this," Leslie thought aloud. "And that slut he's leaving me for is going to get hers."

Leslie's friend, Nicky, had successfully planted a seed of revenge.

Chapter 21
Life or Death

*A*fter Alex's plane landed in Baltimore, Maryland, he ordered a limo to take him to Johns Hopkins. His heart sped up as the limo drove in front of the hospital. Without waiting for the chauffeur, he climbed out the backseat and rushed through the entrance of the Charlotte Bloomberg Children's Center. The receptionist provided Alex a visitor pass, then directed him to the *Pediatric Intensive Care Unit* on the 4th floor. From there, a nurse guided him to Alexander's room.

Alex's nervousness showed as he strolled into the room and saw a beautiful baby boy sleeping in a small hospital bed. Without taking a blood test, he knew Alexander was his baby. He observed the heart monitor and tubes extending from the EKG machine to the baby's chest.

In the corner of the room, Alecia observed Alex's reaction upon seeing their baby for the first time. Sympathetic to his purview, she stood up, walked toward him and placed her hand on the back of his shoulder.

Hope was in her voice, as she said, "I believe Alexander is going to be fine after the surgery. The doctor has arranged for you to have a DNA test before the bone marrow transplant procedure."

Alex looked at her with cold eyes. "I've been thinking about our conversation since you left my office yesterday. Is there a good reason why you didn't tell me about my baby earlier?"

"I thought it was for the best," she replied, after a short pause.

"I had a right to know."

"I trapped you into being with me," she admitted under her breath. "I was embarrassed."

"I deserved to know."

"If it were not for my actions, I would not have gotten pregnant. I thought it was best if I raised our baby by myself."

"You denied me the first three months of my baby's life. And you did this, because you were thinking about yourself."

Looking back, Alecia realized her actions were not reasonable. She tried to soothe her guilty conscience by lying. "I wasn't sure if Alexander was your baby."

"Are you serious?" Alex asked in disbelief. "Without a DNA test, that baby is mine and you know it."

"I'm sorry," she said in a soft whisper.

Alex glared at Alecia in disgust before he turned to leave.

"Wait!" she called out. "You can't leave. My baby needs you."

When Alex turned around, he said, "I'm not leaving. I'm going to get tested to see if I'm a match for the bone marrow transplant."

"Thank you."

"I'm not doing this for you. I'm doing this for *my* baby. Then I'm going to pray the surgery is successful."

Alex walked away from Alecia in despair. He kept his focus on his baby, but he also thought about Evian, the love of his life. He hoped she would be accepting of his child.

Upon walking through the corridor of the testing center, Alex checked in with the receptionist. Then a nurse guided him to a small room, and took a saliva sample from him by inserting a long Q-tip in the side of his mouth. Then she placed the swab in a container for testing.

"How long will it take to get the DNA results?" Alex asked the nurse.

"We should know in a matter of minutes."

"That fast?" he asked in amazement.

The nurse snickered. "Technology is amazing, isn't it?"

Ten minutes later, she confirmed what Alex already knew. He was Alexander's father. A smile spread across his face and joy filled his heart. That was, until reality set in about his baby's critical condition. He quickly turned to the nurse, and asked, "What about the blood work for the bone marrow procedure? How soon can we get started?"

"Wait here. I'll go let the phlebotomist know you're ready."

Eager to get the process started, Alex rolled up his sleeves and pumped his arms, to make it easier for the phlebotomist to find the veins. His blood was drawn on the first attempt.

Shortly after, Alex was deemed the perfect match for the bone marrow transplant. He was ecstatic.

When the doctor tried to explain the risks of the procedure, Alex interrupted him. "I know all about it. Let's get started now."

"You need to be aware of the risks," the doctor insisted.

"I don't care about the risks. I'm trying to save my baby's life."

"Very well." The doctor handed Alex a pen and a document. "Please complete this form."

"What's this?"

"A statement that says you understand the bone marrow transplant procedure, and the risks involved."

"What's going to happen next?"

"We're going to put you under anesthesia. Do you need to contact your family members?"

"I'll call them later," Alex said, after thinking about the doctor's question. He realized his family would pump him for information, and it might take too long to explain everything. He thought the time would be better spent saving his baby's life.

The doctor said, "Make sure you list a contact person in case something goes wrong."

After the paper work was completed, Alex was asked to change into a hospital gown. Then he was taken into surgery. Removing a sample of his bone marrow lasted fifteen minutes, but it took a little longer for the doctor to transplant the bone marrow in his baby's spine.

Alex became fully alert after both procedures were completed. Even though he was groggy, he asked the nurse about the baby's condition.

The nurse said, "The transplant was successful. The doctor is waiting for Alexander to wake up from the anesthesia."

"I want to see my baby," Alex told the nurse, as he struggled to sit up in the hospital bed.

The nurse stood in front of Alex to keep him from getting out of bed. "You need to rest a while longer," she insisted.

Alex ignored the nurse as he went around her and climbed out of bed.

Sighing, the nurse gave up on debating the matter. "Mr. Simmons, I'll take you to see your baby. Please wait here while I go get a wheelchair."

Alex complied with the nurse's directive. In the interim, he slowly stood up, removed the hospital gown, and dressed in his own clothes.

The nurse wheeled him into ICU where Alexander was recovering from surgery. Once Alex spotted Alecia sitting in the chair next to the baby's bed, he told the nurse she could leave. Then he used the remote buttons to move the wheelchair to the opposite side of the baby's hospital bed. His heart melted when he noted a breathing mask over Alexander's nose and mouth.

"The doctor believes he's going to pull through," Alecia said with a sense of relief. "I can't thank you enough for saving my baby's life."

Alex tensed up upon hearing her parental reference to Alexander, especially since the DNA test proved he was the father. He did not say anything to her, but kept his eyes focused on their baby.

"Alex," she said with caution, "I know you're mad at me, but for Alexander's sake, can we put our differences aside."

Nodding, he agreed. Then he noted the bags under Alecia's eyes and grew concerned. "You look like you need some rest."

She forced a thin smile. "I'm fine."

Their conversation ended as quickly as it began. Both Alex and Alecia were focused on their son's recovery. They were elated after Alexander's eyes flickered before opening.

Alecia rushed to his bedside, and cried out, "Thank God! My baby is going to be okay!" She wanted to hold him, but extensions from the heart monitor prevented that from happening.

Quickly, Alex wheeled out of the room to inform the doctor.

The doctor returned to the baby's room moments later, to take his vitals. He smiled as he reported the good news. "Alexander is going to be fine."

"So the surgery worked?" Alex asked to be sure.

The doctor nodded in the affirmative. "We're going to keep Alexander in the hospital for a couple of weeks just to monitor him."

Alex was excited to hear the good news about the baby. He guided the wheelchair out of the room and retrieved his cell phone from his pants pocket. He called his stepmother's cell number but his call went straight to her voicemail. So he called her at work, and learned she was out of town on business.

Alex was puzzled because Jeanine had always kept him abreast of her business ventures. Anxious to get ahold of her, he dialed his brother's cell number.

Guy looked at the familiar number on his cell phone, and smiled before answering the call. "Hi Alex."

"Hi Guy. I was wondering if you heard from Mom."

"No, why?"

"Her secretary told me she was out of town on business."

"That's strange. Normally, mom would have called and told me she was going out of town."

"Yeah, I know."

"I'll call you as soon as I hear from her."

"Please do. I have some news to share."

"What's going on?"

"If you don't mind, I'd rather tell everyone in person."

Guy had a feeling his brother was going to tell him his plans to marry Evian this fall were on again. He decided to toy with his brother by asking, "Is it good news or bad news?"

"It's good news." Alex was dying to tell Guy about his baby, but chose to keep it a secret. Suddenly, his phone beeped. It was Evian. "Guy, I have another call coming through. I'll see you soon."

"Sure thing."

"Hi Evian," Alex said, after answering her call. "How are you?"

"I'm okay. I was worried about you," she whined. "I haven't heard from you since you left Tampa."

"I had to do some blood work and...."

"Is the baby yours?" she interrupted, to get straight to the point.

Alex grinned. "Yes, he is. The doctor said my son is going to pull through."

"That's good to hear." In all honesty, Evian was not sure how to take the news. She wanted to give Alex his first child, but that option was no longer on the table.

"Are you there?" Alex asked when she remained quiet.

"Uh...yes," she stammered. "What about the baby's mother?"

"She's hanging in there, considering."

"That's good," Evian muttered, as hot tears coursed down her cheeks. She wiped away the wetness, while biting her lips to keep from bawling. "I...have to go." She lied to get off the phone.

"I understand. I'm going to stay in Baltimore the rest of the week to make sure my son is okay."

"Okay." Her voice was soft and fragile.

Evian hurriedly disconnected the call. Suddenly, it dawned on her that she was no longer number *one* in Alex's life. His baby would come first; that was a given. But the baby's mother, Evian thought, could be a problem. She was not going to stand by and allow Alecia Kellam to waltz back into Alex's life.

Chapter 22
Sneak Attack

*D*an parked his SUV up the street from Justina's home. He waited patiently for her husband to get in his car and leave. Then he climbed out of his car, strolled to the front door, and pressed the doorbell. He stood back with a sly grin on his face.

Justina was still in bed when the doorbell chimed. She climbed out of bed, put on her robe, and strolled downstairs to the front door. She opened the door and greeted her visitor with a warm smile.

"Hello."

"Hi, are you Justina Bishop?" Dan asked for the sake of asking.

Even though it had been a while since he laid eyes on her, he could not forget her features even if he tried. Compared to when he last saw her, Justina had gained a little weight and looked happy. But in his mind, she was the same devilish person he met several years earlier.

"I'm Justina Bishop. How may I help you?"

"I stopped by because I'm a friend of your sister's."

"I see. Is she all right?"

"Your sister is fine."

"Have we met before?" Justina thought Dan looked familiar but she could not register his face.

"I don't think so. Can I come inside to talk?" he asked, as he quickly maneuvered himself inside her home.

"What did Carmela do this time?" Justina asked, after shutting the door behind him.

Sporting jeans and a T-shirt, Dan's physical appearance was different from the suits he wore in the past. He had since grown a beard and mustache, which made him look older and common-looking, and his face exhibited old scars.

Dan stood toe to toe with Justina, while peering into her eyes. In a way, he was hoping she would recognize him.

His silence sent chills up her spine. She felt threatened by his presence. Backing up, she nervously stated, "I don't know who you are, *Mister*, but you better leave. My husband will be home soon."

"I don't think so!" He barged toward her with an icy glare.

Justina continued to back up until she was against the wall. "I need you to leave! If you don't get out of my house, I will call the police!"

"Listen, bitch!" Dan exploded. "You don't give me orders! Sit down!"

Justina's knees felt like jelly as she wobbled to the sofa in the sun room. Lips trembling, she asked, "What…do you…want with me?"

"I need you to do me a huge favor."

She looked at him as if he was crazy. A favor was the last thing she was going to give him.

Dan warned through clenched teeth, "If you don't comply with my wishes, you will regret it."

"What do you want?"

"I know you love your family, especially your *wayward* sister."

"Where is she?"

"She's in my custody."

Dan held up a silver Rolex watch as proof.

Justina's eyes grew big at the sight of the watch. The enormity of the situation overwhelmed her. "Please…don't…hurt my sister."

"As long as you do as you're told, you have no worries."

"What do you want me to do?"

"Go to the bank and withdraw five-hundred thousand dollars."

"I don't have access to that kind of money."

"Think of one of your fantastic lies, to convince your husband to give you the money. Or, simply tell him the truth."

"You won't get away with this," Justina bellowed.

"Oh yes I will," Dan said with confidence. "If you go to the police, I'm going to deliver your sister's body to your parents' doorstep. I just may deliver yours," he added to his benefit. "Two burials for the price of one. That sounds like a deal."

Justina thought about what he was saying, and knew she could not let that happen. Her parents would be devastated. She was ready to cooperate. "I need…time to get the money," she said in a shaky voice.

"I'll give you forty-eight hours."

Dan checked his watch, before continuing, "I will call you at four pm tomorrow, with further instructions. You better answer my call. If you don't, I'll make my own assumptions."

"What if I can't convince my husband to give me the money?"

"I'm going to enjoy torturing your sister," he countered with a wicked grin.

"Oh God!" Justina cried out. "Please don't hurt her."

"As long as you do as you're told, your sister is safe with me."

When Dan walked out of the house, Justina picked up the phone to call Carmela. She was disappointed to discover her sister's cell phone was no longer in service. The last thing she wanted to do was call her parents. She feared this news would affect her father's heart condition.

Frantically, Justina called her husband. "Aaron!" she screamed, as soon as he answered her call. "I need you! Please come home right away!"

Aaron gripped the steering wheel after hearing panic in his wife's voice. "What's the matter?" he asked, while pulling to the side of the road.

"I need five-hundred thousand dollars."

Justina was expecting her husband to flip out. Several months earlier, Aaron had made it known her extravagant shopping sprees had to stop. So she relied on money from her own personal account, which was significantly less than what was required for Carmela's ransom.

"That's a lot of money," Aaron thought aloud. "What's going on?"

Justina was still shaken up, as she explained, "If I don't have the money in forty-eight hours, he's going to kill my sister."

"Who?"

"The man who barged in our home a few minutes ago."

With deep concern, Aaron said, "I think you should call the police."

"No!" Justina said with the quickness, while pacing the floor. "The man threatened to kill Carmela if I go to the police."

"How do you know she's in his custody?"

"He showed me the watch I gave her on her sixteenth birthday."

"How do you know he won't kill her even if we give him the money?"

With her head held low, Justina said, "I thought about that. I have to believe him. I don't have a choice."

Aaron heaved a sigh. "We'll talk about this when I get home."

"What about the money?"

"I have a meeting in an hour. We'll go to the bank in the morning."

"My sister has been kidnapped!" Justina screamed with steam coming from her ears. "And all you care about is your meeting!"

"Justina, calm down. It's the same meeting that's going to make us enough money to pay your sister's ransom."

"But we have money in the...."

Aaron cut her off in mid-sentence. "Baby, trust me. We will go to the bank first thing tomorrow morning."

"Okay," she conceded.

Justina relaxed after realizing Carmela's kidnapper had given them sufficient time to come up with the money. Besides, she concluded, the money for the ransom was in their bank account.

Chapter 23
Bull's Eye

Spending time with Jeanine had forced Raymond to realize how much he missed his own children. His son was thirty-years old, and his daughter was thirty-five. After their mother died five years ago, Raymond and his children grew apart.

He told her his daughter lived in Italy and they talked from *time-to-time*. That was the truth. But Raymond lied about his son. He told Jeanine his son was deceased. That was a hard lie, but it was the first thing that came to his mind. He was hurt after his son told him he never wanted to see him again. Despite their estrangement, Raymond loved his children more than he loved his own life.

One evening, Raymond and Jeanine were sitting on the deck in her backyard. He noticed she seemed to drift off into her own little world. "A penny for your thoughts," he said, after she remained quiet for several minutes.

Jeanine turned to him with furrowed brows. "Excuse me."

"Do you want to tell me what's on your mind?"

"I don't trust Regine's business partner."

"Why do you feel that way?"

"I believe Lamar Greene is the reason behind the friction in Guy and Regine's marriage." Jeanine sighed, before stating, "I see the way he looks at her. I believe he's in-love with her."

Tilting his head to one side, Raymond stared into Jeanine's eyes and cupped her chin. "Please promise, you won't get involved."

"I promise." Jeanine forced a smile while crossing her fingers.

Raymond was satisfied with her response. Though, he acknowledged Jeanine would be worried about her son and daughter-in-law until Lamar became a nonissue.

The next day, he hired someone to investigate Regine's business partner. In less than twenty-four hours, he learned Lamar had a live-in girlfriend and seemed to live a squeaky-clean life.

"Mr. Greene's business deals are legit," the investigator made clear. "But there is one thing you should know about him."

"What is it?" Raymond asked.

"Lamar is in-love with Regine Croswell-Simmons?"

"How do you know?"

"I witnessed them together. He's been flirting with her, and she doesn't seem to mind."

"That doesn't mean they're having an affair."

The investigator continued, "I found out the grand opening for their new restaurant is in two weeks. Lamar is planning on flying to Miami ahead of Regine. They made reservations at the same hotel."

Raymond shrugged. "That's not unusual for business partners."

"But Lamar made arrangements for Regine to dine with him, in his hotel room."

"That can't happen," Raymond replied in a neutral but firm tone.

"Do you want me to follow Lamar to Miami?"

"No, I'll go."

The last time Raymond was involved in any criminal activity was five years ago. It was when his wife was murdered in the middle of the night. She was found naked with a gunshot hole in the head. The police never found the killer. But what disappointed Raymond the most was the police detectives were so focused on making him the prime suspect, they failed to follow up on other potential leads.

Desperate to find his wife's killer, Raymond hired a private investigator. He was shocked when the investigator told him he believed his wife's boyfriend killed her. Taking justice into his own hands, he shelled out a substantial amount of money to make sure the boyfriend was wiped off the planet earth.

Just like he felt a sense of relief knowing his wife's murderer was dead, Raymond wanted to set Jeanine's heart at ease. He thought he could speak to Lamar *man-to-man*, and encourage him to leave Regine alone. If that tactic failed, Raymond was prepared to do the unthinkable.

***

Upon arriving at the Miami International airport, Lamar picked up a rental car and drove to the Hilton hotel in Miami, which was not far from his and Regine's new restaurant. He had reserved a suite overlooking the skylines. He stopped by the reception desk to confirm his dinner reservations for two in his hotel room.

Since Guy would not be coming to Miami for the grand opening, Lamar took advantage of the opportunity to *woo* Regine. The first thing he did after entering his room was order a bouquet of roses, and had them delivered to Regine at her restaurant in Tampa, Florida. He attached a note that read: *I look forward to sharing my love with you, forever. Love, Lamar.*

After unpacking, Lamar called Regine but received her voicemail. He left a message for her to call him back. Then he decided to go grab a bite to eat. He stopped in his tracks after he heard a knock at the door. He thought it was someone from guest services.

Lamar opened the door and was surprised to see Raymond Brown standing in front of him. He had only seen and spoken with his new acquaintance on two occasions. He first met Raymond through Jeanine when they stopped by the restaurant in Tampa for dinner, a couple of months ago. The other run-in occurred at Alex's engagement party.

"What are you doing here?" Lamar asked.

"Like you," Raymond said, "I'm here on business. Do you mind if I come inside? I need to talk to you about something important."

"Sure."

Lamar stepped aside to allow Raymond's entry. He closed the door behind them, and asked, "How did you know where to find me?"

"I thought I saw you checking into the hotel earlier. I wasn't sure, so I asked the receptionist for your room number."

"Oh…okay," Lamar said, thinking Raymond's explanation sounded odd. He made a mental note to question the hotel manager about the disclosure of his room number. Someone at the hotel was going to get fired as far as he was concerned.

Raymond had paid the receptionist one-hundred dollars in exchange for Lamar's room number. But he kept that minor detail to himself.

After Lamar noticed Raymond had made himself comfortable on the sofa, he followed suit and sat on the loveseat across from him. Cutting to the chase, he asked Raymond, "What can I do for you?"

"I need to know what's going on between you and Regine."

"That's none of your business."

"That's where you're wrong," Raymond replied in a measured tone. "Jeanine Benedict and I are an item. And because her son is married to Regine, I am very much involved." He sat on the edge of the sofa, before continuing, "I won't stand by and watch you destroy their marriage. So I'm going to give you an ultimatum. Either you stay away from Regine, or face dire consequences."

Lamar frowned. "Are you threatening me?"

"It's not a threat, it's a promise." Raymond retrieved a document from his coat pocket, and handed it to Lamar.

Lamar hesitated before he snatched the document and reviewed its contents. Then he peered into Raymond's eyes with a scowl on his face.

"What is this?!"

"A contract that ends your business relationship with Regine."

"I'm not going to sign this."

"Yes you are," Raymond said, as he stood up to leave. Despite the intensity of the conversation, his demeanor was calm, cool, and collected.

"Regine's signature is not even on this," Lamar explained.

"That's a minor detail."

"But the grand opening is in two weeks."

"That's more than enough time for you to decide your destiny. I'm in room 404," Raymond made known, as he turned to leave. "Leave the signed contract under my door."

"This is bullshit!" Lamar complained to Raymond's back. "I'm not going to sign this!"

Raymond did not look back or say another word as he opened the door and walked out of Lamar's room. He pondered his conversation with Lamar as he strolled down the hallway to the elevator.

After pressing the button to go to his room on the fourth floor, Raymond was inclined to return to Lamar's room and force him to sign the document, by any means necessary. But the woman of his dreams was on his mind. He called her as soon as he entered his hotel room.

His call was directed to her voicemail after the third ring. He left her a message: *Hello Jeanine. This is Raymond. I had to go to Miami to take care of some business. Call me when you get a chance. I love you.*

Long after Raymond's surprise visit, Lamar reviewed the contract over and over. The more he read it, the angrier he became. He picked up the phone to call Regine, but his call was routed to her voicemail. He left a message: *Regine, please call me when you get a chance. It's urgent.*

Still rattled by Raymond's visit, Lamar called room service and ordered a bottle of VS Cognac Hennessy. Then he called Regine a couple more times, but she did not return his phone calls. Even his text messages to her went unanswered. A little part of him could not help but wonder if she knew about the contract Raymond had given him to sign.

Lamar was relieved when his liquor with a bucket of ice was delivered. He tipped the hotel attendant and closed the door without locking it. Then he poured himself a drink and downed it within seconds.

He repeated this act three times before he sat on the sofa with another refill.

After emptying the glass for the fourth time, Lamar's thoughts were spinning at the speed of lightning. His eyes became red and blurry. Lamar sensed he was good and drunk. Then he heard a knock at his door. He became anxious after the knocking grew louder.

Chapter 24
Motive

*C*urious to learn more about her nemesis, Evian opened her laptop and typed in Alecia Kellam's name. Alecia was listed as the daughter of Dr. Kellam, the same doctor who invented the cure for Stage IV breast cancer. Since her first internet search did not provide useful information, she searched the Florida court records and hit the jackpot.

The records showed Alecia was arrested for allegedly shooting Alex, but she was later acquitted of all charges. The actual shooter was Rhaunda Coleman, who remained locked up in a mental institution. Further research revealed Rhaunda's father was jailed for obstruction of justice.

"I wonder what happened to her mother, Elizabeth Coleman," Evian thought aloud, as she continued to review the contents on the website.

Quickly, she typed 411.com in the URL field on her computer, to locate contact information for Elizabeth.

"Bingo!" Evian happily screamed, as she dialed the phone number listed online.

The phone rang several times before Elizabeth reached for the phone next to her bed. "Hello," she answered the phone on the forth ring.

"Hello Mrs. Coleman. My name is Evian Gant. I called to speak with you about Alecia Kellam."

Elizabeth sat up in bed in a fit of rage. "Why are you calling me about that *hussy?!* I haven't seen her in a while, and I don't care if I ever see her again!"

"I understand how you feel, but I was wondering if you can tell me what you know about her."

"All I know is that she ruined my life."

"I'm sorry to hear this." Evian pretended to sound sympathetic.

Elizabeth heaved from anger. "If I ever get my hands on that girl, she won't live to see tomorrow."

Hearing this comment was music to Evian's ears. She needed an ally, and thought Elizabeth fit the mold. "What if I told you that I could help you destroy Alecia Kellam for all the pain you suffered?"

Evian's question appealed to Elizabeth. She had been thinking of ways to hurt Alecia but never thought about carrying out the actual acts. Curiously, she asked, "What do you have in mind?"

"Can we meet to talk about this in person?"

"Yes, but it'll have to be in the morning. I'm going to visit my husband around noon. He's in jail. Thanks to Alecia," Elizabeth added with malice.

Evian exhaled. She was certain Elizabeth had the motive and incentive to help her destroy Alecia. But she wanted to give her new ally something to look forward to, so she asked, "What if I told you I have a friend that can help your husband get out of jail?"

"I don't see how. My husband was convicted."

"Has he appealed his conviction?"

"No, not yet."

"If you help me get back at Alecia, I'll ask my friend to help your husband file an appeal, *pro bono*."

"You will do that for me?"

"Of course." Evian smiled, mischievously. After reviewing the address online, she asked, "Are you still at Thirty-Three South Twenty-First Street, Apartment 32?"

"Yes."

"Good. I'll meet you at your apartment first thing tomorrow morning."

"I'll be here."

The brief conversation with Evian forced Elizabeth to dwell on her living situation. Ever since her husband was sent to jail and her only child was institutionalized, life as she knew it had quickly deteriorated. The church she had attended as First Lady voted to kick her out after it was discovered her husband had an affair with one of the church members.

Consequently, Elizabeth's income from the church came to a halt. Her social security checks were her sole source of income. To add to her angst, her five-bedroom home went into foreclosure. She currently resides in a one-bedroom apartment in St. Petersburg, Florida.

She thought Evian's phone call was just what she needed to exact revenge on both Alex and Alecia, for ruining her life.

98

Chapter 25
Soldier Boy

*A*fter Dan left Justina's home, he circled her block several times to look for signs that she might have contacted the cops. He was satisfied the coast was clear. He drove onto the highway and headed back to Tampa. Instead of going straight to the hotel, he made a detour to the local store to pick up a new cell phone for Carmela.

Dan knew she was in his hotel room waiting for him. He assumed Swag dropped her off in the middle of the morning, to make sure the kidnapping plan was carried out.

Carmela jumped out of bed as soon as she heard him using the key card to enter the hotel room. "Hi Dan. Did she go for it?" she asked, as soon as he walked through the door.

Dan frowned. He wondered who she was talking to. As if a light bulb came on, he remembered he was using a fictitious name. "Yeah, I think she went for it," he answered, while throwing his car keys on top of the dresser drawer.

Carmela was happy to hear the good news. She found it hard to believe Justina had fallen for their prank.

Dan looked at Carmela and smiled. For a brief moment, he debated over whether to tell her his real name. But he quickly dismissed that idea. He retrieved her watch from his pocket and handed it to her. "This is yours."

Carmela reached for the watch and put it on her wrist.

Next, Dan retrieved the newly purchased cell phone from his back pocket, and handed it to her with a warning. "Do not call your sister."

"Why would I do that? I don't even like her."

"I figured that much."

"Can we order something to eat?"

"Sure, what do you feel like eating?"

"Chinese."

Dan picked up the phone on the nightstand and ordered two orange chicken dinners with steamed vegetables and fried rice. Then he called his job and reported he would be out sick for the next couple of days. He thanked his employer for letting him keep the SUV while absent from work. He disconnected the call, then sat on the edge of the bed with his hands clasped under his chin. He had botched a kidnapping scheme in the past. But this time, he believed his plan was going to be a success.

"What is it?" Carmela asked, after Dan remained mum for several minutes.

"Nothing. What time is your boyfriend coming over?"

"He'll be here tonight."

"When he gets here, I'll fill him in on the rest of our plans."

Fully clothed, Carmela laid across one of the queen-size beds and turned on the TV with the remote control.

Dan peered at her from the corner of his eyes. He had a feeling Swag was going to abandon her after everything was said and done. Discreetly, he had put his phone number in the cell phone he had given her. He figured she might need his help later on.

When Swag arrived later on that evening, he was grinning as he walked into the hotel room. He was happy to see Carmela. Lately, he had been treating her like his one and only girlfriend. He had even retired her from his *Call Girl* business. "Where's my Sweet Pea?" he asked, after he spotted her on the bed.

"Hi Baby!" Carmela squealed, as she jumped out of bed and ran into his open arms.

Swag hugged and kissed her on the lips. Then he turned his attention to Dan. "So, what's the *deal*?"

"Deal?" Dan asked, seeking clarity.

"Yeah man. What's going on?"

After catching on to what Swag was asking, Dan said, "I paid Justina a visit this morning. I was able to convince her that Carmela is in my custody. I gave her forty-eight hours to get ahold of the ransom."

"Cool. What do you want me to do?"

"I need you to help me stake out Justina's home."

"Why?"

"That's the only way we'll know whether she contacted the police. I'll take the nightshift. You need to go to her house first thing in the morning."

"I got your back," Swag said with assurance.

Next, Dan gave Carmela her instructions. "I need you to write a letter to your sister."

She frowned. "A letter?"

"Yes."

He grabbed a pad and pen from the nightstand and handed them to her. "Make sure she understands you were not kidnapped. You can even tell her you were in on the kidnapping scheme."

Swag nodded his approval. "That's straight. When are you going to contact Justina?"

Dan said, "I told her I will call around four pm tomorrow."

"Cool."

Swag looked over and saw Carmela scribbling on the writing pad. "Are you finished writing that letter?"

"Almost."

After signing her name, Carmela reviewed the letter to make sure she covered everything.

Dear Big Sis,

Thank you for paying the ransom. To be honest, I didn't think you would come through but I'm glad you did. As you probably figured out, I have not been kidnapped. I am with my man. The money will give us a new start in life, far away from you and your lame ass husband.

By the way, your husband has been keeping secrets from you. He even paid me $25,000 to keep my mouth shut about his sexual activities. So let me be the first to tell you that your husband has been a regular customer of my man's escort service. You can check your bank account for the large transactions if you don't believe me.

Please tell mom and dad I love them, but they love you more.

Carmela

Satisfied with the contents of the letter, Dan cupped his chin and pondered the next plan of action. As if the light bulb came on, he swung his head in Carmela's direction. "We have to find some place to hide you."

Swag said, "I'll take her with me to my apartment in Tarpon Springs."

Dan nodded his approval. "After we get the ransom, you should think about taking her to Mexico for a little while."

"Oh hell no!" Carmela hollered out. "I'm not going to Mexico! I don't even like Mexican food."

"You don't have a choice," Swag firmly stated, giving her the stink eye. "Get up and get your shit. We're leaving."

Sizzling inside, Carmela remained quiet as she stood up, grabbed her purse, and met Swag at the door. She had the right mind to tell him *to go to hell*, but figured the consequences would not have been worth it.

"I'll holla at you tomorrow," Swag said to Dan, before exiting the hotel room with Carmela.

Chapter 26
Curveball

*R*egine's heart was torn between Guy and Lamar. She was still upset with her husband after they got into a dispute at the restaurant. But she was also upset with herself after she told Lamar she loved him. She had avoided his calls all day because she felt conflicted.

Regine noticed Guy was short with her as she laid in bed next to him. She was unable to sleep. In her head, she was thinking about the pros and cons of remaining with her husband versus leaving him for her business partner. Eventually she thought it was best to sever all ties with Lamar.

Quietly, she climbed out of bed, slipped on her robe and bedroom slippers, and grabbed her cell phone from her purse. Then she headed downstairs to the library.

Her cell phone showed four missed calls and several text messages from Lamar. The first few text messages made her smile.

"Just calling to let you know I made it," he said in his first text.

"I miss you already," his second text message read.

Next, Regine listened to her voicemail. She noticed Lamar sounded desperate in his last message. She immediately returned his call, but his phone rang nonstop. So she redialed the number. This time her call was routed to his voicemail.

"Lamar," Regine said in the receiver, "I received your messages. I will call you tomorrow."

Regine wondered about Lamar's whereabouts. To make sure he made it to Miami, she called the Hilton hotel and the receptionist confirmed he had checked-in earlier. Per her request, the operator routed her call to his hotel room. She became worried after the phone in his room rang nonstop.

Earlier, Guy heard his wife when she got out of bed and walked out of their bedroom. He walked downstairs and discovered Regine in the library on her cell phone.

"Is everything okay?" he asked, after she disconnected the call.

Startled by Guy's presence, Regine's hand flew to her chest in surprise. "Whoa! You scared me."

"I'm sorry. What's going on?"

"Lamar is not answering his phone. He left several messages for me to call him. In his last message, he said it was urgent that I call him right away."

Guy shrugged his shoulders.

"Did you hear what I said?"

"Yeah, but Lamar is a grown man. He can take care of himself. This is probably a stunt he pulled to get your attention."

"Why are you being so insensitive? Something terrible could have happened to him."

"I should care about Lamar, because?"

"He's my business partner!" Regine exclaimed.

"So." Guy's comeback was short for *'I don't give a damn.'*

Frustrated with her husband and his flippant responses, Regine thought it was pointless to continue this discussion. She walked past Guy without looking in his direction. Then she went into the kitchen to fix a cup of tea. She sat at the kitchen bar with her head held low.

Shortly afterward, Bessie walked in the kitchen and looked at her granddaughter with a grim expression. "You all right?"

Regine's head flew up in bewilderment. "Grandma, what are you doing up?"

"I couldn't sleep," Bessie admitted with sleepiness in her voice. "What's going on between you and Guy?"

"It's nothing."

"Don't lie to me."

"Grandma, please. I don't want to talk about this."

Bessie walked over to the kitchen bar and sat on the stool next to Regine. "What happened to your business partner?"

Regine frowned. "Why are you asking me about Lamar?"

"I overheard you and Guy talking about him."

"You shouldn't be eavesdropping," Regine admonished. "That was a private conversation."

"It didn't sound private to me, especially when another man is involved. So talk to me. What's going on?"

"I couldn't get ahold of Lamar," Regine explained.

"Is that unusual?"

"Not really. Lamar has always answered my calls."

"Don't say anything else," Deacon Franklin told Regine, when he appeared in the kitchen with his robe on.

Bessie gasped in surprise. "Honey, what are you doing up so early?"

"You weren't in bed, so I came looking for you."

"I'll come back to bed soon. I'm talking to my granddaughter."

In a firm tone, the deacon told his wife, "You need to stay out of whatever is going on between Regine and Guy."

"But...."

"Enough!" the deacon interjected, before turning to Regine. "Me and your grandmother are leaving when the sun rises."

Regine's mouth flew open in shock. "You don't have to leave."

The deacon said, "It's better this way."

Bessie wanted to say something, but she had known her husband long enough to know she could not win this argument. With sad eyes, she turned to her granddaughter and patted her hand. "We will talk later."

Regine remained at the kitchen bar in near tears. She was disappointed to see her grandmother and the deacon leave, but accepted their position. The last thing she wanted to do was get them involved in her marital problems.

Deacon Franklin waited for his wife to stand up and walk toward him. Then he enclosed his hand in hers and returned to their bedroom. As soon as the bedroom door closed, Bessie gave the deacon a piece of her mind.

"Why did you do that?!" she screamed. "My grandbaby is in trouble, and you expect me to leave like this!"

The deacon said in a calm manner, "Regine is not a baby anymore."

"But...."

"But nothing!" the deacon made clear, while raising his voice. "We're going home, and that's all I'm going to say." He climbed in bed, threw the blanket over his body, and turned his back to her. Then he closed his eyes, hoping his wife would get the message.

With a scowl on her face, Bessie climbed in bed next to the deacon and turned her back to him. She was livid after he came between her and her granddaughter. She was also upset with her husband for disappearing most of the day. When she questioned him about his absence, he told her he had to take care of some business. He did not bother explaining what the business entailed.

Bessie remained wide awake as she started to put things into perspective. Suddenly, she saw a silver lining. She thought, with Lamar possibly out of the picture, there might be hope for Regine and Guy after all. She could not help but believe her granddaughter's father, Kevin, had something to do with why Regine could not reach Lamar.

Guy remained in the library long after Regine left. He thought his wife was being overly dramatic. Though, their conversation about Lamar had caused him to sweat, *a little*.

Earlier, Guy called Lamar, who was on his way to the airport at the time. Their conversation was heated and laced with threats.

"We need to talk," he told Lamar.

"There's nothing to talk about."

"I want you to stay away from my wife."

"Is that what she wants?"

"Listen, you *son of a bitch*!"

"No, you listen," Lamar replied, matching Guy's fury. "Regine and I are meant to be together, whether you like it or not."

"I will kill you, if you come near my wife!"

Lamar pretended to chuckle, before asking, "What are you going to do? A little over a year ago, you couldn't even rescue her from her kidnapper without her father's assistance."

"You don't know what you're talking about!"

"You are *weak* just like Regine's father said you were. He could not rely on you, so he asked me to watch over her."

"You're lying!" Guy countered, finding it hard to believe what Lamar told him.

"This conversation is over." Lamar abruptly ended the call.

Guy repeatedly redialed Lamar's phone number, but his calls went straight to voicemail. So he left threatening messages.

Headstrong on getting even Lamar, Guy called his best friend, Mike Solomon, who owned a reputable private investigation firm in Tampa, Florida.

Mike *aka Big Mike* was not big in size. He was only five feet, eight inches tall; and weighed one-hundred, sixty pounds. Big Mike was a childhood nickname that stuck throughout his adult life.

"Hello Guy," Mike said, after answering his phone. "How are you?"

"I'm fine. I'm calling to see if you can help me out."

"What's going on?"

"I have a feeling Regine's business partner is coming on to her." Guy went on to explain why he felt that way.

"What do you want me to do?"

"I want you to take Lamar Greene out of the picture."

"Are you saying what I think you're saying?"

Guy read between the lines. "Yes," he answered, after deep thought.

"You got it, but I will not share the details of the outcome. The less you know the better off you are."

***

Reflecting on his conversation with Big Mike, Guy could not help but wonder if his actions would come back to haunt him. He made a mental note to call his friend for an update on his initial request.

Chapter 27
Devil Wears Gucci

The next morning, Evian dressed in a green, strapless Gucci dress with matching shoes. Then she stopped in the kitchen to grab an apple for breakfast. She was in a *happy-go-lucky* mood, when she grabbed her purse, rushed out the front door, and climbed in her BMW. It took her forty-five minutes to drive to Elizabeth Coleman's apartment, which was located in a rundown area on the south side of St. Petersburg, Florida.

Nearing her destination, Evian checked to see if the car doors were locked. Then she removed her jewelry from her neck and wrists and put them in her Gucci purse.

When Evian drove into the parking space in front of Elizabeth's apartment complex, she spotted young men loitering. They were drinking out of forty-ounce beer bottles and smoking pot. She climbed out of her car and held her purse under her arm. Then she ran upstairs to the second floor while ignoring catcalls from the young men. She took a deep breath before she knocked on Elizabeth's front door.

The door opened and revealed a light-complected, short, stocky, elderly lady with droopy shoulders and sad eyes.

Evian looked past the straggly gray hair into the eyes of the woman who could change her life, forever. "Are you Mrs. Coleman?" she asked to be certain.

"Yes."

"I'm Evian Gant. I spoke with you over the phone."

"Hi honey, come on in." Elizabeth stepped aside to let Evian enter her apartment. Then she pointed to the sofa, and said, "Have a seat."

Evian walked inside and sat down on an old tattered sofa. She noted the apartment had very little furniture. "I hope this is not a bad time."

"Not at all," Elizabeth said with enthusiasm. She swatted at the air to make her point.

Elizabeth asked Evian, "Can I fix you something to drink?"

"No thank you."

"So," Elizabeth said as she plopped down on the sofa next to Evian, "what do you have in mind for Alecia Kellam?"

Evian looked around the room, before asking, "Is anyone else here with you?"

"No, we're alone."

"Good. Let me get straight to the point. I need you to steal Alecia's baby."

Elizabeth frowned. "I didn't know she had a baby."

"Unfortunately, Alex Simmons is her baby's father."

"I knew it!" Elizabeth said, while pounding her fists in the air. "I knew he was cheating on my baby with that *whore!* Alex and Alecia are going to pay for what they did to my family. They're out gallivanting and having babies, while my husband is in prison and my daughter is rotting away in a mental institution. It's not fair!" Elizabeth complained, as tears welled up in her eyes.

"That's why I'm here," Evian explained in a comforting voice. She gently put her hand on top of Elizabeth's. "I want to see to it that Alecia pays for what she did to your family. Can you do it?"

"Do what?"

"Steal her baby."

Elizabeth heard Evian the first time, but she thought she was hearing things. "I can't do it," she said, while shaking her head. "I can't risk going to jail."

"I will help you,' Evian encouraged. "I promise you won't get caught."

Frustrated, Elizabeth said in a stern tone, "I told you my family is locked up. Now you want me to go do something stupid."

"But you won't get caught," Evian said with confidence. She retrieved a pen and checkbook from her purse, and made out a check payable to cash for *three thousand dollars*.

Frowning, Elizabeth asked, "What are you doing?"

"I want you to buy something nice," Evian said, as she handed her the check.

Elizabeth gawked at the amount of the check. In her head, she was already thinking of ways to spend the money.

Smiling inside, Evian gloated over her new friend's reaction to the money. "If you steal the baby," she egged on, "the money is yours."

Prior to Evian's visit, Elizabeth had been praying for a miracle. She started to view her new friend as an angel sent by God. She asked Evian, "What do you want me to do with the baby?"

"Bring the baby to me." Evian made the request seem simple. She acted as if it was normal to steal someone else's baby.

"What are you going to do with the baby?"

"I'm going to put him up for adoption. I know there's a market for babies, and any number of adoption agencies would want first dibs."

Elizabeth frowned. "Are you serious?"

"I'm as serious as a heart attack. We're going to take Alecia's baby, just like she took your daughter from you."

Thinking in overdrive, Elizabeth had several questions swirling in her head. But she asked the one question that might be the deal-breaker.

"How am I going to steal the baby without getting caught?"

"So you're interested?"

"Possibly."

Elizabeth chose not to fully commit. Though, she had no intentions of returning the check. Her husband was in desperate need of commissary items, and she needed to pay the phone bill. She eagerly said, "Tell me what I would have to do."

"Well," Evian said in a low but audible tone, "this is what we're going to do."

Sitting on the edge of the sofa, Elizabeth listened while Evian outlined the details of her plan. The longer she listened, the more she believed she could get away with stealing Alecia's baby.

Evian finished her spiel, by adding, "Alecia will be feeling your pain for the rest of her life."

"When do you want me to take the baby?"

"I haven't figured that part out yet. I'll let you know soon."

"Do you really think we can get away with this?"

"I wouldn't have told you about my plan if I didn't think it was possible."

"I'll do it."

Evian smiled. "You won't regret it."

Beaming inside, Elizabeth always wanted Alex and Alecia to feel her grief. It was the same grief she felt since the day her daughter and husband were taken from her. She believed carrying out Evian's plan would make her feel whole again.

Chapter 28
Ripple Effect

*C*armela did not like Swag's one-bedroom apartment in Tarpon Springs, Florida. First of all, it was in the middle of nowhere. The closest store was twenty miles away. Secondly, the apartment lacked character. There were no pictures on the walls, and there was barely any furniture. Carmela quickly became depressed in her new environment.

Out of curiosity, she asked Swag, "When did you get this place?"

"A couple of months ago. It's my getaway spot."

Carmela sat on the sofa and turned on the TV with the remote. She blew out air in frustration, before complaining, "This place doesn't have cable."

Swag pointed to a rack of DVDs with old movies. "I have a DVD player. Watch a movie."

With her bottom lip poked out, she continued to whine, "I don't understand why I can't stay at your place in Tampa."

Swag sat on the sofa next to her and cupped the side of her face. "Trust me, babe. If things work out like we planned, *I* will be a half-million dollars richer."

Carmela frowned. "What do you mean?"

"Huh?"

"You said *you* would be a half-million dollars richer."

"I did?" he asked in amazement.

"Yes, you did. Are you going to leave me after we get the ransom?"

"Why would I do that? You're my prize. What I meant was — what's mine is yours." Just the thought of getting his hands on a half-million dollars made his face light up like a Christmas tree.

Thoughtfully, Carmela asked, "What about Dan?"

"What about him?"

"I think Dan deserves some of the money. It's his plan, remember?"

"He wouldn't have a plan if it wasn't for you." Swag paused, before asking, "Do you have a thing for that white dude?"

"No, he's just been really nice to me."

110

"Don't let his niceness fool you. He's only nice, because he wants the money as bad as *I* do."

Swag stood up and retrieved his car keys from his pants pocket. Then he checked his watch, to make sure he was on schedule to monitor Justina's home for any signs of the police or suspicious characters.

Before he walked out the front door, he looked over at Carmela, who was lounging on the sofa. "Make sure you stay put until I get back," he ordered in a firm tone.

Carmela stood up and grumbled, "You mean I have to stay cramped up in this apartment all day?"

"Yeah. If your sister calls the police, your picture might be all over the news."

"Is that why you brought me here, in *no man's land*?"

"Yep."

Swag frowned after Carmela plopped down on the sofa, folded her arms, and pouted. "What?!" he asked in a harsh manner. "You don't want to do this anymore?"

"No, that's not it."

"Well, what is it?"

"Nothing."

Swag sighed before he gave her a kiss on the cheek. "I love you, Babe." He lied with ease. "I'll be home soon. As soon as *I* get the ransom money, I'm going to buy you something nice." He forced a smile before he walked out of the apartment.

He climbed in his car feeling lucky and in control. Though, Swag did not always feel this way. As a youngster, he was abandoned by his drug-addicted mother, and he never knew his father. Raised in the streets, Swag had endured a hard-knock life.

Several years earlier, Smokey, Washington DC's most notorious pimp spotted Swag hustling on the streets. He hired Swag to look after his prostitutes after noting his muscular build and street smarts. Smokey equipped his new employee with a gun and told him to take matters into his own hands if there were any signs of trouble. He paid Swag handsomely for his minor role.

With Swag watching his girls, Smokey's prostitution business prospered. But one day it all came to an end, after Smokey went to jail during a sting operation. He was subsequently convicted and sentenced to twenty-five years in federal prison.

Shortly afterward, Swag relocated to Tampa, Florida and continued where Smokey left off, but on a smaller scale and with much younger girls. He had personally handpicked his escorts, preferring the naïve and gullible. Unsuspecting Carmela was strategically targeted.

Swag was proud he had been able to accomplish so much without his former employer. He reflected on the time Smokey cheated him out of his full pay. It was only one-hundred dollars, but he thought he was being swindled.

When Swag tried to resolve the issue, Smokey ordered his men to beat the crap out of him. Swag had survived the brutal beating, but he wanted revenge.

"He doesn't know who he's dealing with," he told an acquaintance, who also worked for Smokey.

"Man," his acquaintance said, "I don't know what's up your sleeve, but you need to chill out."

"Forget that!" Swag countered in anger. "I'm not taking no *shit* from Smokey! He got me fucked up. He doesn't know who he's dealing with."

"Are you crazy?! Smokey will kill you."

"Not after I get through with him."

Swag had remained true to his word. He became a self-appointed snitch, providing police detectives with enough information to land Smokey in prison for the next twenty-five years. He felt relieved to be from under Smokey's control. And he was looking forward to breaking free from Dan and Carmela, once he got ahold of the ransom.

Chapter 29
Funny Money

*J*ustina woke up early and urged her husband to do the same. They had planned on going to the bank to get the ransom for Carmela. It did not take Justina long to shower and dress, but she noticed her husband was moving at a snail's pace. She went downstairs to eat a light breakfast, while Aaron went into the master bathroom to shower.

After eating breakfast, Justina checked her watch a dozen times before marching upstairs with an attitude. "What's taking you so long?" she griped, as soon as Aaron exited the bathroom.

Aaron's arrogance showed as he dried off with a towel, and coolly asked, "Isn't it obvious? I had to take a shower."

"We're running out of time. I have to have the money in my possession by four o'clock."

"We have plenty of time."

Aaron walked over to the closet and retrieved a light gray suit. When he caught Justina glaring at him, he said in a harsh tone, "Why don't you just call the police, and let them take care of this matter?"

"I told you before. I don't want to risk putting my sister's life in danger."

"Are you going to call your parents?"

"I can't. Not now."

"You don't think they have the right to know their child has been kidnapped?"

"My father is not well," Justina made clear, after softening her stance. "He recently had heart surgery. This news would probably kill him."

Aaron did not understand Justina's explanation for not wanting her parents involved. He knew her father loved his daughters, and would want to know if something happened to either of them.

He moved like a turtle as he stepped into his pants. Then he sat on the lounge chair in the corner of their bedroom, and stared into space.

Growing impatient, Justina asked, "Why are you stalling?"

Aaron sat up on the edge of the chair with his hands folded. "I want to make sure you thought this whole thing out. What if we give the kidnapper the money, and he doesn't have Carmela in his custody?"

"He showed me her watch. That's proof enough for me."

"Are you sure Carmela's not behind this? What if she thought of this scheme to swindle money out of us, *again*?"

"Again?" Justina asked in confusion.

"Uh…I mean…in this instance."

Justina was too upset to process her husband's tongue slip. "Please Aaron," she begged, "let's go to the bank."

"Okay."

Aaron's response was slow and methodic. He stood up to put on his dress shirt, socks, and shoes. He was hesitant as he grabbed his suit coat and walked downstairs with Justina leading the way. Suddenly, Aaron stood still on the last step.

Justina turned around, and asked, "What's the matter with you?"

"Uh…nothing," Aaron stammered, after snapping back to reality. "Let's go. I'll drive."

When they arrived at the bank, they filled out a slip to withdraw five-hundred thousand dollars and handed it to the teller. They were later directed to an office to speak with the president of the bank.

"Are either of you in any danger?" the bank president asked, trying to decipher whether Aaron and Justina were victims of extortion.

"No, we're not," Justina spoke up. "We're in the process of re-modeling our home, and the contractor will only accept cash." Her lie was not well thought-out but seemed plausible. At least, that was what she believed.

The bank president eyed Justina for signs of deception before deciding to honor her request. Turning to the computer monitor, he typed in their account number. There was a long pause before he spoke. "I don't know how to tell you this, but our records show you don't have enough money in your account to cover your withdrawal request."

"I'm sure you're mistaken," Justina rushed to say, finding it hard to believe what she just heard.

"I'm afraid not." He printed their bank account statement and handed it to Justina.

When she reviewed the statement, her eyes remained glued on their account balance. It showed they had one-hundred thousand dollars in their savings account. The last time she checked, the balance was a little over a million dollars. She turned to her husband with slanted eyes.

Aaron's eyes drifted downward as he thought of a way to address their dilemma. Turning to the bank president, he asked, "Can we borrow the difference?"

"No!" Justina directed her sharp response at Aaron. "You need to tell me what is going on!"

"It's a long story."

In a nasty tone, Justina said, "Explain why we're here, when you knew we didn't have five-hundred thousand dollars in the bank."

Aaron felt the blood drain from his face. He wiped his sweaty palms across his pants, before saying, "I didn't know how to tell you."

"Tell me what?!" Justina spat. "That we're broke."

"We're not exactly broke," Aaron said in a low voice. "We just don't have as much as we used to."

Justina narrowed her eyes while looking at her husband with disdain. She wanted to kill him on the spot.

The bank president cleared his throat to get Justina and Aaron's attention. "Perhaps I should leave you two alone, to talk about this matter in private."

"No, that won't be necessary," Justina countered. She suspended her anger to deal with the matter at hand. "Can we get a loan for the difference?" she asked, after deciding to piggyback off Aaron's earlier suggestion.

"Four-hundred thousand dollars is a lot of money. We have to run a credit check."

"That's fine."

The bank president printed Justina and Aaron's credit reports and reviewed its contents. He was trying to delay the bad news.

Justina asked, "Is there a problem?"

"I don't know how to tell you this, but your credit score is too low to qualify for the amount you're requesting."

Exasperated, Justina said, "Please explain how *our* credit score dropped from over eight hundred points a year ago."

The bank president turned the credit report around and placed it in front of her. "You see these negative accounts," he said, while pointing to the creditors in question. "These accounts are in default, and they are affecting your credit rating."

Justina eyes nearly popped as she zoomed in on the negative balances. Then she swiveled her head in her husband's direction. "I thought you were paying our creditors. What have you been doing with *our* money?"

Wrestling for a comeback, Aaron stuttered, "I've...made a lot of...bad investments."

"What about the rental properties?" Justina asked, curious to know more about their finances.

"We lost a lot of properties to foreclosures. The renters were not paying their rent on time, and I could not afford to maintain the mortgage payments."

"Why didn't you tell me?"

"I didn't want you to worry. Trust me. I have a lot of things in the works that will replenish our savings in no time."

Truth was, more than half of Aaron's explanation was a lie. It was true that some renters were not paying on time. But he did not tell Justina he had squandered most of the money on *Call Girls*.

Justina sighed as she turned to the bank president. "Please give us what we qualify for."

"Considering your credit history, we can only give you a secured loan for one-hundred thousand dollars."

Justina squinted her eyes. She found it hard to believe what she was hearing. She leaned toward the bank president, and said, "You mean, we'll be borrowing money against the money we have in our bank account?"

"I'm afraid so. Besides, your recent withdrawal of twenty-five thousand dollars prevents us from loaning you additional money."

Justina frowned. "We did not withdraw that much money."

"Are you sure?" the bank president asked with grave concern. "We have an electronic copy of the withdrawal slip on file. If you'd like, I can retrieve it for you."

"That won't be necessary," Aaron blurted out. He did not want to admit he gave Carmela twenty-five thousand dollars to keep quiet about his *sex-capades*.

Justina eyes shifted in Aaron's direction. "Tell me what's going on."

"Can we talk about this when we get home?"

"I think that's a good idea," the bank president cut in, feeling uneasy about being in the middle of a domestic dispute.

"You don't understand," Justina told the bank president. "We desperately need the full five-hundred thousand dollars."

"Why? Are you in trouble?"

"No," Justina answered. "Please give us the one-hundred thousand dollar loan. We'll get the difference from our other bank." She cut her eyes in Aaron's direction as a gesture to keep quiet about her little white lie. She was trying to maintain some level of dignity.

"Wait here while I draw up the paperwork."

As soon as the coast was clear, Justina stared at her husband with contempt. She did not want to cause a scene, so she said, "I'll deal with you later."

Aaron remained quiet. He knew there was nothing he could say that would appease Justina. He did not want to lose his wife; not this way.

The bank president returned with the contract for the loan, and placed it in front of Justina. "I need you and your husband to read the terms of the loan agreement and sign at the bottom."

Justina reviewed the contents and signed the agreement. Then she gave the pen and loan contract to her husband to sign.

Hastily, Aaron scribbled his signature and handed the form to the bank president.

"Very well. I'll be back with the loan."

"Cash only," Justina requested aloud.

Moments later, the bank president returned to his office with one-hundred thousand dollars in cash. He counted the money, then put it in an envelope and handed it to Justina.

Both Justina and Aaron thanked the bank president before they stood up to leave. When they exited the bank, Justina walked in the opposite direction of Aaron's car.

"Where are you going?!" Aaron hollered out.

Justina closed her eyes while taking a deep breath and exhaling. Then she swirled around and glared at her husband. She calmly explained, "I have to find a way to get the rest of the money for the ransom."

Aaron held out his hands, and begged, "Let me see what I can do."

"You've done enough!" Justina walked away and hailed a cab.

Chapter 30

Spooked

*D*eacon Franklin and Bessie got up early to pack and leave. They had just descended the stairs with their suitcases, when they ran into Guy, who was up from a restless night of sleep. "What's going on?" Guy asked, before they walked out the front door.

Bessie remained mum, as her husband explained, "We have things to take care of back home."

Speechless, Guy stood still as he watched Grandma Bessie and the deacon leave with their suitcases. Then he noticed Regine walking down the hallway and toward the front door. She was fully dressed for work. He stood in her path, and asked, "Did you know they were leaving?"

"Yes." Regine's reply was short. She gave her husband a blank stare as she walked around him and out the front door.

Guy galloped to catch up with her. Standing next to Regine, he bid her grandmother and the deacon farewell with hugs and kisses.

"Give KC a kiss for me!" Bessie yelled out, after climbing in the passenger side of the car.

Regine smiled. "Will do."

The deacon shook Guy's hand, and said, "Take care of your wife." Then he climbed behind the wheel of the car and started the ignition.

Guy was not sure how he felt about the deacon's advice. A couple of days earlier, Deacon Franklin pulled him aside and told him he needed to get his house in order. Guy guessed it was the deacon's way of hinting he knew their marriage was in trouble.

After Bessie and the deacon drove away, Guy walked back in the house without saying anything to Regine. He assumed she was still upset with him. And he assumed correctly.

Regine pretended as though he was not present as she walked to her car and climbed in. She headed to her restaurant in Tampa, Florida. As soon as she entered the restaurant, she made a *bee line* to her office to call Lamar. She was disappointed when her call was forwarded to his voicemail.

Suddenly, her phone rang. She smiled after she looked at the caller ID. "Hi Lamar!" she said with excitement in her voice.

"Who is this?" the deep sounding voice inquired.

Regine frowned. "Who is this?"

"I'm Detective Baily, from the Hollywood Police Department. Now answer my question."

"I'm Regine Simmons. Where's Lamar?"

"Who are you to Mr. Greene?"

"I'm his business partner. What's going on?"

"I can't tell you until we speak with his family members."

"Lamar's parents died several years ago," Regine recalled aloud. "He does not have any children. And he has been estranged from his siblings for quite some time." In fact, Regine did not know how to begin contacting Lamar's family members.

"Does Mr. Greene have a wife or girlfriend?" the detective probed.

"He has a girlfriend. Her name is Leslie Holloway."

"Do you know how we can reach her?"

"I'm sure it's jotted down," Regine explained, while browsing through the rolodex on her desk. "Can you tell me what is going on?"

The detective was not sure if he should divulge information about Lamar. Then he reasoned Regine had been cooperative, and might be able to help him solve the case. "Mr. Greene is missing."

"Missing…what…when…how?" Stunned and choked up, the questions fumbled out of Regine's mouth at once.

"We found his rental car abandoned on the side of the highway in Hollywood, Florida. The keys were still in the ignition, and his cell phone and wallet were in the glove compartment."

Regine frowned. "Hollywood? That doesn't make any sense. Lamar made hotel reservations at the Hilton in downtown Miami."

The detective recorded her statements on his writing pad, before asking, "Do you know if Mr. Greene has any enemies?"

"Not that I know of."

"Have you been able to locate his girlfriend's phone number?"

"Not yet. Can I have your phone number? I'll call you back when I find her number."

After the detective gave Regine his number, she disconnected the call and searched through the Rolodex again. "It's got to be here," she said aloud. She was relieved when she found Leslie Holloway's contact information on the index card with Lamar's name. Quickly, she picked up the phone and dialed her number.

"Hello," a sleepy sounding voice said.

"Good morning, Leslie. It's Regine."

"Oh, it's you. What do you want?" Leslie grumbled.

Regine hesitated before responding. She sensed Leslie had a problem with her phone call.

When they first met, it was not a pleasant experience for Regine. It was Lamar's idea for him and Leslie to go on a *double date* with Guy and Regine, so they could get to know each other better. Things did not turn out as Lamar had expected. Leslie had made the evening uncomfortable for everyone. She made snide remarks about Regine's conservative attire throughout the evening.

"I apologize for calling so early," Regine explained, trying to get to the reason why she called Leslie in the first place. "I received a call from a police detective."

"What does that have to do with me?"

"Lamar is missing."

"Again, what does that have to do with me?"

"I thought you should know. You're still his girlfriend, aren't you?"

"No *bitch!* And you know it!" Leslie blasted with venom on her lips.

Regine was caught off guard by the hostility. She paused for a few seconds, before stammering, "I have no idea what you're talking about."

"*Miss Goodie Two-shoes* is trying to play innocent. You weren't satisfied with your man, so you had to go after mine."

Regine took quick shallow breaths before speaking in a calm voice. "Lamar and I are business partners. We are not in a relationship."

"Answer this," Leslie pressed on. "Did he tell you he loved you?"

Regine remained mum.

"Your silence has answered my question. You can have Lamar!" Leslie screamed like a mad woman.

"I told you there's nothing going on between me and Lamar."

"Save it! You can't convince me you didn't know Lamar broke up with me before he went to Miami. He told me he was *in love* with you."

"He did?" Regine Lamar would be so forthright about his feelings for her, especially with Leslie.

"So I wonder what this phone call is really about. Do you need proof that Lamar broke up with me?"

"That's not why I called. I told you before, Lamar is missing."

"I don't give a damn!" Leslie abruptly disconnected the call.

After Regine returned the phone to its cradle, she sat in her chair analyzing everything Leslie had just told her. She was surprised when a bouquet of roses was delivered to her office an hour later. She felt hopeful after learning the flowers were from Lamar.

Immediately, she picked up the phone and dialed the detective's phone number. "Hello Detective Baily, this is Regine Simmons. I need to know if you were able to locate Lamar."

"I'm afraid not."

"Are you sure? I just received flowers from him."

"Flowers? Why did he send you flowers?"

"He always makes nice gestures like this."

That was true. Lamar was always sending Regine flowers and gifts. Though, she failed to tell the detective this was his first time signing a note that read: *I love you.*

"Oh, one more thing," Regine said to Detective Baily. "I found his girlfriend's phone number." After she gave the detective Leslie's number, she asked, "Can you let me know when you find Lamar?"

"Sure thing," the detective said. "We're trying to get a warrant to search Mr. Greene's hotel room. A case like this goes cold if we don't have any leads within the first forty-eight hours."

"I understand."

Even though she was worried sick about Lamar, Regine decided to keep herself busy at work. She received a couple of messages from Guy throughout the day, but she purposely ignored his calls. She was still seething from their most recent argument.

***

Leslie disconnected the phone in a fit of rage. Regine's phone call had unnerved her. Talking aloud, she said, *"First that bitch takes my man. Now she wants to rub it in my face. I got something for her."*

She rushed to the bedroom to grab a gun from the lockbox Lamar had kept hidden in the bedroom closet. It took her awhile before she figured out how to load the bullets in the gun. She threw the gun in her purse and was headed toward the front door.

Hastily, she stopped in her tracks. She had the sudden urge to have a V8. Rushing to the refrigerator, she grabbed a small can of the vegetable juice and downed it in five seconds. "Ahhh…. That's exactly what I needed," she remarked, feeling rejuvenated.

After throwing the empty can in the garbage, she grabbed her purse and bolted out the front door. She ran to her car, climbed in, and sped off. Leslie had one thing in mind and that was to kill Lamar's business partner. She did not realize she had more than exceeded the speed limit until she arrived at Regine's restaurant in record time.

To be discreet, she parked in the back parking lot. She looked around to make sure she was not being watched before she opened the car door. Suddenly, a large man charged toward her, forcing her to tumble into the driver's seat. Leslie grew scared after the man opened her car door and forced her to get out.

"What's going on?" she asked in a shaky voice.

"Don't worry about all that."

"And what if I don't?" she asked with an attitude.

"Make my day. Either way, you're going with me."

Leslie looked around and acknowledged no one was in sight. Slowly, she climbed out of her car with her purse.

The man nudged her toward a black SUV, which was parked a couple of feet from her car. He instructed her to get in the backseat.

Leslie did as she was told. After climbing in, she came face-to-face with Regine's father, who was puffing on a cigar.

"What do you want with me?" she asked Kevin.

"I want to stop you from doing something you will regret."

"I don't know what you're talking about."

"What's in your purse?"

Leslie's eyes shifted downward.

"If you came here to hurt Regine, you got another thing coming to you."

"What is it to you?"

"That's my daughter you're trying to *fuck* with!" Kevin leaned toward Leslie and got up in her face. "I have never killed a woman, but you will be the first."

Leslie started shivering out of fear.

"I know your kind," Kevin continued. "This is not the first time you played second-fiddle to a man."

Her eyes widened in surprise. "What are you talking about?"

"You know exactly what I'm talking about."

Gasping for air, Leslie found it difficult to breathe. She read into what Kevin was intimating.

He snatched her purse and opened it. "You won't be needing this," he said, as he held up her gun. "Just so you know – you're being watch. If you come near my daughter again, consider yourself dead." He threw the car door open as a way of letting her know she had been dismissed.

Leslie was sweating bullets as she climbed out of the SUV and ran back to her car. Her wheels screeched as she peeled out of the parking space and drove onto the main road. She kept her eyes glued to the rearview mirror to see if she was being followed. Scared straight, she was no longer interested in hurting Regine.

Chapter 31
Unequally Yoked

*W*hen Evian returned home from medical training at the hospital, she was surprised to see Alex's car in the driveway. She wondered what prompted him to return home earlier than expected. "Alex!" she called out, after rushing in their condo. "Where are you?!"

Upon hearing her voice, he walked down stairs and met her in the foyer. "Hello, *Babe*," he said, after hugging her and giving her a kiss on the lips.

Evian stared at Alex as if he had four eyes. "What are you doing here? I thought you were staying in Baltimore the rest of the week."

"I decided to come home early, to share the news about the baby with my family. Besides, the doctor assured me that the surgery was successful, and my son is going to be fine." Alex held up his car keys. "I'm on my way to visit Guy and Regine. Would you like to come with me?"

"Sure."

Alex waited until Evian climb in the passenger seat and buckle up before starting the ignition. He was in a good mood when he backed out of the parking space and drove onto the highway.

Evian thought it was a great opportunity to obtain some information about Alecia and the baby. She cleared her throat, before asking, "Is the baby still in the hospital?"

Alex nodded. "The doctor said he should be home in a few weeks."

"Do you plan on returning to the hospital?"

"Yes. I'm going to make arrangements to return to Baltimore on Friday."

"Oh...." She sounded disappointed.

Alex glanced at Evian, and asked, "Would you like to come with me?"

"No, I don't think that's a good idea."

"Someday you're going to be my son's stepmother. I think now is a good time to introduce you."

"It's just a baby."

At the traffic light, Alex turned to Evian and held her hand. "It would make me happy if you came with me."

"I'll go," she conceded, after pondering his request.

Alex smiled. "Thank you. Having you by my side means a lot to me."

When the light turned green, Alex focused on the cars ahead of him. Evian did not know it but she had taken a lot of weight off his shoulders. He wanted her to be accepting of his baby.

During the drive, Evian wrestled with the idea of getting married this fall. She was timid as she broached the subject. "Um…Alex. I know we talked about delaying our wedding plans."

"That's what you wanted. I want to get married this fall."

"Do you still want to marry so soon?"

"Yes, especially now that I have a baby."

"Okay, we'll do it."

"Are you serious?"

"I love you," Evian dreamily admitted. Though, her heart fluttered from fear of becoming a bigamist. This was a new low for her.

"Are you sure you want to get married?"

"Yes. I would marry you tomorrow if it were possible."

Alex grinned. "Now we have two things to tell my family."

He drove in to the driveway of Guy and Regine's home and spotted his big brother throwing a softball to his nephew in the front yard. Alex had envisioned doing the same thing with his son one day.

Guy approached his brother with a high-five and a brotherly embrace. "Hey bro. I'm glad you made it over."

Alex smiled. "It's good to see you. I see KC is getting bigger."

"Yeah," Guy gushed with pride in his voice. "That's my little man. I don't know what I would do without him."

Alex stooped low and opened his arms to give his nephew a hug. "Hi there, he said to KC. "I got something for you." He retrieved a toy fire truck from the trunk of his car.

"This is for you," he said as he handed the toy to KC.

"Thank you!" KC made a joyful sound of appreciation.

"Anything for you, *Buddy*."

Guy stood back and smiled at his son's reaction to Alex's gift. Then he spotted Evian climbing out of the passenger side of the car. He walked over and greeted her with a warm embrace.

"It's good to see you, Evian. Why don't both of you come inside?"

"C'mon on, KC," Guy said to his son. "We're going inside."

"Okay Daddy!" KC ran inside the house and upstairs to his bedroom with his fire truck.

A few steps ahead of Evian and Guy, Alex walked through the front door and looked around the house before turning back to his brother. "Where's Regine?"

"She's at work."

"That's too bad. I wish she was here."

"She'll be home soon. So Alex, tell me the good news."

Alex grabbed one of Evian's hands and kissed the back of it. Then he turned to his brother with a knowing smile.

"Well," Guy egged on. "What is it?"

"We're getting married," Evian announced with a wide grin.

Guy smirked. "I was at the engagement party, remember?"

"But we're getting married in two months," Alex clarified.

"I thought you were going to wait."

"I changed my mind about the wedding date," Evian chimed in. "I just had cold feet."

Alex nodded in agreement. "Evian and I talked about it and she assured me she was ready to be my wife."

"Congratulations to both of you!" Guy hugged Alex and Evian and stood back with a wide grin.

"We have more good news," Alex announced with a cheesy smile. "I have a beautiful baby boy."

Guy's eyes shifted from Alex to Evian's stomach. He was confused because there was no evidence of a baby bump. Stammering, he said, "How? When?"

Alex teased, "Well, my sperm fertilized an egg that produced a baby."

"You know what I mean," Guy replied with a light chuckle.

"Do you remember Alecia Kellam?"

"I can never forget her."

"She and I had a baby."

Guy's brows scrunched as he stared at Alex. He could not believe his ears. "I didn't know," he uttered under his breath.

"I recently found out I was the father of her baby." Alex was too embarrassed to tell his brother Alecia had raped him. So he provided his own watered-down version. "A little over a year ago, Alecia and I had an affair, and she became pregnant with my son."

Evian's eyes flickered. It sickened her to know Alex was tricked into having a baby with Alecia.

"What is his name?" Guy asked Alex.

"Alexander Simmons."

"When am I going to see him?"

"He's in the hospital," Alex explained. "He needed a bone marrow transplant. The doctor was able to use a sample of my bone marrow to save his life."

Guy's jaw dropped. "When did this happen?"

"Two days ago."

"So the baby is going to be all right?"

"The surgery was successful. If my son continues to do well, he should be released from the hospital sooner than expected."

This was news to Evian. Her brain was in overdrive trying to think of a way to kidnap baby Alexander before he was released from the hospital.

"Do you want me to come with you to the hospital?" Guy asked Alex.

"Not this time. If the custody arrangement goes well, you will be able to see Alexander soon enough."

"Do you have a picture of him?"

"Yes." Eagerly, Alex pulled out his wallet and showed Guy the picture Alecia had given him.

"He's handsome," Guy bragged, as he eyed the picture. Then he pulled out his cell phone and snapped a picture of Alexander. "Now I have my own picture. He looks like his *Uncle Guy* if I must say so myself."

Alex laughed. "You mean he looks like his daddy."

Evian became annoyed. This was the first time she was aware of the baby's picture. She wondered why Alex did not bother to show it to her.

Guy walked over to the bar and opened a bottle of champagne from the wine cooler. "This is cause for a toast," he said, as he handed Evian and Alex empty wine glasses and put an empty wine glass on the bar in front of him. Then he carefully filled the glasses with champagne.

"To Alexander!" Guy cheered, as he held up his wine glass.

"Here, here," Alex said, as he clicked his glass of wine with Guy's. Then he turned to Evian and did the same.

Guy said, "You should contact our family attorney."

"I'm one step ahead of you. I called him as soon as I returned from Baltimore." Alex glanced around and noticed the house was eerily quiet. He turned to Guy, and asked, "Where are Grandma Bessie and the deacon?"

"They had to go back to Virginia. The deacon told me they had some things to take care of at home."

Alex frowned. "That's too bad. I wanted to tell them the good news."

"You can call and tell them later. Were you able to reach mom?"

"Not yet. I left a message for her to call me."

"Um…Guy," Evian cut in, "when will Regine be home? I'd like to get some advice from her, on how to sustain a happy marriage."

Guy thought his wife was the last person he would recommend for any advice. He simply said, "Regine should be home soon."

***

Regine got off early because she was unable to stay focused at work. She drove into the driveway of her home and pulled up next to her brother-in-law's Lamborghini. She climbed out of her car just as Alex and Evian walked out the front door.

"Hey Sis!" Alex greeted, while giving Regine a bear hug. "How's my favorite sister-in-law?"

Regine giggled. "I'm your only sister-in-law." Then she gave Alex's fiancé a hug. "What are you guys doing here?"

Alex said, "We stopped by because we have good news to share." He held Evian's hand as he repeated everything he told Guy.

"He looks just like me," Alex bragged, as he retrieved the picture out of his wallet and showed it to Regine.

Regine gawked at the picture with an open mouth. "Wow! He does look like you. He is so handsome. When am I going to see him?"

"You'll be meeting Alexander Simmons soon. Evian and I are going to see him on Friday."

"I'm so happy to hear this."

Guy peered out the bay window and noticed Alex and Evian talking with Regine in the driveway. He walked out the front door, approached his wife, and gave her a peck on the cheek. "Hi Regine." His voice was dry and void of emotion. "I told Evian you would be a good person to talk to about marriage."

Regine turned to Evian and smiled. "Maybe we can get together and have lunch next week."

"That sounds like a great idea!" Evian was ecstatic.

"Yeah," Guy muttered under his breath, "that should be an interesting conversation."

"I think we should be leaving," Alex said to Evian. "We have a lot of things to do before we fly to Baltimore."

"Thanks for stopping by." Guy shook his brother's right hand and gave him a shoulder bump. Then he gave Evian a warm hug, and said, "Welcome to the family."

Evian smiled. "Thank you."

Regine watched until Evian and Alex climb in their car and back out of the driveway. Then she turned to Guy, and asked, "Can we talk?"

"Not now." Guy turned his back to her, walked inside their home, and headed to his office. He thought drowning himself in work was the only way to deal with the fact that his marriage was likely doomed.

Chapter 32
Déjà vu

*A*fter climbing in the cab, Justina buried her head in her hands. She was beating herself up for not staying abreast of her and husband's finances. She had a feeling Aaron was not telling her the truth about what happened to their savings, but she could not dwell on it.

She sat upright in the cab to pull herself together. Her focus was on getting the money to pay her sister's ransom. She contemplated calling her parents to ask for the money, but knew the phone call would prove futile. For one, her parents would want to know why she needed so much money. Secondly, her parents did not have sufficient money for the ransom; they had recently refinanced their home to stay above water.

Halfway home, Justina became hopeful after realizing there was only one person she could think of that had the money she needed. It was none other than her ex, *Guy Simmons*.

She retrieved her cell phone from her purse, and searched through her contact list for Guy's cell number. The last time she used it, he had come to her rescue. She was praying for another miracle.

The phone rang two times before he answered her call. "Hello."

Justina gasped. The sound of his deep rich voice made her feel excited and bubbly inside.

"Is anyone on the line?" he asked, after he was met with silence.

"Uh...hi Guy, it's me," the timid sounding voice replied. "I'm glad you answered my call."

"Why are you calling me?"

"I need your help," Justina said in desperation. "It's an emergency."

Shaking his head, Guy could not believe her audacity. Several years ago he tried to help her but it backfired. He remembered how Justina went through great lengths to sabotage his marriage. He could not let that happen again.

"I suggest you dial 911," he offered.

"I can't," Justina weakly admitted. She was in tears, as she stammered, "My sister...is in trouble."

"Carmela?" Guy questioned with furrowed brows.

"She's...been kidnapped," Justina muffled between sniffles.

After hearing this, Guy's heart fluttered. "What do you want me to do?"

"Carmela's ransom is five-hundred thousand dollars. I need to borrow four-hundred thousand dollars. I was able to get one-hundred thousand from my bank."

Guy brooded over Justina's dilemma for a few seconds before responding. "I'll see what I can do to help you. But there's no guarantee that if you gave the kidnapper the money, he would be willing to return Carmela. I think it would be a good idea if my friend looked into this matter."

"Who's your friend?"

"Do you remember Mike? He owns a private investigation firm."

"I remember him."

Justina recollected that it was the same Mike who helped find the person that assaulted her several years earlier.

Guy said, "Give me your phone number."

After he got off the phone with Justina, he called his friend. "Hi Mike. It's good to hear your voice."

"Hey Guy, what's going on?"

"Can you give me an update on Lamar Greene?"

"I'd rather not."

"Why not?" Guy questioned with raised brows. "Does it have anything to do with the fact that he's missing?"

"Again, the less you know the better off you are. I don't want to tell you anything that you might be forced to divulge later on."

Big Mike wanted to desperately to tell his best friend what he had witnessed. To do that, he thought, would put his friend at risk of becoming a potential suspect.

Guy said, "I have another problem."

"What's up?"

"It's Justina...."

"Are you serious?!" Big Mike sharply interjected. "Don't tell me you're talking about the same Justina Reyes that tried to destroy your marriage."

"Yeah," Guy muttered, feeling his friend's wrath. "But she needs help. Actually, it's her sister who's in trouble. She's been kidnapped, and there's a ransom."

"Damn!" Big Mike exclaimed. "Those cases are complex if not solved quickly."

"Do you think you can help?"

"I don't know." Big Mike paused, before adding, "I hate to say this, but your father-in-law might be her only hope."

"Are you sure?"

"Yeah, I'm afraid so. The only other option is to get the police involved." After a brief moment of silence, Big Mike said, "I can't tell you what to do, but I suggest you stay out of it."

"I appreciate the advice, but I want to help Justina find her sister." Guy hung up the phone contemplating his next move.

"Who was that on the phone?" Regine asked, after he returned the phone to its cradle.

Guy was not sure how Regine would feel if she knew Justina called him for help. He tightened his lips and thought of a lie. "It was a wrong number."

"Don't do this!" Regine snapped. "Tell me what's going on."

"That was Big Mike."

"Is he okay?"

"Yeah, I wanted him to do me a favor." Guy stalled, before explaining, "Justina asked me to help her."

"Why?"

"Her sister has been kidnapped."

"Oh God, no!" Regine cried out, as her hand flew to her chest. "What are you going to do?"

"Big Mike suggested that I call your father."

Regine understood why Guy's friend wanted her father involved. Her father had connections all over the United States.

"Please call him now," she insisted, as she walked to the phone on the desk, dialed her father's phone number, and handed the receiver to Guy.

"What?" Kevin gruffly answered, making it clear he did not have time for idle chitchat.

"Uh…this is Guy. I need your help."

"How's my baby?"

Guy looked into his wife's big brown eyes before responding. "She's fine."

"So what's up?"

"I have a friend who's in trouble."

"What kinda trouble?"

"She's been kidnapped, and there's a ransom."

"Why are you calling me?!" Kevin grumbled. He was only seconds away from disconnecting the call.

Guy surmised his father-in-law was giving him a hard time. His lack of confidence was clear, as he stuttered, "I was told…you can help her."

"Again, why are you calling me?!" Kevin barked.

Guy's head jerked back with furrowed brows. He was taken aback by his father-in-law's curt response.

Regine pried the phone out of her husband's hand and put the receiver to her ear. "Dad, it's me. My friend's sister needs your help. Her life is in danger."

Sighing, Kevin pondered his daughter's request. Regine was his heart. He could never tell her *no* for anything. "What is your friend's name?"

"Justina Bishop. You probably remember her as Justina Reyes."

"Why do you want me to help her? From what I could recall, she was never your friend."

"We've patched up our differences."

"Are you sure you can trust her?"

"Yes."

"How can I reach her?"

After Regine gave him Justina's phone number, she asked, "Do you think you can help her?"

"I need more information. Let me call your friend to see what I can do."

As soon as she heard the dial tone, she returned the phone to its cradle. Thinking aloud, she said, "I wonder why Justina didn't call me for help."

Guy explained, "Justina wanted to borrow money to pay the ransom."

"I see."

Regine noted visible lines scrunched across Guy's forehead. "Don't worry," she said with assurance. "My dad is going to find Carmela and bring her home."

At that very moment, finding Carmela was the least of Guy's worries. When Lamar told him Kevin did not trust him to take care of Regine, Guy thought he was lying. Now the writing was on the wall. He believed he was no longer in good standing with his father-in-law.

Chapter 33
Dead Give Away

*K*eeping his promise to his eldest daughter, Kevin decided to contact Justina Bishop. He thought about his dealings with her several years earlier. The encounter was brief but powerful. He was responsible for hiring a flunky to marry Justina who swindled her out of her money and assets. It was Kevin's clever plan to get Justina out of his daughter's life for good. He dialed her number with reservations.

Justina rushed to answer the phone as soon as it rang. "Hello Mike," she rushed to say. "I'm so happy you called."

"This is not Mike," Kevin corrected in a husky voice.

"Who is this?"

"Don't worry about all that. Do you have the money for the ransom?"

"I don't have all of it."

"How much do you have?"

"One-hundred thousand."

"I won't charge you more than that for helping you find your sister."

She frowned. "I didn't know I had to pay you."

"My services are not free," he countered in a harsh tone. "You want your sister back or what?"

Justina was thrown off guard by Kevin's harsh demeanor. She was expecting a call from Big Mike, who was much nicer.

"What do you want to do?!" he barked, after Justina remained silent.

"I'll do it. I'll give you the money."

"Good. When are you supposed to make the exchange?"

"I'm not sure. The kidnapper told me he was going to call me today at four o'clock. If I don't answer his call, he said he will kill me and my sister."

Kevin cupped his chin while mentally sizing up Carmela's kidnapper. "Did you call the police yet?"

"The kidnapper told me he would hurt my sister if I got the police involved."

"Give me your address."

"Uh…okay."

Justina felt vulnerable divulging so much information to a stranger. After providing her address, she asked, "What's going to happen next?"

"I'm going to send one of my men over to your house," Kevin stated, as he turn to his most loyal friend and associate.

"What is the man's name?" Justina asked Kevin.

"Thorny."

Justina silently questioned, *"Why does that name sound familiar?"*

"Do not ask him any questions," Kevin continued to bark over the phone. "He's going to appear at your back door. Be there to let him in."

"Why is he coming to my back door?"

"Someone might be watching your house. We can't take any chances."

"Thank you," she said in a hushed whisper. It never dawned on Justina that someone might be lurking outside her home.

Kevin sighed as he disconnected the call. Then he turned to Thorny, his partner in crime. "I appreciate you helping me out like this."

"No problem."

Thorny had been Kevin's right hand man for over twenty years. He was always present when his associate ordered several young men killed because they harmed his daughters. Though, he could not help but wonder if Kevin's actions would be enough to prevent the inevitable.

Aaron walked into the living room just as Justina returned the phone to its cradle. He asked her, "Who were you talking to on the phone?"

"Why do you care?!" Justina snapped.

Feeling the sting of her backlash, Aaron sat next to her on the sofa to plead his case. "I'm sorry we don't have all the money for the ransom, but I'm getting ready to make a deal that will make us a lot of money."

"You don't get it, do you?"

"Get what?"

"You withdrew twenty-five thousand dollars from our bank account. What did you do with the money?"

"I needed collateral for a business deal." His lie was quick and well thought out.

"And I'm stupid," Justina retorted. "Okay, let's play your game. Tell me about the business deal you've been bragging about."

"Uh…uh," he stuttered, "…um…it's not as simple as that."

"You're such a liar!" Justina stood up to leave.

"Wait! What are you going to do about the money?"

Justina turned around with a look of satisfaction. "I called a very good friend who's sending someone to help me find my sister."

"Who did you call?"

"The man I should have married."

"Guy Simmons." Aaron recited her ex-lover's name with hatred in his heart.

Justina smirked. "That's right, the one and only Guy Simmons." She was satisfied to have gotten under Aaron's skin.

"You're still *in love* with him, aren't you?"

"That's for me to know, and for you to find out," she sassed, before she turned to leave.

"Justina, please be reasonable. Don't do this."

Spinning around, she shouted, "Do what?! You did all of this! Every weekend you've been going out of town on *business trips*, but you're not making any money."

Aaron said with stress in his voice, "I can explain."

"Really?" she asked with bulging eyes. "I'm listening. Explain why you've been robbing our savings account."

Aaron remained mum. The lies in his head were in conflict with the lies he had already told her. He thought silence was his best response.

"You're such a *loser!*"

To calm her nerves, Justina rushed to the kitchen to get a cup of coffee. While sipping the strong black liquid, she peered out of the kitchen opening, which was in clear view of the living room. She spotted her husband on the sofa with his head held low. Lately, she had been questioning whether she should divorce Aaron and cut her losses. She acknowledged her husband was not the same man she fell *in love* with.

Aaron felt Justina's gaze but was afraid to look in her direction. He was dealing with inner demons. Even in times like these, he had sex on his mind. Thoughts of his last sexual encounter with professional escorts caused his manhood to rise. He headed upstairs to the master bedroom to pleasure himself.

135

Chapter 34
Fast and Furious

Evian was in a good mood when she and Alex returned home. In her heart, she had forgiven her fiancé for not showing her his baby's picture. She had more important things on her plate, and that included ensuring Alex would be a part of her life forever.

She and Alex went separate ways when they entered the condo. Evian grabbed her laptop and sat on the sofa in the living room. She browsed the internet for the perfect honeymoon location.

Alex went into his home office to make travel plans for his and Evian's trip to Baltimore. He also contacted his attorney to add his baby to his will and insurance policy. Then he walked into the living room and spotted Evian on the sofa. "Hi there, what are you up to?"

She looked up from the laptop and smiled. "How do you feel about us going to St. Lucia for our honeymoon?"

Alex grinned. "Are you sure you want to marry me this fall?"

"I've never been surer of anything." Evian stood up and approached Alex, and in a soft loving voice, she said, "I want to be your wife and the stepmother of your child."

Alex cupped her face and kissed her on the lips. "I love you," he whispered.

Evian blushed. "I love you too. We will *forever be* inseparable."

"I agree." Alex was taken in by her charm and beauty.

Happily, she said, "I'm going to call Joyce to ask her to be my *Maid of Honor*. You think your twin sisters would agree to be my bridesmaids?"

"The twins would be honored. I'll call my wedding coordinator in the morning."

"Why not call her now?"

"I don't know. It's kind of late."

"It's not too late to plan the wedding of our dreams. I would like to call her now if that's okay with you."

Alex took out his wallet, retrieved the coordinator's business card and handed it to Evian. "You can reach her at this number. I'm going to go lie down to shake off this jet lag. Maybe we can go out to dinner later on."

"Sounds like a plan." Evian kissed Alex before strolling to his office. She closed the door behind her so she could talk freely.

"Hello, Doris Bell." She cited the name on the card, as soon as the wedding coordinator answered her call. "My name is Evian Gant, Alex Simmons' fiancé."

"Hi Evian. It's so nice to hear from you. But Alex told me to cancel the wedding plans."

"I'm sure you're mistaken." Evian purposely flipped the script. "I called to see if I can meet with you tomorrow to discuss the wedding plans. You're still our wedding coordinator, aren't you?"

"Sure." Though, Doris was puzzled as to why Alex did not call her himself, to resume the wedding plans.

After talking things over with Evian, Doris believed she would be able to fulfill Alex's original requests and incorporate a few of Evian's ideas. They agreed to meet the next day.

Instead of returning the phone to its cradle, Evian called her best friend, Joyce, to ask her to be the Maid of Honor.

"Of course I will!" Joyce said with glee. "I'd be honored. Can I invite Brian?"

Evian frowned. "I guess," she said with little enthusiasm. "I'll swing by in the morning, so we can go to the wedding boutique."

"I'll be ready."

Next, Evian called her parents. "I'm getting married this fall," she happily announced, as soon as they answered her call.

"That's not possible," her mother protested over the speakerphone.

"Yes, it is!" Evian hastily countered.

"But you're married to Pierre," her father interjected. He was sitting next to his wife in the family room listening to their conversation.

Evian inhaled and exhaled. "The United States does not have a record of my marriage to Pierre."

"Evian, don't do this," her father pleaded. "You can't be married to two men at the same time. You will be breaking the law."

"Dad, I called to invite you and mom to my wedding. Are you trying to ruin the happiest day of my life?" Evian's voice was strained.

Mrs. Gant shushed her husband by placing her hand on top of his knee. She did not want him to push the issue.

The silence on the other end of the phone was deafening. Evian asked in anger, "Are you coming to my wedding or not?!"

"We'll be there," her mother answered with a sour face. Though, her father remained quiet. He had already made up his mind he was not going to partake in his daughter's shenanigans.

Excited to hear her mother's reply, Evian bounced back to her joyful self. "I'll send you a wedding invitation soon."

After disconnecting the call, Evian went to the door to lock it. Then she picked up to phone to dial another phone number. "Hello Elizabeth," she said in a hushed voice. "This is Evian. I need you to take the baby this Friday."

Elizabeth was taking a nap when Evian called. It took her a few seconds to register the caller's voice. Then it took a few more seconds to figure out what Evian was talking about. "You need me to take the baby on Friday?" she asked. "But that's in a couple of days."

"Yes, I know. This will be the only window of opportunity for you to take the baby."

Elizabeth mentally questioned whether she should be involved. "Are you sure you know what you're doing?"

"Of course I do."

"How am I going to get to Baltimore?"

"I'll make the arrangements tonight." As an afterthought, Evian asked, "What is your dress and shoe size?"

"Why?"

"It's all a part of the bigger picture."

"I'm a size sixteen, and wear size six shoes. But I don't understand."

"I'll come by your apartment tomorrow to explain everything."

Evian went online to make hotel and airplane reservations for Elizabeth. Then she called Johns Hopkins hospital to ask questions about *baby* Alexander's condition. She knew exactly what to say to elicit information from the head nurse at the hospital, especially since she had interned at Johns Hopkins hospital for a short period.

After disconnecting the call, she went in the closet in the home office to retrieve a box with her personal items. She dug in the box and found her old hospital security pass for Johns Hopkins hospital. She put it in her purse after figuring it would prove useful later on.

Then she went into the bedroom to celebrate her accomplishments. She undressed to pure nakedness and crawled in bed next to Alex. Then she rubbed her flesh against his.

Alex was immediately aroused by her touch. He turned over and gave her what she wanted: *uninhibited, unadulterated, hard-core sex.*

Chapter 35
Wolf in Sheep's Clothing

*L*ong before Raymond decided to confront Lamar Greene, Jeanine had taken matters into her own hands. She feared Guy was getting ready to lose his wife, and had a feeling Lamar Greene was the culprit of their marital woes. She contacted her private detective, Tim Carter, to probe her suspicions. He later reported he did not find anything unscrupulous about Lamar's background or his business dealings.

Tim added, "Lamar is headed to Miami. I think I should go talk to him, about dissolving his relationship with Regine."

"I'm going with you," Jeanine replied.

"I can't let you do that. It could be dangerous."

"I'm going," she persisted.

"Okay, but you must stay out of my way so I can do my job."

"Agreed."

Upon arriving in Miami, Jeanine stayed at the Bal Harbor hotel in Miami. It was one of Trowne Key Estates' many luxurious hotels. She agreed to wait there until Tim returned from speaking with Lamar.

Several hours later, he returned to the hotel, and told Jeanine, "Lamar was no longer an issue."

"Are you sure?"

"I'd rather spare you the details. But I have a feeling no one will be hearing from Lamar Greene for quite some time."

"Are you saying what I think you're saying?"

"Yes."

"Thank you," she said with a look of satisfaction.

"No problem. Now let's get you back home."

"I want to stay another day to take care of unfinished business here at the hotel."

Tim nodded in understanding.

After Jeanine returned home from Miami, she listened to her voicemail and noted several messages from her youngest son. She eagerly dialed Alex's phone number.

Alex was pooped after his intense love-making session with Evian. But he was not too tired to answer his stepmother's call. He rolled out of bed and sat on the edge. "Hi Mom, it's so good to hear from you."

"I'm sorry I missed your calls earlier. I was out of town."

"Is everything okay?"

Jeanine smiled. "Everything is fine. I wanted to make sure one of the resorts was operating smoothly. It's nothing you should concern yourself with. What's going on?"

"Well Mom, I have good news to share with you."

"What is it?"

"You have another grandson."

"I do?" Jeanine asked in surprise.

"Yes, his name is Alexander. He's three-months old."

Jeanine frowned. "I'm confused. I didn't know Evian was pregnant."

"Mom, do you remember Alecia Kellam?"

"Yes."

"She's my son's mother."

Jeanine paused. She was shocked to hear the news.

"Mom, are you there?"

"Yes…um…," Jeanine stuttered, after recovering from shock. "How did that happen?"

"It's a long story."

A smile spread across her face, after she became excited over the prospect of having another grandchild. "When am I going to see the baby?"

"Soon." Alex figured he would tell Jeanine about the details of his son's medical condition at a later time.

"Son, I'm so happy for you."

Alex smiled. "I love you, Mom."

"I love you too."

After talking with his stepmother, Alex crawled back in bed and cuddled with his fiancé. He was still reeling from the excitement in his mother's voice, but Evian was seething inside.

Focusing on the bigger picture, she asked Alex, "What time are we going to meet with Alecia when we get to Baltimore?"

"Around noon. The meeting should not last more than an hour."

"Is Alecia always at the hospital?"

"For the most part. Why?"

"I'm just curious," she said in a soft voice, pretending to act innocent. "Are you ready to get up, to go out to dinner?"

Alex grinned. "Yeah, especially since *we* worked up an appetite."

***

Next, Jeanine returned Raymond's calls. She was elated to hear from him. More often than not, she had envisioned spending the rest of her life with him. When she dialed his number, her heart fluttered while waiting to hear his rich, captivating voice.

"Hello Raymond."

"Hello, love," he greeted with a warm smile.

Jeanine smiled, feeling giddy.

Raymond said, "I'm happy you finally returned my call. Do you have any plans this evening?"

"No, what do you have in mind?"

"I would love for you to come over, so we can spend time on my private beach."

"Sounds heavenly. I'll be there in an hour or so."

"I look forward to being in your presence."

Raymond smiled as he returned the phone to its cradle. He had just returned home from Miami. He had stayed there a couple of days longer to make some business deals. Now that he was home, he wanted to put his confrontation with Lamar Greene behind him.

Spending time with Jeanine would at least make him feel better about his actions the past few days. At least, that was what he thought.

As soon as Jeanine appeared at his front door, Raymond's mouth flew open in awe. She had on a white see-through wrap over a multicolor Prada bathing suit that accentuated her slim physique. Her long flowing hair was shiny and her light brown eyes sparkled.

"Wow," Raymond said. "You are breathtaking."

"Thank you. You're not bad looking yourself," she commented, while eyeing Raymond's buff chest and muscular legs.

Raymond guided her to his golf cart, which he used to take them to his private beach.

During the short drive, Jeanine asked, "How was your trip?"

"It was great. I was able to take care of some business."

"That's great. My trip was also a success."

"Where did you go?"

"Miami."

"You were there?" Raymond asked in surprise.

Jeanine nodded. "It was an unscheduled business trip. I spoke with managers about upgrading the interior of some of my hotels."

"Why didn't you tell me you were there? We could have met and had dinner together."

"It was an impromptu trip. I didn't want to bother you."

In a way, Raymond was relieved she did not tell him she was in Miami. He did not want Jeanine to know about his visit with Lamar. "Maybe you and I can plan a vacation soon," he suggested, purposely changing the subject.

Jeanine smiled. "That sounds like a great idea."

Raymond parked his golf cart a couple of feet from the beach. Then he retrieved a blanket and a basket of wine, fruit and cheese bites from the back of the cart. He and Jeanine laid out the blanket before they sat down and poured themselves a glass of wine.

"This is nice," Jeanine remarked, as she looked across the horizon and spotted a colorful rainbow over the clear blue water.

He smiled. "I wanted us to have some privacy."

Jeanine fell under Raymond's spell every time she was in his presence. Unlike her deceased husband, he had his own money and made her the center of his universe.

Raymond noticed the sparkle in Jeanine's eyes. Her face was glowing. "There's something going on with you," he acknowledged aloud. "You look so relaxed."

"Let's just say I had a problem, and now my worries are over."

"Would you care to elaborate?"

"Not really."

It was Jeanine's turn to change the subject. "I have good news to share with you," she proudly boasted. "Alex told me he has a beautiful baby boy."

"Congratulations!" Raymond cheered with bright eyes.

"Thank you. I can't wait to see my bundle of joy."

"I didn't know his fiancé was pregnant."

"Actually, he had a baby with one of his old flings."

Raymond held up his glass of wine and waited for Jeanine to do the same. "Here's to being a wonderful grandmother."

Clicking her glass with his, Jeanine added, "And here's to no more trouble in paradise."

Raymond smiled but wondered about the meaning of her last statement.

Chapter 36
When Hope Fails

Justina had been waiting on pins and needles for the person who was sent to help her find her sister. She sat up on the chair in the den when she heard someone knocking at her back door. Slowly, she strolled to the door and opened it. Standing before her was a tall, statuesque, middle-age man. She gaped at her new visitor's bald head and long grayish goatee. Then she peered into his beady brown eyes protruding from his face.

"Thorny?" she questioned, to be sure.

He gave a slight nod.

Justina stepped aside. "Please come in."

Thorny entered her home, and asked, "Where's your phone?"

"It's in the den." Justina pointed to the phone on the end table.

Thorny walked over to the phone and sat on the edge of the sofa.

Justina followed his lead, and sat on the sofa next to him. "Have we met before?" she asked, as she eyed him closely. "Your name sounds familiar."

"No we haven't."

Thorny did not care to mention that he had spoken with Justina over the phone several years earlier. Nor did he explain he had helped take part in swindling her out of her assets and money. "Have you tried contacting your sister?" he asked her.

"Yes, but the number is no longer in service."

"I figured that much."

Thorny retrieved a recording device from his pocket, and attached it to the phone.

"What is that?" Justina asked out of curiosity.

"It's a GPS tracking system. I'm going to use it to record the kidnapper's location."

"I see. What do you want me to do?"

"When the phone rings at four o'clock, answer it and keep the caller on the line for at least three minutes. Do you think you can handle that?"

Justina nodded. She checked her watch and noted it was five minutes before four o'clock.

Aaron walked in the den and spotted Thorny sitting on the couch. He wondered about this strange man. "Who are you?" he asked with a chip on his shoulder.

"Don't worry about who he is and why he's here," Justina told her husband. "This matter does not concern you."

Aaron felt small, but it did not stop him from asking Thorny, "Are you the police?"

"Do I look like the *damn* police?!" Thorny yelled, losing his patience by the second.

Aaron flinched. He assumed Thorny had street credentials, and guessed he could be a professional killer.

Justina walked over to her husband, and said in a hushed voice, "He's here to help us find Carmela."

Aaron's eyes grew wide. "Are *we* going to pay the ransom?"

Justina rolled her eyes. "You know *we* don't have all the money."

"What?" Aaron said with a smirk on his face. "Guy Simmons didn't come through for you?"

"He told me it was no guarantee the kidnapper would release Carmela, even if we paid the ransom."

"That's the same thing I told you."

In a huff, Aaron turned his back to his wife and walked toward his office. The unexpected twists and turns surrounding his sister-in-law had caused him to yearn for sex. He needed it badly. His manhood was erect by the time he made it to his office.

The phone rang just as Justina decided to go after her husband, to explain everything. She followed Thorny's demand to answer it on the third ring. "Hello," she said, shakily.

"Hello Justina," Dan said in a casual manner. He did not know he was on the speakerphone, when he asked, "You have all the money?"

Justina looked to Thorny who told her to lie. "Yes, I have the money."

"Good, now this is what I want you to do."

"Wait!" Justina interrupted Dan, after remembering Thorny told her to keep the kidnapper on the phone for three minutes. "Where's my sister?"

"I told you. She's in my custody."

"Can I talk to her, to make sure she's okay?"

"No can do. You can talk to her once I get the money."

Justina cleared her throat, before asking, "How do I know my sister is still alive if I can't talk to her?"

"You just have to trust me."

"But I don't know you."

"That doesn't matter. You want your sister back or not?"

Dismissing the question, Justina asked, "What do you want me to do?"

"Meet me at the *Down Beat* restaurant at eight o'clock in the morning, and bring the ransom with you. If I see cops in the vicinity, Carmela is dead. Do you understand?"

"Yes. Please don't hurt my sister," Justina begged. Fear had taken over every fiber of her being.

"As long as you do as you're told, you don't have to worry about me hurting anyone."

Turning his thumb upside down, Thorny signaled for Justina to end the call. She did as she was told.

"Do you think he's going to kill my sister?" she asked, after returning the phone to its cradle.

Without answering her question, Thorny said, "We were able to track the location of the caller. Sit tight until I call you. Do not call the police." He retrieved his cell phone to record the caller's address. Then he detached the recording device and stood up to leave.

Justina asked, "When will I hear from you?"

"In a day or so."

"Why so long?"

"When we locate the kidnapper, we have to find your sister. It's possible that he's hiding her in a different location."

"I see."

"Don't worry," Thorny said. "We're going to find her."

After he left, Justina went upstairs to talk to her husband. She found him in his office in front of the computer, watching porn and jacking off. "What are you doing?" she said with disgust.

Aaron fumbled to *click* out of the porn site on the computer. Then he quickly jammed his warped penis in the small opening of his boxer shorts. "It's...not what...it seems," he struggled to say.

Justina crossed her arms and leaned on one leg. "Explain it to me."

"I...uh...uh...." Aaron could not think of a logical explanation.

"Just what I thought!" Justina snapped. "My sister has been kidnapped, and all you can do is watch porn?!"

Aaron stood up and stretched out his arms to his wife. "I'll never do it again," he said in a pleading tone. "You must believe me."

"Carmela's not your sister," Justina said with an attitude. "And you made it clear that you didn't like her. So I gave you a pass for not understanding. But the least you could do is pretend like you care."

"I do care."

"That's bull!" Justina shouted at the top of her lungs. "Instead of supporting me, you're in here watching porn. Who in the hell did I marry?!" she screamed, while throwing up her arms in despair.

"Uh…um…this is not something I normally do."

"Yeah, right." Justina dashed out of his office and headed downstairs. She needed to distance herself from Aaron before she said something she would probably regret.

Overcome with guilt, Aaron remained in his office long after Justina left. He was unsure of what to do next. One side of his brain told him to find Justina and plead his case; but the other side of his brain negated that option. He picked up his phone in his office to call Swag. When his call went straight to Swag's voicemail, his message was simple and to the point. *This is Aaron. I need an escort right away. Call me back.*

Swag was sitting outside monitoring Justina and Aaron's home when his phone rang. It was his favorite customer. He did not know if he should answer it, for fear it would thwart the kidnapping scheme. So he let the call go straight to his voicemail. Then he listened to the message a few minutes later. Shaking his head, he thought it was too risky to arrange a *Call Girl* during this critical period.

Aaron was still feeling the sting of getting caught with his zipper down. But his desire for sex intensified. He was disappointed after his call to Swag had gone unanswered. He agonized over the idea of warming up to his wife, to satisfy his sexual needs.

Justina was in their bedroom when Aaron walked in. She glared at him out of the corner of her eyes. "What do you want?" she grumbled.

"I want to see if we can patch up our differences."

"What differences?! You're the problem!" she fired off. "You are the only one that can fix your problem."

In his defense, Aaron said, "If my wife gave me sex on a regular basis, maybe I wouldn't have to look at porn."

"You're blaming me? I cannot believe this," she stressed with disgust. "First, you spend most of our savings on *God knows what*. Then I catch you watching porn. Now you're blaming me for not giving you sex. You're pitiful, and ought to be ashamed of yourself."

"Uh…I didn't…mean…."

"Save it!" Justina trounced past Aaron and rushed out of their bedroom.

Aaron blew out air in frustration. He was fed up with Justina, and how she was using every opportunity to make him feel bad. He grabbed his car keys and hurried downstairs. He stopped in his tracks after he spotted Justina's purse on the sofa.

Thinking clearly, Aaron headed for her purse and peered inside. The envelope filled with the ransom money was visible. He looked toward the stairs to see if Justina was present before he peeled off two one-thousand dollar bills and stashed them in his wallet. Then he jetted out of the house.

Aaron climbed in his car and sped out of the driveway. He was headed to Tampa, to acquire sexual services. But first, he stopped by a local check-cashing store to get change. He was desperate for sex, but he wanted it dirt cheap, especially since Justina had taken a loan against what was left in their bank account.

Cruising along the strip, he carefully searched for his prey. He preferred girls with big boobs and big apple bottoms. Though, his sudden erection inspired him to pull over to the first girl he saw. She was a tall, skinny blonde, dressed in six-inch hooker shoes, a very short mini skirt, and a tight-fitting blouse that *oozed* double-D cleavage. "Hey sexy!" he yelled out the passenger window. "You need a ride somewhere?"

"Does it look like I need a ride?" she retorted, rolling her eyes.

"No, but…."

"If you're 5-0," the prostitute threatened while leaning in the passenger window of Aaron's car, "you might as well keep it moving."

"I'm not a cop. You can trust me."

"Yeah, right," the prostitute rebuffed.

"I can show you my ID if that'll help." Eagerly, Aaron pulled out his wallet, retrieved his driver's license, and showed it to her.

The prostitute chewed her gum like a cow as she looked at his ID and mentally questioned Aaron's motives. "You want some action, huh?"

"Yeah, something like that." Briefly, he glanced down at his erection. Just looking at the prostitute had excited him beyond measure.

"How much?" she asked, deciding to give Aaron a chance.

"Two hundred." He retrieved two one-hundred dollar bills from his wallet and held it up.

"Make it five hundred, and I'll make your dreams come true."

Aaron showed her the money and unlocked the passenger door.

As soon as the prostitute climbed in his car, sirens blared all around them. He turned to the prostitute and was caught off guard when she flashed her police badge. "What is this?" he frantically inquired.

The undercover prostitute said, "You're under arrest."

147

"No! No! Don't do this!" Aaron pleaded for mercy. "I'm married!"

"You should have thought about that beforehand."

"Put your hands up and get out of the car!" another police officer ordered, as he approached the driver's side of Aaron's car.

When Aaron turned to his right, the undercover prostitute had climbed out of his car. Stunned, he sat still and stared straight ahead.

"Put your hands up and get out of the car!" the officer repeated.

Aaron did as he was told. When he spotted the camera crew, he tried to shield his face with his hand. But it was too late. His predicament was slated to make the evening news.

Chapter 37
Blind Ambition

*T*he next morning, Evian picked up her best friend, Joyce, from her condo and drove to the wedding boutique in downtown Tampa. Evian told the owner of the boutique that she pictured herself in a pure white ballroom gown worn in fairytale stories for her wedding. She made clear that the price of the gown was not a factor, especially since Alex had agreed to pick up the tab.

After trying several gowns, Evian was drawn to a gown suited for a royal wedding. The white satin, strapless dress was a mixture of modern and traditional craftsmanship. The body of the dress was made of French Chantilly lace. Attached to the gown was a six foot embroidered train.

"This is beautiful," Evian raved in the mirror, while admiring how the dress accentuated her figure.

"It is," Joyce concurred. "But don't you think it's a tad much for a small wedding chapel.

"I think it's perfect." Evian stood in front of the mirror and turned from side to side.

"You look like the perfect bride-to-be," the owner chimed in.

Evian turned to the owner with a broad smile. "I'll take it."

The owner clasped her hands. "Good. Now what do you have in mind for your maid-of-honor and bridesmaids?"

"I want something black and sleek for the bridesmaids." Evian turned to Joyce, "and said, "I want my maid of honor to pick her own gown."

Feeling special, Joyce picked a black chiffon floor-length dress with bedazzled jewels.

After leaving the wedding boutique, Joyce and Evian decided to go to lunch. They stopped by her future sister-in-law's restaurant in Tampa Florida. Regine was not there, but it did not stop Evian from bragging about her.

"Wow," Joyce gushed. "She seems like an amazing woman."

"Yes she is. She had a very humbling upbringing." Evian proceeded to tell Joyce about how Regine was raised by her grandmother and her mother was strung out on drugs.

Joyce looked around the elegant upscale restaurant, before saying aloud, "I would never have guessed."

"If you think her life story is something, Alex and Guy also had it rough."

Joyce frowned. "But their mother is rich."

"Jeanine Benedict is their stepmother. Their parents died when they were kids."

"I didn't know."

"I think the Simmons' family is amazing. I look forward to becoming a part of their legacy."

"What about medical training?" Joyce asked, while eating salad.

Evian sipped her soup before responding. "I figure with a man like Alex, who needs a medical license."

"So you're going to drop out of the program?"

"I may," Evian coyly remarked.

"What about your dreams of becoming a doctor?"

"I'd rather spend the rest of my life becoming the perfect wife and mother."

Joyce frowned. She and Evian had discussed this subject in the past, and they were both adamant about not having children.

"I would love to have Alex's baby," Evian admitted, while fantasizing about the possibility. She paused, before stating, "Can I tell you something in confidence?"

"Sure."

"Alex just discovered he has a baby."

Joyce gasped. "Are you serious?"

"Yes, but not for long. I have a plan to steal his baby."

"Are you crazy?!" Joyce asked with a look of amazement. Then she searched around to see if anyone was in earshot of their conversation. "You can go to jail," she said in a hushed whisper.

Evian shrugged off her friend's concerns. "I'm not going to steal the baby, per se. I have an ally who agreed to do it for me."

"You do?" Joyce's brows flew up in surprise.

"Yes. Her name is Elizabeth Coleman. She just happens to be the mother of Alex's ex-girlfriend."

"*Shut the front door!*" Joyce exclaimed, finding it hard to believe what her friend just told her.

Evian continued, "The baby was on its deathbed. Can you believe Alex gave the baby some of his bone-marrow, to save his life?"

"Well, yeah," Joyce stated, matter-of-factly.

Evian dismissed her friend's flippant response. "Instead of letting nature take its course, now the baby has seven more lives."

"The baby is not a cat. It's someone's child, for Christ sake."

"Not when I get through with it."

Joyce sat stunned. She suddenly lost her appetite.

Sipping her soup, Evian noted her friend was eerily quiet. She wondered if it was a good idea to tell Joyce about her plans. "I can trust you, right?"

Joyce nodded *yes*, even though she was unraveling inside. She wanted to get as far away from Evian as she possible.

Oblivious of her friend's feelings, Evian said, "After we leave here, we're going to meet with my wedding coordinator. It shouldn't take too much of your time. You're coming with me, right?"

"Sure," Joyce reluctantly agreed.

After climbing in the car and buckling up, Evian started the ignition and pulled onto the highway. She noticed Joyce was quiet and reserved. "I'm not going to harm the baby," she said to ease Joyce's conscience.

"What are you going to do with it?"

"I'm certain an adoption agency would find a perfect family for the baby. I can make a ton of money. Of course, that depends on the highest bidder. Some people are willing to pay a large sum of money for a baby."

"Evian, the baby is not a piece of expensive furniture. It's a real live human being who needs his mother, someone who cares about him. Didn't you tell me the baby was sick?"

"The operative word is *was*. That baby was conceived by a *bimbo* who drugged and raped Alex. The way I figure it, I'm sparing the baby the embarrassment of ever finding out his mother was a conniving whore."

"Is that what you're going to tell your son?"

"What are you talking about?"

"Are you going to tell your baby that you stole his brother, so he could be his father's first child?"

Evian slammed her hands on the steering wheel, while keeping control of the car. "Why are you making this so difficult?!" she yelled to the top of her lungs. "I thought you were my friend."

"I am your friend, but I think you're going about this the wrong way."

"Can't you see?!" Evian exclaimed. "I can't stand by and let that *bitch* waltz back into Alex's life."

"What makes you think that?"

"I know women like Alecia Kellam. They would stop at nothing to get their hands on the prize," Evian said, as she drove into the parking space in front of the wedding coordinator's office.

Joyce paused, before asking, "Why did you confide in me about your plans to steal the baby?"

"I need you to help me transport the baby to the adoption agency."

"I don't want anything to do with this."

"But I need you. Besides, are you forgetting what I did for you?"

Wincing, Joyce remembered when she recruited Evian to torture her ex-boyfriend. One day she caught him cheating on her, and wanted to make sure he never had an opportunity to cheat on anyone else.

She and Evian broke into his apartment in the middle of the night while he was alone in bed, snoring and resting peacefully. Joyce woke him up by swiping him across the back of the head with the barrel of a gun.

Her boyfriend jumped out of bed in his birthday suit. It took him a second to register Joyce's face, and the gun aimed at his head. "What are you doing?" he asked, while trying to remain cool under pressure.

Joyce said, "I want to make sure you never hurt another woman."

"Baby," he pleaded with outstretched hands, "let's be reasonable. You don't have to do this."

Evian looked at Joyce's soon-to-be-ex with disgust. "It's *mother-fuckers* like you that give all men a bad name."

Shaking inside, he peered at Evian through slanted eyes. "You need to stay out of this. This has nothing to do with you."

"That's where you're wrong. Joyce is my best friend."

Unable to reason with Evian, he turned to Joyce with fear in his eyes. "You don't have to do this. Let's go somewhere and talk."

With bitterness in her heart, Joyce said, "It's too late for that. Lay in bed and stretch out your arms and legs."

Evian warned, "If you don't want to die, you will do as you're told."

Reluctantly, he did as he was told.

While Evian tied his arms and feet to the bed posts with rope, Joyce went in her purse and removed a needle filled with solution she and Evian concocted in the science lab. Then she aimed the needle at his penis.

Her boyfriend's eyes nearly popped out of his head after it dawned on him that his pride and joy was in jeopardy. "Joyce, don't do this!" he hollered in vain, while twisting from side to side, trying to free his hands and feet from the rope.

Joyce hesitated. She was unsure if she should follow through with the plan to sterilize him. She began to question her actions.

Snatching the needle from her friend's hand, Evian said, "I'll do it!" She jammed the needle in his groin, then seemed to take joy in watching him scream for mercy. His cries subsided as the anesthesia took effect.

"Are we hurting him?" Joyce asked Evian with genuine concern.

"Just his ego."

Evian grabbed her bag full of surgical supplies and rested them on the side of the bed. With Joyce's help, she performed a castration procedure.

She made an incision in the scrotum of his right testicle to remove the tube that connected the testes with the urethra. After she stitched up the incision, she repeated the same procedure on the other testicle.

An hour later, Evian stood up and smiled. "He should be awake from the anesthesia soon. Let's untie him and get the hell out of here."

Joyce asked, "What if he goes to the police?"

"He won't," Evian said with certainty.

"How do you know?"

"He'd be too embarrassed to tell anyone about how his manhood was reduced to the size of a lottery pencil."

Joyce said, "We could go to jail if anyone ever found out what we did."

"That's why this is going to be our little secret."

That was the last time they seen or heard from Joyce's boyfriend. Evian assumed he moved to another state because he was embarrassed. However, Joyce had her own suspicions, but decided to keep them to herself. The entire ordeal had consumed her thoughts. She had asked God to forgive her for her sins. It had taken a long time, but she also learned to forgive herself and pledged to do right by people.

Snapping back to the present, Joyce turned to Evian and somberly admitted, "I regret what we did to him. He didn't deserve it."

"Yeah, but it was a lot of fun," Evian countered with a burst of laughter. "I could only imagine the look on his face when he woke up and discovered his limp penis."

"Yeah, but that was different. What you're thinking about doing could permanently damage lives."

"C'mon Joyce. I can't be in two places at one time. Elizabeth Coleman is going to steal the baby from the hospital and take him to a motel. I told her that I would meet her there. But just in case I can't make it, I need someone to take the baby off her hands. You're the only one I trust."

"And if I get caught?" Joyce asked with raised brows.

"You're not going to get caught. Once you drop the baby off at the adoption agency, you can return home."

"Just like that." Joyce was being cynical on purpose.

Evian snapped her finger, while singing, "It's as easy as *1-2-3*."

Chapter 38
Likely Suspect

Detective Baily used the information Regine had provided to explore leads on Lamar Greene's disappearance. He drove to the Hilton hotel in Miami to ask questions and search the victim's hotel room. He identified himself and explained the purpose of his visit. He told the hotel manager, "We have reason to suspect foul play."

The manager nodded in understanding. "We cannot give you any information about any of our guests. You will need a court order."

Detective Baily held up the search warrant as two uniformed police officers stood next him.

The manager cooperated after he reviewed the court order. He led the detective and the uniformed officers to Lamar's hotel room, and stood by while they conducted a thorough search.

The detective noticed there was an empty bottle of VS Cognac Hennessy on the cocktail table. He ordered that the bottle be sent to the forensic lab for testing.

Then he turned to the hotel manager, and asked, "Can you check to see if Mr. Greene ordered this brand of liquor from your hotel?"

"Sure."

"Do you know if Mr. Greene seemed anxious about anything when he checked into the room?"

"According to my staff, Mr. Greene did not have many requests. He just wanted to make sure we received his dinner reservations for two."

The detective's brows shot up. "Dinner reservations?"

"Some of our guests prefer dining in their room, in private. So we assign two of our staff members to their room to provide the same services guests would normally receive if they were frequenting in our restaurant."

"You said Mr. Greene made reservations for two. Did he specify the other person's name?"

"No."

Detective Baily walked in the bedroom and noticed the blanket missing from the bed. Then he spotted Lamar's briefcase on the side of the bed. He opened it and shifted through the contents. Most of the paperwork was related to the new restaurant in Miami. Further research revealed an unsigned contract. A sticky note with a room number and a person's name was attached to it.

The detective turned to the hotel manager with the sticky note, and asked, "Can you give me the names of the guests who checked in this hotel room within the last week or so?"

"That's against our policy. We cannot disclose that information without another court order."

"Can you make an exception, this one time?" the detective asked with puppy dog eyes.

"Yes, but I can't make any more exceptions."

Detective Baily found out Raymond Brown had checked into the hotel room in question. It was around the same time Lamar went missing. He attempted to ask questions about this particular guest, but the manager refused to cooperate without another court order.

Back at the precinct, the detective browsed through the database system, and learned Raymond Brown was investigated for allegedly killing his wife, heiress to the world's largest outlet mall in the United States. Raymond was listed as the primary suspect. But he had an alibi the night his wife was murdered.

Next, Detective Baily obtained a request to search Lamar's cell phone records. He heard several voicemail messages from Guy Simmons, who threatened to kill Lamar if he did not stay away from his wife. He also heard voicemail messages from Leslie Holloway. Detective Baily thought she sounded like a woman scorned. He thought it was odd that she continued to leave messages long after Lamar went missing.

Since Raymond Brown was unlisted in the phone directory, Detective Baily searched the motor vehicle database system. He learned Raymond lived in the suburbs of Tampa Bay, Florida. He contacted the local police department in Tampa, to let them know he was on his way to question persons of interest, in connection to Lamar Greene's disappearance.

***

Upon arriving on the Gulf Coast, Detective Baily drove up the path to Raymond Brown's sprawling ten-bedroom estate in Tampa Bay, Florida. A twinge of jealously overcame him as he eyed the beautiful exotic trees and flowers surrounding the lakefront view. The detective's eyes were drawn to an arc-shaped waterfall in the middle of a lake. He guessed Raymond had hired help to maintain the luxurious landscape.

He climbed out of his car and walked up the path to the massive double door. The housekeeper opened one of the doors before he had a chance to ring the bell. "May I help you?" she asked.

"I'm here to see Raymond Brown."

"May I ask your name?"

"I'm Detective Baily, from the Hollywood Police Department." He removed his badge from his hip pocket and showed it to her.

"Wait here," she said, closing the door behind her.

Minutes later, Raymond opened the door and greeted the detective with an extended hand. "Hi, I'm Raymond Brown. What can I do for you?"

After shaking hands, Detective Baily said, "I'm investigating the disappearance of Lamar Greene. Do you happen to know him?"

"I'm afraid not," Raymond said with a straight face.

"Are you sure?" the detective probed, hinting he had evidence that proved otherwise.

Raymond's eyes shot up in the air, pretending to rethink the detective's question. "Did you say Lamar Greene?"

The detective nodded.

"I do know Lamar. We met through a mutual friend."

"Were you in Miami recently," Detective Baily asked, getting to the heart of the matter.

"I was there on business."

"Did you happen to run into Mr. Greene while you were there?"

"Why? Is there something wrong?"

"Mr. Greene is missing, and I'm investigating his whereabouts."

"Am I a suspect?"

"I wouldn't say that."

"So what is it?"

"We're questioning everyone who may have had contact with Mr. Greene within the last forty-eight hours."

"Why are you questioning me?"

"Your name and room number was jotted on a sticky note we found in Mr. Greene's hotel room."

"That doesn't mean anything," Raymond defensively replied.

The detective continued, "The sticky note was on top of a contract dissolving Mr. Greene's businesses relationship with his partner, Regine Simmons."

Raymond flinched. He was kicking himself for being so careless.

Detective Baily asked, "Do you know anything about the contract?"

"Am I under arrest?"

"No."

"I'm not saying another word until I speak with my attorney." Raymond took a step back and closed the door in the detective's face.

The detective closed his writing pad and retreated to his car. As far as he was concerned, Raymond had just been elevated from a *person of interest* to *prime suspect*.

Chapter 39
Spooked

*O*n day two, Swag left Carmela alone in his apartment *again*. She noticed he had become increasingly impatient with her. She also noticed he had left early without a kiss good bye.

After brushing her teeth, she sat on the sofa in the living room to watch another movie. She popped in her third DVD when her gut tuition kicked in. She stood up and started snooping around his apartment. It did not take long before she found a one-way plane ticket to Jamaica in Swag's dresser drawer. It was buried under his clothes. Carmela frowned after she noted Swag was scheduled to leave the U.S. tomorrow morning.

"That mutha…," she whispered under her breath. Carmela wanted to be sure her mind was not playing tricks on her. So she rummaged through the dresser drawer once more to see if there was another ticket.

Deep down, Carmela always had a feeling Swag was going to abandon her once he got his hands on the ransom. The one-way plane ticket made her suspicions a reality. She stood up and paced the room, looking lost and sad. Without thinking twice, she grabbed her purse, opened the front door and bumped into a very handsome man that looked to be in his mid-forties.

"Oh, I'm sorry," she sincerely apologized.

The man smirked. "It's okay. Can I come inside?"

"No…um…no. I don't know you like that."

"I'm harmless. Swag sent me here to check on you."

"He did?" Carmela said with wide eyes.

"Yeah."

Carmela stood back to let the man in. This was not the first time Swag sent someone to check up on her so she felt comfortable with her decision. "I'm not sure when Swag is coming back," she told the stranger.

"It's okay. He told me to wait for him. What's your name again?"

"Carmela, what's yours?"

"You can call me Smokey."

"Smokey," Carmela said aloud, as she thought of R&B singer, Smokey Robinson. "It's because of your light complexion and green eyes, isn't it?"

He smiled. "Yeah, something like that."

After Carmela sat on the sofa, Smokey sat next to her. Mentally, he determined he would use her to get to Swag. But first he decided to use his charm and good looks to glean information from her.

"You seem like a smart girl," he began. "How did you meet Swag?"

Carmela reminisced about her first encounter with Swag, while Smokey focused on how he was going to exact revenge on his former employee.

Smokey was recently released from prison after his attorney filed an appeal. In addition to prostitution, the police report showed Smokey had guns and drugs in his possession. It was later discovered that the arresting officers falsified the police report with trumped charges.

The attorney had also discovered the police interviewed an inform-ant prior to the sting operation. The informant's name was not stated, but the report had described Swag to perfection.

As soon as Smokey was released from jail, he went looking for his former employee. He was surprised to learn from the streets that Swag had relocated to Tampa, Florida and had his own *Call Girl* business.

Smokey had been tailing Swag for the past few days. He had wait-ed all night and most of the morning to try and determine Swag's next move. He was going to follow him earlier, but noticed Carmela was still in the apartment. So he waited until his *ex-partner in crime* backed out of the parking lot and drove away. Then he galloped up-stairs and was pleasantly surprised to bump into Carmela.

"Do you still love him?" Smokey asked, after Carmela finished telling him how she fell in love with Swag.

"I used to."

"What changed?"

Carmela grabbed the plane ticket from the cocktail table and hand-ed it to Smokey.

He looked at it and frowned. "Is he leaving you?"

"That's what it looks like."

"Damn. That's messed up. What are you going to do?"

"I don't know," she thoughtfully admitted. "I have nowhere else to go."

Chapter 40
Ride or Die

*W*hen Evian and Joyce met with the wedding coordinator, Doris Bell, to go over the wedding plans. The coordinator informed Evian that she had already contacted local caterers for the food and wedding cake. "Oh, one more thing," Doris said as an afterthought. "Alex called me earlier, and asked me to include his son in the wedding plans."

"What is a three-month old baby going to do?!" Evian spouted in anger. "He's too young to be a ring bearer." She chuckled at the thought.

Evian's reaction prompted Doris to offer a suggestion. "I think it would be a great idea to take pictures of Alex and his son together, to be projected on the wall as the guests enter the wedding hall."

"But the wedding is not for his son!"

"You must respect Alex's wishes. Do you have any suggestions on how you would include his son in the wedding?"

"He shouldn't be there," Evian rebuffed. "After this weekend...." She stopped talking in mid-sentence, after realizing she almost revealed her plans to get rid of the baby.

"I think we should think on this a little longer," the coordinator determined. "In the meantime, I need a list of your guests."

"What about Alex's guest list?" Evian asked.

"He has already provided his list to me."

"Can I see it?" Evian sat on the edge of her chair with puppy dog eyes.

"Sure." The coordinator went through her folder, retrieved a document and handed it to Evian.

Evian perused the list, but her eyes zoomed in on the one guest whose name was penciled in. She looked up at the coordinator, and asked, "What is Alecia Kellam's name doing on this list?"

"Alex called me this morning to add her name."

Incensed, Evian turned to Joyce with rage in her eyes. "You see what I mean? I figured this would happen."

Joyce bit her bottom lip. She sympathized with her friend.

"Remove Alecia Kellam's name from the guest list," Evian demanded of the coordinator.

"I can't do that." Doris's response was firm and unyielding.

"Yes, you can," Evian countered in the same manner.

The coordinator gazed at Evian over the rim of her glasses. She did not want to argue, so she said, "Let me see what I can do."

"What does that mean?"

"I will review the list and make any necessary changes." Doris said anything to appease Evian. She had already decided that Alecia's name would stay on the list, especially since Alex would be footing the bill.

Evian said, "I have one more request."

"What is it?" Doris' tone was sharp and short. She was fed up with Evian's demands.

"I do not want to include Alex's son in *my* wedding."

The coordinator removed her glasses and sunk back in her chair. "Do you have any other concerns?" she asked in a curt manner.

"Yes, do not tell Alex about my requests. If you do, I will gladly fire you as our wedding coordinator."

"Understood." Doris' response was terse and short.

"Well, that's that," Evian said, as she stood up to leave with a look of satisfaction. "C'mon Joyce, it's time to go."

Joyce was baffled over Evian's interaction with the wedding coordinator. She thought it was a sign that her friend's future with Alex was destined to fail.

Evian, on the other hand, was grinning and feeling jubilant. As soon as they walked outside, she asked Joyce, "Can you believe Alex pulled a stunt like that? He changed our wedding plans without telling me."

"What did you expect? He wants his child in the wedding."

Evian rolled her eyes. "What about Alecia Kellam? Alex did not have to add her to the guest list."

"That's his baby's mother."

"Fine, I get that. But he did not have to invite her."

"Calm down," Joyce insisted. "Why don't you go home and talk it over with Alex? I'm sure he has a logical explanation for inviting his baby's mother."

"No, I'm not going to do that because after this weekend, Alecia and her baby are going to be a figment of Alex's imagination."

"Are you going to follow through with your plans to take the baby?"

"Yes, why?"

"I was hoping you changed your mind."

"What are you going to do if I don't?"

Joyce opened her mouth to respond but did not know what to say. Contacting the police about her friend's scheme had crossed her mind.

Evian's eyes narrowed as she got up in Joyce's face. "That's fine if you don't want to help me. But if you tell anyone about my plans, you're going to wish you hadn't."

"Are you threatening me?" Joyce asked with raised brows.

"Let's just say you've been warned."

Evian was satisfied she had gotten her point across. She pretended to smile and act as if she and Joyce were on good terms. "You feel like shopping?" she asked with glee in her voice.

Joyce hesitated before responding. "I'm sorry, but I have to go home to get ready for my date with Brian." In her mind, she could not wait to get away from her so-called friend.

"I can't believe you're still dating him," Evian said with malice. She did not want Joyce to be happy with Brian or any man for that matter.

Rolling her eyes, Joyce said, "You don't have to like Brian, but you must respect the fact that I love him."

"Fine, whatever," Evian said in a nonchalant manner. "I'll drop you off at your place. I have to meet my new friend in an hour."

"Your new friend?" Joyce asked in amazement.

"Do you remember when I told you the mother of Alex's ex-fiancé is going to help me steal his baby?"

Joyce nodded. She hesitated before she climbed in the car with Evian. She had already concluded her friend was a deranged lunatic, who would stop at nothing to get what she wanted.

As soon as Evian drove in front of her friend's condo, Joyce quickly climbed out of the car and waved *goodbye*. She did not look back as she ran up the path to her front door. Breathing hard and erratic, Joyce unlocked the door, rushed inside and locked the door behind her. She was relieved to get away from Evian.

For a second, Evian questioned her friend's urgency. She eventually concluded that Joyce was probably eager to go out with her boyfriend.

She checked her purse to see if the Johns Hopkins hospital security pass was still in her purse. Then she started the ignition and drove to the medical supply store to buy a small bottle of chloroform, nursing garb and shoes. Next, she stopped by Wal-Mart to purchase a prepaid cell phone and a brown life-size baby doll. She put the baby doll in the same bag as the nursing garb and threw the cell in her purse.

When Evian drove into the parking space in front of Elizabeth's apartment building, she was pumped up and in rare form. She grabbed the bag from the backseat of her car. Then she briskly walked upstairs, acting like a woman on a mission.

Elizabeth opened the front door with a wide smile. "Come on in, honey," she said in a sweet voice. "I've been waiting for you all day."

As Evian entered her apartment, Elizabeth noted the frown on her young friend's face. "Honey, are you all right?"

Evian nodded *yes* but it was a lie. Mentally, she wondered if she could trust Joyce to remain quiet about her plans to steal the baby.

"Are you sure you're okay?" Elizabeth asked. "If you've changed your mind about taking the baby, we'll find another way to get back at Alecia."

Sounding pitiful, Evian said, "I just found out my best friend died a little while ago." She figured she did not tell a complete lie. In her heart, Joyce was dead to her.

"I'm sorry to hear this, honey." Elizabeth embraced Evian and told her everything was going to be all right. "Is there anything I can do?"

"No, I'm going to miss her." Speaking sorrowfully, Evian played the *'woe is me'* role to perfection.

"God will see you through this," Elizabeth said with assurance. "Maybe we should rethink our decision to take the baby right now. Losing a loved one is hard, and you need time to heal."

"No," Evian quickly replied, forcing herself to perk up. "We have to follow through with our plans." She held up the bag in her hand and gave it to Elizabeth.

Elizabeth took the bag and looked inside. Seeing the nursing uniform and shoes had shed light on their mission. She frowned when she pulled the baby doll out of the bag and held it up. "What is this for?"

Evian explained, "After you take Alex and Alecia's baby, you are to put the doll in the bed to make it look like the baby is still there."

"Oh...I see."

"You have a pen and a piece of paper?" Evian inquired. "I need you to take some notes."

Elizabeth stood up and grabbed a pen and a slip of paper from the kitchen drawer, then hurried back to the living room. "I'm ready."

She took notes, as Evian explained, "I paid for a roundtrip ticket for you to go to Baltimore in the morning. From there, you are to pick up a rental car I reserved in your name, and drive to Johns Hopkins Hospital. Do you have a valid driver's license?"

"Yes."

"What about a passport?"

Elizabeth frowned. "Why do I need a passport?"

"If something goes wrong, you may have to leave the country."

"I'm not leaving my home!" Elizabeth exclaimed.

Lightly patting her new friend on the thigh, Evian said, "I can assure you that it's highly unlikely that you would have to leave the country, and if you do, it'll only be for a couple of days."

"I have a passport," Elizabeth answered, after acknowledging she had one from her days of traveling abroad with her husband, when she was First Lady of her church.

"Good. Now before you arrive at Johns Hopkins hospital, change into the nursing uniform. Do not park in the garage. Park in the metered parking space on North Wolf Street. You are to use the back entrance to enter the hospital. Go down the hall and on your left you will see the Bloomberg Children's Center. From there, go to the Pediatric Intensive Care unit on the fourth floor."

"I've never been a nurse," Elizabeth pointed out. "I don't know what to do."

"I suggest you watch nurse characters on T.V. to get a better feel of the nursing role."

"Okay...but what if the baby starts crying?"

"I put a small bottle of *chloroform* in your *bag*. Dab a little on a cloth and put it under the baby's nose. He'll be knocked out in seconds. One more thing," Evian said after thinking long and hard. "Make sure you stop by the store to buy pampers, a bottle and baby milk."

Nodding, Elizabeth's heart fluttered from anticipation.

Evian continued, "You are to take the baby and drive to the motel off Security Boulevard in Woodlawn, Maryland."

"Then what?" Elizabeth asked.

"I will meet you at the motel to take the baby off your hands."

Elizabeth remained quiet. She was nervous about getting caught.

"Trust me," Evian said with confidence, "you will feel vindicated after everything is said and done."

Elizabeth took a deep breath and exhaled. *Vengeance* sounded like music to her ears. "How are you going to reach me? I don't have a cell phone."

"Here's the cell phone and the hospital security pass to show the guard," Evian added, after retrieving the items from her purse and handing them to Elizabeth. "The guards never pay attention to the picture on the security pass, so you don't have to worry about getting caught."

"Is that it?" Elizabeth asked, to be sure.

"Pretty much. Carry the cell phone with you at all times, in case we have to change our plans." As Evian stood up to leave, she said, "Make sure you follow the instructions I gave you. We cannot afford to make any mistakes."

Chapter 41
Red Flags

*D*etective Baily arrived at Regine and Guy's home, hoping to find out more information about Raymond Brown's connection to Lamar Greene. He was in awe of the size of their mansion as he parked in their driveway. Looking around, he noticed the lawn was adorned with colorful rose gardens throughout. *"What is this? The life of the rich and freakin' famous?"* he questioned himself.

The detective climbed out of his car, walked up the pathway to the front door, and pressed the doorbell twice.

Regine opened the door with a pleasant smile. "May I help you?" she asked, as she looked into the detective's blue eyes.

"Are you Regine Simmons?"

"Yes, I'm Mrs. Simmons."

"Hi, I'm Detective Baily from the Hollywood Police Department. We spoke on the phone. If you don't mind, I'd like to come inside to ask you and your husband some questions."

"Did you find Lamar?"

"No, that's why I'm here. We've searched Mr. Greene's hotel room, and we're following up on potential leads."

"I see." Regine stepped aside, unblocking the door entrance. "Please come inside and wait here. I'll go get my husband. He's in his office."

Detective Baily walked in the foyer and his eyes were drawn upward. He whistled when he saw the gold and crystal chandelier hanging from the ceiling. Then he looked on the other side of the living room and spotted the wraparound staircase, which led to six bedrooms and four bathrooms.

When Regine walked into the office, Guy sensed her presence but kept his eyes focused on his paperwork. He feared she was going to ask him for a divorce. "I told you," he said in a harsh tone. "I'm not ready to talk to you. Not now."

"You made that clear," Regine spat, matching his grumpy attitude. "Detective Baily from the Hollywood Police Department is here to speak with us."

Guy's breath got caught in his lungs. He was nervous. Sitting upright in his chair, he asked, "Did he say what he wanted?"

"I think he's here to ask us some questions about Lamar."

"I see."

Regine took note of Guy's fidgety hands. She had known her husband long enough to realize he was hiding something. She had a feeling it had something to do with Lamar's disappearance. Peering into his eyes, she asked, "Is there something I should know?"

Guy's eyes shot up, as he stuttered, "No...um...why do you ask?"

"You don't seem like your usual self."

"I'm fine!" Guy raised his voice, but not on purpose.

Regine frowned but managed to deflect her husband's rude behavior. "We can meet with Detective Baily in the den, if you prefer."

"If you don't mind, can you please escort him to my office?"

Regine nodded before she walked out of the office to get the detective.

Minutes later, Detective Baily walked in Guy's office with his pen and writing pad. His large body frame seemed too small for the office.

Guy stood up and greeted the detective with a firm handshake. After the introductions, he turned to his wife, who stood in the door entrance. "That'll be all, Regine."

"Detective Baily is here to speak with both of us."

"I think it's best," the detective interjected, "if I speak with both of you separately. Don't you agree?" he asked, as he turned to Guy.

"Yes," Guy answered, while nodding.

Regine lowered her head as she left the office, quietly closing the door behind her.

The detective asked Guy, "Did you contact Mr. Greene three days ago?"

Guy bit his bottom lip. To lie, he thought, would be senseless, especially since he left unfriendly messages on Lamar's voicemail. He hesitated, before admitting, "I left a couple of messages."

"So you admit you threatened Mr. Greene?" The detective alluded to the messages Guy had left on Lamar's voicemail.

"Yes, I threatened him. But I didn't mean anything by it."

"What prompted you to threaten him?"

"Lamar has a thing for my wife. I was trying to scare him off."

Detective Baily opened his writing pad and retrieved a copy of the contract found in Lamar's hotel room. He slid it across Guy's desk, and asked, "Is this the agreement you asked Mr. Greene to sign?"

Guy frowned as he read the contents of the contract. He looked up at the detective, and asked, "Where did you get this?"

"It was in Mr. Greene's hotel room."

With his eyes glued to the document, Guy said, "I didn't know Regine was trying to dissolve her business relationship with Lamar."

The detective sat on the edge of the chair, and asked, "Do you know, for a fact, that your wife gave Mr. Greene the contract?"

"I'm not sure."

"Are you sure you don't know anything about this?"

"What are you saying?" Guy griped. "You think I gave Lamar the contract to sign?"

"Isn't that what you wanted?"

"Yes, but I do not have a stake in my wife's restaurant business. Did you ask Regine about this?"

"No, not yet."

"Wait here. I'll go get her."

Guy stood up to leave his office. Minutes later, he returned to his office with Regine on his heels. He picked up the contract from his desk and showed it to her. "Do you know anything about this?"

Regine took the document from Guy and read it in its entirety. With scrunched brows, she slowly lifted her head. Her eyes shifted from the detective to her husband, as she asked, "What is this?"

"I found it in Mr. Greene's hotel room," Detective Baily offered. "We need to know if it was your idea to dissolve your business relationship with Mr. Greene."

"I would never think of doing anything like this," Regine replied, clearly offended by the detective's question. Then she turned to her husband with narrow eyes. "Did you talk Lamar into doing this?"

"No, but it sounds like a great idea." As soon as Guy responded, he instantly regretted his frankness.

"I'm sure this is what you wanted," Regine flippantly replied.

"So neither of you knew anything about this?" the detective asked both of them.

Regine frowned. "Of course not."

"No," Guy definitively replied.

Detective Baily directed his next question to Guy. "Do you know Raymond Brown?"

Both Guy and Regine looked at each other with concern before turning to the detective. "Yes, we know him," Guy confirmed. "What does Raymond have to do with this?"

"We found a sticky note with Raymond's name and room number attached to the contract."

Regine's mouth flew open in surprise, while Guy froze in one place. Both had acknowledged the implications.

"How do you know Raymond Brown?" the detective continued.

Guy said, "He's dating my mother."

"That answers my question." The detective scribbled Guy's response in his writing pad.

Regine asked the detective, "Do you think Raymond had something to do with the fact that Lamar is missing?"

"It's hard to say," Detective Baily stated, while cupping and rubbing his chin. Then he turned to Guy, and asked, "Do you think Raymond Brown gave Mr. Greene the contract to sign?"

Guy shrugged. "I'm not sure." In all honesty, he assumed his stepmother was possibly behind this. Since Raymond was her suitor, it made sense. *"But why?"* he silently asked himself.

But Regine believed her Grandmother Bessie had something to do with Lamar's disappearance. Two months earlier, she spotted Raymond and her grandmother talking during her son's birthday celebration. Regine thought they seemed unusually friendly, considering it was their first time meeting each other.

After jotting Guy's response on his writing pad, the detective asked, "What is your mother's name, and how can I reach her?"

"Her name is Jeanine Benedict. If you don't mind, I'd rather obtain your contact information and ask her to give you a call."

"No problem." Detective Baily went in his wallet and retrieved his business card. He handed it to Guy as he stood up to leave. "Thank you both for your cooperation. I'll see myself out."

Regine asked, "Will you let us know if you are able to locate Lamar?"

The detective nodded in agreement before leaving Guy's office. He was certain he was on to something. It was just a matter of time before Raymond Brown confessed about what happened to Lamar Greene.

Regine had remained in Guy's office after the detective left. She watched him pick up his phone and slam it on the receiver. Then he fumbled with paperwork on his desk. He was jittery and it showed.

"What did you and the detective talk about when I left your office earlier?" she asked, hoping he would open up to her.

Guy picked up his pencil and put it down. He thought about her question, and answered her in a low voice, "I didn't tell you this before, but I told Lamar I would kill him if he ever came near you again."

"What?! You threatened him?" Regine asked in anger. "So you know what happened to Lamar?"

"What are you implying? You think I killed him?"

Regine opened her mouth to respond but closed it. Without thinking, she had unintentionally implicated her husband in Lamar's disappearance.

"I'm sorry...I didn't mean to accuse you."

"Yes you did!" Guy sharply countered. "Please leave my office!"

"I'm sorry."

"I'm sure you are," he snarled. "Please leave. I have work to do."

Feeling ashamed, Regine backed out of his office and closed the door behind her. She did not want to believe Lamar was dead or that her husband had anything to do with the fact that he was missing.

She walked in their bedroom and sat on the edge of the bed. She was thinking about the business contract that dissolved her and Lamar's business relationship. She asked herself, *"Did Raymond Brown give him the contract? If so, did her Grandmother Bessie ask him to do this?"* There were so many red flags swirling around in her head, she could not think straight. She wanted desperately to call her grandmother with her questions, but she was afraid of the answers.

Guy had his own suspicions. As soon as the coast was clear, he phoned his stepmother to ask her if she knew anything about Lamar's whereabouts. He was disappointed when he received her answering machine.

"Mom, this is Guy," he said on her voicemail. "Call me when you get a chance. It's important."

Chapter 42
Nosedive

*D*an was beginning to feel vindicated for all the hell Justina had put him through in the past. He was eager to get his hands on the ransom. But a strange feeling overcame him. He retrieved his cell phone from his pocket, and dialed his new *partner-in-crime's* cell number.

"Hi, this is Dan," he stated, after Swag answered his call. "Is everything okay on your end?"

Swag was hunkered behind his steering wheel, when he answered in a low voice, "Yeah, I've been over here all day. Justina didn't leave the house yet. But her husband left a little while ago."

"He did?" Dan questioned in surprise.

"Yeah, but don't worry. I know what he's up to."

"Are you sure he's not going to the cops?"

"Nah man," Swag answered with a head nod. "You don't have anything to worry about. What's happening on your end?"

"I told Justina to meet at the Down Beat restaurant in the morning." Dan checked his watch, before stating, "I'll be headed your way soon."

"Okay, I'll holla atcha," Swag bellowed with a slight nod.

Swag was going to make sure Justina never made it to the Down Beat restaurant in the morning. He had planned on intercepting her meeting with Dan, with the goal of keeping one-hundred percent of the ransom for himself.

The day before, he had followed Aaron and Justina to their bank. But he was perplexed after they exited the bank, and went in opposite directions. He had followed Aaron to his home, and Justina had arrived in a cab several minutes later.

Swag's plans to highjack them were on hold, especially since he did not know if they had the ransom money in their possession. To add to his frustration, Carmela was becoming annoying. She was complaining about everything, from the food she ate to the lumpy uncomfortable bed. He could not wait to be done with her. He had purposely left the house earlier than expected, just to get away from her. But he had a plan in place to free him from his life for good.

172

Shortly after disconnecting the call with Swag, Dan heard a knock at the door. He walked over and opened the door but was shoved back with blunt force, by Thorny and his henchmen. They barged in the hotel room and closed the door behind them.

"What's going on?!" Dan shouted hysterically.

Thorny raised his gun and aimed it at Dan's head. "Where is she?!" he asked through gritted teeth.

Shivering from fear, Dan's hand flew up in surrender. He backed up as far as he could go before he fell onto the bed. Quickly, he sat up and stretched out his hands. His voice was shaky, as he sputtered, "I don't know what…you're…talking about."

"Yes you do," Thorny determined. His face was inches away from Dan's. "If you don't tell me where she is, I'm going to blow your fucking head off!"

"I swear," Dan pleaded with clasped hands. "Please don't shoot. I don't know where she is."

"So this is how you want to play games. Fine, I'm going to enjoy breaking every one of your fingers until I get some answers!"

"Carmela's boyfriend took her!"

"Where did he take her?"

"I don't know."

"When did she leave?"

"I believe it was last night." Dan quickly retrieved Carmela's letter from his pocket and handed it to Thorny. "This is the note she left for her sister," he offered, making a concerted effort to spare his own life.

Thorny took the note and read it. Then he looked at Dan, and asked, "Who wrote this?"

"It was Carmela. She wasn't coerced."

"Damn!" Thorny said in disbelief. "Why?"

"Carmela hates her sister," Dan explained, hoping Thorny would take the focus off him.

Thorny was pissed. He could not believe he was a part of a wild goose chase. "So this was some *bullshit* scheme?!"

"I'm sorry," Dan cried out. "Her boyfriend was in on it too."

"What is her boyfriend's name?"

"I only know him as *Swag*."

"Where is he?"

"He's in his car, not far from Justina's home."

"What is he doing there?"

"We wanted to make sure Justina didn't involve the cops. So I asked him to watch her home."

Thorny retrieved his cell phone from his coat pocket to call his street associate, *Killa*, to deal with Swag.

Happily, *Killa* told Thorny he would oblige his request. He also told him it should not take more than fifteen minutes to get to Justina's home from his current location.

Satisfied with *Killa's* response, Thorny disconnected the call and turned his attention to Dan. "I'm curious. Did you approach Carmela, or did she approach you about the kidnapping plan?"

"It was her decision," Dan fibbed.

"How did you meet her?"

"Uh…um…." Dan struggled to come up with a good lie.

"Don't even think about lying to me. I want the truth."

Dan did not want to risk upsetting Thorny. So he volunteered information about his past dealings with Justina.

Thorny was stunned by what Dan had told him. He was going to ask additional questions but realized it had been ten minutes since he last spoke with *Killa*. He instructed Dan to use his own cell phone to lure Swag back to the hotel.

Dan dialed his associate's number and waited to hear his voice.

When Swag's cell phone rang, he looked at his Caller ID and saw that it was Dan. "What's up?!" he hollered over the receiver.

"I'm…having…car…problems," Dan stuttered, while trying to remain calm. "Can…you return to…the hotel? I need a ride."

"Man, are you kidding me?! A half-million dollars is at stake and you're calling me with some damn car problems!"

"C'mon Swag," Dan persisted, almost begging. "I need your help."

"You need to get in a cab or steal a car! I'm not coming to Tampa when the money is right here in Bradenton."

Thorny snatched the phone from Dan and spoke into the receiver. "Your name is Swag, right?" he said, as a way to introduce himself.

"Who wanna know?"

At that very moment, Swag was caught off guard when *Killa*, Thorny's associate, broke the car window on the driver's side with his fist. Then *Killa'* put his hand around Swag's neck and squeezed.

Swag struggled to get free. But the grip around his neck was strong and unbreakable.

Killa opened the car door, pulled Swag out of his car, and dragged him to another car. After shoving his abductee in the backseat, he climbed in behind him and signaled for the driver to head to Tampa.

Swag tried to resist by throwing weak punches, but he was overpowered when *Killa* drew back his tight fist and punched him in the face in one swift motion. Swag dropped back in his seat and saw stars. He was unable to comprehend what happened. Within seconds, he passed out on *Killa's* lap. He drifted off into a deep, painful sleep.

Thorny stayed on the phone until the commotion subsided. Then he turned to Dan. "Your friend is on his way here."

Dan knew what that meant. Swag had conformed against his will. He was certain his associate did not go down without a fight.

Swag slept like a baby during the entire trip to Tampa. He was still unconscious when he made it to the Cameroon hotel. Killa had carried his abductee inside the room and tied him up to a chair.

Swag was aroused when Thorny splashed a bucket of water in his face. The coolness of the water sent chills up Swag's spine. He shook his head vigorously trying to remove some of the dripping water from his face. It took a while before he opened his eyes and realized he was in a familiar place. He glanced over at Dan who was tied up in a chair next to him.

Thorny teased Swag, by asking, "How was your beauty rest?"

Swag opened his mouth to respond, but found it difficult. His jaw was swollen and his bottom lip was twice as big. Anyone would have assumed he had been in a major fight, never getting past round one.

"Where's Carmela?" Thorny asked.

Balling up his mouth, Swag decided not to cooperate.

"You're tough, huh?" Thorny asked. "I got something for that." He beckoned *Killa* to stand in front of Swag. "You remember my friend, don't you?"

Swag drew his head back, after Killa towered over him with a mean grill. He was terrified of the tall statuesque man standing in front of him.

Sensing fear, Thorny asked, "Do you want to cooperate, or do you want to die a losing fight?"

"What do you want from me?" Swag replied in a cooperative tone.

"Now we're getting somewhere," Thorny said, after asking *Killa* to step aside. "Where is Carmela?"

Swag remained tight-lipped.

"Even if you tell me," Thorny explained, "you're not getting the money for the ransom."

"So why should I tell you a *damn* thing?!" Swag spouted in anger.

"To save your life."

"How do I know you won't kill me after I tell you?"

"You have my word."

"Humph...yeah, right."

"With or without your cooperation, we will find Carmela. If you give us the information we need, we will let you walk away."

"Just like that?"

"Yeah, just like that."

Swag did not believe Thorny. Though, he acknowledged he had only one card to play. After weighing his options, he volunteered the address of the apartment in Tarpon Springs.

Thorny frowned. "What is she doing there?"

"I took her there."

"Call her?"

Swag did as he was told. He was surprised Carmela's phone rang several times before his call was routed to her voicemail. "She's not answering her phone," he reported with disappointment in his voice.

"Don't bullshit me!" Thorny grumbled.

"I'm not."

Through squinty eyes, Thorny sensed Swag was telling the truth. He ordered his men to keep an eye on Dan and Swag, while he walked outside the hotel room to make an important call.

"What's up?" Kevin answered, after receiving Thorny's phone call.

"We have the kidnapper and his partner in our custody," Thorny explained. "Carmela's hiding out in an apartment in Tarpon Springs. She wasn't really kidnapped. She was in on the scheme to get the ransom from her sister."

Kevin frowned. "On the real?"

"Yeah."

"Good looking out. What's the address in Tarpon Springs?"

After receiving the address from Thorny, Kevin and his henchmen headed to Swag's apartment, where they expected to find Carmela

Chapter 43
Liar, Liar

*E*vian walked out of Elizabeth's apartment feeling good. She was satisfied her plans to steal Alex and Alecia's baby was on course. But she had other things on her mind. The last conversation with her friend, Joyce, saturated her thoughts.

Instead of going home, she drove to her friend's home and parked a couple of yards up the street. She put the gear in park, climbed out of her car, and sneakily walked up the path to Joyce's front door. She made sure no one was looking when she grabbed a big rock on the ground, and used it to break the window panel on the right side of the door.

Joyce was upstairs in her bedroom when she heard the glass break. "Hello!" she cautiously called out. "Is anyone there?"

Evian remained quiet as she stuck her hand in the panel opening and unlocked the door. Then she eased the door open, and slowly ascended the stairs. She held on to the same rock she had used to break the window panel. When Joyce peered out of her bedroom, Evian used the rock as a weapon to pummel her friend in the head.

Screaming from pain, Joyce tried to fight back but the blows to her head were overpowering. Blood poured down the side of her face and her vision became blurred. She dropped to the floor and blacked out.

Evian hovered over Joyce to look for signs that she might still be alive. "Joyce," she softly called out. "Open your eyes if you can hear me." When she did not get a response, she stood up, ran down stairs and fled the scene. She shielded her face with her purse as she briskly walked to her car, climbed in, and sped off.

"Why Joyce?!" Evian cried out, as tears streamed down her face. "Why did you make me kill you?! You were my best friend."

When she returned home, she flipped open her compact mirror and looked at her red teary eyes. She had been crying off and on ever since she pummeled her best friend in the head with a rock. "Pull it together," she scolded herself, before she grabbed her purse from the backseat of her car.

Evian continued to babble between sobs. "Tomorrow things will be back to normal. Alecia and her baby will become a thing of the past.

And my dear friend, Joyce. I suppose I'll be asked to speak at her funeral." Her last statement was followed by a river of tears.

After drying her eyes, she took a deep breath and exhaled before climbing out of her car. Then she put on a happy face as she walked through the front door of the condo, yelling, "Alex, honey! I'm home!"

Alex smiled upon hearing her voice. "Hi Evian!" he shouted out. "I'm upstairs in the bedroom."

Trouncing upstairs, Evian felt as though she had the weight of the world on her shoulders. She grew concerned after she noticed Alex packing an empty suitcase.

Brows perched upward, she asked, "What are you up to?"

"I figure I'd get a jumpstart on packing for our trip tomorrow morning."

"That's a great idea. I'll start packing after you finish up."

Frowning, Alex took a closer look at Evian's face. "Is something wrong? Your eyes look red and swollen."

"It's my allergies," she lied, hoping he would change the subject.

"Oh, okay."

Alex walked over to the closet, grabbed two suits and a couple of dress shirts. Then he walked over to the bed and placed them in the suitcase. "How was your day?" he asked, after he noticed his fiancé was unusually quiet.

"It was fine." Slowly, Evian walked over and sat on the bench in front of their king size bed.

"Did you make progress on our wedding plans?"

"Yes. Joyce and I stopped by the boutique to pick out my wedding gown and the dresses for the bridal party. Then we met with Doris Bell to finalize the wedding plans."

"How did that go?" Alex asked, as he retrieved a couple of boxer shorts from the top dresser drawer and put them in his suitcase.

"Doris is a wonderful wedding coordinator. I hope you don't mind, but I gave her some last minute ideas."

"Not at all," Alex made clear, while putting toiletries in his suitcase. "Did Doris tell you I asked her to include Alexander in the wedding plans?"

"Um…yeah. She did."

"How do you feel about it?"

"I think it's a wonderful idea," Evian said with fake excitement in her voice. She struggled to keep a straight face. But deep down, she felt slighted.

Alex walked over and gave Evian a peck on the lips. "You're going to be a wonderful stepmother."

Evian thought to herself: *More like biological mother, after baby Alexander is sold to the highest bidder.*

Alex walked over to the bed and closed his suitcase. "I'm all done."

Evian chose her words carefully, when she asked, "Why didn't you tell me you invited Alecia Kellam to our wedding?"

"She's my baby's mother. I didn't think you would mind."

Alex detected sadness in her voice. He felt bad for how his decision affected her. He strolled over and sat next to her on the bench. "I'm sorry," he said, as he cupped the side of her face.

"I would never do anything to intentionally hurt you. From now on, I will not make any changes to our wedding plans until I discuss them with you first." Alex dried her eyes with his fingers. "How's Joyce?" he asked, to lessen the tension between them.

"She's fine."

"Is she excited about being your Maid of Honor?"

"Um…well…something came up unexpectedly. Joyce told me she wouldn't be able to make it. She and her boyfriend made plans to elope."

"On the same day we're getting married?"

"Yes."

"That's different." Alex was confused. He thought Joyce's decision to elope on their wedding day was more than a coincidence, but he kept his thoughts to himself. He asked, "When are we going to meet her fiancé?"

"Soon." Evian was feeling uncomfortable lying to Alex in his face. She stood up, and said, "I hope you don't mind, but I need the bedroom to myself. I have to pack for our trip to Baltimore."

"I understand. We're only going for the weekend, so make sure you pack lightly." Alex closed his suitcase and kissed Evian on the lips before exiting their bedroom.

Evian remained seated long after Alex left their bedroom. She was pleased with her decision to kill her best friend, Joyce, and her impending plan to steal Alex and Alecia's baby. But there was one more obstacle in her way: *her husband, Pierre Michel.* To make sure he did not become a problem later on, she mentally devised a plan to kill him.

In the meantime, she picked up the phone in the bedroom and contacted several adoption agencies in Baltimore. She was relieved when she found a black market adoption agency that did not ask any questions.

"How much am I going to get in exchange for the baby?" she asked the owner of the adoption agency in Baltimore.

"That depends on how soon we can get the baby."

"I can drop the baby off tomorrow."

"Well, if that's the case, we'll give you seventy-five thousand."

"Make it one-hundred fifty thousand, and we have a deal."

The owner paused before giving in to Evian's wishes. He said, "We expect to see you tomorrow afternoon."

"Great. We have a deal."

Evian inhaled and exhaled with relief after disconnecting the call. She knew Alex would be heart-broken after his baby up and disappeared. On second thought, she believed he would forget all about Alexander once she became pregnant with his child.

"That's an excellent idea," she thought aloud. Then she strolled in the master bedroom and threw the entire pack of birth control pills in the garbage container. She had planned on making sweet, passionate love to Alex later on, with the hope of conceiving his child in the process.

***

Pierre was surprised his temporary visa to visit the U.S. was approved so quickly. When his plane landed in New York, a limo and chauffeur was there to take him to the magazine's corporate building in downtown Manhattan.

The change in weather was instantly noticeable. Pierre did not know how to dress or what to pack. He had settled for a couple of his best suits. The problem was his suits were too heavy for New York's summer weather. He removed his suit jacket before climbing in the backseat of the limo.

An hour later, the magazine's owner, Mr. Hodges greeted Pierre as soon as he walked in the building. "Pierre Michel!" he announced with an overzealous handshake. "I'm so glad you made it. How was your flight?"

"It was nice, thank you."

"I'm glad to hear that. Please follow me. We have a lot to talk about. After the meeting is over, we're going to put you up in the Trump Towers, one of the finest hotels in the United States."

Mr. Hodges escorted Pierre to his office. He sat behind his desk while his guest sat across from him. Getting down to business, he asked, "Did you bring the pictures we requested?"

"Yes, I only have one." Pierre retrieved the lone picture from his shirt pocket and handed it to the owner.

After Mr. Hodges viewed the picture, he bore a wide grin. He looked as if he had just struck gold. Evian had on a simple wedding dress and Pierre had on an outdated suit. He thought they seemed like an odd couple.

"This is perfect!" Mr. Hodges said with excitement in his voice. "Do you have the marriage certificate?"

"Yes, but what about helping me find my wife?"

"You came to the right location. When the time is right, everyone will get what they want. You, Mr. Michel, are getting ready to become famous."

"Excuse me. I don't understand."

"We have been wondering what happened to that particular Miss America. It was as if she disappeared off the planet earth. Now we know what she's been up to. She was married to a poor *pauper*. Then she ran off and left you after she realized you were not what she dreamed of. No offense," Mr. Hodges added, as he held up his hand and swatted at the air.

"If she's in the U.S., finding her is going to be easy. I have feeling this is going to be the biggest story this company has ever written."

"I'm here to find my wife and take her back home," Pierre made clear.

"I'm sure you are."

Mr. Hodges was laughing inside. He had a feeling Evian would never return to St. Kitts to be with the likes of Pierre Michel.

Pierre did not know the company's research department had recently learned of Evian's residence and the details of her impending nuptials with Alex Simmons. The research department also learned Alex had donated a sample of his bone marrow to Alecia Kellam's baby, and was planning a return trip to Baltimore, Maryland.

Because the details of Alex and Evian's actions seemed unclear, the owner of the magazine made arrangements to fly Pierre to Baltimore or Tampa on a moment's notice.

The publicity department was trying to figure out the perfect time and location to reveal the truth about Evian, at her husband's expense. One of the illustrators presumed Evian and Pierre's cover story would read: *"Miss America is Engaged to a Rich Man, while Married to a Poor Man. Does it make her a Bigamist or a Gold-Digger?"*

Chapter 44
Conflicted

*J*ustina was fuming mad after she caught her husband watching porn. She did not think it would have bothered her as much if her sister's life was not at stake. It did not escape her that Aaron did not return home last night. Emotionally shaken, she was trying to think of someone she could talk to, to explain her dilemma. Guy was the only other person she thought she could turn to. She felt drawn to him.

After trying to reach him on his cell phone without success, Justina called the house phone. But Regine answered her call. She did not know how to respond. She was wrestling with the idea of asking her best friend to speak with her husband. "Uh…hi Regine. How are you?"

"I'm fine. How are you?"

"Did Guy tell you what was going on with my sister?"

"Yes, why wouldn't he?"

"I just assumed…."

"I care about Carmela," Regine cut Justina off in mid-sentence. "Why didn't you ask me for help?"

Justina was timid, as she answered, "I don't know. I figured I'd ask Guy for the money to pay the ransom."

"But I'm his wife." Regine's voice began to tremble from anger. She felt betrayed.

Justina did not want to argue with Regine. Though, she understood her friend's hostility. "Is Guy there? I need to talk to him."

Regine rolled her eyes. "Yes, he's here."

If Carmela's life was not in jeopardy, Regine was certain she would have hung up on her *so-called* friend. She put the phone on the kitchen counter, and walked downstairs to Guy's office.

"Justina is on the phone. She'd like to speak with you."

Guy hesitated before he picked up the phone in his office. "Hello."

Justina smiled after hearing his voice. "Hi Guy."

"Are you okay?" he asked with grave concern.

"Yes, I'm hanging in there, considering." She proceeded to tell Guy how unhappy she was.

As Justina spoke, Guy sat up in his chair and gave her his undivided attention. Every now and then, he nodded without verbally responding.

Regine observed Guy's body language while he conversed on the phone. She questioned her husband's feelings for Justina. It was the way he said her name. His heart and soul was with Justina at that very moment.

Guy did not notice his wife's departure, as he began to question Justina. "Did someone contact you yet?"

"An older man showed up at my house yesterday. He assured me he has located the kidnapper."

"That's great news!" Guy replied with a broad grin. "What about Carmela? Is she okay?"

"I hope so. I'm waiting to hear from her."

"Don't worry. Everything is going to work out fine."

Comforted by Guy's words, Justina allowed her thoughts to slip from her mouth. "I feel so alone."

"You're not alone. I'm here for you," he said, wishing he was there to wrap his arms around her. "We're going to find your sister and bring her home." His voice was soothing and comforting.

"I can't thank you enough. You've always been there for me."

Guy felt honored to be of assistance to Justina. Though, it bothered him that his wife had not asked him for help in a long time.

"When this is over," Justina continued, "I want to see you."

"Regine and I would be happy to meet with you and your husband."

"It sounds like a plan." Justina knew Guy had twisted her words to his advantage. "I'll call you when Carmela comes home."

"Please do."

The phone rang as soon as Guy returned it to its cradle. It was his stepmother. He was relieved to hear her voice. "Hi Mom. I'm glad you called."

"Hello Guy. What's going on?"

"A detective stopped by to ask me questions about Lamar, Regine's business partner."

"Why?"

"He's missing."

"Are you a suspect?"

"I'm not sure. I left threatening messages on Lamar's voicemail but it wasn't anything serious."

Jeanine gasped. "Why did you do that?"

"Mom, I didn't have anything to do with Lamar or his disappearance, if that's what you're thinking. As far as I'm concerned, he might be on an island somewhere, basking in the sun and drinking a margarita."

"Let's hope you're right."

"The detective searched Lamar's hotel room and found an unsigned contract dissolving his and Regine's business relationship."

"Really?" Jeanine asked with raised brows.

"I guess that's why the detective wants you to call him."

Jeanine frowned. "Why?"

"Supposedly, Raymond's name and room number were written on a note attached to the contract. Do you have a pen and paper?" he asked, after picking up the detective's business card on his desk.

"I'll call the detective later," she explained, after Guy gave her the phone number. "Have you heard from Alex?"

"Yes I did. He told me about the baby."

"Isn't that something?" Jeanine said with pride in her voice. "I cannot wait to see the baby."

The thought of seeing his nephew made Guy smile. For a millisecond, he had forgotten about the matter at hand. His thoughts shifted to his marriage after his eyes connected with the picture of him and Regine on his desk. They seemed so happy and *in love*.

Jeanine grew concerned after she was met with silence on the other end of the line. "Guy, are you okay?"

"Yes Mom. I'm fine."

"Are you sure? You seem a little distracted."

Guy decided against revealing his marriage was on the brink of failure. So he lied, "I'm just tired, that's all."

"You've been working hard. Maybe you should take some time off work and spend time with Regine."

"Mom," he said with sadness in his voice, "now is not a good time. I'm getting ready to close a business deal, and Regine is getting ready to open a restaurant in Miami."

Jeanine nodded in understanding. Then she peered at her watch. "Let's plan on getting together soon, to talk in-person."

"Sounds like a plan."

"Give Regine my love, and give little KC a big kiss for me."

"Will do."

After disconnecting the call, Guy lowered his head in despair. He found it hard to believe Lamar was missing. He racked his brain trying to decide whether he should question Raymond about Lamar's disappearance. Without thinking twice, he grabbed his car keys and headed out the front door.

***

Upon arriving at Raymond's estate, Guy spotted a brand new Jaguar parked in the driveway. He climbed out of his car, lumbered up the path to the front door, and rang the doorbell.

Raymond's housekeeper warmly greeted him. "Hello, may I help you?"

"Hi, I'm Guy Simmons. I'm here to see Raymond Brown."

"Mr. Brown is not expecting any visitors."

"Please tell Mr. Brown that it's urgent that I speak with him right away. I'm Jeanine Benedict's son."

"You are?" she asked with surprise in her voice. She did not see the resemblance. Raymond had introduced her to Jeanine as soon as they started dating.

"I'm her stepson," Guy clarified. Although Jeanine is not his biological mother, he felt that she was in every sense his true mother.

"Please wait here," the housekeeper insisted. "I'll go see if Mr. Brown is able to see you." She did not have to go far. When she turned around, Raymond was standing in front of her. "Oh…hi. Mr. Guy Simmons is here to see you."

Raymond walked around her and greeted Guy with an extended hand. "Hello Guy, come on in."

After shaking hands, Guy asked, "Did I catch you at a bad time?"

"It's okay. Come on in?"

Guy followed Raymond through his house and outside on the deck in the backyard. He took a seat at the patio table.

Earlier, Raymond looked at his surveillance camera from his den, and spotted Guy's car pulling up in the driveway. He wondered what prompted the unexpected visit.

Raymond walked over the patio bar and filled two glasses with Vodka. He sat a drink in front of Guy and joined him at the table. "What brings you to this side of town?"

"A detective from the Hollywood police department just questioned me about Lamar, Regine's business partner. Apparently, he is missing."

"Is that so?" Raymond replied, after sipping his drink.

"He asked me about you."

"Why?"

"He wants to know your connection to Lamar Greene."

"I've only met Lamar a couple of times."

Guy had a feeling Raymond was beating around the bush. So he cut to the chase, by asking, "Did you go to Miami to see Lamar?"

"Yes and no," Raymond admitted. "I went to Miami to take care of some personal business. I ran into Lamar while I was there."

"Did you give him a contract to sign?"

"Contract?" Raymond asked, feigning ignorance.

"The officer found a contract dissolving Lamar and Regine's business relationship. Would you happen to know anything about that?"

"I'm afraid not."

"There was a sticky note with your name and room number affixed to the contract. Can you explain that?"

"I told you," Raymond said while spreading his hands in the air. "Lamar and I ran into each other by coincidence. When I found out we were staying in the same hotel, I invited him to my room for drinks." Raymond paused and leaned toward Guy. "Can I ask you a question?"

"Sure."

"Why are you asking me about a man that tried to come between you and your wife?"

"I don't know what you're talking about."

"I believe you do. It's obvious to everyone that Lamar is smitten with Regine."

Guy felt his blood pressure rise. He was embarrassed. It dawned on him that Lamar had made him look like a fool.

Affectionately, Raymond patted Guy's shoulder. "Why don't you go home and try to patch up things with your wife?" With a wide grin, he added, "Please give my love to Regine."

"Will do."

Feeling deflated, Guy stood up to leave. He opened the sliding door and walked through the house and out the front door. His conversation with Raymond did not put his mind at ease. Instead, he suspected Raymond was not being forthright with him.

Chapter 45
Ace in the Hole

*C*armela purposely turned the ringer off her cell phone, to avoid Swag. She was still upset with him after she found his plane ticket to Jamaica. She thought it was best to speak with him about the matter in-person. Besides, she was enjoying Smokey's company. She let her guard down, when she began talking to him about how she felt betrayed by Swag. "Looking back," she said aloud, "I think he's just using me."

"I thought you were his girl."

"I'm one of many. After today, Swag won't need me anymore," Carmela added, before looking down at her feet.

"I'm sure you wouldn't have any trouble finding a man. You're smart and beautiful," Smokey stated to get in her good graces.

Internally, Carmela wondered if she could trust Smokey. She followed her heart. "I want to tell you something." She took a deep breath and exhaled, before telling Smokey about Dan and Swag and their involvement in the kidnapping scheme. She also told him about the ransom.

Smokey's eyes bulged out of his head, as he slowly recited, "Your ransom is a...half...million...dollars."

"Yeah."

"Your sister is worth that much?"

"It's her husband's money. He owns a lot of property."

"What's going to happen once your sister pays the ransom?"

"We already took care of that. I wrote a letter to my sister telling her that this was all a scam. She's going to get the letter in exchange for the money."

"Damn," Smokey muttered, while shaking his head. He could not believe Carmela was double-crossing her own sister. "So when do you get your share?" he asked, after a short pause.

She shrugged. "I'm not sure."

"What do you mean you're not sure?"

"I'm not sure if I trust Swag to give me my share of the ransom."

"What makes you think that?"

"It's just some of the things he's been telling me." She paused, before continuing, "I've been with Swag long enough to realize he has always done any and everything for a dollar. He even told me about his plans to take Dan's share of the ransom money."

"You mean that white dude you told me about?"

"Yeah."

"That's jacked up."

With a sullen face, Carmela explained, "I guess I was holding on to hope that Swag truly loved me.

"If you don't trust him, why don't you call your sister and tell her about the hoax?"

"Because I hate her."

"What you're saying doesn't make any sense. You have a feeling Swag is getting ready to scam you out of your share of the ransom. But you're letting him take advantage of your sister."

Carmela remained mum. Smokey was making her think long and hard about the situation and her feelings for Swag. "What do you think I should do?"

"You need to go after the ransom."

Carmela turned to Smokey with wide eyes. "What are you talking about? Swag and Dan already contacted my sister about the ransom."

"If you call your sister and tell her to send you the money, I believe she will do it."

Carmela frowned. "You think she'll fall for that?"

"I believe so."

"What about Swag?"

"What about him? We're going to screw him, just like he tried to screw you."

"I thought Swag was your friend."

"He was...I mean he is, but I don't like the way he's trying to screw you over."

Carmela reflected on Smokey's remarks. Then she asked with renewed hope, "Do you think I should call her now?"

"Yeah."

After rehearsing what they were going to tell Justina, Smokey asked Carmela, "Are you sure you know what to say?"

"Yes, don't worry."

Taking a deep breath, Carmela made up her mind to play a convincing kidnapped victim. She retrieved her new cell phone from her purse to call Justina. The phone rang several times before her sister answered her call.

On purpose, Carmela made the tone of her voice seem shaky. "Hi Sis... it's me."

"Carmela!" Justina screamed and jumped for joy. "I'm so happy to hear from you! Are you all right?! Did the kidnapper harm you? Where are you?"

The questions were so rapid, Carmela did not know which one to answer first. "Justina, I'm fine. I'm with the kidnapper now," she said, as she eyed Smokey. "He wants you to wire the money to him."

Justina frowned. Thorny had assured her he had located the kidnapper yesterday. Maybe he was not successful, she thought to herself. Confused and conflicted, she told Carmela, "Your kidnapper wants me to meet him at the Down Beat restaurant in the morning."

"The plans have changed."

"Where are you?"

"I can't tell you," Carmela said in a frazzled whisper, for added affect.

"Can I talk to the kidnapper?"

Without answering Justina, Carmela handed the phone to Smokey.

"Hello." Smokey's voice was strong and husky.

"Who are you?" Justina asked, after she did not recognize his voice.

"Your worst nightmare," he said with a threatening tone. "I need you to send me the money. Otherwise, you will never see your sister again."

"But I thought I already spoke with the kidnapper, earlier."

"Are you sure it was the kidnapper?"

Justina's heart was beating one-hundred miles per hour. She was scared and dumbfounded. "What are you saying?"

"I allowed you to talk to your sister. So who do you believe is the real kidnapper?"

"Please don't hurt my sister," Justina pleaded, her lips were quivering.

"Don't worry," Smokey calmly replied. "If you do as you're told, you won't have to worry about that."

"I'll do anything you want me to do."

"Go to Western Union and wire the money to your sister. Send the money to Alabama."

"You're in Alabama?" Justina asked to be sure she heard him correctly.

"Maybe." He did not tell her they were only eight hours away from the nearest city in Alabama.

"I have to be honest with you," Justina admitted in an uneasy sounding voice. "I don't have the full five-hundred thousand. I need more time to get the rest of the money."

"How long will it take you?"

"I'm sure I'll be able to get the rest of the money today. I have a friend that'll loan me the money." She hesitated, before asking, "When can I see my sister?"

"As soon as you send the money." Smokey abruptly disconnected the call. He could not believe he was able to convince Justina he was the real kidnapper.

"What did she say?" Carmela asked.

"She said she'll send us the money."

Carmela's mouth flew open in surprise.

"Let's go," he said as he stood up to leave. "We're going to Alabama to get the money."

Carmela grabbed her purse and left the apartment with Smokey. They drove off in his car and headed northbound.

Several minutes later, Kevin Graham and his henchmen arrived at Swag's apartment in Tarpon Springs. They busted the door in and searched around, but Carmela was not there.

***

During the drive to Alabama, Smokey thought of a clever idea. He wanted to taunt his former employee. He turned to Carmela, and said, "I think we should let *your boy* know he's not going to get the ransom. Get him on the phone. I'll do all the talking."

Carmela retrieved her phone from her purse and noticed two missed calls from Swag. Her heart beat rapidly as she dialed his number and handed the phone to Smokey.

Thorny became alarmed when Swag's cell phone rang. He turned to his detainee, and asked, "Where's your phone?"

"It's in my pocket."

"Answer it!" Thorny demanded.

Swag was nervous when he answered his phone. He put the phone to his ear, and said, "Hello."

"Hey Buddy!" Smokey chuckled at his new reference to Swag.

Swag froze in place after hearing his former employer's voice. "I thought...you were...in prison."

"I'm sure you did, seeing that you're the reason I went to prison in the first place."

Swag stammered, "I don't...know what...you're talking about."

"I believe you do. You should thank your girl. She saved your life, at least temporarily."

Unable to stay calm, Swag started fidgeting and swaying back in forth in his chair. "Why…are you…on my girl's phone?"

"Don't worry about all that!"

"Please don't hurt Carmela."

"Why would I hurt this priceless jewel?" Smokey glanced at Carmela with a smirk on his face. "She's getting ready to make me a boat load of money."

Perplexed, Swag's brows shut up. "What are you talking about?"

"Carmela's ransom. She told me about your little scheme. This is a courtesy call to let you know I'm going after the money. Then I'm coming after you for snitching." On that note, Smokey slammed the phone shut.

Swag poked out his bottom lip after hearing the dial tone. He knew his life was doomed.

"Who were you talking to?" Thorny asked.

"A guy I used to work for."

"Explain."

Swag sighed before rehashing his past dealings with Smokey, from beginning to end. He even included the part about being an informant for the police.

"So you're a snitch, huh?" Thorny asked in amazement.

Swag dropped his head in shame.

"Since you're a snitch, I need to know everything you know about Smokey, and don't leave nothing out."

After listening to Swag, Thorny called Kevin and told him everything he had just learned about Smokey aka *Donald Newvall*. He was certain Kevin would find both Smokey and Carmela within 24 hours.

Chapter 46
Without A Trace

*T*he next morning, Alex and Evian arrived in Baltimore as planned. Evian was anxious to meet the baby's mother, but for reasons unknown to Alex. In her heart, she believed this would be the last time she would see or hear from Alecia again.

When they arrived at the hospital, Evian excused herself to go to the restroom, while Alex waited for her in the lobby. She entered one of the stalls and whipped out her cell phone, then breathed a sigh of relief after hearing her ally's voice. "Are you here in Baltimore?"

"Yes," Elizabeth confirmed. "I just picked up the rental car. I'm on my way to the hospital."

"Did you remember to rent the car seat for the baby?"

"Yes, I got it."

"Good. After you steal the baby, go straight to the motel. I will meet you there around noon."

"Okay, I'll be there."

After disconnecting the call, Evian started sweating profusely. She dashed her face with water and dried it with paper towels. Then she saw her reflection in the mirror. For a split second, she was overcome with guilt. She bounced back after envisioning light at the end of the tunnel. Exhaling, she exited the restroom with renewed confidence.

Alex snickered when she walked out of the restroom. "Everything come out all right?" he joked.

Chuckling, Evian lightly punched Alex's arm. "You are too much."

"Are you ready to meet Alecia?"

"I sure am."

Alex and Alecia had agreed to meet in the Family Meditation Center, a private room on the fifth floor of the hospital. It was the only vacant room in the hospital they could use to talk in private.

Alecia rose from her chair as soon as Alex and Evian walked in the room. "You must be Evian," she said, as she extended her hand.

With a fake smile, Evian limply shook Alecia's hand. "Nice to meet you." But the tone of her voice depicted hatred.

Alecia smirked after guessing Evian viewed her as a threat. "Why don't we have a seat?" she suggested, while pointing to the vacant chairs.

"That's a good idea," Alex chimed in.

Quickly, Evian grabbed his arm and requested he sit next to her. He obliged her request.

Alecia took note of Evian's possessiveness. She said to herself, *"This girl has a lot of growing up to do."* To set Evian at ease, she sat across from them.

With clasped hands, Alex sat on the edge of the chair, and asked, "How's Alexander?"

"He's doing great," Alecia boasted with a broad grin. "I can't thank you enough for saving my baby's life."

"*Our baby*," Alex corrected.

"You're right, I'm sorry."

"It's okay. You raised Alexander by yourself for the first three months of his life. Now you have us," he said, as he turned to Evian.

"Yes, you do," Evian felt compelled to say, but her heart was as cold as ice. "We're going to love *your baby* as if he was ours."

Perplexed, both Alecia and Alex frowned as they gazed at Evian.

Realizing they caught on to her purposeful statement, Evian tried to correct herself, by saying, "I mean. We're going to love Alexander as if he was our very own."

Alex figured his fiancé was nervous, and did not know what she was saying. However, Alecia was not buying it. She could easily foresee problems with Alex's fiancé in the near future.

Suddenly, Alex's cell phone rang. It was his secretary. "I'm sorry," he apologized to both Alecia and Evian. "This is important. I have to take this call," he said, before he stepped outside the private room.

As soon as Alex left the room, Evian gave Alecia a piece of her mind. "Let's not beat around the bush," she said in a tone that was meant to scare Alecia. "I don't like you."

Alecia bore a fake smile. "The feeling is mutual."

"For Alex's sake, let's make sure this meeting is as painless as possible."

Alecia nodded in agreement.

"One more thing," Evian said as she sat on the edge of her chair, "you are never to be left alone with my man."

Before Alecia could respond, Alex returned to the room. "Sorry ladies, there was a little problem at the office. I hope you two had the opportunity to get acquainted."

"Yes we did!" Evian cheered in a high-pitched voice. "We have a very good understanding of one another."

"That's good to hear. Before I forget, I have something for you." Alex retrieved a personal check from his shirt pocket and handed it to Alecia.

"What is this for?" she asked, after noting the check amount was fifty-thousand dollars.

"I want to make sure my baby has everything he needs. I have asked my attorney to start sending you checks on a monthly basis."

"You don't have to do this. My father left me enough money."

"That's your money. Just like your father took care of you, I have to step up to the plate to take care of my own child."

"Alex, you're being unreasonable."

"No, you are. I cannot make up for being absent for the first three months of my baby's life. But I will not miss the rest of his life. I'm going to help you raise our child."

Alecia remained quiet. She did not know what else to say.

"When Alexander gets out of the hospital," Alex continued, "I'm going to arrange for both of you to return to Florida for a couple of weeks."

"I don't know about that."

"My child needs to know my family, especially my fiancé," he said, as he briefly turned to Evian. "I want joint custody."

"Are you serious?"

"Yes I am."

Alecia felt overwhelmed by Alex's demands. All she ever wanted from him was to save her baby's life. She did not expect anything more or less.

Alex said, "I want to see my baby as often as I can. What do you think is fair?

She pondered his questioned, before saying, "I'll agree to one weekend a month and alternate holidays."

"That's fair. But I would like the baby to visit me every other summer."

Alecia and Alex ironed out the details involving his visits with Alexander and child support payments. They also agreed to confer with their respective attorneys to make everything official.

Evian was sizzling inside while watching Alex and Alecia finalize the arrangements for their baby. She could not wait for the meeting to end.

***

Elizabeth made it to the hospital dressed in a nursing uniform, and carrying a large duffel bag. She parked near the back entrance on North Wolf Street, and entered the hospital with the hospital pass Evian had given her. As predicted by Evian, the guard did not look closely at her face to make sure it matched the picture on her pass. She took the elevator to the fourth floor and casually approached the nurse's station.

Pretending to fit in, she picked up a pad on the desk and jotted gibberish, all while looking around to make sure no one was watching her. Then Elizabeth looked up and found a chart on the wall. It listed the patients' names with corresponding room numbers.

After mentally taking note of Alexander's room number, Elizabeth found an empty baby cart in the hallway. She commandeered the cart and pushed it toward baby Alexander's room. She noted his room was void of visitors. Exhaling, she felt a sense of relief when she discovered Alexander was sound asleep.

Elizabeth checked her watch to make sure time was on her side. Then she looked around to make sure no one was watching before strolling in the baby's room.

When she placed a rag soaked in *chloroform* over Alexander's nose, he fell into a deeper sleep. She disconnected the heart monitor and wrapped Alexander in a small blanket she had retrieved from her bag. Next, she retrieved the baby doll from her bag and placed it in the hospital bed. She used the blanket on the bed to cover up the baby doll from the neck down.

Nervously, she rushed and placed baby Alexander inside the cart and covered him with the blanket in her bag. Then she pushed the cart out of Alexander's room without being deterred. She took the elevator to the ground level and headed for the rear exit.

She made sure the coast was clear before she grabbed Alexander out of the cart, exited the rear entrance of the hospital, and rushed across the street to the rental car. After placing the baby in the car seat, Elizabeth sped away from the hospital, burning rubber.

"Oh God!" she screamed with pride in her voice. "I did it!"

She drove straight to the motel in Woodlawn, Maryland, as Evian had instructed.

Chapter 47
Roll of Thunder

Regine was torn over whether she should ask her husband for a divorce, to put them both out of their misery. She did not like the way Guy had been treating her; nor did she believe his repulsive behavior was warranted. After picking up the phone, she was certain her grandmother would give her some much-needed advice. "Hello Grandma, it's me."

"Hi Regine," Bessie cooed with excitement. "It's good to hear your voice. I'm sorry we had to cut our visit short."

"It's okay. I want...." Closing her mouth, Regine questioned whether she should involve Bessie in her decision to divorce Guy.

Alarmed by Regine's pause, Bessie sat up in her chair, and asked in a voice filled with worry, "What is it, *Baby*?"

Regine decided to approach her grandmother with another matter. "Lamar is still missing." Her voice was filled with sadness, but her grandmother smiled inwardly.

"The way I see it," Bessie boldly stated, "that might be a blessing in disguise. Now you and Guy can work on your marriage."

"I'm afraid it's not that simple."

"It's that girl, Justina. Isn't it?"

"I'm not sure," Regine admitted. "They've been communicating a lot lately."

"I knew it!" Bessie hollered. "That girl ain't nothing but a *heathen!*"

"Justina's sister was kidnapped. That's why she's been calling Guy. She asked him to help her get her sister back."

"She could have called the police!" Bessie said in a huff. "When are you going to learn? That girl wants your husband."

"I don't think anything is going on between Justina and Guy."

"Not now," Bessie made clear. "It's just a matter of time."

"Maybe things are meant to be," Regine admitted in a soft voice. "What if I gave them my blessing?"

"What are you saying?"

"Maybe Guy and Justina were destined to be together, like me and Lamar."

"You're not saying what I think you're saying, are you?"

"I'm no longer *in love* with Guy. I think I've known it for quite some time, but I didn't have the courage to tell him." Then, she professed in a soft-spoken voice, "I love Lamar. I didn't know how much until he turned up missing. I'm worried something bad has happened to him."

Bessie fell silent. When she finally spoke, she asked, "Have you prayed about this matter?"

"Grandma, did you hear a word I said? I don't love Guy, at least not the way I used to." Regine paused, before admitting, "I want a divorce."

Bessie sighed. "I had a feeling this would happen," she said with sadness in her heart. "You were too close to Lamar."

"No Grandma, you're wrong. Lamar is the first man that ever made me feel complete. He treats me as if I'm the only one that matters."

"What about Guy?"

"What about him?" Regine rebuffed without waiting for a response. "Guy has always put others before me. First Justina, then his siblings...."

"Regine," Bessie interjected, "think about what you're saying. Guy has made mistakes, but so have you."

Bessie's words stung, and made Regine think back to the time she aborted her first baby. No matter how hard she tried, she could never forget. "It was a mistake," she told her grandmother, after deep thought.

"I know, *Baby*. That's why I think it's important for you to pray and ask for God's divine intervention. Fight for your marriage," Bessie encouraged. "Do it for KC. He needs both of his parents." Regine did not respond, so Bessie continued, "Please pray over the matter."

"Thank you, Grandma."

"You're welcome. I want you to be happy."

"I know."

After disconnecting the call, Regine reflected on her conversation with her grandmother. She recognized it felt good to reveal her true feelings about Guy and their marriage. Then suddenly, as if a light bulb came on, she remembered the new restaurant in Miami would be open for business next week. With so much going on around her, she did not know whether she should postpone the grand opening.

Regine phoned her accountant, who told her too much was at stake. He further stated that several news reporters and food critics were scheduled to be in town for the big event. She thanked her accountant before disconnecting the call. Then she went online to reserve a flight to Miami. She thought it was best to leave as soon as possible.

When Guy returned home from visiting Raymond, he walked upstairs to the master bedroom and discovered Regine packing her suitcase. "What are you doing?" he asked her with raised brows.

"I have to go to Miami."

"I thought you were going to wait to leave for Miami next week."

"Since Lamar is missing, I have to leave now to make sure everything is taken care of, for the grand opening."

Sadly, just the thought of not seeing or hearing from Lamar again was too much for Regine to bear. Her shoulders dropped and her heart ached as she resumed packing.

Guy noticed Regine's mood changed, and wondered if it had something to do with Lamar's disappearance. On a whim, he asked, "Do you want me to go with you?"

"No. That's not necessary."

Guy grimaced. He was hurt because Regine did not need him, not the way Justina needed him. "Am I not good enough for you?!"

Sighing, Regine sat on the edge of the bed to face Guy. Against her grandmother's advice, she announced, "I want a divorce."

"What did you say?" He was taken aback by his wife's announcement.

"I haven't been happy for a long time."

"Why didn't you tell me?"

"Don't act surprised. The last time we had sex, things did not turn out right."

"It's not my fault we hadn't had sex in over a month. And when we finally did, you called out another man's name."

"Don't do this," Regine chastised. "Can you honestly say you're still *in love* with me?"

Guy remained mum while pondering Regine's question. He recognized the love he had for his wife was waning.

Regine was not surprised Guy did not answer her question. For most of her young adult life, she had fought to be a part of his life. She loved her husband but wondered if her love had anything to do with the fact that they were both parentless when they first met.

Guy's parents died in a car accident when he was fifteen years old, and Regine's parents were nonexistent for most of her childhood and young adult life. In fact, her mother was strung out on drugs and she was told her father was deceased. She was shocked to later discover her father was very much alive.

Both Guy and Regine acknowledged they were drawn together by their past, and now they were unsure of their future.

"I want to make this marriage work," Guy pleaded, "for KC's sake."

"My heart belongs to someone else."

Guy knew Regine was referring to Lamar but did not want to say his name. "How long have you been seeing him behind my back?"

"I never cheated on you, if that's what you're suggesting." Regine took a deep breath before repeating her earlier statement. "I want a divorce."

"So you can marry Lamar?"

"Lamar is missing and may never be found, so he has nothing to do with my decision." Her heart was heavy, as she continued, "I'm doing this so we can both be happy."

"I'm not...happy...without you," Guy choked out, trying to stop the pain from piercing his broken heart.

"You will be happier with Justina."

"There's nothing going on between me and Justina," Guy muttered. Though, he was not sure how he felt about the woman he had asked to marry several years earlier.

Out of curiosity, Regine asked, "Are you still *in love* with her?"

Guy frowned. "What kind of question is that? I love you."

Regine opened her mouth to respond but closed it after realizing it was pointless to debate the matter.

Coincidentally, the repeated mention of Justina's name had forced Guy to reconcile his past. Every time he was in her presence, she still had a way of making his heart flutter.

"Is there anything you want to tell me?" Regine quizzed, trying not to sound accusatory.

"About what?"

"Lamar."

Frowning, Guy asked, "What are you saying?"

"I think it's odd that you've shown nothing but hatred toward Lamar. Then he suddenly disappears."

"I had good reason to hate any man that tries to take my wife from me!"

Regine did not want to argue with Guy. She stood up and resumed packing. "You need to be with Justina, especially now. She needs you."

"She's married."

Without malice, Regine said, "That did not stop her from turning to you after her sister was kidnapped."

"She needed money to pay Carmela's ransom."

"Justina didn't have to call you. We are, or *were* friends. She could have called me."

Guy fumbled with his chin and bit his bottom lip. He admitted to himself, *"His wife was right. Justina could have called her."*

Regine closed her suitcase before she turned to her husband, and declared, "It's over."

"Just like that," Guy said with sorrow in his voice. "You're going to give up on us."

"No Guy, it's more like moving on and finding true happiness."

"What about KC?"

"We can share custody."

Regine lifted the suitcase off the bed and put it on the floor. "I'll move out when I return from Miami."

"You don't have to do this. We can get counseling."

"I think we need a counselor, but not a marriage counselor. We need to learn how to raise our child, while living apart."

Guy rubbed his hand across his head and around the side of his neck out of frustration. "I...don't know...what to say."

"There's nothing else to say."

Sizzling inside from rage, Guy turned around, ran downstairs, and out the front door. He needed to get out of the house before he did or said something he would probably regret. He found it hard to accept that Regine was giving up on him, and their marriage.

***

"What's wrong?" Deacon Franklin asked, after Bessie disconnected the call with her granddaughter.

"That was Regine. She told me Lamar is still missing."

"That's a good thing, isn't it?"

Bessie frowned. "Why would you say something like that?"

"Isn't that what you wanted?"

"No!" Bessie bellowed. "That's not what I wanted!"

Concerned his wife was getting riled up, the deacon held her hand while lightly squeezing her shoulder. "Calm down, *Baby*. I thought you had problems with Lamar."

"What makes you think that? That man saved my grandchild's life, remember?"

"But you told me...."

Bessie held her hand up to silence the deacon. "I told you I was concerned Regine was spending too much time with Lamar. I never told you I didn't like him."

Deacon Franklin massaged his chin while staring into space.

Bessie analyzed her husband's gestures, as she enveloped her hand in his. "Hon', did you do something to Lamar?"

The deacon kissed Bessie on the cheek. "I gotta go to church for Morning Prayer." On that note, he turned his back to Bessie and walked out the front door.

Bessie did not know how to interpret the deacon's response. The more she thought about it, the more she realized he never answered her question.

Chapter 48
Unscrambled

*G*uy felt like his life was caving in around him. His wife's allegations about his feelings for Justina were not substantiated by proof. So he could not understand why Regine was trying to tie his past to the present. He was seething in anger as he climbed in his car, backed out of the driveway, and drove onto the main street.

Suddenly, his cell phone rang. It was Justina according to the caller ID. He thought about not answering her call, because he blamed her for causing the rift in his marriage. On second thought, Guy wanted to know why she was calling him. He activated the blue tooth system in his car, and answered in a testy manner. "What do you want?"

"Hi Guy. I'm sorry if I called you at a bad time, but I don't know who else to call."

"What's going on?" he continued in a curt tone.

"I heard from Carmela," Justina explained, sounding uneasy.

Guy could not help but smile. His tone softened, as he said, "That's good news. When is she coming home?"

"That's why I'm calling. A different man called and told me he kidnapped her."

Perplexed, Guy paused for a few seconds. "What are you saying? Two different people claim to have kidnapped Carmela?"

"Yes. One of the kidnappers asked me to meet him at the Down Beat restaurant in Bradenton in the morning. He told me to bring the money, and he'll release Carmela in my custody."

"So Carmela is with *that* kidnapper?"

"I don't think so. Your friend told me he located that particular kidnapper, and was on his way to confront him."

Guy assumed Justina was referring to his father-in-law, Kevin Graham. He probed further. "What about the other kidnapper?"

"I just received a call from the other kidnapper. He let me talk to Carmela. He also asked me to wire the ransom to Alabama."

Cupping his chin with his free hand, Guy thought something sounded fishy about what Justina was telling him. He was about to respond, but her phone beeped, signaling another call.

"Guy, please hold on," she said, after eyeing the unfamiliar phone number. She clicked over to the other call. "Hello."

"May I speak to Justina Bishop?"

"This is she. Who's calling?"

"The Tampa Bay Police Department. Your husband is in our custody."

"For what?" Her voice sounded strained with worry.

"We picked him up last night. He was on skid row, soliciting sexual services from a prostitute."

Justina's heart dropped. "What did you say?"

"Your husband is in jail for soliciting a prostitute."

Stunned into silence, Justina could not believe Aaron was on skid row looking for a prostitute. That was the seediest place in downtown Tampa.

"Mrs. Bishop, are you still there?" the officer asked.

"Why didn't Aaron call me himself?"

"I'm not sure."

"How long will he have to stay in jail?"

"The rest of the weekend. Mr. Bishop's bail review hearing is scheduled first thing Monday morning."

"I see." Justina was choked up but pushed through her emotions.

"Do you have any more questions?" the officer inquired.

"No. Thank you for calling."

"No problem."

Justina clicked back to the other call. "Hi Guy. I'm back."

"Was that one of the kidnappers?"

"No. I just found out my husband is in jail."

"What did he do?"

"It doesn't matter," Justina sadly replied. "I'm leaving Aaron, for good." This, she had decided while she was on the phone with the police officer. Unable to hold it together, she broke down crying.

"Everything around me is crumbling," she admitted, while sobbing.

"Justina," Guy softly cooed, "it's going to be all right. Let me come over and help you through this. Give me your address."

After Justina gave him her address, Guy disconnected the call and headed over to her home. Every fiber of his being told him he was doing the right thing. *"But why do I feel guilty?"* he asked himself.

Chapter 49
Surreal

*A*lex was happy his meeting with Alecia to discuss their son had ended on a good note. He was particularly satisfied with the child support and visitation arrangements. More importantly, he thought Alecia and Evian were getting along better than he had expected. Though, Alex was not naïve. He knew it was a matter of time before Evian's jealous streak reared its ugly head.

When they left the waiting room, Alex grabbed Evian's hand while Alecia led the way to their baby's room. He was anxious to see his baby. He became alarmed when Alecia stopped in her tracks upon entering the room. She stared at the baby doll in disbelief.

"Where is he?" Alex asked, as he walked around Alecia, and moved toward the bed. He frowned after taking note of the baby doll.

"Maybe he's with the nurse," Alecia nervously explained, before she grabbed the baby doll and sprinted to the nurse's station. Her motherly instincts kicked in. Something was wrong.

Alex was going to follow her, but Evian grabbed his hand. "Why don't we wait here" she insisted, "in case the nurse returns to the room with the baby?"

"I suppose you're right," he replied, while staring at the empty bed. He was worried about the baby but did not know why.

Evian, however, was smiling inside. She could not wait to see the look of panic on Alecia's face. "Let's have a seat," she said to Alex, while pointing to the only two chairs in the room.

"I'll stand. You can have a seat."

Evian strutted over to the chair and sat down. She was teetering on the edge of her seat, while waiting for a grief-stricken Alecia to return to the room with the bad news. She knew she did not have to wait long.

At the nurse's station, Alecia did not wait for the head nurse to finish her phone call, before she screamed, "Where is my baby?!"

"Who are you?" the nurse asked, after disconnecting the call.

"Alecia Kellam. My baby was in his room about an hour ago, and now he's not there. And I found this doll left in his bed," she said, as she threw it on the counter.

The nurse looked at the doll with wide eyes. "What is the patient's name?"

"Alexander Simmons."

The nurse typed in Alexander's name on the computer and waited two seconds for the results. "Isn't he in his room?"

"No he's not!" Alecia sharply answered. "And someone left a baby doll in his place!" She wanted to strangle the nurse for asking a stupid question. "Where's the nurse that was supposed to be caring for him?!" she demanded to know.

"Wait here. I'll page her." The head nurse grabbed the speaker-phone and called for Alexander's nurse. When she did not get a response, she roamed the halls looking for her. She found her in the lunchroom taking a break.

"What are you doing in here?" she asked the nurse. "You should be watching the patient, Alexander Simmons."

"I just checked on the patient a few minutes ago. He was sound asleep."

"But the baby is not there," the head nurse made clear.

"Why? What's going on? Is something wrong with the patient?"

"The patient is missing."

Alexander's assigned nurse gasped in horror.

The head nurse tried to maintain her cool, but her harsh demeanor spoke volumes. "I'll deal with you later." She rushed back to the nurse's station, where she found Alecia pacing back and forth. Quickly, she flew to the phone on the desk to call security.

"Have you located my baby?" Alecia asked the head nurse.

"I'm afraid not."

Alecia broke down crying and yelling, "Somebody better find my baby!!" She thought she was going to have a heart attack. Her heart was racing, and she found it difficult to breathe.

When Alex heard the screeching sounds in the hallway, he ran outside Alexander's room and discovered Alecia bent over on the floor weeping, profusely. He rushed over to her, knelt down and lightly touched her shoulder. "What's the matter?"

Tears flowing nonstop, Alecia explained between sobs, "Alexander …is…missing."

"What do you mean?" Alex asked.

"Alexander is missing," Alecia stammered between sniffles. "Someone took him."

"How do you know?"

"They can't find him."

The enormity of the situation was a tall order for Alex to swallow. He was in shock and could not speak.

Standing near the door entrance of Alexander's room, Evian witnessed Alex and Alecia falling apart in the middle of the hallway. She thought they were making spectacles of themselves. Putting on her game face, she walked over to them, and asked, "What's going on?"

"Alexander is missing," Alex explained, somberly.

"*Missing?!*" Evian stressed in an exaggerated voice. "What do you mean he's missing?"

"I think…someone stole…my baby," Alecia sobbed, before resting her head on Alex's shoulder for support.

Evian wanted to walk over and yank Alecia away from her fiancé, but knew he would not be pleased with her behavior. So she walked over, knelt beside Alecia, and said, "Why don't we go to Alexander's room, until someone at the hospital is able to find out what's going on?"

"That's a good idea," Alex said, as he stood up and reached for Alecia. When she stood up, he wrapped his arms around her waist and escorted her to Alexander's room.

Evian was speechless as they walked by her. She followed behind them, rolling her eyes and shooting daggers at Alecia's back.

Alex and Alecia sat in the only two chairs in the room, comforting each another. Evian stood next to Alex with her arms crossed and pouting.

The hospital security guard and two Baltimore City police officers rushed into Alexander's room. "Ma'am," one of the officers said to Evian, "are you the mother of the missing baby?"

"No," Evian answered with an attitude.

"I am the baby's father," Alex interjected. Then he pointed to Alecia and clarified, "She's the mother."

Choked up, Alecia stuttered, "Did…you see…who took my baby?"

The officer said, "The hospital security staff is viewing video footage of this floor, and other areas throughout the hospital. We hope to find some leads."

"Can I see the video?" Alex asked.

The officer was going to protest, but he noted the look of desperation in Alex's eyes. "Follow me."

When Alex stood up to follow the officer, Evian and Alecia insisted on going with him. The officer did not object to their wishes.

In the security room, the video of Alexander's room in the past two hours were shown. Nothing seemed out of the ordinary. That was, until Elizabeth Coleman was shown entering Alexander's room. Seconds later, she was pushing a cart to the elevator and exiting the hospital.

The officer put the video of Elizabeth on pause, then turned to Alex and Alecia, and asked, "Do you know this person?"

Holding her breath, Evian stood back and watched Alex's reaction. Since Elizabeth did not do anything to shield her face, Evian thought Alex would recognize his ex-fiancé's mother.

Narrowing his eyes, Alex struggled to hone in on the woman's features but could not register her face.

Alecia, who stood next to Alex, moved closer to the video monitor. The longer she focused on the video image, the more she realized the features belonged to the woman she had confronted a year earlier. "Oh my God!" she cried out, as tears flooded her face. "She took my baby!"

"Do you know this woman?" the officer asked.

"Yes...I know her," she answered while weeping. "That's Elizabeth Coleman."

Alex took a closer look at the video image, and agreed with Alecia. He added, "Mrs. Coleman is the mother of my ex-fiancé."

"Are you sure it's the same woman?" the officer asked.

Both Alex and Alecia nodded.

"Why would she do this?" the officer asked Alecia.

"I think Elizabeth feels betrayed by me," Alex interjected. "I was sorta dating Alecia, while I was dating her daughter."

The officer's eyes shifted between Alecia and Alex. Then the officer browsed the videos for more clues. He spotted Elizabeth exiting the hospital and rushing to a car with the baby. When she peeled out of the parking space on North Wolf Street, he could not get a clear view of the Maryland tags but was able to distinguish the make and model of the car. He also determined that the car was fairly new.

The officer grabbed his walkie-talkie from his hip and ordered an APB on Elizabeth Coleman. He also requested assistance from the FBI. Then he turned to Alex and Alecia, and said, "We're in the process of issuing an Amber alert, which could help us find the baby."

Evian's nerves became unraveled. She was trying to figure out a way to make sure she was not implicated for helping Elizabeth steal baby Alexander. Turning to the officer, her voice trembled, when she asked, "What's going to happen next?"

"We have to find Elizabeth Coleman."

"What if the baby is not in her custody?"

"We're hoping that is not the case. But if it is, we will interrogate Mrs. Coleman, to find some answers."

Alex asked, "How soon will we hear from you?"

"We will contact you as soon as Mrs. Coleman is in our custody."

Alecia felt dizzy. Her knees gave out on her as she fainted and fell to the floor. Alex knelt down and gathered her in his arms.

"She's in shock," the officer surmised. "I'll go get a doctor."

Evian grew furious as she witnessed Alecia lying in Alex's arms. Suddenly, she lost control of her emotions. "Why are you tending to her like that?!" she threw a fit. "You need to let the doctors here at the hospital do their job!"

Scrunching his brows, Alex looked at his fiancé in a state of confusion. "Evian," he calmly said, "I want to be here for my child's mother. If you have a problem with that, you can just leave."

Angry beyond comprehension, Evian marched out of the security office in a huff. Had she turned back, she would have noted the scowl on Alex's face. He was disappointed in her. Her wicked behavior made him question whether he should marry her.

When Evian turned the corner, she was bombarded with news cameras from every major news station in Maryland. "What's going on?" she asked one of the news reporters.

"Do you know Alecia Kellam?" the reporter asked.

"Why do you ask?"

"Is it true that Alecia Kellam's baby was stolen from the hospital?"

Evian bit her bottom lip. She did not know how to respond. She was surprised the news crew was there to report the abduction, especially since it had just happened.

Unbeknownst to Evian, Alecia became somewhat of a celebrity in Maryland after her father died. Her father had saved thousands of lives, after he invented the cure for stage IV breast cancer.

"How is Ms. Kellam doing?" one of the news reporters asked. Before Evian could respond, another reporter came forward with knowing eyes, and asked, "Are you Evian Gant, the Miss America title holder?"

Evian panicked. The camera crew was headstrong on videotaping her.

"Mrs. Gant, who are you to Ms. Kellam?" the reporter asked.

"No one!" Evian screamed. She used her hand to conceal her face as she walked past the reporters in a hurry.

As soon as she turned the corner, she hid in a vacant waiting room on the first floor of the hospital. Welcoming the privacy, she retrieved her cell phone from her purse to call Elizabeth Coleman.

Chapter 50
Lukewarm

*D*etective Baily showed up at the condo Leslie Holloway shared with Lamar Green, and knocked on the front door. He waited several seconds before knocking again. He turned to leave after assuming no one was home. But, suddenly, the front door flew open.

"What do you want?!" Leslie greeted the detective with a chip on her shoulder. She had been drinking and hiding out in her condo ever since Regine's father threatened to kill her.

The detective turned around and was caught off guard by Leslie's crazed appearance. The alcohol on her breath filled in the space between them.

"Are you Leslie Holloway?"

"Why do you want to know?" she asked with an attitude.

"I'm here to investigate the disappearance of Lamar Greene."

"Lamar is missing for real?" Her mouth flew open as she placed her hand on her chest from shock.

"You didn't know?" The detective figured she should have known something was amiss, since Lamar did not return her calls.

"So she was telling the truth," Leslie muttered under her breath.

"She?" the detective asked with arched brows.

"Regine Simmons," Leslie offered. "She's Lamar's business partner."

"Do you know if Mrs. Simmons was having an affair with Lamar Greene?'

Leslie brows shut up in fury, as she yelled, "That slut stole my man!"

The detective nodded in sympathy. "Ms. Holloway," he continued to probe, "can someone vouch for your whereabouts after Mr. Greene left for Miami?"

"Why?"

"I must investigate everyone associated with Lamar Greene."

"My friends can verify my whereabouts?"

"What are their names?"

"Nicky Cannon and Marissa Carey," Leslie answered.

"Can you prove you did not travel to Miami recently?"

"I most certainly can." She rolled her head and twisted her mouth to get her point across.

The detective jotted down her statement and closed his writing pad. Then he gave her a direct order. "Stay in town in case we have further questions."

"I'm not going anywhere. Lamar signed the deed of this condo to me."

"Duly noted." He tipped his hat before turning to leave.

Leslie closed the door and started pacing back and forth. The detective's visit had her shaking in her pants. She picked up the phone to get answers. "Hi Nicky, this is Leslie. The detective just appeared at my door, asking me questions about Lamar."

"I don't know why. My girl, Charlotte, put a substantial amount of GHB in Lamar's liquor. There is no way he could have survived the overdose. Why are you worried?" Nicky asked, after Leslie fell silent.

"Lamar's body is missing."

Suddenly, Nicky became speechless. She was worried but tried not to show it. "Just stay cool, Leslie. There's no evidence that'll pinpoint you as a suspect in his disappearance, and you don't have to worry about Charlotte talking."

"I hope you're right."

Leslie was devastated after Lamar broke up with her. She believed she was well on her way to becoming his wife. That was before he started displaying signs he was infatuated with his business partner. He could not stop talking about her. So it came as no surprise when Lamar told her he was leaving her for Regine.

But this revelation had pushed Leslie over the edge. She thought to herself, *"If she can't have Lamar, no one else can."*

Shortly after Lamar left for the airport to go to Miami, Leslie recruited her girlfriend to help her exact revenge on Lamar. She became excited after Nicky told her about a friend of hers that worked at the Hilton. It was the same hotel Lamar had checked into.

"Are you sure she will do it?" Leslie asked Nicky.

"Yeah. Charlotte is my girl. Give her a thousand dollars, and she'll be straight."

Leslie asked, "What about you? What do you want?"

"We'll talk about that another time. Let's take care of your *boy* first."

"What do you have in mind?"

"What is Lamar's favorite drink?"

"VS Cognac Hennessy."

"That's good. I'll ask my girlfriend to put some GHB in his drink order when she delivers it to his room."

"What is GHB?"

"It's a date rape drug. But I'll make sure she puts enough in his liquor to knock him out."

"As in death?" Leslie asked, for clarity.

"My girl, Charlotte, is going to make sure he never recovers." Nicky paused, before continuing, "You need to continue calling Lamar, even though you will never hear from him again. Leave messages on his voicemail, so the police won't suspect you had any involvement."

Leslie did as she was told. She thought Nicky's suggestion was smart. But their actions backfired after Lamar disappeared. All kinds of thoughts were going through Leslie's head, long after the detective's visit. She asked herself, *"What if Lamar is alive? Or, what if he never drank the liquor?"*

Chapter 51
Busted

*W*hen the detective returned to the police station in Tampa, he learned there was video footage of the hallway leading to Lamar Greene's hotel room. Raymond and another person, whose identity was blurred by dark sunglasses, a dark overcoat, and a hat, were seen entering and leaving Lamar's room around the time he disappeared. They were carrying a large item out of the room. It was wrapped in a blanket.

The video footage also showed a hotel staff member delivering a bottle of Hennessy to Lamar's room. The forensic specialist tested the empty bottle, and discovered it contained traces of GHB or *gamma hydroxybutanoic acid*. Detective Baily was aware the drug was often used as a date-rape drug but could be lethal if taken in large doses.

In light of the new evidence, the detective was certain Lamar was murdered, and Raymond Brown was the main suspect. He ordered two unmarked cars to follow the suspect until he was able to obtain a warrant. It had taken several hours before the detective was able to present his findings before the district court. The judge believed there was enough evidence to issue a warrant for Raymond's arrest.

Detective Baily contacted the undercover officers to get an update on the suspect's whereabouts. He was told Raymond had just arrived at Jeanine Benedict's home. The detective ordered the officers to notify him of Raymond's next destination.

As soon as Jeanine exited her home, Raymond stood back and took note of her stupendous beauty. Her hair was tied back in a bun, and her makeup was flawless. She looked radiant in a black slim-fitting Versace dress.

Raymond smiled. "Hello Ms. Benedict. You are by far the most beautiful woman I have ever known."

Jeanine giggled. "If you keep lauding me with compliments, my head is going to explode."

They both laughed.

Raymond wrapped his arm around Jeanine's waist and guided her to the passenger side of his brand new Jaguar. He checked his coat pocket to make sure the ring box was there. Then he strutted around his car and climbed behind the steering wheel. Earlier, he had purchased a five-carat diamond engagement ring, which he planned on giving to Jeanine when the time was right.

They arrived at the restaurant an hour later. After the host seated them at their table, Raymond ordered filet mignon and Jeanine ordered lobster soufflé. Their dinner was accompanied with a bottle of red wine.

Raymond had prearranged to have two violinists come to their table, to play a love ballad. Jeanine was enchanted as she swayed to the beautiful melody. She clapped with a burst of excitement after the ballad ended. The violinists bowed before leaving.

Jeanine gave Raymond a knowing smile. "You never cease to amaze me."

"I plan on showering you with love and attention, for the rest of our lives."

"That sounds promising." Sitting across from Raymond, Jeanine was excited to be in his company. Though, she could not help but think about what Guy told her earlier, about Raymond's possible involvement in the dissolution of Regine and Lamar's business relationship.

When her private investigator, Tim Carter, told her she did not have to worry about Lamar posing a threat to Guy and Regine's marriage, he did not share any specifics. Tim led her to believe that Lamar was dead. She could not help but wonder if Raymond had something to do with Lamar's demise.

Raymond became concerned after Jeanine's blissful smile turned upside down. He asked, "Are you okay? You barely touched your food."

Jeanine paused before she spoke. "I was wondering if you met with Lamar Greene while you were in Miami."

"We met briefly," he admitted without elaborating.

"Why didn't you tell me?"

"I didn't think it was important."

"So that explains why the detective wants to talk with me."

"The detective?"

"Guy told me a detective asked him questions about a contract dissolving Lamar and Regine's business relationship. Did you give Lamar the contract?"

Raymond hesitated, before admitting, "Yes, I gave Lamar the contract."

"Why?"

"Because I saw how Lamar and Regine's business relationship was affecting their marriage, *and you*."

"Did you have anything to do with his disappearance?"

"No."

"Were you in his hotel room around the time he disappeared?"

"Yes," he slowly admitted.

Jeanine's response was stifled after she heard commotion in front of the restaurant. She and Raymond turned around and saw police officers heading toward their table, with Detective Baily leading the way.

"What's going on?" Raymond asked, after the detective stood before him with a scowl on his face.

"We have a warrant for your arrest."

"What is this about?" Jeanine asked, as she removed her napkin from her lap and put it on the table.

While keeping his eyes focused on Raymond, the detective said, "We have proof Mr. Brown was involved in Lamar Greene's disappearance."

"Me?!" Raymond rebuffed. "I didn't have anything to do with that!" he shouted, after the officers forced him out of his chair. When he stood upright, Raymond quickly retrieved the ring box from his coat pocket and threw it on the table. "I love you!" he declared to Jeanine. "I want you to be my wife! Will you marry me?!"

The police officers handcuffed Raymond and read him his Miranda Rights, then escorted him out of the restaurant.

Jeanine was stunned by what she had just witnessed. She spotted the ring box on the table and covered it with her hand. She was not sure how she felt about Raymond's bizarre proposal.

Coincidentally, Detective Baily stayed behind and sat in Raymond's vacant chair.

"What do you want?" Jeanine demanded to know.

"My name is Detective Baily from the Hollywood Police department. I would like to ask you some questions."

Jeanine remained mum. She refused to cooperate with the officer, fearing anything she said to the detective could possibly be used against Raymond. Especially, as it seemed, Raymond had made a daring effort to save her son's marriage.

Detective Baily stood up to leave, after he was met with silence. "I'll be in touch."

"Not any time soon, I hope."

After the detective left the table, Jeanine opened the ring box and welled up upon seeing a five-karat engagement ring. She quickly closed the ring box and put it in her purse. Then she paid the bill at the restaurant and ordered her driver to pick her up. Luckily, her driver was in the vicinity.

The limo driver got out of the car to open the door for Jeanine. She climbed in and tried to get a grip on what transpired at the restaurant. Suddenly, her cell phone rang. It was Alex. Jeanine put up a front to hide the fact that she was feeling glum and distressed.

"Hi son," she said with a plastered smile. "How's my grandson?"

"Mom, I'm afraid I have bad news."

Jeanine frowned. "What is it?"

"Alexander was abducted from the hospital."

"What happened?"

"It's a long story."

Jeanine instructed the limo driver to take her to the airport. Then she told Alex, "I'm on my way to Baltimore."

"Mom, that's not necessary."

"I'm on my way," Jeanine insisted. "I'll call you when my plane lands."

"Thank you, Mom."

"Try not to worry. We're going to find the baby, I promise."

Alex nodded. Though, he was not optimistic. Earlier, he called his twin sisters and told them what was going on.

Dana asked, "Do you think Evian had anything to do with Alexander's disappearance?"

"No, why would you say that?"

"I don't have proof, but I never trusted her."

"Why didn't you tell me how you felt about Evian earlier?"

"Mom told me not to worry. Besides, you seem happy with her. I didn't want to spoil things for you."

Alex quickly dismissed his sister's question about Evian's involvement in his baby's abduction. He found it hard to believe.

"Dana, I just called to tell you what was going on. I'll keep you posted if I hear anything else."

"Please do. I'll tell Cassie what's going on."

"Thank you."

Next, Alex called Guy. He tried calling him earlier but his went straight to voicemail.

Chapter 52
Living Hell

*B*ack in jail, Aaron was placed in a holding cell with several men, who all fit the mold of hard core criminals. He was scared but tried to put up a brave front. He thought by sitting in a corner and staying to himself, it would stop the inmates from bothering him. But the inmates sensed fear. They taunted Aaron to the point his bladder became weak. When he eyed the only unsanitary toilet in the back of the cell, he became sick to his stomach. He could not imagine using the toilet in front of the inmates.

Aaron prayed the nightmare would end, and soon. What was even more daunting was the fact that he was told he had to wait until Monday to be released from jail. Of course, that depended on the outcome of his bail review hearing.

Earlier, he was entitled to one free phone call and blew it on trying to call the 1-800 *Call Girl* service. He thought Swag would loan him the bail money, considering he was a faithful customer of his escort service for the past two years. After Aaron did not get an answer, he asked the officer to call his wife. He was hoping against hope that Justina would be open-minded and forgive him for trying to solicit a prostitute. He understood this latest incident might destroy their marriage.

When Aaron looked up, another inmate was thrown in his cell. There was something about the inmate that spooked him. His eyes grew wide, as he muttered under his breath, *"It can't be."* Blocking his face with his hand, Aaron hunkered over and hoped his new cellmate did not see him.

But Raymond Brown could spot his one and only son a mile away. With caution, he walked over to Aaron and sat next to him on the hard bench. "Son," he said, as he lightly touched Aaron's shoulder. "What are you doing in here?"

Aaron yanked his shoulder away from Raymond, yelling, "Get your hands off of me!"

"Son, I know you're still angry...."

Aaron cut Raymond off in mid-sentence, and glared at him with blazing eyes. "You killed my mother, and now you have the nerve to call me your son."

"I did not kill your mother."

"So why did you ask me to lie for you?"

"It's a long story."

"I had to go to court to learn the truth about my mother's death. Can you imagine how I felt when I saw my father listed as the primary suspect?"

"Aaron...."

"No! I don't want to talk to you."

One of the inmates joked, "I sense there's trouble in paradise."

Raymond shot daggers at the inmate, who eventually retreated. Then he redirected his attention to his son. "I know you don't believe me, but I did not kill your mother."

Aaron wanted to cry. He missed his mother so much, his heart ached.

Raymond persisted, "I was with another woman the night your mother was murdered."

"Is that why you used me as your alibi?" Aaron asked, after recalling that his father urged him to lie to the police the night his mother was murdered.

"I did not kill your mother."

"Who was she?" Aaron asked, as he turned to his father with droopy shoulders and sad eyes.

Raymond frowned. "What are you talking about?"

"Your mistress. The same woman you claim you were with while my mother was being murdered."

Raymond sighed. "She didn't mean anything to me. I broke up with her after your mother was killed."

"How convenient," Aaron sarcastically replied.

"It wasn't serious."

"Is that supposed to make me feel better?"

"No, but I found your mother's murderer."

Shocked by this revelation, Aaron's eyes bulged out of his head. He could not believe what his father had just told him. "What are you talking about?"

"It was the young man she was seeing. He murdered your mother."

"Are you suggesting that my mom was cheating on you with another man?"

"We both had affairs. It was a mutual agreement."

"I don't want to hear about this," Aaron bemoaned, covering his ears with his hands.

Despite the circumstances, Raymond was happy to see his son. He felt relieved to get the truth out in the open. He never imagined that it would be behind bars. He was curious to know why Aaron was in jail, but decided not to push the issue. Instead, he asked, "Does your wife know you're in here?"

"How did you know I was married?" Aaron asked in surprise.

"Your sister. We talk from time to time."

"Oh," Aaron said in amazement.

"I'm sure your wife is beautiful."

Aaron cracked a smile. His father's assessment about Justina was right on.

Raymond said, "Maybe when we get out of here, I can meet her."

Aaron's smile faded. "I don't think so."

"Son, we need to work through our problems. I miss you."

Aaron missed his father as well, but was afraid to admit it. He peered at his father before he paid attention to his surroundings. Suddenly, his cellmates seemed less intimidating. With Raymond by his side, Aaron had a feeling the weekend in jail was not going to be as stressful.

He started to relax and look forward to the future, and hopefully get back on good terms with his wife. Though, he was not kidding himself. He knew regaining Justina's trust would be an uphill battle.

The conversation with Aaron had forced Raymond to reconcile his past. He regretted being with his mistress the night his wife was murdered. Raymond was with her for the sex, and his mistress stayed with him for his money. Both were giving each other what they wanted.

Raymond had rented a penthouse apartment for his mistress with the stipulation that he could come and go as he pleased. Their relationship soured after his wife was murdered. He decided to end their relationship after feeling guilty for not being able to protect his wife.

His mistress did not take the news of the breakup well. "You owe me!" she shouted at the top of her lungs.

"I owe you nothing!" Raymond rebuked. "Can't you understand? My wife is dead."

"What about me?" she whined. "You told me you wanted to marry me."

Raymond sighed, before explaining, "You're young. I'm sure you won't have a problem finding someone else." He dug in his pocket and pulled out his wallet. Then he retrieved a wad of cash and handed it to her. "This should be enough to help you get on your feet."

His mistress counted five thousand dollars and looked at Raymond with a frown on her face. "This is not enough. I need more money."

"You're not getting any more money from me."

In a huff, she crossed her arms and leaned on one leg, before spouting, "What if I tell the police detectives you were with me the night your wife was killed?"

Raymond stepped to her with evil eyes. He was only inches from her face. "Are you threatening me?" he asked through gnashed teeth. His question had a deadly undertone.

Stepping backward, she feared Raymond was capable of killing her. She stammered, "No…I didn't mean…anything by it. I'm sorry."

He asked, "Do I have to worry about you running your mouth?"

"No."

"Get your things and get out of my apartment. I never want to see you again."

Reluctantly, she did as she was told. But Raymond had a feeling he would be crossing paths with his mistress in the future. One thing he knew for certain: he did not want Jeanine to ever find out about her.

Raymond was afraid of what Jeanine would think of him, especially after she told him about her experience with her deceased husband's mistress. He knew he should have been upfront with Jeanine about his wife and his mistress, but he did not want to risk losing her.

Chapter 53
Brazen

Elizabeth checked into the motel room with the baby, and waited for her *partner-in-crime's* phone call. She grew nervous after the baby woke up and started crying. Alexander was hungry, she assumed, so she dug in her small suitcase for a bottle. She banged her hand on her forehead in anger after realizing she forgot to buy a baby bottle, milk, and diapers.

The baby's crying grew louder by the second. Elizabeth picked him up and rocked him back and forth in her arms, but that did not stop him from crying. "Where is Evian?" she asked with worry in her voice. "She should have been here by now."

At that very second, her cell phone rang. It was Evian. She hesitated before answering her cell phone. "Is this you?" she asked, to be sure.

"Yes, this is me. You still have the baby?"

"Don't you hear him crying?!" Elizabeth complained. "He's been crying nonstop."

Evian rolled her eyes skyward. She thought her accomplice was a doe-doe head. "Why don't you give him a bottle? Or, check to see if his diaper needs to be changed."

Elizabeth frowned. "If I had those things, it wouldn't be a problem, now would it?" She did not wait for Evian to answer her, before she asked in a huff, "Are you on your way?!"

"I can't come right now."

Incensed, Elizabeth's nose flared. "What do you mean, 'you can't come right now?' This baby is crying and I don't know what to do with it."

"Calm down, I'll think of something."

"You got me involved in this scheme of yours, and now you have to think of something," Elizabeth flippantly replied. "I'll tell you what, I'm taking this baby back to the hospital. Then I'm going back home."

"You can't do that!" Evian retorted, her nervousness showed.

"Why not?!"

"There is video footage of you leaving the hospital with the baby."

Grabbing her chest from shock, Elizabeth slowly sat down on the edge of the bed. She began shivering from the thought of going to jail.

"Elizabeth!" Evian called out. "Are you there?!" She did not get an answer, but knew her ally was still on the phone. "I'm going to get you out of this," she said with certainty.

"How?" Elizabeth asked, sounding pitiful.

"When I take the baby to the adoption agency, they're going to give me one-hundred fifty thousand dollars."

"Which adoption agency?"

"The one downtown, in Baltimore."

"Oh." Elizabeth perked up a little.

"Did you bring your passport?"

"Yeah, why?"

"I'm going to give you some money, so you can leave the country."

Astonished, Elizabeth said in defiance, "I can't leave the country. I can't leave my family."

"Either you leave the country, or risk going to jail." Evian knew she had gotten Elizabeth's attention. "You need to go to the store and get the baby some milk and diapers. Make sure you change out of your nursing uniform and put on your hat and sunglasses when you leave the room. I'll call you later."

After disconnecting the call, Evian returned to the security station and was relieved the news camera crew was not there. She asked Alex, "Did they find Alexander?"

"No, not yet."

"How's Alecia?" Evian asked, for the sake of asking.

"She's going to be okay. The hospital admitted her and gave her a sedative to calm her nerves."

"What's going to happen next?"

"I want to stay here a bit longer, to make sure Alecia is okay."

"Is that necessary?" Evian bickered.

Alex glared at her. Earlier, she had given him a glimpse of her wicked side. Now she was showing outright contempt for his baby's mother. He told her in a cool tone, "I think you should go to the hotel. I'll call you when I need you."

Evian was tempted to respond but changed her mind after observing Alex's icy demeanor. She walked away from him with her head held low. She needed Alex more than he ever knew. He was her alibi in case Elizabeth got caught with the baby.

In the meantime, Evian had some business to take care of. She needed to meet with Elizabeth Coleman before her plan blew up in her face. She sprinted out of the hospital and caught a taxi to the motel off Security Boulevard in Woodlawn, Maryland.

During the drive, Evian called the adoption agency and told them she would be dropping off the baby in an hour or so. She also requested the payment in exchange for baby Alexander be in the form of cash, preferably one-hundred dollar bills.

Evian's confidence was at an all-time high when the cab drove in front of the motel. She paid the driver, climbed out of the cab, and rushed to her ally's room.

Elizabeth exhaled with relief upon seeing her new friend. "It's about time. Here you go," she said, as she picked up the baby and handed him to Evian.

Feeling awkward holding the baby, Evian sat on the bed with the baby slumped over her arms. He had cried himself to sleep before she arrived. She turned to Elizabeth, and said, "I need to borrow your rental car, to take the baby to the adoption agency."

Elizabeth dug in her purse and retrieved the car keys. "Then what?"

"I'm going to drop you off at the bus station, and buy you a one-way ticket to Canada."

"Why Canada?"

"Besides Mexico, Canada is the only country you can get into without a passport."

"What if I want to go home?"

"We'll talk about that later." Evian did not want to burst Elizabeth's bubble by telling her that it would not be wise to stay in the United States.

***

Evian's parents had a feeling something was amiss with Evian. Lately, their daughter seemed short with them over the phone, or she would ignore their phone calls altogether. Worried sick, Mrs. Gant had convinced her husband to fly to Tampa, Florida to see about Evian. Their plane had just landed in Tampa airport and they were waiting for their bags in the baggage claim area, when Mr. Gant asked his wife of twenty-seven years, "Are you sure this was a good idea?"

"We didn't have a choice. Evian is not answering our calls."

"What if she gets upset when she sees us?"

"We will deal with that later. For now, I just want to see if she's okay. I don't trust her husband. I have a feeling Pierre is up to something."

"Why do you think that?"

"Do you remember he threatened to go after Evian?"

"Yeah, I do, but I thought he was bluffing."

"I don't put anything past him. He seemed determined to find her."

"Pierre doesn't have the financial means to come to the United States to look for her."

"As a mother, I have to trust my gut instincts. I have a feeling our daughter is in trouble, and it is our responsibility to keep her safe."

Mr. Gant nodded in understanding. He retrieved the suitcases from the carousel and put them on a cart. Then they took the elevator to the car rental office on the third floor of the airport.

After climbing into the rental car, Mr. Gant waited for his wife to buckle up in the passenger seat, before saying, "Hon, is there a reason why you are worried about Evian's safety?"

Mrs. Gant sighed. "This whole thing about Evian not being honest with Alex is bothering me. For the life of me, I don't understand why she didn't tell him she was already married. "What if this whole thing blows up in her face?" she stressed. "Evian could possibly lose the most pleasant and generous man she has ever met. 'And for what?' Over foolishness."

"What can we do?"

"Convince Evian to do the right thing."

Mr. Gant understood his wife's internal conflict. He, too, had been questioning his daughter's irrational decision to remain secretive.

They drove to the hotel in Tampa to unpack their bags. Then they drove to Alex and Evian's condo, but no one was home.

"Maybe they went out to eat," Mrs. Gant explained.

"Or maybe they're out of town," her husband countered. "And if that's the case, we flew to the U.S. for nothing."

Swatting at the air, Mrs. Gant said, "Don't be silly. Evian would have told us if they were going out of town."

"Can we call her to be sure?"

Mrs. Gant smiled as she retrieved her cell phone from her purse to call her daughter.

During the drive to the adoption agency, Evian's cell phone rang. She grew nervous after her mother's cell number appeared on her caller ID. She knew if she did not answer their call, they would worry, needlessly. Putting on a cheery face, she answered the phone with joy in her voice. "Mom, how are you?"

Mrs. Gant was happy and relieved to hear her daughter's voice. "Evian, honey, you had us worried. Are you okay?"

"Yes, I'm fine. What makes you think something is wrong?"

"You didn't return our phone calls."

"Alex and I are out of town taking care of some personal business."

"Why didn't you tell us?"

"Because it's no big deal. I want to be here for Alex."

"What happened?" her mother asked with genuine concern.

"A woman from Alex's past told him he was the father of her child."

"Is he?"

"Yes," Evian muttered under her breath, "but not for long."

Mrs. Gant frowned. "What do you mean by that?"

"I'm just kidding." Evian pretended to laugh, but her mother became alarmed.

"Evian, where are you?"

"Baltimore, but we should be back in Tampa in a few days."

Mrs. Gant wanted to tell her daughter that she and her husband were in the United States. But she did not want to alarm Evian.

"Let us know when you return to Tampa. Okay, honey?"

"Sure thing, Mom. Tell Dad I said 'hello.' I love you both."

"We love you too."

Chapter 54
Missing in Action

At Broward General Hospital in Fort Lauderdale, Florida, a John Doe was held in the mental ward against his will. He was admitted to the hospital after a Florida State Road trooper found him on the off ramp of I-95, wandering aimlessly and narrowly escaping ongoing traffic. He was incoherent and hallucinating from a drug-induced high.

On day one, the patient had to be constrained to his bed after yelling and screaming, "Someone is trying to kill me!" He was heavily medicated, but it did not lessen his erratic behavior.

The next day the patient started banging his head on the wall. Flash images of Regine, Leslie, Raymond and Guy swirled around in his head. He could not make sense of what these images meant or who these people were. He started yelling something unintelligible. Again, he was given medication to calm his abrasive behavior.

Day three was slightly better. The patient knew where he was but could not understand why he was there. The psychiatrist told him he was admitted after they found a large amount of GHB in his system.

The patient frowned. "What is that?"

"It's a drug typically used to treat insomnia."

The patient sat in a chair across from the doctor's desk with furrowed brows. He could not understand what the doctor was telling him.

"Do you know your name?" the psychiatrist probed.

Tapping into his memory bank, the patient closed his eyes and struggled to remember his name. He grew frustrated because he could not answer this simple question.

"Do you remember anything?"

The patient tried concentrating. He was hoping something from his past and present would come to his consciousness. "I don't remember," he finally said.

The doctor nodded in sympathy. "I'm going to recommend that you stay in the hospital a little while longer."

Bouncing out of his chair, the patient screamed, "I need to get out of here!"

The doctor stood up and backed up. "Calm down, sir," he said with outstretched arms.

"I don't want to be here!"

"I know, but we're trying to help you."

"I want to go home!" the patient cried out, while foaming at the mouth. He did not know where he lived but knew it had to be better than staying in the hospital.

"Sir, if you don't calm down, we will be forced to constrain you."

Lunging at the doctor's throat, the patient yelled, "Get me out of here!"

In that instant, two hospital orderlies ran into the office, grabbed the patient, and held him down long enough for the psychiatrist to inject meds in his arm. Within seconds, the patient became lethargic.

Several hours later, the drugs wore off. This time, the patient's mind was clear. He even knew his real name, where he lived, and why he was in South Florida. The problem was no one believed him.

"My name is Lamar Greene," he told the psychiatrist with confidence. "I am a businessman."

"Mr. Greene, if that's what you want to call yourself, what type of business do you own?"

"I'm an investor, but I also co-own two restaurants."

"Yeah, okay." The psychiatrist decided to entertain Lamar by asking, "What type of food do you serve at your restaurants?"

"We specialize in gourmet food," Lamar said, proudly. "Each restaurant has a different name."

The psychiatrist stared at Lamar before turning serious. "If you want to get out of here, I need you to be honest with me."

"I am telling the truth. If you don't believe me, please contact my business partner. Her name is Regine Simmons."

"Okay, I'll go along with your little charade," the doctor said, after picking up his pad and pen on his desk. "What is her number?"

Lamar gave the psychiatrist Regine's home phone number because it was the first and only phone number that came to his mind.

After jotting down the number, the doctor picked up the phone on his desk and called Regine. The phone rang three times. He did not wait for the call to be routed to her voicemail before he returned the phone to its cradle. "Sorry, there was no answer."

Disappointed, Lamar asked out of curiosity, "What is today?"

"Friday."

"Regine's probably here in Florida."

The doctor looked at Lamar suspiciously, before stating, "It's obvious that you're still delusional. I'm going to up your meds, and...."

"I don't need any more meds!" Lamar shrieked. "I need to get the hell out of here!"

"Sir, you need to calm down."

Lamar started looking wild and crazy. He was tempted to take a swipe at the psychiatrist.

In fear of his safety, the doctor stood up and stepped back. "Listen John…."

"My name is Lamar Greene!" he shouted in vain. "How many times must I tell you this?!"

Quickly, the psychiatrist reached for the phone and dialed zero for the operator. "I need help!" he hollered into the receiver.

Within seconds, two orderlies barged in his office. They held Lamar down and tied his hands behind his back. Then they took him to an empty windowless room and tied him to the bed. The psychiatrist later entered the room and injected meds in his patient's arms. Instantly, Lamar became drowsy and fell into a deep sleep.

The psychiatrist returned to his office moments later. Cupping his chin, he sat at his desk and mentally rehashed his meeting with Lamar. He questioned whether his patient was telling the truth. Following his instincts, he redialed the number Lamar had given him earlier. He was surprised a young woman answered his call on the first ring.

"Hello, are you Regine Simmons?"

"This is she. How may I help you?"

"Hi, I'm a psychiatrist at Broward General Hospital in Fort Lauderdale. I have a patient who claims his name is Lamar Greene. Do you know him?"

"Yes, he's my business partner. Have you seen him? I'm worried sick about him."

The doctor realized Lamar was telling the truth. To be sure, he asked, "Can you describe him?"

"Yes, he's Caucasian, about five feet' nine inches tall, has a medium build, and his dark black hair has specks of gray. Is he okay? Can I speak with him?" Regine asked with a sense of urgency.

"Mr. Greene is fine, but he's not available."

"Thank God he's alive," Regine remarked, breathing a sigh of relief. "I'll be there as soon as I can."

"Okay, I'll let him know."

Regine disconnected the phone with a broad smile. As an afterthought, she called Detective Baily and told him Lamar was in the hospital.

"What happened to him?" the detective asked.

"I'm not sure. I just got off the phone with his psychiatrist at Broward General Hospital. What's going to happen next?"

"That depends on what Mr. Greene tells me. Right now, Raymond Brown is in our custody."

"He is?" Regine asked with raised brows.

"Before you called, we believed Mr. Brown had something to do with Lamar Greene's disappearance."

"Oh, wow," Regine said in surprise. "I didn't know that."

"Thanks for letting me know about Mr. Greene. I'm happy he's okay, for your sake." To make sure she fully understood his meaning, Detective Baily added, "Mrs. Simmons, everyone deserves to be happy."

"I'll be sure to remember that." Regine was ecstatic to know Lamar was very much alive. She walked into her son's room and found him playing with his toy truck. "Hi KC," she lovingly cooed.

KC turned to Regine and smiled. "Look at my truck, Momma."

"I see it," Regine beamed, before she knelt beside him on the floor. "Momma is getting ready to go out of town. Can I get a big kiss?"

KC kissed her on the cheek.

Smiling, Regine patted the top of her son's head. "I love you, KC."

"I love you too, Momma."

"Are you going to be good for the babysitter?"

"Yes Momma."

Regine gave her son another kiss before she stood up and left the room. Earlier, she had arranged for the nanny to take care of KC, until Guy returned home.

***

Lamar was tied to his bed for a couple of hours before his mental state returned to normal. Though, his memory was still fuzzy. He scanned the windowless room in the mental ward. Then he stared at the shackles tied around his hands and feet. He became edgy when the psychiatrist entered his room.

"Mr. Greene, how are you feeling?"

"Please get me out of here," Lamar pleaded, his voice cracked. "I don't deserve to be treated like an animal. I didn't do anything wrong."

"I know," the psychiatrist said, as he walked toward Lamar's bed.

"Why am I here?"

"You were admitted to the hospital several days ago. We found drugs in your system and your behavior was unpredictable. Do you know of anyone that might want to cause you harm?"

Raymond Brown was the first person that came to Lamar's mind, but he did not want to tell his psychiatrist. First, he needed to talk to Regine. He wanted to see if she had anything to do with Raymond's actions. "I need to call my business partner."

"I've already spoken with her. She should be here soon."

"Please untie me."

"Do you promise not to get violent with me or my staff?"

"You have my word."

"I'll call the nurse so she can get your things for you. I apologize for any misunderstanding."

"No apology necessary."

***

The night Lamar went missing, he was left on the side of the high-way in a drug-induced state. He had opened the car door and climbed out, wobbling and almost tumbling to the ground. Headlights from oncoming cars blinded him. At one point, he walked into the outer lane, and cars sharply moved to the right, to avoid hitting him. Then Lamar walked back to the side of the highway and began removing all of his clothes except his boxer shorts.

A state road trooper had spotted Lamar on I-95 walking several yards from his car. He climbed out of his car with his flashlight zoomed in on Lamar's face. "Sir," he said in a calm manner, "are you okay?"

Lamar yelled, "I'm going to die!"

"Sir, what is your name?"

"Leave me alone!"

Realizing Lamar was incoherent and might be under the influence, the state road trooper wrestled him to the ground and handcuffed him. Then he drove Lamar to Broward General Hospital for an evaluation. From there, he was admitted to the hospital against his will.

Coincidentally, Detective Baily spotted the abandoned rental car on the shoulder of the highway. He was unaware Lamar was taken to the hospital for psychiatric treatment several hours earlier.

Chapter 55

In Reverse

*W*hen Guy drove in Justina's driveway, he spotted her outside pacing back and forth. He was distressed by her distraught appearance. Her head was held low, and she was wiping away tears with the back of her hand. Guy ignored his ringing cell phone as he hurriedly climbed out of his car and ran toward her. "Don't cry," he said, pulling Justina in his arms. "Everything is going to be okay."

Justina wrapped her arms tightly around his neck. She was afraid to let go. "I don't…know what…to do," she cried out, as tears continued to flow down her face. "My life is falling apart."

"It's going to be okay. Let's go inside so we can talk."

Once inside her home, Justina guided Guy to the living room where she told him about her husband's predicament. She also told him Aaron had depleted most of their savings.

"I'm so sorry you're going through this," Guy sympathized.

Justina's voice was soft and weak, as she said, "I never had a reason to question Aaron about our finances until now. Before you came over, I browsed our bank statements for the past two years. Aaron withdrew large sums of money from the bank on a weekly basis. Now he's in jail for soliciting a prostitute."

Guy's brows shot up in surprise, before asking, "Do you think your husband used the money for that purpose?"

"I went through his cell phone records and found a 1-800 number to a *Call Girl* service."

"Did you call the number?"

"Yes, but I received a voicemail recording."

"What are you going to do?" he asked out of concern.

"I'm going to leave him. But I can't think about that right now. I need to get the rest of the money for Carmela's ransom. Can you lend it to me?"

"Yes." But Guy thought it was strange that two different kidnappers were after the ransom. His gut instincts told him to call his father-in-law, but he was afraid of the backlash.

Suddenly, Justina's home phone rang. She gazed at Guy for direction. "What should I do?" she asked in panic.

"Answer it."

Justina picked up the phone on the second ring. "Hello."

"It's me," Thorny stated.

"Did you find the kidnapper?" Justina asked after recognizing his voice.

"He's in our custody."

"What about the other kidnapper? The one who called and let me talk with my sister. He told me to wire the money for the ransom to Alabama."

Thorny knew Justina was referring to Smokey. "Did you send the money?"

"Not yet. I told him I didn't have all of it."

"I don't think you'll be hearing from him anytime soon."

"Why not?"

Thorny checked his watch, as he said, "Right about now, the other kidnapper should be in our custody." He did not have proof but knew *Kevin Graham* was very resourceful.

Justina frowned. "I don't understand."

"Your sister was in on this," Thorny bluntly replied.

"Are you saying Carmela was never kidnapped?"

"Exactly."

Justina briefly closed her eyes and forced herself to hold back tears. Her voice cracked, when she asked, "Why...did she...do it?"

Thorny did not think it was his place to tell her the truth, so he remained quiet.

"When can I see my sister?" Justina probed.

"Soon enough."

"Thank you for everything," she solemnly replied, before disconnecting the call.

"Who was that on the phone?" Guy asked.

"One of the men you sent to help me find my sister."

"What did he say?"

"He told me they found the kidnappers."

"Including the one that has your sister?"

Justina nodded. Then she became bitter as reality set in. "Carmela was never kidnapped!" she spat in anger.

Guy frowned. "Come again?"

"Carmela was in on the kidnapping scheme to extort money from me and my husband. How could she do this to me?" Justina asked, as tears welled up in her eyes.

Understanding her anger, Guy stood in front of Justina and cupped the side of her face. Then he forced a thin smile. "Look on the bright side of things. Carmela is alive and well."

Justina rested her head on Guy's chest. "I suppose I should be relieved. Hopefully, my parents will never find out about this."

"Try not to worry." Guy brushed her hair to soothe her broken heart.

Justina tilted her head upward and kissed Guy on the lips. The moment felt right. She wanted him, and hoped he felt the same way.

Guy pulled out of her embrace. "This isn't right. I mean…you know I'm married."

"I know, but it doesn't change how I feel about you. I can't pretend anymore. I love you."

"I shouldn't be here. I gotta go."

"Where are you going?" she asked with panic in her voice.

"I'm going to Miami to support my wife, for the grand opening of her new restaurant. Then I'm going to sit down with her to discuss our plans for the future."

"What about me?"

Guy glanced down. Deep in his heart, he knew he still had feelings for Justina. In fact, he loved her. He looked into her eyes, and kissed her passionately on the lips, then took a step back. "I need time to talk to Regine. She is the mother of our child."

"I understand. I'll respect whatever you decide, but I cannot change the way I feel about you. I love you, and nothing or no one can change that."

"We will talk when I return."

Guy kissed her on the forehead, then rushed out of her home and climbed in his car. Before starting the ignition, he reached for his cell phone in the console and noticed two missed calls from his brother. He immediately called his Alex.

"Hello." Alex answered the phone with sadness in his voice.

"This is Guy. What's going on?"

Alex sobbed, as he said, "My baby…is gone."

"Gone? What are you talking about?"

"Rhaunda's mother, Elizabeth Coleman, took my baby."

"Oh God!" Guy frantically replied. "When? Why?"

Between sobs, Alex said, "I think she did it to get back at me."

"I don't understand."

"I didn't tell you this before, but Mrs. Coleman called me several months ago. I think she took my baby to get back at me for cheating on her daughter. She believes I'm the reason Rhaunda is in a mental institution."

Guy gasped from shock. "Are the police involved?" he asked, after regaining his composure.

"Yes, they issued a nationwide Amber alert."

Guy checked his watch, after figuring he would go to Baltimore on his private jet. "Be strong Alex. I'm going to see what I can do on my end. I should be there in a couple of hours."

"That's not necessary. Mom is on her way here."

"I'm on my way," Guy persisted.

After disconnecting the call, Guy called Big Mike on his cell phone, and told him about Alex's dilemma. He asked his friend to put out a million dollar reward for whoever finds Alexander Simmons.

"I need a picture of the baby," Big Mike said.

Guy remembered he had a picture of Alexander in his cell phone. Briefly, he held the phone away from his ear, searched through the photos on his cell phone, and forwarded the baby's picture to his friend. Then he returned the phone to his ear. "I just sent the picture to your cell phone. Make sure the reward is posted worldwide."

"I'm on it."

Guy peeled out of Justina's driveway and sped onto the highway. Too many things were on his mind. He was perplexed about Justina and her ordeal; he was worried about how Regine would react when he fulfilled her wish for a divorce; and he was in a frenzy after learning his brother's baby was abducted from the hospital.

As he turned onto the highway, he was distracted and did not see the car in the left lane. His car skidded into the side of the other car before it careened across the highway and flipped upside down. The air bags stopped his head from crashing through the front window pane. But the blow from the air bags knocked him out cold. He remained unconscious long after the ambulance arrived.

Chapter 56
Clueless

*T*he magazine owner had one of his staff to check Pierre out of Trump Towers in New York. Then he arranged to have Pierre flown to Maryland on a private jet. Pierre was subsequently taken to the Marriott hotel near the Baltimore Inner Harbor, and was told to wait in the room for a phone call.

Pierre did not know what prompted the sudden change in his location. He grew antsy sitting in his hotel room. He had a feeling the people he was dealing with were withholding information from him, but did not know why. At his wits end, he picked up the phone on the nightstand and made an important phone call. It took several tries before his call was forwarded to the right person.

"Mr. Michel," the magazine owner said, as he reclined in his leather office chair. "What can I do for you?"

"I need to know what's going on. First I was in New York, now I'm in Maryland."

"Mr. Michel. We need for you to be patient."

"When am I going to be able to see my wife?"

"I told you, when the time is right, you will see her."

"Why do I have to wait for a particular time? If you know where she is, why can't I see her now?" Pierre was angry. His tone lacked the usual coolness.

Smiling inwardly, Mr. Hodges was unmoved by Pierre's outburst. "Mr. Michel, please be patient. We've been in this business for the past two decades. We know exactly what we're doing."

"Why do I get the strange feeling you're pulling my leg?"

"Do you think we would go through the trouble of getting you a passport and a temporary *visa* to come to the United States if we were pulling your leg?"

"I suppose you're right," Pierre concluded, feeling somewhat grateful. "Can you give me an idea of how long I have to wait?"

The owner simply said, "It'll be soon."

Unbeknownst to Pierre, Mr. Hodges was already informed that Evian was spotted at Johns Hopkins Hospital in Baltimore, Maryland. When the time was right, he had planned on surprising Evian with an unexpected visit from her husband.

After Pierre disconnected the call, he grew more and more frustrated by the second. He felt hopeless, sitting around in the hotel room doing nothing. He grabbed the remote control, sat on the edge of the bed, and turned on the television.

Across the TV screen was a banner that read: *Amber alert for Alexander Simmons.* Then side-by-side pictures of the missing baby and Elizabeth Coleman appeared on the screen with a 1-800 number for any leads to their whereabouts. Shortly afterward, video footage of Alecia and Alex were shown. A woman in the background tried to shield her face with her hand, while running away from the camera crew.

Blinking, Pierre was not sure if his eyes were playing tricks on him. That was, until the news reporter confirmed the woman was Evian Gant. The reporter questioned why she was at the hospital, and wondered if she had any connection to baby Alexander or his parents.

Running to the phone, Pierre punched in the phone number to the magazine company. "I just saw her," he rushed to say, as soon as Mr. Hodges was on the line.

"Saw who?"

"My wife, Evian Gant."

Mr. Hodges sat on the edge of his chair, and asked, "Where did you see her?"

"She's here in Baltimore, at Johns Hopkins Hospital. The news reporter questioned Evian's connection to a missing baby."

Mr. Hodges ears perked up upon hearing the news of the baby. "Mr. Michel," he finally said, "I'm going to have my car service pick you up and take you to the hospital. Be ready."

Pierre disconnected the call with a sense of relief. After all this time, he would have the opportunity to see his wife. He smiled at the thought of repairing his marriage.

Chapter 57
Snatch and Grab

*K*evin recruited a police officer as his informant to help him find Donald Newvall *aka* Smokey. The officer discovered Smokey had recently registered a black town car in his name. So he put out an *all-points bulletin and discovered* Smokey's car was spotted at a restaurant in Tarpon Springs, Florida.

The officer relayed his findings, and told Kevin, "Once Donald Newvall cross the Florida State Line, it might take longer to get more up-to-date information."

"What does that mean?" Kevin asked with raised brows.

"It means we would have to get approval for a nationwide search."

Kevin disconnected the call and pondered the situation. He acknowledged he was going to need help, so he called one of his associates for a favor. His directive was short and to the point: *Go to the restaurant and transport Smokey and Carmela back to Tampa, by any means necessary.*

Within thirty-minutes, his associates spotted Smokey and Carmela sitting at a mom and pop restaurant in Tarpon Springs. They were waiting for Justina to come up with the money for the ransom.

Sitting across from Carmela, Smokey was relaxing in his chair. He felt confident his ploy to divert Swag's plans and get ahold of the ransom would work. He leaned toward Carmela with a big grin. "You're pretty. You know that?"

Carmela beamed. Suddenly, she felt warm and bubbly all over. She shyly said, "You're not bad looking yourself."

Smokey blushed, before asking, "What are you going to do with your share of the money?" Earlier, they had decided to split the ransom fifty/fifty.

Carmela shrugged. "I'm not sure. I figure *we* might travel the country."

"We?" Smokey asked in surprise.

"Uh…yeah…I thought maybe you and I could…." Carmela stopped talking in mid-sentence. She knew what she wanted to say, but acknowledged she was being presumptuous.

"Do you want me to come with you?" Smokey asked, unsure if this was what she meant. He reached across the table and held her hand. "We're in this together."

Curiously, she asked, "Do you have a girlfriend?"

"I have a couple of lady friends I kick it with from time to time. But it's nothing serious."

"Like the way Swag kicked it with me," Carmela sassed, while poking out her bottom lip.

"Nah...nothing like that. When I see you, I see a strong young lady who's willing to do anything to help her man. Swag is a lucky man to have you by his side."

"You mean *was*," Carmela said with emphasis on the "s".

"You're right." Smokey chuckled.

Oblivious of their surroundings, neither knew they were being watched by Kevin's associates. The men approached their table and glared at them.

Startled, Smokey and Carmela looked at each other before they looked at the men with bewildered expressions.

"What do you want?" Smokey asked one of the men.

The taller of the two men said, "We were sent here to transport you to Tampa."

"Who sent you?" Smokey asked, his nervousness on full display.

"Don't worry about all that. Let's go!" the other man barked.

"I'm not going anywhere with you!" Carmela snapped.

One of the men grabbed her arm and dragged her out of her chair. She tried resisting, but she was no match for the broad-shouldered man.

"Get your hands off of me!" she screamed animatedly, causing a scene. The patrons and employees pretended not to witness the raucous.

"You don't have to handle her like that," Smokey said in Carmela's defense.

"Tell her to calm down, and act like a lady," the man who accosted Carmela warned. "Otherwise, I will force her to shut up."

Carmela and Smokey's eyes connected. They knew the man's threat was not to be taken lightly. Both agreed to go with the men, and not put up a fight.

They were driven to the Cameroon hotel in Tampa as instructed. When Kevin's associates pulled into the parking space, he drove up beside them. Then he watched Smokey and Carmela get yanked out of the backseat of the town car.

"Follow me," Kevin said to his associates and captives. He led them to Dan's hotel room.

When he knocked, Thorny opened the door and greeted him with a handshake. Kevin entered the room and eyed Swag and Dan, who were still tied up. "We got more company," he told Thorny. He stepped aside as Smokey and Carmela were shoved to the forefront.

After Smokey was tied to a chair, Kevin paced the floor with a smirk on his face. "Well...well...well. Look at what we have here. What I want to know is why?"

Smokey said, "This was not my idea." He turned in Swag's direction, and said, "This was his plan."

"Don't put this *shit* on me," Swag exclaimed, before he turned to Carmela. "It was her idea!"

"Oh hell no!" Carmela yelled, as she turned in Dan's direction. "Dan, this was your idea, and you know it."

Caught off guard, Dan was about to lie but the look in Kevin's eyes stifled his tongue. "It was my idea," he slowly confessed.

Thorny had already provided the facts about Dan, but Kevin wanted details. So he asked, "Why did you do it?"

Dan paused and balled up his mouth, before mumbling under his breath, "I used to work with Justina at her law firm in Atlanta."

"You were her partner?"

"Yes," Dan answered. "She's the reason I went to jail. But I escaped."

Everyone except Thorny was astonished by this revelation.

Kevin asked, "How?"

"The guy I shared a cell with hung himself. I took on his identity."

"How did you get away with that?" Kevin probed. "What about fingerprints?"

"It was easy. Security was lax. My cellmate was scheduled for release the same day he hung himself. I took his identity bracelet and walked out of jail."

"Damn," Kevin said in amazement, shaking his head in disbelief. "What is your real name?"

"Roger Salvador." He hesitated, before asking, "What are you going to do with me?"

Kevin cupped his chin while thinking Roger might prove to be a valuable asset in the future. "Are you in contact with your family?"

"I don't want my family to know I escaped from jail."

"Why not?"

"They would try to help me. I don't want them to get in trouble for harboring a fugitive."

"You're a smart man," Kevin stated with a look of satisfaction. "Are you interested in working for me?"

"Yes," Roger readily agreed, nodding his head with vigor. "I would love to work for you."

"Good." Then Kevin turned his attention to Swag. "What's your part in all this?"

"I'm with her," Swag said, pointing to Carmela.

"No you're not," Carmela flippantly replied. She huddled close to Smokey, and said, "I'm with him."

"She's not with him," Swag insisted. "She's with me."

"Not for long." Kevin glanced at his watch, before adding, "There's still time for a last kiss good-bye."

"What...do you...mean by that?" Swag choked out.

"It means you messed with the wrong girl."

"Will...you...let me go?" Smokey said in a shaky voice. "I didn't...do anything."

"You just made matters worse," Kevin replied with disgust. He detested men who exploited women for a living. He turned to his henchmen, and ordered, "Take them out of here and leave no trace of their existence."

Everyone in the room knew Kevin's order was code for *kill*. Swag and Smokey started shaking in their pants.

Carmela asked Kevin, "What are you going to do with me?"

"We're going to take you to your sister's home. I'm sure she's worried about you, even though it's obvious you don't give a damn about her." Then he turned to Roger, and said, "Get up. You're going with me."

***

Shortly after Guy left Justina's home, the phone rang. It was her mother according to the Caller ID. She knew if she did not answer the call, her parents would worry and call nonstop until they were able to reach her. Nervously, she answered the phone on the third ring. "Hi Mom."

"Hi Justina. Have you spoken with Carmela yet, about coming back home?"

"Yes," she slowly answered. "But it's going to take some time for me to convince her."

"I understand. Can we talk to her?"

"She's not here at the moment, but I'll tell her to call you."

"Where did she go?" her father asked.

Stammering, Justina did not know her father was on the call. "Uh…hi Dad. How are you feeling?"

"I'm fine. How's Carmela?"

"She's fine."

"Don't lie to me."

Justina stalled. She had a hard time telling her parents the truth. No matter how hard she tried, she could not think of a clever lie.

"What is it, honey?" her mother asked, after Justina did not respond.

"I'm on my way over. I need to talk to you and dad in person."

Justina disconnected the call in a hurry, to prevent her parents from asking further questions. Quickly, she got dressed, grabbed her car keys and purse, and sprinted out the front door.

On the way to her parents' home, she saw a terrible accident on the main highway. She scanned the scene and spotted a jumbled car that looked like Guy's. She quickly retrieved her cell phone from her purse to call him, but her call went to his voicemail. Instinctively, she pulled over to the side of the road and ran toward the accident.

The closer she got to the scene, the faster her heart beat from fear. She sped up as she got close enough to make out the image of the man that was extracted from the car. "Oh God! That's Guy!" she screamed, hysterically.

The police officer blocked her from getting closer.

"Let me through!" Justina urged, as she began to cry.

"Do you know this man?" the officer asked.

"But I'm his wife!"

That little white lie was enough to get Justina through the barricade. She ran toward Guy, who was being lifted into the ambulance. Then she climbed in the ambulance and went to the hospital with him. Justina broke down crying when she perused Guy's banged-up face and bruised body.

While in the ambulance, Guy's eyes were shut the entire time. Though, flash images of his wife occupied his mind. He imagined smelling her hair, kissing her plump lips, and making love to her. He needed her and hoped she felt the same way.

He did not know Justina was in the ambulance with him. She had been crying and praying for his quick recovery.

"Is…he going…to be okay?" she asked the paramedic. Her voice was weak and shaky from weeping.

"Your husband is unconscious but breathing on his own."

Upon arriving at the hospital, Justina was told to remain in the waiting room to allow the emergency room doctors and nurses to examine the extent of Guy's injuries. Her cell phone rang as soon as she sat in one of the vacant chairs in the waiting room. She hurriedly retrieved her phone from her purse and answered the call on the second ring. "Hello."

Without a formal greeting, Kevin Graham said, "We have your sister. We'll be at your house in an hour." He disconnected the call without waiting for her response.

Justina was torn over whether she should leave. But the nurse at the reception desk assured her that Guy was in good care. She hesitated before she grabbed her purse and caught a cab to her car, which was left at the scene of the accident.

Chapter 58
Nitty Gritty

*J*oyce's boyfriend, Brian, rang her doorbell to take her out on a date. He waited several seconds but did not get a response. He was getting ready to knock on the front door but hesitated after spotting the broken window panel. Instinctively, he knew something was wrong. He used caution as he turned the door knob and opened the door.

"Joyce!" he called out, while peering inside. "Are you here?"

When she did not respond, he slowly walked into her condo and closed the door behind him. He picked up a huge bronze vase on the end table and held it up in the air like a baseball bat. He was ready to do bodily harm, if necessary.

Ascending the stairs, Brian spotted Joyce on the floor in the middle of the hallway. Her body was scrunched over and her eyes were closed. He threw the vase down and knelt down beside her. He bent over and whispered in her ear, "Joyce, can you hear me?"

He became alarmed when she did not respond. Then he noticed blood seeping from the back of her head. His heart leapt as he rushed to the phone in her bedroom and dialed 911.

When the police and ambulance showed up, Joyce was taken to the hospital where the surgeon performed brain surgery. She had suffered a concussion and a blood vein had ruptured in the back of her head. The surgery was a success.

Twenty-four hours later, Joyce's eyes fluttered open. Brian grabbed her hand, and spoke to her in a soft and soothing voice. "Joyce, I'm here for you. Do you know who I am?"

After she nodded, he asked, "Do you remember what happened?"

Joyce briefly closed her eyes and thought back to the day she and Evian met with the wedding coordinator. Suddenly, tears poured down her face after she recollected that it was Evian, who mercilessly pummeled her in the head with a rock.

Brian nervously asked, "What's wrong?"

Opening her mouth to respond, Joyce found it difficult to speak. She placed her hand on her neck to signal her throat was dry. In response, Brian poured her a cup of water.

Joyce sipped the water through a straw, before admitting in a hoarse voice, "It was Evian. She tried to kill me."

"Do you feel up to talking to the police? They're standing right outside your room."

"Yes," she slowly answered.

"I'll be back."

The officers entered her room with a pen and writing pad. During the interview, Joyce stated that Evian attempted to kill her. She also told them about Evian's plan to steal baby Alexander.

After the officers left Joyce's room, they contacted the Baltimore City police department to relay their findings. One of the officers stationed at Johns Hopkins hospital told Alex and Alecia about Evian's involvement.

Frantically, Alex asked the officer, "Why would she do this?!"

"We don't know. Our goal is to find her before it's too late."

Sobbing, Alecia asked, "What is she going to do with my baby?"

"We were told Ms. Gant planned on selling the baby to an adoption agency."

"She sold my baby?!" Alecia cried out in horror. "How could she get away with this?"

When Alex tried to reach out to comfort Alecia, she backed away from him with a scowl on her face. "Get away from me!" she shouted. "You let that maniac take my baby!"

"I didn't...know she...would do this. You have to believe me." He turned to the officer, and asked, "What can I do?"

"Do you know where we might find Ms. Gant?"

"Earlier, I suggested she go to the hotel."

"Which hotel?"

"We have a room at the Hilton, near the harbor."

"I'll send someone over to the hotel to see if she's there. If she's not, we're going to ask you to help us lure Ms. Gant back to the hospital."

Perplexed, Alex asked, "How would I do that?"

"Make her believe you don't know about her involvement, especially since the focus has been on Elizabeth Coleman."

Alex nodded in understanding.

***

After she was admitted in the hospital, a man Joyce had known her entire life snuck in her room looking distraught. He eyed the bandages wrapped around her head as he moved closer to her bedside.

Like the rest of his children, Joyce had inherited his chiseled nose, shapely lips and deep dimples. His daughters had even inherited their father's serious and goal-oriented disposition.

"Hi baby," he said to his youngest daughter, "how are you feeling?"

She slowly opened her eyes. Then tears began to pour down her face. Unlike her stepfather, she had not seen her biological father in years but had a feeling he had been watching over her.

In a soft and loving tone, Kevin Graham said, "I'm sorry I wasn't there for you when you needed me most. But I swear on my life, your girlfriend won't get away with this."

Kevin knew Evian Gant assaulted his daughter. He had already devised a plan to kill her. He was furious after learning one of his henchmen did not keep a closer eye on Joyce and her acquaintances. In response, Kevin beat the crap out of him with his pistol, causing the man to black out. Then he walked away as the man gasped for his last breath.

Painstakingly, Joyce peered into her father's eyes. "You killed him, didn't you?"

"I don't know what you're talking about."

"My ex-boyfriend," Joyce explained. "The one I help Evian castrate." Her voice trailed off. She was ashamed to admit that she took part in a heinous act. "Did you kill him?" She seemingly held her breath and hoped for the truth.

Kevin did not answer right away, but his blank stare spoke volumes. He distinctly remembered setting the young man on fire. He explained, "I'm supposed to protect you."

"But not like this. All I ever wanted was for you to be a part of my life."

Kevin held her hand. "I don't know what I would do if anything ever happened to you and your sisters.

Joyce's brow shot up in surprise. "Sisters? I have sisters?"

Now that the cat was out of the bag, Kevin figured he had to come clean. He smiled after remembering Grandmother Bessie had pleaded with him to share this secret earlier.

"You have three sisters," he admitted. "Two live in New York, and one lives in Clearwater. Her name is Regine Simmons."

"Regine? Why does that name sound familiar?"

"She owns several restaurants in Florida."

Joyce's eyes widened after recalling she and Evian had frequented Regine's restaurant in Tampa. It was the same day her friend attacked her.

"I think I know her, not personally. But I heard so many good things about her. I can't believe she's my sister. Why didn't you tell me?"

"I was trying to protect you."

Despite her father's criminal history, she loved him immensely. She also knew his past had a lot to do with why she never knew about her sisters.

"When can I meet my sisters?" she asked, her eagerness showed.

"Soon." Kevin smiled. He was certain of their union.

Chapter 59
XOXO

*A*fter Regine's plane landed at the Fort Lauderdale International airport, she grabbed her bags and hailed a cab to Broward General Hospital. Her heart was so heavy with worry and anticipation, the ten minute drive felt like an hour. Before the cab came to a complete stop, she paid the fare, then climbed out the car and rushed up the path to the hospital entrance.

She approached the receptionist, and said, "I'm here to see Lamar Greene."

The receptionist searched her computer before responding to Regine. "Mr. Greene is in the process of being discharged from the hospital."

"Where can I find him?"

"If you wait here, he should be downstairs any moment."

On pins and needles, Regine sat in the lobby and waited for Lamar. She did not have to wait long.

Lamar walked out of the elevator and smiled upon seeing his business partner. "Hello Regine. It's good to see you," he said, as he stood in front of her with a broad smile.

Regine jumped out of her chair and embraced him. "Lamar! I'm happy to see you. Why didn't you call and tell me you were in the hospital? I would have been here sooner."

"It's a long story."

Regine eyed Lamar's empty hands. "Where are your things?"

"A detective from the Hollywood Police department came to visit me. He gave me my wallet and cell phone, but told me my rental car was impounded for inspection. I guess the rest of my things are at the hotel. Have you checked in your room yet?"

"No, I came straight here from the airport."

"Let's swing by the hotel," Lamar suggested, as he grabbed her hand and walked out of the hospital. "We need to freshen up before we go to the restaurant."

"Are you sure you feel up to it?" Regine asked with deep concern.

"I'm sure. The grand opening is in a few days. Did Guy come with you?"

"No."

"Good."

Lamar hailed a cab to take them to the Hilton hotel. During the drive, he told her, "Detective Baily told me he arrested Raymond Brown because he was deemed a suspect in my disappearance." Lamar paused, before continuing, "He also asked me about a contract dissolving our business relationship."

"I know," Regine admitted, lowering her eyes in shame. "Detective Baily asked me and Guy about it a couple of days ago."

"So you didn't have anything to do with Raymond giving me the contract to sign?"

"Of course not. I was just as shocked as you. Did you say anything to the detective about Raymond or the contract?"

"No, I wanted to speak with Raymond first, and ask him why he went through such extremes to try and rid me from your life."

Regine asked herself the same thing. She had her own suspicions but kept her thoughts to herself.

Casting his eyes downward, Lamar muttered, "I was supposed to look out for you."

"What are you talking about? You are not responsible for me."

"But your father...."

"My father?" Regine interrupted with raised brows. "What does he have to do with this?"

"He was concerned about your safety. After you were kidnapped a year ago, he asked me to look after you."

"Wow," Regine whispered aloud.

"Promise you won't tell your father I told you about our arrangement."

Regine smiled to put Lamar at ease. "I promise, but looking after me is not your responsibility."

At the hotel, Regine checked into her room while Lamar attempted to retrieve his belongings from the hotel manager. The manager told him Detective Baily had confiscated his briefcase and other items. He gave Lamar another room at the hotel and offered to replace most of his personal items.

Lamar took the manager up on his offer, and arranged to have the concierge order a couple of suits and dresser shirts from the Brooks Brother store. He also asked the concierge to buy hygiene products, and have them delivered to his room.

Next, Lamar stopped by his hotel room to drop off his things. Then he walked across the hall to Regine's room and knocked on the door.

She opened her room door with a broad smile. "Hi there. What can I do for you?"

"Do you mind if I come inside?"

After Regine stepped aside to allow Lamar passage, he turned to her, and said, "I'll be returning to Tampa immediately after the grand opening."

"Why so soon?"

"I gave Leslie the deed to my condo. I need to go home and pack my things." He paused, before adding, "There's something you should know about me."

"You're not going to tell me you're a murderer, are you?" She remembered her father's obscure warnings about Lamar.

Lamar snickered. "No, but it is serious. Please sit down."

Regine sat on the edge of the bed, and listened attentively while Lamar admitted, "Before I met you, I was the CEO of DuPont Inc."

"Isn't that the biggest paper supply company in the world?"

"Yes, it's my family's business. My real name is Charlton DuPont."

Regine could not believe her ears. She thought if what he was saying is true, she was in the company of a billionaire.

Lamar explained, "I gave it all up for you. I have always been *in love* with you, ever since the day we first met."

Regine stared at Lamar without blinking. She could not believe her ears. "What...about Leslie?"

"I never loved her. She pushed herself in my life and I let her."

Swallowing hard, Regine was at a loss for words.

"I also thought your husband would have issues with you doing business with a single man. But your husband saw right through me. He knows how I feel about you."

Regine stood up and paced the room. Then she turned to Lamar, and uttered aloud, "All this time, I never knew."

Lamar strutted toward her with dreamy eyes. "I love you," he confessed. "I want to share my future with you."

Standing still, Regine felt her knees buckle. Her feelings for Lamar were mutual but she had reservations. She slowly shook her head. "I can't do this."

"I know. You're married. Are you *in love* with him?"

Regine opened her mouth to respond but nothing came out but hot air. The answer was *no*. Her prince was standing before her, and she desperately wanted and needed him.

Lamar embraced Regine, then whispered in her ear, "I can achieve anything as long as you're in my life. I want you to be my wife."

Regine was afraid. Her fears were ignited as soon as Lamar picked her off her feet and guided her to the king size bed.

"What...are...you doing?" she staggered.

"Something I wanted to do since I first laid eyes on you."

Lamar ravished her lips with wet kisses. Then he chuckled after nuzzling her nose with his.

Confused, she asked, "What's so funny?"

"I have always dreamed of this moment."

Without further prompting, Lamar smothered Regine's lips and neck with small pecks. Then he caressed her breasts.

Hot and bothered, Regine had dreamt of this moment. She surrendered to his desire, and allowed Lamar to undress her.

He cracked a smile before kissing her on the lips. Receptively, Regine hungrily kissed him back. Their yearning and desire for one another grew by the second. Each was trying to show how much they needed to be loved and feel loved.

After disrobing her, Lamar touched and kissed her skin as if he was touching priceless jewels. Then he devoured her breasts as if it was his last meal. The room was filled with passion as he picked her off her feet and carried her to the king size bed.

Regine laid across the bed while Lamar planted kisses on the inside of her thighs. The closer he moved toward her *kitty*, the more she creamed with delight. She arched her back and helped him to the goal line.

After licking on Regine's cherry jubilee, Lamar slowly climbed on top of her. As soon as he inserted his tool, the fireworks began. His rapid thrusts caused Regine to emit screams and moans of pleasure. The room was hot, and their hearts were beating as one.

Over the next hour, they were in rhythm, grinding and making love to each other. Both had breathlessly surrendered to each other's touch.

"Oh Lamar!" Regine called out before creaming with delight.

Sweat dripping down his face, Lamar climaxed before crashing on top of Regine. Fully satisfied, he rolled on the side of her to look into her eyes. He caught her staring at the ceiling. "What are you thinking about?"

"KC," she slowly mouthed, before turning to face Lamar.

"What about him?"

"I'm not sure how he's going to handle his parents not being together anymore."

Lamar grinned. "KC is very young. He will adjust. You know I'm going to love him like he's my very own."

"Do you really mean that?"

"Of course I do." Lamar kissed Regine on the forehead. "Sweetie, I think we need to get up and get ready to go to the restaurant." He stood up and put on his pants and shirt. "I'm going to my room to freshen up. I'll pick you up in thirty minutes. Will you be ready?"

"Yes. I just need to take a quick shower."

After Lamar left her room, Regine could not contain her excitement as she retrieved her cell phone from her purse, to make an important phone call. "Hello, Grandma, it's me!" she excitedly announced, after hearing her grandmother's voice.

"Hi, *Baby*."

"I have wonderful news!" Regine rushed to say with a broad grin.

"What is it?" Bessie glanced at her husband with a grim expression.

"I found Lamar!"

"You did?" Bessie eyes grew wide.

"Yes. Lamar is here in Miami with me."

"Does he remember anything?" Bessie asked out of concern for her husband.

"All he knows for sure is that Raymond Brown was involved."

"Has Raymond been arrested?"

"Yes he has." Regine glanced over at the clock on the end table. "Grandma, I gotta get dressed to go the restaurant. I'll chat with you later."

"Okay. I love you."

"I love you too."

Bessie took a deep breath and exhaled after disconnecting the call.

"What did she say about Raymond?" her husband asked, curious to know what information Regine divulged.

"He's in jail."

"Damn," the deacon muttered under his breath.

"What's the matter?"

Eyes closed, the deacon placed his elbows on the dining table and folded his hands. He was in deep thought.

Bessie put her hands on her hips and shook her head. She assumed her husband had something to do with Lamar's brief disappearance, but knew he would not tell her anything. She strolled over to the dining table, and gingerly rested her hand on her husband's shoulder. At this point, she decided to stand by her man, through thick and thin.

Chapter 60
Train Wreck

Evian had just received $150,000 in cash from the adoption agency in exchange for baby Alexander. The money was burning a hole in her purse. She planned on giving half of the money to Elizabeth to help her leave the country. With the other half, she looked forward to going on a huge shopping spree for herself.

She drove onto the beltway when her cell phone rang. After fumbling through her purse for her cell phone, she noted her fiancé's name displayed across the screen.

"Uh...hi Alex." Evian did not let on that she was still angry with him for dismissing her earlier.

"Where are you?"

"I'm at the hotel."

Wincing, Alex knew she was lying but remained neutral. He was fully aware the Baltimore City police officers had the Hilton hotel near the harbor staked out, and had already confirmed that Evian was nowhere in sight. "Can you return to the hospital?" he asked her, in a somber tone.

Evian frowned. "I thought you didn't want me there."

Alex wanted to give her a piece of his mind but remembered his baby's life was at stake. "I'm sorry for the way I treated you earlier," he forced himself to say. "I was wrong. I need your support." After Evian remained quiet, he added, "I need my *future wife* by my side, to help me through this."

Evian's fist went to her chest. She was moved by Alex's heartfelt words. "I'll be there as soon as I can."

Alex disconnected the call and turned to the police officer. "I believe she'll be here soon."

But Evian had other plans. She pulled into a parking space in front of the motel in Woodlawn, Maryland, and sprinted to Elizabeth's room. She banged on the door with a sense of urgency.

"Open the door!" she hollered out.

Elizabeth swung the door open, and frowned. "What took you so long?"

"Are you ready?" Evian asked, after she stepped into the motel room.

251

"What kind of stupid question is that?"

"Grab your things and let's go!"

Evian ignored Elizabeth's snippy temper. She had too much on her mind. She was in a rush to get back to the hospital. When they climbed in the car and buckled up, she told Elizabeth, "I'm going to drop you off at the Greyhound bus station."

"Why?"

"I figure that'll be a safer route for you. It's likely that your face is all over the news by now."

Elizabeth balled up her lips in anger, before spouting, "If it weren't for you, I wouldn't be in this mess!"

"You can't blame me for this," Evian calmly replied. "You should have hid your face."

"In a nursing uniform?" Elizabeth questioned with a hint of sarcasm. "Why didn't you tell me about the cameras?"

Blowing out hot air, Evian was growing tired of bickering with Elizabeth. She cut her eyes at her ally, and said with an attitude, "I didn't put a gun to your head to make you to steal the baby."

"But you told me I wouldn't go to jail."

"And you're not going to jail. That's why you're leaving the country."

Elizabeth started crying. She instantly regretted her decision to get involved with Evian.

While guiding the steering wheel with her free hand, Evian dug in her purse, retrieved half of the money she received from the adoption agency, and handed it to Elizabeth. "This should be enough to get you by."

Elizabeth stopped sobbing long enough to ask, "What good is money if I can't see my family?"

"You can't see them anyway. Both your husband and daughter are locked up, remember?"

Tears flowing, Elizabeth chopped up her words in anger, before stating, "But at least...I was...able to...visit them in-person!"

"Now you can send them money, and take care of them from afar."

Drying her eyes, Elizabeth asked, "What about you?"

Evian smiled while imagining her upcoming nuptials with Alex. "I'm going back to the hospital to support my fiancé."

"Fiancé?"

"I plan on marrying Alex. Then I'm going to give him his first child."

Elizabeth started boiling over from rage. "You selfish no-good bitch!" she spat in anger. "You had me do *all this* for you! It was never about me!"

"You did get something out of this!" Evian exclaimed. "You wanted vengeance for the way Alecia and Alex wronged your family, you got it."

"But...."

"But nothing!" Evian sharply countered. "You've been on my *ass* ever since we left the motel. I'm trying to get you out of this jam, and now you're being ungrateful. I could have easily turned you in to the police. Did you think about that?!"

Feeling deflated, Elizabeth rested her head against the passenger window and whimpered. She resented the way her new friend turned on her.

Evian dropped Elizabeth off at the Greyhound bus station in downtown Baltimore, then headed back to Johns Hopkins to be with Alex. She felt confident her plans had been carried out, successfully. She parked the rental car in a parking garage near the Baltimore harbor. Then she caught a cab to the hospital, which was only a couple of blocks away. She refreshed her makeup before climbing out of the cab.

Evian entered the hospital and noticed several police officers in the lobby area. She assumed they were there because baby Alexander was missing.

When the officers began moving toward her, she panicked and started backing up. "What's...going on?" she asked in a shaky voice.

"Please do not cause a scene," the officer closest to her said. "We need you to come with us."

Evian screamed, "I'm not going anywhere with you!" Looking beyond the officers, she was relieved when she saw her fiancé walking toward her. "Alex!" she shouted out in panic. "I'm so glad you're here. Please tell these officers they're making a big mistake."

One of the officers stopped Alex from getting close to Evian, so he yelled over the officer's shoulder, "Why did you take my baby?!"

"I didn't do anything!" Evian cried out. "I would never harm Alexander." She motioned toward Alex, but the officer pulled her back and handcuffed her.

"Don't do this!" she wailed, struggling to pull her wrists out of the cuffs. "You've got the wrong person!"

"Ma'am," the arresting officer said to Evian, "you are under arrest. You have the right to remain silent...."

Alex confronted Evian after the officer put the handcuffs around her wrists. "Where is he?!" he shouted out. "Where's my baby?!"

Evian shook her head and squeezed her lips together. She wanted to confess but, in her heart, she knew the baby would only push Alex closer to Alecia.

When the officers escorted her out of the hospital, they ran into a slew of news reporters. Evian was bombarded with questions about her status as Miss America, and for her alleged involvement with stealing baby Alexander. She had successfully tuned everyone out but froze in place at the sight of her husband, who was standing near the hospital entrance.

"Evian!" Pierre called out over the news reporters and camera crew. "What's going on?"

"Do you know this woman?" the reporter from the magazine company asked, shoving a microphone in Pierre's face.

"That's my wife."

When Evian passed by Pierre, he reached out to her but she stared straight ahead. She wondered how he was able to find her.

The cameras flashed incessantly. A photo of an open-mouth Evian facing her husband, with Alex standing in the background was what the magazine company envisioned for the front cover.

"Sir," the magazine reporter said to get Pierre's attention. "Did you know your wife was engaged to marry Alex Simmons?"

Pierre was stunned and unable to digest what the reporter had told him. "What did you say?" he asked, after swallowing hard.

"Your wife, Evian Gant, Miss America," the reporter emphasized. "She was engaged to marry Alex Simmons. Now it seems she's going to jail on child abduction and endangerment charges. How do you feel about that?"

The reporter did not wait for Pierre's response, before he continued, "Your wife's fiancé had a baby with another woman. This is just speculation, but we believe your wife stole the baby because she was jealous of the baby's mother."

Pierre listened attentively as he stared at the news reporter in a state of confusion.

"Mr. Michel," the reporter pressed on, "you traveled from St. Kitts to find your wife. Based on what you learned today, do you think it's possible to save your marriage?"

Head bowed and feeling let down, Pierre walked away from the reporter, and away from the hospital. He was ready to go back to St. Kitts without his wife.

Pierre was not the only person hurt from the magazine reporter's revelations. Evian's parents were sitting in their hotel room, looking at the news on TV. They sat in horror as they witnessed their daughter in handcuffs, and listened to the details surrounding her arrest.

"What are we going to do if she goes to jail?" Mrs. Gant frantically asked her husband.

"I'm not sure," her husband said, as tears welled up in his eyes. It dawned on him that their daughter could possibly spend the rest of her life in jail.

Chapter 61
Cold Case

Raymond Brown was transported from the holding cell and taken to the interrogation room. The guards guided him to a table in the middle of the room and sat him in one of the vacant chairs. Detective Baily walked in shortly afterward, and sat across from Raymond.

"Mr. Brown," the detective began, "I need to know your involvement in Lamar Greene's disappearance. For your cooperation, I will guarantee that you get a reduced sentence."

"I have no idea what you're talking about," Raymond replied, while shrugging his shoulders.

"Don't play games with me." The detective stood up and closed in on Raymond's face. "Either you talk now or spend the rest of your life in prison."

"If you don't mind, I would like to speak with my attorney. Is he here?"

Detective Baily returned to his chair after he motioned the guards to escort the attorney to the interrogation room.

Raymond's attorney walked in the room carrying a suitcase and looking dapper in his black Armani business suit and shiny Ferragamos shoes. He greeted his client and the detective with a handshake. Then he sat in the vacant chair next to his client and turned his attention to the detective. "I am Mr. Brown's attorney."

"I know," Detective Baily replied, his tone was flat. He had a feeling he would not get any answers during the interrogation process, especially since Raymond hired a high-profile attorney with impeccable credentials.

"I am asking for my client's immediate release."

"That's not possible. We believe your client carried Lamar Greene's body out of the hotel room."

"You have no proof that shows a body was carried out of the room."

The attorney appeared confident, but Raymond's tensed up upon hearing the detective's allegation.

"I know what you're trying to do," Detective Baily rebuffed, "and it's not going to work."

The attorney retrieved a document from his briefcase and slid it across the table in front of the detective. "This is proof that Lamar Greene was just released from Broward General Hospital in Fort Lauderdale." He remained quiet to give the detective time to browse the hospital discharge papers.

"Lamar Greene is alive?" Raymond asked his attorney in disbelief.

The attorney nodded as he kept his eyes focused on the detective. "You had the opportunity to interview Lamar Greene at the hospital. Did he tell you my client carried him out of the hotel?"

The detective winced. Earlier, he was disappointed when Lamar Greene refused to answer his questions or admit that Raymond was involved in his disappearance. To answer the attorney's question, Detective Baily stated, "There is video footage that shows Mr. Brown and his accomplice were in Mr. Greene's hotel room." He turned to Raymond, and asked, "What was in the blanket you and your partner carried out of Mr. Greene's hotel room?"

"Do not answer that question," the attorney told Raymond. He stood up with his briefcase to conclude the interrogation. Then he turned to the detective, and said, "I am asking for my client's immediate release."

"But we have evidence...."

"No you don't," the attorney cut the detective off in mid-sentence. "Without eyewitnesses or a statement from Mr. Greene, your baseless evidence would not hold up in court and you know it."

Detective Baily sat motionless for a few seconds, while thinking about the attorney's remarks. He knew the attorney was right on all accounts.

"If you do not release my client," the attorney continued, "I will file a lawsuit against this police department, which will ensure your resignation or early retirement. Take your pick."

"That won't be necessary," the detective replied, feeling somewhat deflated. He asked the guards to remove the handcuffs from Raymond's wrists.

After Raymond was released from jail, he retrieved his personal belongings and met his attorney in the waiting area. He felt good to be free.

"What's going to happen next?" Raymond asked his attorney, as they walked out of the police precinct.

"We have to get ahold of Mr. Greene."

"Why?"

"Just to cover our bases."

"How did you know he was in the hospital?"

"I have a reliable source," the attorney replied, choosing not to reveal specifics about his informant. "While I search for Mr. Greene, I need you to lay low and refrain from discussing your case with anyone."

"What about my son?"

Earlier, Raymond called his attorney to represent his son without knowing why he was in jail.

The attorney sighed, before explaining, "Your son was involved in a prostitution sting operation."

"Can you make the charges go away?"

"I wish it were that simple. Your son's face was plastered all over the local news stations, and several women came forward claiming he gave them the AIDS virus. So the State's Attorney is in the process of charging him with aggravated assault with a deadly weapon. If it's proven he has AIDS and knowingly spread the virus, no amount of money will be able to get your son released from jail right away."

"How much time are we looking at?"

"He could be facing a life sentence behind bars. The best I can do is make sure he doesn't get the death penalty. In the meantime, I'll make sure he's transported to a facility with better amenities."

"Do the best you can. Money is not a problem. I'll be in touch," Raymond said, before he turned to head upstairs.

"Where are you going?" his attorney called out.

Raymond turned back. "I need to see my son."

"Please tell him I will be making arrangements to meet with him soon. I plan on finding out as much as I can about his case."

"What about my son's wife? Are you going to contact her?"

"That's one of my first priorities. If his wife stands by him during this ordeal, I believe a jury would sympathize with him."

"If not?"

"We will think of another way to garner public support. I'm not going to lie to you. This is going to be a hard case to win."

"Do your best?"

"You have my word."

***

The guards transported Aaron from his cell to the visitor's room. He appeared distraught as he sat down and picked up the phone on the other side of the Plexiglas window to speak with his father.

Raymond felt saddened after taking note of Aaron's haphazard appearance. He picked up the phone, and asked, "How are you holding up?"

Aaron broke down crying. "Dad, you…have to…get me out of here. Why don't they kill me now?"

"You don't mean that. You have a wife that loves you."

Sobbing, Aaron mumbled, "I have a feeling she's not going to want anything to do with me."

"Can you blame her?" Raymond asked in anger. "Why did you do it?"

Aaron assumed his father found out why he was in jail. Feeling ashamed, he avoided eye contact, and said in a low and sorrowful voice, "I don't know."

"Son, do you have the AIDS virus?"

Aaron nodded *yes*.

Raymond briefly closed his eyes. "Did you sleep with women without using protection?"

Confused, Aaron asked, "Why are you asking me these questions?"

"Charges are being brought against you for aggravated assault with a deadly weapon."

Aaron panicked. *"What?! I didn't kill anyone!"*

"Knowingly spreading the AIDS virus is considered a weapon."

Feeling hopeless, Aaron started wailing nonstop.

"Son, you have to be strong. My attorney is going to see if he can get you transported to a better facility."

Aaron was too ashamed to continue facing his father. He returned the phone to its cradle, stood up, and walked toward the guards.

Raymond bit his bottom lip response. He was worried about his son's safety behind bars.

Chapter 62
Mission Accomplished

*J*ustina was an emotional wreck. The man she was *in love* with was in the hospital; her husband was in jail for soliciting a prostitute; and she almost fell victim to extortion plot. She was home awaiting her sister's arrival, but Carmela was the last person she wanted to see.

Startled by the knock at the door, Justina sat up in the chair and jumped out of her daze. She slowly stood up and walked over to the front door. Her nose flared and her heart fluttered after eyeing her sister through the tiny peephole.

Incensed, Justina opened the door, and lashed out at Carmela. "Why?!" she screamed to the top of her lungs. "Why did you do it?!"

Carmela did not flinch. She stared at her sister as if she lost her mind. Her reaction only escalated the tension between them.

Suddenly, Justina raised her fists and charged at Carmela with all her might. She struck her sister twice before Kevin grabbed her around the waist and threw her over his shoulder.

"Chill out," he told Justina, as he walked through her front door with Thorny, Carmela and Roger (*aka Dan*) on his heels.

"Put me down," Justina yelled, swinging her arms and legs to get out of his grasp.

Kevin put her down but blocked her path to Carmela.

Justina looked at him sideways, before asking, "Who are you?"

"He's my partner," Thorny stated from behind, after closing the front door. "You wanted us to help you find your sister, and we did our part. What you do to your sister after we leave, is on you."

Arms crossed, Justina was huffing and puffing while looking at her sister with rage in her eyes. With a hint of sarcasm, she said, "I'm glad your kidnappers did not hurt you. But it pales in comparison to what I plan on doing to you."

Carmela drew back with alarm. This was her first time witnessing her sister's fury. She was afraid her sister was going to follow through on her threat.

Justina looked over Carmela's head and caught a glimpse of the man that accosted her days earlier. "What are you doing here?" She took a closer a look at his features, and noticed he resembled her former business partner. "Roger, is that you?" When he nodded, she asked, "Why are you here? I don't feel comfortable with you in my home."

"We brought him here," Thorny interjected, "to apologize."

"I'm sorry for everything," Roger weakly admitted.

Justina charged toward him, and blasted, "It wasn't enough that you threatened to take my life several years ago! Now you got my sister involved in this so-called scam of yours!"

Roger bore a hard scowl, before exploding, "You ruined my life! You turned my parents against me! You stole my career! It's because of you, I have nothing!"

Suddenly, Justina became remorseful. But she also thought back to the time Roger was incarcerated for his past actions. She gawked at him as if she was looking at a ghost. "I...thought you...were dead," Justina uttered in disbelief. "I was told you hung yourself in jail."

Roger remained silent, while Justina put two-and-two together. He was a fugitive, she thought to herself. She turned to Thorny, and asked, "What is going to happen to him?"

"It's up to you."

"This is all too surreal." Justina mulled over the situation before turning to Roger. "I'm ashamed of the way I treated you in the past. I want you to go on with his life. But I want you to promise to leave me alone."

"I promise," Roger gladly proclaimed with a wholesome smile.

"Now that that is settled," Thorny said to Justina. "Do you have the money you owe us?"

"Yes, I'll go get it."

Justina went upstairs to get the money she borrowed from the bank. She was in near tears when she strolled downstairs and handed the money to Thorny. "Two thousand dollars is missing. My husband must've taken it."

Thorny counted the money, before asking, "Where is your husband?"

"He's in jail, but I promise I will get the rest of the money I owe you."

Kevin massaged his goatee while assessing the situation. "Don't worry about it," he finally said. "We're even."

Justina bore a thin smile. She was grateful for his understanding.

Kevin turned to Roger and Thorny, and said. "Let's go."

"Don't leave me here with her!" Carmela begged, pulling on Thorny's arm.

Snickering, Thorny looked at Justina before he turned to Carmela. "I doubt if your sister will raise a hand to hurt you. But if she does, you deserve it." He shook Carmela's hand off of him and followed Kevin and Roger out the door. He closed the door behind him on purpose.

Carmela started shivering as she backed up against the door.

Justina shot daggers at her sister as she slowly stepped in her direction.

"What are you going to do to me?" Carmela's voice shook from fear.

"Nothing." Justina had second-guessed her decision to beat the crap out of Carmela. On that note, she walked in the den and sat on the sofa. She was blown away by Roger and Carmela's actions to extort money from her. Her feelings were hurt as tears welled up in her eyes.

It took Carmela a while before she moved from one spot and crept toward her sister. Suddenly, her consciousness kicked in. She felt guilty for her actions.

"Justina," she said in a low tone, "why is your husband in jail?"

Lowering her eyes, Justina was overcome with shame. She did not want to tell her sister the truth. When she remained quiet, Carmela sat on the sofa next to her. "I know what Aaron has been doing behind your back."

Justina looked up at her sister. "Carmela," she timidly said, "please tell me everything you know."

"Aaron has been cheating on you." Carmela did not wait for Justina to respond, before continuing, "I worked for the same *Call Girl Service* Aaron used. He was a loyal customer."

Justina's hand flew to her chest, as she cried out, "Oh God! Tell me it's not true! Did you and Aaron....?" She tried in vain to block out the possibility that her sister and husband had sex.

"Don't get it twisted," Carmela sassed. "Nothing happened between us, but he paid me dearly for services I never rendered."

"What are you saying?"

"Aaron paid me twenty-five thousand dollars to keep quiet about his sexual activities. But it did not stop him from prowling. That's why he's in jail, right?"

Briefly closing her eyes, Justina flashed back to the day she and Aaron went to the bank for the ransom money, and the bank president told her Aaron had taken out a loan for twenty-five thousand dollars. She opened her eyes and asked her sister the one question that troubled her most. "Why did you do it?"

"Do what?"

"The kidnapping scheme."

"I had to teach you a lesson. You're selfish, and you never cared about anyone but yourself."

Justina's mouth flew open to protest. "How could you say that? I opened my home to you."

"You only did it because you felt guilty for not being there for me when I needed you most. It's a shame you're not helping mom and dad when you know they're struggling."

"They didn't ask me for help."

"Why should they? You know dad lost his job over a year ago, and mom has been working nonstop to pay the bills. You're a smart girl; you could have figured it out."

"I'm sorry," Justina admitted with distress in her voice.

"I am too." Carmela stood up and headed toward the front door. "I'm going home."

"To mom and dads?" Justina asked with yearning in her voice.

Carmela nodded before she walked out the front door.

Justina sat still thinking about her recent visitors. She was grateful to Thorny and Kevin for locating her sister, but could not get Roger out of her mind. She felt confident that no one was looking for him.

Now that Carmela was safe, Justina grabbed her purse and car keys. She was headed to the hospital to visit Guy. As she opened the front door, her home phone rang. She hesitated before she rushed in the den to grab the phone on the table top.

"Hello."

"Is this Justina Bishop?"

"Yes, this is she."

"Mrs. Bishop, I am your husband's attorney."

Justina rolled her eyes. "Why are you calling me? I already know about Aaron's bond hearing. It's not scheduled until Monday morning." Her tone was short and impatient.

The attorney paused. He did not know how to respond to the negative tone in Justina's voice. "Mrs. Bishop, your husband was charged with aggravated assault and battery."

Justina frowned.

"Mrs. Bishop...."

"I can't do this!" Justina screamed. "I have to go to the hospital."

"I understand. When you get a chance, please turn on the local news. Then call me back as soon as possible. I need to discuss your husband's case. My number is...."

Abruptly, Justina disconnected the call. But she was curious to find out what Aaron did this time. She sat on the sofa in the living room, turned on the television, and flipped through the channels until she found the local news station. Her eyes grew wide as the news reporter showed her husband's mug shot. Then her heart dropped after the reporter announced Aaron was charged with *aggravated assault with a deadly weapon* for knowingly spreading the AIDS virus to several women.

Justina needed to see Aaron, to hear his side of things. She needed to know if the news report was true. So instead of going to the hospital, she went to see Aaron in jail.

***

In an orange jumpsuit, Aaron was led to the visiting area to meet with Justina. He was happy to see her. With hope-filled eyes, he sat in the chair on the opposite side of the Plexiglas window. The phone on each side of the divider was their only means of communication. Aaron picked up the phone and encouraged his wife to do the same.

"Hi Justina."

The scowl on Justina's face spoke volumes. "How did you contract the AIDS virus?" she asked, even though she figured it had something to do with his encounters with prostitutes and *Call Girls*.

Aaron's smile turned upside down.

"Why did you marry me, knowing you were involved with prostitutes?"

"I thought it was under control," he admitted, clearly embarrassed.

At that very moment, Justina made a life-changing decision. She remained calm, cool and collected, when she looked him in the eyes, and said, "I want a divorce."

"Why?! So you can be with Guy Simmons?!" Aaron said in anger. "Please don't leave me. Not like this. I need you."

Justina sighed. "Aaron, I can no longer live a lie. You will be hearing from my attorney." She returned the phone to its cradle, stood up and left.

After visiting her husband in jail, Justina cried all the way to the hospital. She was upset because the man she thought she knew turned out to be a stranger.

Several years earlier, Justina was devastated when she first discovered she had the AIDS virus. But she felt hopeful after the doctor told her she could live a long time, as long as she practiced safe sex and took her medications. With renewed hope, Justina started anew. Then the unexpected happened. She met Aaron, her prince in shining armor.

When Aaron told her he, too, was HIV positive, Justina never questioned her husband about how he contracted the virus. That was not important to her. Up until now, he never gave her a reason to question him about his past.

Chapter 63
Destiny

*A*fter Elizabeth stepped off the Greyhound bus in Niagara Falls, New York, she stood in line to cross the Rainbow Bridge to Canada. Her hands were trembling when she presented her ID to the security officer behind the Immigration booth.

The officer eyed her with suspicion, before he turned to his computer monitor to browse the FBI's most wanted list. When Elizabeth's picture appeared on his screen, he stood up and put his hand on his gun. "Ma'am, I need you come with me."

"Why? I didn't...do anything...wrong."

"Please follow me," he insisted.

Without resistance, the officer escorted Elizabeth to a vacant room and locked the door behind them.

Stammering, she asked, "Is...there...a problem?"

"There's a warrant for your arrest," the officer replied.

"No, you're mistaken."

The officer showed Elizabeth the printed copy of the wanted poster. "Is this you?"

Elizabeth looked at the picture and could not lie. That was her image on the poster. "What's going to happen to me?"

"The FBI is going to extradite you back to Maryland to face charges."

Shortly after, Elizabeth was flown to Baltimore and escorted to the police precinct where she was questioned for hours. Then she was put in a holding cell with none other than her newest friend.

Evian watched in horror as the guard removed the handcuffs from her co-conspirator's wrists, opened the gate, and motioned for Elizabeth to enter the cell.

Elizabeth dragged her feet as she walked in the cell, sat next to Evian and stared into space. She did not utter one word.

"What happened?" Evian asked her ally in a hushed voice.

"What do you think happened?" Elizabeth said, as she turned to Evian with a scowl on her face. "Your plan didn't work."

Evian grinned. "But our plan did work. Alex and Alecia will never see their baby again."

"We had no right to take the baby. I hate that you got me involved in this foolishness."

"I didn't force you," Evian replied with a dirty look on her face.

"Yes you did. You and your cunning ways. When you gave me a check for three thousand dollars, I thought you were being generous. But you wanted to use me to steal the baby."

"It was all a part of the plan and you knew this."

"Yeah, but I didn't know I would go to jail."

"Why are you complaining? I gave you seventy-five thousand dollars after I sold the baby."

"And what good is the money when I can't spend it? Do you at least know if the baby is all right?"

"The baby is fine."

"Do you know where the baby is?" Elizabeth probed with wide eyes.

Evian shrugged. "I don't know and I don't care. It might be on the paperwork the adoption agency gave me."

"Did the adoption agency know the baby wasn't yours?"

"I'm sure they did. They never asked any questions. Like me, they wanted to pretend like it was a legitimate transaction."

"Where's the paperwork?" Elizabeth asked out of curiosity.

"I left it in the rental car."

"Where's the rental car?"

Evian paused as she looked toward the cell gate. She wanted to make sure no one was in earshot. "I parked it in a garage near the Baltimore harbor," she admitted in a low voice.

"Oh, okay," Elizabeth said, before she went to the front of the cell to get the guard's attention.

Although the guard was not in clear view of Elizabeth, he was close enough to hear her. He quickly walked to the cell gate and opened it.

Evian frown. "Where are you going?"

Elizabeth waited until she was on the other side of the cell, before responding, "I'm getting the *hell* out of here."

Stunned, Evian stood up and asked, "How?"

"I have immunity. I told the FBI everything they wanted to know." Then she revealed the recording device that was hidden under her shirt. "And now I have your confession on tape."

"Why did you do that?"

"Revenge," Elizabeth coyly replied. "When you asked me to take that baby, it was never about me."

"You bitch!" Evian snarled, as she put her arms through one of the cell slits to try and beat the crap out of Elizabeth.

Elizabeth backed away from Evian and followed the guard to the holding area, where she was subsequently released to Protective Custody. The deal she cut with the State's Attorney assured her two years of probation with no jail time.

Evian returned to the lone bench in her cell, to ponder her situation. Earlier, she was questioned for hours but she never opened her mouth to provide any information on the whereabouts of the baby or Elizabeth Coleman. All of that was in vain because, thanks to Elizabeth, her confession to the crime was recorded on tape.

***

Despite Amber alerts and Guy's offer of a one-million dollar reward to find *baby Alexander*, there were no new leads. The police investigators had already warned that if the baby was not found within the first twenty-four hours, the likelihood of finding him was grim.

This news did not bode well for Alecia. She sunk into a deep depression. The doctor admitted her in the hospital and gave her some sedatives. Both Alex and Jeanine remained by her bedside to console her, to no avail.

"Alex," Jeanine said as she looked at the worry lines etched across his forehead, "we're going to find the baby."

He turned to her with a thin smile.

Suddenly, two police officers approached Alecia's room. "We have good news," one of the officers stated. "We may have a new lead on your baby's whereabouts."

Alecia's spirit bounced back, as she sat up in bed, and asked, "When will you know for sure?"

"We were able to locate the adoption papers. We don't want to get your hopes up, but we believe the baby was flown to London. Representatives from the State Department are now in the process of identifying the baby. If everything checks out, your baby will be returned to the U.S. no later than tomorrow morning."

"This is good news," Jeanine said with a burst of excitement.

"It's too soon to say for sure," the officer said, "but we are hopeful."

Chapter 64
The Truth

*A*fter Raymond visited his son in jail, he called Jeanine to tell her he was okay. He also wanted to come clean with her about everything that went on between him and Lamar. He was relieved when she answered his call. "Hello Jeanine. I just got out of jail."

She forced a thin smile. "That's nice to hear Raymond."

He instantly knew something was wrong based on the sound of her voice. "Are you okay?"

Jeanine had been crying tears of joy before he called. "We just received some promising news about the baby."

"What are you talking about?"

"Alex's baby…he was taken…from the hospital."

Raymond frowned. "What do you mean? Who took the baby?"

"It's a long story."

"Where are you?"

"At Johns Hopkins hospital in Baltimore."

"I'm on my way."

Raymond quickly made arrangements to fly to Baltimore. Then he heard specifics about *baby Alexander's* abduction on the radio broadcast. Throughout his and Jeanine's relationship, he tried to protect her and anyone close to her but he believed he failed her in this instance. Even his actions dealing with Lamar Greene backfired.

Several days earlier, Raymond had returned to Lamar's hotel room to talk some sense into him. He knocked on the door, but there was no answer. The next time he knocked harder and with so much force the hinges trembled. "Lamar!" Raymond called out. "Open the door!"

Sloppy drunk, Lamar wobbled to the door and swung it open. He was displeased to see the man that asked him to dissolve his relationship with Regine. Frowning, he squawked, "What in the *hell* do you want?!"

"I want to make sure there's no room for any misunderstanding."

"I don't…care what…you say," Lamar slurred. "I'm not going to do what you want me to. I love Regine." His confession was honest and heartfelt.

Raymond barged in the room, pushing Lamar backwards. "You're going to sign the contract!" he shouted, after closing the door behind him.

Lamar hissed. "No I'm not, and you can't make me!"

Eyes blazing, Raymond grabbed the collar of Lamar's shirt and punched him in the stomach.

Losing his balance, Lamar tumbled to the floor. It took a while before he got over the shock. He charged at Raymond with a vengeance. But he was too slow.

Raymond put Lamar in a headlock. Then he repeatedly punched him in the face.

Lamar fell backward and hit his head on the edge of the marble countertop before crashing to the floor with a loud thump. The blow to his head caused him to blank out.

Suddenly, Raymond grew nervous after he did not notice movement. He was going to kneel down and search for a pulse but stopped in his tracks after hearing a knock at the door.

Raymond tiptoed to the door as if he was walking on eggshells. "Who is it?" he asked through the closed door.

"A friend of a friend."

Raymond thought the voice sounded familiar. He opened the door, and thought it was peculiar that the man standing before him was wearing dark sunglasses, gloves, a hat, and a trench coat. "Deacon Franklin, is that you?" he asked in surprise. "What are you doing here?"

"I'm here to see Lamar."

"Lamar is not available," Raymond said in a hushed voice but loud enough for the deacon to hear him. "He had a little accident."

"Can I come in?" the deacon persisted, stepping closer to the door.

Raymond paused. He had only met the deacon a hand full of times, and was unsure of whether he could trust him. He opened the door with caution.

Upon entering the room, the deacon stopped in front of Lamar's motionless body. Then he turned to Raymond and asked, "Is he dead?"

"I think so."

"What happened?"

"We…uh…had a little misunderstanding."

The deacon walked over to the body and knelt down next to it. Then he lifted Lamar's eyelids with his thumb. He became stone-faced when Lamar's pupils rolled to the back of his head.

"What are...*we* going...to do?" Raymond asked, hinting he was terrified.

"*We?*" Deacon Franklin's brow shot up in surprise.

Raymond was hoping to get out of this situation unscathed. He assumed the deacon would help him.

Without uttering a word, the deacon stood up and walked into the bedroom to grab Lamar's car keys, wallet and cell phone from the nightstand. Next, he snatched the blanket off the bed and spread it on the floor next to Lamar's body.

"What are you doing?" Raymond asked, as the deacon moved around like a thief in the night.

"We have to move the body."

"Why can't we call the police?"

"Do you want to go to jail?"

"Of course not."

"You need to help me lift the body and put it in the blanket," the deacon told Raymond. "I also need you to retrace your steps and wipe down anything that has your fingerprints."

Raymond did as he was told. Next, he and the deacon carried the body out of the rear entrance of the hotel. They were able to find the rental car by pressing the keyless remote starter. After looking around to make sure no one was in sight, they put Lamar's body in the trunk of the rental car.

"I'll drive the rental car," Deacon Franklin said to Raymond. "I want you to follow me in your car."

The deacon drove northbound on I-95. He pulled off on the side of the highway when he reached Hollywood, Florida. Raymond drove up behind him and climbed out of the car after the deacon opened the trunk of the rental car.

"Help me carry the body and prop it up in the front seat," Deacon Franklin instructed Raymond.

Raymond looked around to see if anyone was looking before he helped the deacon transfer the body.

Both were sweating and moving quickly as they positioned the body behind the steering wheel. Then the deacon put Lamar's cell phone and wallet in the glove department. He purposely left the keys in the ignition.

"Now what?" Raymond asked, after waiting for the deacon to climb in the passenger seat of his car.

"Lamar's body will be found in the morning," the deacon stated with confidence.

"Can I ask you a question?"

The deacon nodded.

"Why did you come to Lamar's hotel room?"

"To take care of some business."

Raymond noticed the deacon did not elaborate. But he assumed it was the same reason he was there, to find a way to make sure Lamar did not disrupt Guy and Regine's marriage.

Raymond dropped the deacon off at his car, which was parked across the street from the hotel. Before the deacon climbed out of the car, he turned to Raymond, and said, "Make sure no one knows about this."

"You have my word."

The deacon nodded before he walked across the highway. He was on his way back to Guy and Regine's home in Clearwater, Florida, where he and Bessie had been staying while on vacation.

When Raymond parked his car in the hotel garage, his heart was beating rapidly. He was looking forward to taking a shower, to wash off all the griminess of the day's event. He was nervous when a stranger caught up with him before he entered the hotel lobby.

Staring straight ahead, the man asked Raymond, "What did you and the deacon do with Lamar Greene's body?"

Raymond turned to the man with wide eyes.

"I was there when you and the deacon carried Lamar's body out of this hotel and put it in the rental car."

"Who are you?" Raymond was curious to know.

"Tim Carter. I'm Mrs. Benedict's private detective."

Raymond's brows shot up in surprise. "Jeanine Benedict?" he asked to be sure.

"Is Lamar Greene still alive?"

"No," Raymond answered. "Are you going to tell Jeanine what happened?"

"No."

Tim gave a slight nod before he turned and walked away from Raymond.

Raymond had already made up his mind not to tell Jeanine about his run-in with her private detective.

***

Detective Baily was at his wits end. He had determined that the investigation on Lamar's disappearance was a standstill. He retraced his steps, and realized there was one more lead he did not explore.

The forensics lab confirmed that the liquor bottle found in Lamar's hotel room contained traces of GHB.

Following his instincts, the detective returned to the hotel and asked to speak with the hotel staff member who delivered the liquor to Lamar's room. A young lady appeared before the detective with her eyes cast downward. There was something about her that told him she was hiding something.

"What is your name?" he asked her.

"Charlotte Smith." Her reply was soft and timid.

"Do you mind going with me to the police station? I need to ask you some questions."

"What is this about?" she feebly replied. "I didn't do anything."

"I'm investigating a homicide," the detective fibbed. "And I need your help."

Charlotte started fidgeting with her hands. Then she looked to her manager, and asked, "Is it okay if I go?"

"Sure." The manager nodded. "Can you make sure she's back in an hour? We're short-staffed tonight."

"I think you need to make other plans. This may take a while."

Detective Baily sat across from Charlotte in the interrogation room, and stared at her with grave suspicion. He had a feeling she was the missing link in the investigation.

"Ms. Smith," he said to Charlotte, "we need to know who put you up to this."

Charlotte started biting her fingers and her knees were shaking. She looked around the dark room before turning back to the detective. "I don't know what you're talking about."

"Yes you do, and you're not leaving here until we get some answers."

"You can't keep me here against my will." She became defensive and bold.

The detective smiled. "You're absolutely right. You could cooperate with us, or you could go to jail for attempted murder. Take your pick."

Swallowing hard, it dawned on Charlotte that she was stuck between a hard place and a rock. She stammered, "I…didn't…do anything."

The detective knew he had to manipulate her to get to the truth. "We have video footage of you spiking Lamar Greene's liquor bottle," he lied with ease. "We just need to know why. Were you coerced?"

Charlotte experienced a *shock and awe* moment. She thought she was being discreet when she put six ounces of GHB in Lamar's liquor. She did not know surveillance cameras were in the bar area of the hotel's restaurant. "It was my friend, Nicky Cannon," Charlotte started singing like a canary. "She asked me to spike his drink."

"Why did she ask you to do it?"

"Lamar's girlfriend wanted him dead. "Her name is Leslie," Charlotte admitted. "I only know her by her first name."

Detective Baily's eyes shot up, after remembering Leslie Holloway's timid reaction to his visit. He left the room and ordered that Nicky and Leslie be taken into custody.

Chapter 65
Crushed

*J*ustina returned to the hospital and slowly walked into Guy's room. She was delighted to see his eyes were wide open. "Guy!" she screamed with excitement in her voice. "I'm so glad you're okay." As if it was second nature, she rushed to his bedside and gave him a big kiss on the cheek.

Guy appeared to light up when he saw Justina walk in the room. He tried to sit up but he was too weak, and he was connected to the heart monitor. In a hoarse voice, "Guy said, "I'm glad to see you."

"You gave me a scare. I was so worried about you."

"I love you," he admitted in a hush voice.

She beamed in response. "I love you too."

Slowly, he placed his right hand on top of hers, before asking, "Where do we go from here?"

Justina clasped her hands in his. "I'm leaving my husband," she admitted with relief.

"Will you marry me?" Guy asked. It was the one question that occupied his thoughts after he became conscious.

Eyes welling up with tears of joy, Justina nodded with assurance, as she answered, "Yes, I would love to marry you."

Guy grinned before his eyes rolled to the back of his head. Then he started shaking vigorously and foaming at the mouth.

"Oh God!" Justina cried out. "Guy! What's wrong?!"

The beeping heart monitor alerted the doctors and nurses, who rushed into his room with lifesaving equipment. "Miss," one of the nurses said to Justina, "please step aside."

"What's the matter?" Justina questioned, while crying profusely. She thought the worse.

The nurse insisted, "Ma'am, we need you to step out of the room."

Justina became indignant. "I'm not going anywhere until I get some answers!"

The nurse aggressively shoved Justina out of the room while the doctor performed CPR on Guy.

Justina's cries fell on death ears as she paced the floor and prayed for Guy's speedy recovery.

Coincidentally, the nurse came out of the room and told Justina that Guy had a heart attack, and the doctors were doing everything they could to save his life.

"Do you know if your husband wishes to be resuscitated?"

"What do you mean?"

"Should we put your husband on a life support if his heart gives out?"

Tears flooded Justina's face as she clearly understood her options. "Do what you can to save him!" she screamed to the top of her lungs.

Suddenly, Guy's cell phone began to ring. Absentmindedly, Justina forgot the nurse had given her his things earlier. She fumbled through the bag to find his cell phone. "Hello," she said, while sobbing. Her voice was soft and almost inaudible.

"Who is this?" Guy's stepmother asked with raised brows.

"This... is...Justina." She was still crying from the news of Guy's heart attack.

Jeanine's nose started flaring from anger. "What are you doing answering my son's phone?" Her tone was firm and demanding.

Wiping her tears with the back of her hands, Justina said, "Guy is in the Bayview hospital in Bradenton, Florida."

"What is he doing in the hospital?"

Justina took a deep breath and exhaled. She was heart-broken, and tried to remain strong. "Guy was in a car accident, and...."

"Did you contact his *wife*?" Jeanine cut in, not giving Justina the opportunity to report that Guy had just had a heart attack.

"No, I didn't get a chance to call Regine."

"I know exactly who you are," Jeanine said with rage in her voice, "and what you've done to my son and daughter-in-law in the past. I suggest you leave the hospital now."

Justina shook her head, vigorously. "I can't do that. I love Guy."

Angrily, Jeanine disconnected the call and immediately phoned Regine. She was going to persuade her daughter-in-law to go see about her husband. More importantly, she wanted Regine to intercede in Justina's attempts to steal Guy away from her.

At the new restaurant in Miami, Regine answered Jeanine's call but was unable to clearly hear her above the noise from the construction workers and decorators. She went into her office to talk with her mother-in-law in private. "Hi Jeanine. How are you?"

"Hi Regine. I hate to bother you, but your friend, Justina, just told me Guy was admitted in the Bayview hospital in Bradenton, Florida."

"Oh God, no!" Regine said, as she grabbed her chest. "Is he okay?"

"Your friend told me he was in a car accident."

"I'll leave now to go see about him."

Considering the news about Guy, Jeanine decided not to tell her daughter-in-law Alex's baby was abducted. She figured Regine would have enough on her plate to deal with.

Next, Jeanine called the Bayview hospital. The administrator answered her call, by asking, "Are you a relative of Guy Simmons?"

"Yes, I'm his mother. Why?"

There was a short pause before the administrator admitted in a somber tone, "We regret to inform you that your son didn't make it."

Jeanine frowned. "What does that mean?"

The administrator paused, before stating, "Mr. Simmons passed away. He died of a heart attack."

Jeanine dropped her cell phone and started weeping nonstop. "Oh God!" she cried out. "My son...." Choked up, the pain was too much for her to bear.

Alex heard her wails and went in search for her. He stepped outside of Alecia's room and found her crying and hunched over. "Mom," he said, as he slowly knelt down beside her. "Are you okay?"

"It's...your....brother," she said between sobs.

"What about Guy?"

"He's...dead."

Alex was in shock as he sat on the floor next to Jeanine. Tears welled up in his eyes, as he asked, "How? What...happened?"

"He had a heart attack."

"Does Regine know?" Alex asked in a controlled but weak tone.

Jeanine shrugged. "I'm not sure. I just called her. She told me she was going to the hospital to see about Guy."

***

Back at the restaurant, Regine walked out of the office and stood toe to toe with Lamar.

"What's the matter?" he asked.

"It's Guy. He's in the hospital. I have to leave now."

"I'll go with you."

"That's not necessary. One of us has to stay here to make sure the workers have the restaurant up and running before the grand opening."

Regine exited the back of the restaurant and caught a cab to the airport.

After boarding the plane, she sat in the business section. She closed her eyes to relax her nerves. Suddenly, the last ten years flashed before her eyes. Memories of Guy were prominent. They had known each other since they were fifteen years old. She cracked a smile as she thought of the time she was *head over heels in love* with him.

But lately, things had gone awry. She felt like they were strangers, coexisting and taking up space in each other's lives. Making love to Lamar had confirmed what she knew all along. She fell out of love with her husband a long time ago. Lamar had taken her on a new journey.

Regine was ready to give Guy her blessings, to be with her best friend. She had known he was smitten with Justina ever since they were in high school. She did not want to stand in his way of true happiness.

Shaken out of her spell, Regine's eyes flew open when she heard commotion on the plane. There was a lot of turbulence. Then she felt the plane drop at a rapid pace. She asked the flight attendant, "What's going on?"

The attendant ignored Regine to calm the frantic passengers. Suddenly, the passengers became terrified when the turbulence caused oxygen masks and debris to fall from compartments above the seats.

"Attention passengers!" the pilot yelled over the intercom system. "Please return to your seats, buckle your seatbelts, and hold tight. There is a small fire on the left wing of the plane. We have to conduct an emergency landing."

Instinctively, the passengers started panicking, demanding more answers.

"What's going on?!" one passenger yelled at the flight attendants, who were fastened in the seats.

"Get me out of here!" another passenger shouted.

Regine prayed as tears flooded her face. "God, please watch over my son. I love KC so much."

She did not know two of her father's henchmen were on the same flight. Kevin sent his men shortly after Lamar disappeared. Since Regine arrived in Fort Lauderdale, they had been discreetly watching over her. But this time, there was nothing they could do to save her life or themselves from the inevitable.

The plane quickly descended before exploding in midair, and remnants of the plane fell in the Atlantic Ocean.

Epilogue

*G*uy and Regine's double funeral was held at Mount Bethel Baptist Church in St. Petersburg, Florida. It was attended by more than one thousand people, including city officials, and employees and associates from their respective businesses.

Jeanine held KC in her arms throughout the memorial service. KC was too young to understand he would never see his parents again. He kept pointing to their pictures, which were sitting on a tripod next to the caskets. At one point, he yelled out, "I want my mommy and daddy!"

Overwhelmed by his reaction, Jeanine coddled him and told him it would be okay. She had already filed the paper work to become KC's legal guardian.

Sitting next to Jeanine, Raymond held her hand and would not let go. He was by her side during her moment of grief, long after he was cleared as a suspect in Lamar's disappearance. He had planned on being with Jeanine for the rest of their lives. He was happy she had accepted his hand in marriage. But he was going through a difficult time dealing with his son's death.

After Aaron was convicted on ten counts of aggravated assault for spreading the AIDS virus, he was transported to a state-of-the-art prison facility, which normally housed white collar professionals. But Aaron was still unhappy. The next day he overdosed on sedatives after experiencing bouts of depression. Aaron had a very low-key funeral, but his victims used the moment to celebrate in public.

Alex took Guy and Regine's death to heart. He had always looked up to his brother and sister-in-law. He was so busy trying to recreate the love they had for each other he failed to do his research on Evian. He regretted getting involved with her. He breathed a sigh of relief when he learned Evian was behind bars where she belonged.

Though, he was not sure how he felt about Elizabeth Coleman, who was granted probation for her actions. She was further punished after realizing her felony convictions prevented her from going to visit her husband and daughter, who remained institutionalized.

Alex's thoughts were redirected toward Alecia, who was sitting next to him with their baby in her arms. He and Alecia became closer after their son was returned to the United States, two days after his abduction. The baby was deemed to be in good health. Alex and Al-

279

ecia kept a watchful eye on their baby, never letting him out of their eyesight. They had even discussed plans to marry someday.

The twins, Dana and Cassie, sat next to each other crying on each other's shoulders. With Guy gone, they relied on Alex for brotherly advice and support. Both had remained in college and looked forward to graduating in two years.

Lamar Greene took Regine's death the hardest. He stood before her closed casket, crying profusely. He could not believe she was gone. He was escorted out of church after he started professing his love for her. His heart ached too much for him to continue the restaurant business. Lamar decided to sell his stake in Regine's restaurant, and return to his family's business.

Lowering her eyes, Bessie regretted not giving Regine her blessings to be with Lamar, especially since it was obvious they truly loved each other. She and her husband, Deacon Alfred Franklin, were relieved when Raymond told them he did not tell the police about the deacon's involvement in Lamar's disappearance.

Bessie looked over and saw Justina on the other side of the church, sitting alone and dressed in black. Even though she did not like Regine's friend, her heart went out to her.

In a daze, Justina was mourning the loss of two men: her husband, Aaron; and Guy, the man she truly loved. Now she was left alone and lonely. She thought about what her sister told her, in terms of financially helping her parents. After careful analysis, she realized her sister was right. She was so caught up in making a life for herself, she neglected her parents. To make things rights, she cashed in on Aaron's million-dollar life insurance policy, and used some of the money to help her mom and dad and put her sister, Carmela, through college. With time, she repaired her relationship with her sister, despite the faux kidnapping scheme.

Carmela was receptive to Justina's financial support, to continue her education. It took some time but she learned to forgive her sister. She also decided to no longer be a part of the Call Girl business. She looked forward to starting her career as a Social Worker.

Big Mike sat on the front row with his face buried in his hands. Although they were not blood relatives, he viewed Guy as his brother. He felt guilty for not telling his friend about what he had witnessed the evening Lamar Greene went missing. He watched Raymond and the deacon carry a huge object wrapped in a blanket out of the hotel. He assumed it was Lamar's body. He left the hotel immediately afterward. He thought if he told Guy about what he had witnessed, he would have unintentionally put his friend at risk of becoming a murder suspect.

Regine's parents, Sue Croswell and Kevin Graham, were also present at the funeral. Though, both were heavily disguised, because of their criminal past. Throughout Regine's life, both had gone through great lengths to protect their daughter, but the inevitable happened.

Kevin especially felt bad because Regine died without ever meeting her sisters. To make sure he did not repeat this mistake, he made arrangements for Joyce to meet her other sisters after the doctor released her from the hospital. Kevin was happy to learn her prognosis had significantly improved.

***

A week after charges were dropped against Raymond Brown, Leslie Holloway and her friend, Nicky Cannon were charged with attempted murder. Charlotte was also charged but on lessor charges.

However, Nicky sought to get a reduced sentence after learning she could spend twenty-five years in prison. So she blamed Leslie for coercing Charlotte to put GHB in Lamar's liquor. She also agreed to help the prosecutor bring additional charges against Leslie for murdering Raymond Brown's first wife.

Five years earlier, Leslie had recruited Nicky to help her murder Raymond's wife. They had been following his wife for two weeks until they finally caught her in a compromising situation. Raymond's wife was on top of her young boyfriend, riding his manhood when Nicky snuck through the bedroom window and shot Mrs. Brown in the back. Then she sneakily climbed out of the window and disappeared. The boyfriend panicked and left the scene shortly thereafter.

Leslie and Nicky thought they had gotten away with murdering Raymond's wife. So no one was more surprised than Leslie after learning she had been charged with her murder.

Sitting in jail caused Leslie to reflect on her relationship with Raymond, her ex-lover. He told her he was leaving his wife six months into their affair. Three years went by and she was still waiting to become Mrs. Raymond Brown. She went ballistic after he told her his wife was contesting the divorce.

Ideally, Leslie thought by having Raymond's wife murdered it would have brought them closer together. But it had the opposite effect. Raymond became withdrawn and eventually broke up with her.

She was heartbroken but determined to start a new life without him. Leslie thought Lamar Greene was the answer to her prayers. But he ended up falling for Regine Simmons. To make matters worse, Leslie tried calling Lamar from jail but he refused to accept her calls.

Leslie's arrest was plastered all over the news. But she was not the only headliner.

News of Evian Gant's indictment on attempted murder, and child endangerment and abduction charges was publicized worldwide. The judge threw out her *not guilty by reason of insanity* plea, and sentenced her to twenty-five years to life in prison.

Evian thought the judge would have sympathy after she told him she was pregnant. But that tactic failed after he ordered a pregnancy test and learned that it was not true.

Her parents were at a loss for words. They had spent every dime they had on trying to pay their daughter's legal fees. In the end, no amount of money could stop Evian for spending the bulk of her life behind bars.

The court had arranged for Pierre to be present as the State's witness. But the State had so much evidence and witnesses, including testimony from her friend, Joyce, that Pierre's presence played a minor role in her conviction.

A benefactor of Evian's demise was the owner of the magazine company Pierre had contacted to find Evian. The magazine's number one headline involved Evian and her marriage to Pierre; and her engagement to Alex. The article also featured news about the baby's abduction and his recovery. The magazine owner, Mr. Hodges, proclaimed the news story sold more copies than all editions since the company started. Mr. Hodges sent Pierre a check for five thousand dollars for his assistance in making Evian's story newsworthy.

Coming soon....

"Revolving Doors"

Chalandra Davis had a hard life. She and her sister, Angela, had endured a lifetime of grief and abuse at the hands of their father. But one day, they got even. Their actions landed them on the streets, where they learned about life the hard way. Luckily, they survived the pitfalls of life but they lost their souls in the process. Until the very last chapter, you will witness the mistakes, the secrets, and the lies that tear these sisters apart. You will also ask yourself: *Is there room for forgiveness?*

Visit www.dorothyjmorris.webs.com for the excerpt

About the Author

Dorothy J Morris was born and raised in Fort Lauderdale, Florida. She has a master's degree in Human Resources Development and a bachelor's degree in Psychology. *Fatal Blow*, the final installment of the Fatal Trilogy, is her third novel. She is currently working on *Revolving Doors,* a two-part contemporary series.

Dorothy lives in Maryland with her husband and two daughters. Besides reading and writing, she enjoys going on cruises and visiting the Caribbean Islands.